The Secret
Memoirs

— of —

JACQUELINE
KENNEDY
ONASSIS

The Secret Memoirs

of

JACQUELINE KENNEDY ONASSIS

A Novel

Ruth Francisco

ST. MARTIN'S PRESS ❧ NEW YORK

www.stmartins.com

Book design by Maura Fadden Rosenthal

Library of Congress Cataloging-in-Publication Data

Francisco, Ruth.
    The secret memoirs of Jacqueline Kennedy Onassis: A Novel / Ruth
Francisco.—
1st ed.
        p. cm
    ISBN 0-312-33799-X
    EAN 978-0-312-33799-5
    1. Onassis, Jacqueline Kennedy, 1929—Fiction. 2. Presidents'
spouses—Fiction. 3. Women editors—Fiction. 4. Widows—Fiction.
I. Title.

PS3606.R366S43 2006
813'.6—dc22

                                                        2005044592

First Edition: February 2006

10   9   8   7   6   5   4   3   2   1

CONTENTS

EDITOR'S FOREWORD

I cannot say that I was a good friend of Jacqueline Kennedy Onassis or that I knew her well. We met as editors at Doubleday in 1978, both new to the job. She was very interested that I was editing the memoirs of Adlai Stevenson, a great political figure whom she knew as a friend and admired as a statesman and wit. We had lunch together many times. We did not share confidences, but I'd like to think she enjoyed our lively discussions as much as I did. For personal reasons—a messy divorce, a handicapped child—I resigned from Doubleday and moved to upstate New York to run a local newspaper. We lost touch.

So I was surprised to get a call from her in early 1994. She asked me to come to Manhattan. She didn't tell me why she wanted to see me, but I had read in the paper about her fall from her horse and subsequent health problems. I wanted to help in any way I could.

We met at the Metropolitan Museum of Art café at noon. She was very thin and obviously quite ill. She wore a wig and her signature oversize sunglasses. She was cheerful and gracious and seemed particularly interested in my family and my life plans. At the end of our lunch, Jackie handed me a package wrapped in brown paper the size of a manuscript. "Do with it what you will," she said, then got up and left.

I was excited and curious, to say the least. As soon as I settled in for the train ride home, I ripped open the package. Inside were a dozen journals. I slipped one out and opened it. Each page was written on the front and back in Jackie's impatient yet elegant cursive.

Quickly I rewrapped the journals as best I could and placed them under my seat. I wanted to wait for a better setting where I would not be interrupted and could devote my entire concentration.

That evening—after purposefully lingering over dinner—I poured myself a glass of sherry, sat down on my worn velvet couch, and opened the first journal. I read through the night and into the next day. Then I put the journals in a box and stored them in my attic.

I would like to say I hid them there out of respect for Jackie's privacy. It was nothing as noble as that. It was merely indecisiveness, which I admit is a character flaw of mine. I was torn. Should I destroy them? Much revealed in them was so raw, so intimate. Or should I send them to the John F. Kennedy Library? Or to her daughter, Caroline? But if Jackie had wanted her journals to go to either of these places, she would've given them there directly.

I suppose she chose me because she knew of my passion for memoirs, which I continued to edit on a freelance basis. Memoirs may not be entirely honest or accurate, but they nearly always attempt to define the unnameable—to reveal the soul.

A decade passed. Scandal and tragedy continued to rack the extended Kennedy family. Michael Kennedy lost his life in a skiing accident in 1997. John F. Kennedy Jr. and his wife, Carolyn, died in a plane crash in 1999. And on June 7, 2002, Michael Skakel was convicted of murder.

The journals gathered dust in my attic.

Then in the autumn of 2004, the year that marked the tenth anniversary of her death, I retrieved her journals and reread them. After all the books written about her, a play, a musical, an exhibition of her clothes, I felt that it was time for Jackie to speak for herself. I called a colleague at St. Martin's Press, whom I trust and respect and who also had known Jackie as an editor. She agreed that the memoirs should be published.

Jackie was known as an intensely private person, one who seldom talked about herself or expressed her feelings. Her reticence was part of her allure, which created an obsession in our nation and in the world. Yet I suspect Jackie always desired to reveal herself to us. With her ironic sense of humor, she may have enjoyed the thought of debunking her own image.

—Julie Gannon, APRIL 2005

The Secret
Memoirs

———— of ————

JACQUELINE
KENNEDY
ONASSIS

MY STORY

As I leave the squealing-crashing-honking street and step inside Saks Fifth Avenue, the same department store where my father, Black Jack, gave me a charge account at age ten, the gentlest of artificial breezes greets me.

This is the woman the world observes.

Dressed in a deceptively simple sleeveless shift, hair in a scarf, I pull off my windshield sunglasses and wander up and down the aisles of glistening glass shelves. I stop to admire the crystal-cut perfume bottles and seek out my favorite—Guerlain's Jicky. I spray the tester bottle guiltily, like a secretary on her lunch hour with neither intention nor means to make a purchase. Lavender fills the air—Provence lavender warmed by the midday sun.

I move on before memories overwhelm me.

I pass by blue-and-white porcelains and soft leather purses in amber browns and reds—the colors of exotic hardwoods. I admire the cascading silk scarves—trefoils and fleurs-de-lis, posies and primroses, lions, dragons, and unicorns, blue, gold, and red—all carefully displayed so as not to appear cluttered. My eyes drink in the beauty. With each step into the lair of treasures, I forget myself, growing lighter, taller, anonymous.

Beauty calls me to the present, a narcotic, like Circe's seductive caresses, banishing unpleasant thoughts and past humiliations. Long before I knew about grief or suffering or sadness, I found solace in beautiful things. Long after I owned all that one could possibly imagine, without need or desire for more, I found delight in luxury.

Fondly I remember Mummy unwrapping boxes packaged in paisley Florentine papers and golden string, pulling out a second box of shiny enameled cardboard that pulled apart like a plastic egg, revealing inside neatly folded tissue paper too lovely to discard, packaging with no use but to delay, and thus increase, her delight. Then—with a look on her face of almost prayerful reverence—she would hold up something cashmere or crystal or gold.

Mummy had her disappointments, too, and needed beauty's soothing tonic.

I remember shopping together with my sister, Lee, walking side by side like a team of horses, excited by the impression we made, excited to see such beautiful things, excited to be alive. What fun we had. We loved each other, once. My heart crackles with a remorse I can't define.

As I wander the aisles, the saleswomen smile at me pleasantly, eyes sparkling with recognition, yet say nothing, careful not to frighten me off. I give them a nod to show I appreciate their discretion but move on, seeking to buy something that stirs my soul.

I pause in front of a case of men's jewelry—tie pins, cuff links, rings, and chains. An experienced shopper, I realize in a nanosecond that there is nothing of interest here, yet my eyes linger on the money clips. I stand motionless and re-member buying Jack a Saint Christopher money clip from Tiffany, in silver, my first major purchase for a man, shivering with excitement as my world began to spin faster and faster, presenting it to him on my wedding day, wanting him to like it, because it was understated and perfect, yet also teasing him, as I often did, be-cause he refused to carry money.

The only man I ever had to pay for at restaurants.

An icicle lodges in my chest—my panic builds, crushing my heart. I can't breathe. Please, give me one day without thinking about him! I must move on— I must put all that behind me. I shake off the image as I have learned to do—*Look, open your eyes! What do you see now? What do you smell now?*—ordering myself to the present. But my discipline fails me, my thoughts sliding back into dangerous terri-tory, like how these cases are nearly the size of coffins or how jewelry outlives us all.

Is there no escape? Perhaps, I think, it's time for another vacation—although I have yet to unpack from my recent trip to Buenos Aires—perhaps to some place I've never been, which will be difficult because I've been nearly everywhere that has a decent hotel.

Some place—any place—where I can be anonymous.

As I wonder where such a place might be—a remote island in Indonesia or Antarctica—I jump with inspiration. I realize I do need something, a case for my oversize sunglasses, because I have yet to find one big enough that I like and be-cause I have begun to think—in the early mornings after sleepless nights—that the only way to overcome my anxiety is to take off my glasses and look at the world with naked eyes.

I move quickly to a case filled with sunglasses from Paris and Milan and London—lenses from amber to turquoise, frames of tortoiseshell and titanium, displayed naughtily, earpieces spread wide. The salesgirl pulls out a tray of eye-glass cases, her manicured fingers trembling as she snaps open one in black croco-dile skin. In her confusion as to how to address me—Bouvier? Kennedy? Onassis?—the salesgirl quivers with nervousness, her words barely audible. "These are just in from Milan—very chic, very classy," she says, immediately overcome with embarrassment, as if mortified to be telling her famous customer what is chic and classy.

Suddenly I see a quick, furtive movement out of the corner of my eye. *Pop, pop, pop!* Bolts of lightning explode off the mirrors, blinding me, burning my optic nerves. *Oh, my God, no!*

In an instant, I'm back in the motorcade, the Dallas sun shooting off windshields and office windows like broken glass, deafening rifle blasts bouncing off buildings. *Jack! Jack!*

I turn and see him, the Cyclops, crouching near the escalator, lips moist with spittle, his lens pointed at me, his round black eye, silver-lidded, unblinking. He fires his flash.

I panic. Get me out of here!

I shove on my sunglasses and rush to the door. Suddenly everyone seems to recognize me, pointing, as if spotting a fox on a hunt. "It's Jackie!" "Look! Look!" "There she is! Jackie O."

His gumshoes squeak behind me on the marble floors, camera lenses and extra film rattling in his pockets. I twirl out the revolving door into the chaos of Fifth Avenue and sprint across the street. I hear him behind me, puffing, calling my name, "Jackie! Wait!" I run for my life.

Fleeing the past, evading the present, frightened of the future, I can never run fast enough.

He is always there, pursuing me like a guilty conscience, stealing my mortality—he or another Cyclops just like him. He calls my name, his legs akimbo, pelvis tucked as he steadies his lens—"Jackie! Over here! Look at me!" Surprised, I glance at him, then run blindly, my eyes throbbing from his flash.

This is the woman the world sees on the front page of half a dozen tabloids, fleeing across Central Park like Bigfoot in a meadow before darting into an impenetrable forest.

This is the woman the world judges as if they own her.

I know what they say about me. To some I am the perfect mother, a woman of grace and dignity, the courageous widow. To others I am hedonistic and greedy—obsessed with material things. Others say that I am calculating and cold and that I scorn introspection. Still others condemn me for not giving back in my maturity—for not championing a cause—for not wandering through the muddy streets of Third World countries, giving hungry children my money, my love, myself.

Behind the woman in the photos is another woman—a girl, a wife, a mother. Like you, I am a woman of passion and deep emotion who desires and dreams. I am a woman who walks alone by the sea, who rides her horse, who hums to herself as she dabbles with her paints in the shade. Who looks into the eyes of those she loves as if into the face of God.

I have hidden for so long my joy, my pain, my memories, demanding my privacy—"I want to live my life, not write about it!" But as I draw closer to the time when one final Cyclops will take one last photo—that of my casket being lowered into the ground—I have come to understand that privacy is an illusion. After we die, we live only in the memories and imaginations of those who think of us.

Perhaps I've never known myself. I must look and see who I was, who I am. The woman who looks out from the photo.

DEBUTANTE

1942–1953

ARTFUL DODGER

Black Jack screeches to a stop in front of One Gracie Square, taps his special horn signal—*toot, toot-toot, toot*—and jumps out of his black Mercury convertible. Tanned as an Arab sheik, wearing a three-piece suit and spats, with a blue bachelor's button pinned to his lapel, he dashes into our flat, calling our nicknames—"Jacks! Pekes! Pekes! Jacks!"—with Mummy yelling back, "Don't you girls get your dresses dirty! And no ice cream! Jack, I want them back in time for dinner," her voice scraping against the windows like bare branches in a storm, a voice she reserves for fights with Jack.

"Anything you say, Lovey." He blows her a kiss as we fling ourselves into his arms, his sun-aged neck smelling of spice and smoke, then run out the door, *free, free* at last.

"Don't you dare take them to the track, Jack!"

"Wouldn't dream of it, Lovey," and off we go, Lee squeezing my hand tightly, afraid of being left behind. I am too happy to shake her off but ignore her, just as I ignore her hopeful questions late at night after our daily scolding—*She's not our real m-mother, is she, Jacks?*—as she dreams of her perfect world, her imaginary playmates, her beautiful, doting mother. But I know Janet is our real mother—as real as they come.

But no thought of that now. We race through the streets of Manhattan, down First Avenue to the Queensboro Bridge, out Queens Boulevard through Long Island City, doglegging to Hillside Avenue, then down to Hempstead Turnpike to Belmont Park. Such a beautiful day, crisp, smelling of lilac, the wind blowing in our hair. We fly past immense cemeteries, the great Steinway piano manufacturing village, factories, and mile after mile of brick and wood-frame houses. Nothing can stop us now! I yank off my white gloves and throw them into the air, but Lee, afraid of punishment, merely waves hers, tossing back her light brown hair and squealing, then tucks them carefully into her little purse. She plays the fool, but I know better. I'll be the one to come home with horse dung on my shoes and streaks of mud on my dress. I'll be the one who'll get slapped. But Lee will feel it more than I.

Black Jack with one arm around me, Lee in the backseat. We giggle and laugh and point out landmarks to each other. The giant Trylon and Perisphere in Flushing

Meadows, where we among 45 million saw the 1939 World's Fair, "The World of Tomorrow" with Moto-Man the robot and the totally electrified kitchen. On the other side, the rolling hills of Franklin Park. In every direction are towering cranes, huge trucks of lumber and steel, building sites, lying still and ravaged like fraternity row after a night of parties. Gradually the new construction yields to potato fields and salt marshes.

"Can we have pistachio ice cream?" asks Lee.

"Of course, gallons and gallons of it," shouts Jack, "for breakfast, for lunch, for tea," and he and I laugh at Lee, because who could care less about ice cream, and laugh with Lee, because what's more important in all the world, really, than pistachio ice cream, gobs and gobs of it melting down our arms, sweet and sticky, knowing a scolding will follow, but not yet, not for a long wonderful afternoon with Dad.

We stop at a gas station for Lee to pee. Then I let her sit between Jack and me, as if she's our little girl. We sing songs and laugh, so happy to be with a daddy who is debonair and fun, always mistaken for a movie star, ladies swooning under his gaze like wheat in a hot summer wind. So unlike Mummy, who chills a party like a cold draft.

We pull up to a stoplight. A red convertible slides up next to us. Dad nods to the blonde in the passenger seat. She smiles and reaches out with her hand, her face transformed, ecstatic, as if graced by a divine presence. Her boyfriend stares straight ahead, but you can tell he knows what's going on. The light changes. The red convertible pulls ahead.

Black Jack's tongue darts over his lower lip as if savoring the thought of a new flavor. Almost thirteen, I know something about men and women, yet I wonder what he does to make them love him so. They smile at him right in front of husbands and fathers and brothers and boyfriends, as if he were a fertility god traipsing around with grapes in his hair, as if he were visible only to them.

"But he loves his girls," the gossips say. "I've never seen a father love his daughters so."

We smell Belmont Park before we see it, the sweet musky odor of horses, dampened earth, and fresh hay. We are here way before the crowds. The first race goes off at noon.

As the sun burns off the morning mist that blankets the track, Black Jack waves and smiles his way to the backstretch. Everyone knows him—muckers, bug boys, jockeys, groomers, and trainers. He skips over the mud puddles to keep his shoes clean. Lee and I follow. We walk around the concourse to the barns, admiring the azaleas and blossoming cherry trees, the peat beds of irises and tulips, the gardenia bushes and rose arbors.

The horses know it is race day. I sense their excitement even before I see them. I hear neighing, a clomping hoof, a shaking mane—sounds that make my heart flutter.

We walk into Barn 43 and down through a corridor of stalls. At a double stall near the end, a brass nameplate hangs over the door: ARTFUL DODGER.

When we enter the stall, the horse turns his head and looks at us with an expression of amused superiority. He snorts and looks away.

"Jackie, meet Artful Dodger, the greatest horse that ever lived." Black Jack runs his hand down the neck of the seven-year-old chestnut stallion, nuzzling his ear like a lover while making eyes at a woman leaning on a gate across the way. She wears a red ascot. Someone's mistress? A horse owner, perhaps? Not that it matters. He winks at her and fingers his pencil-thin mustache. Clark Gable, take note—this is how you play a rogue, a roué, a rake, a gift to all womankind. Don Giovanni, Casanova, Lothario, step back, make way for Black Jack.

"Have you ever seen a more beautiful horse, Jackie?" He addresses me again for two reasons: to show the pretty female that he is a father, thus harmless and unavailable—but ever so available—and because he wants to teach me, about horses, about power, about flirting, about the game.

I stand back and regard the animal. I know enough about horses to see he's not beautiful—short legs, bunchy knees, heavy chest, unruly mane, tail like a bottlebrush. There's something crafty about this horse. I feel it. He gives me a long look, then rolls his plum-colored eye away. I couldn't be less interesting to him.

"Artful Dodger will be running against Count Fleet next month," says Black Jack. "One-on-one for a mile and a quarter."

"Count Fleet is a three-year-old!" I say indignantly. Everyone knows Count Fleet has won ten of his last thirteen starts and is shaping up to be next year's Triple Crown winner.

"It'll be the race of the century, the champion against the upstart," interjects Clay Baxter, the horse's owner, who strides into the barn. He is tall and beefy, an auto dealer who got out of the market before it crashed, then bought up half the dealerships on the East Coast. "Jack! It's good to see you." He pumps Black Jack's hand. "I saw you drive up in that piece-of-shit Mercury. What happened to the Stutz?"

"Gave her up. Hardly made sense to have a car like that in the city."

"I'll sell you another one whenever you want. Straight from the factory."

"I might take you up on that."

Baxter thumps his left mitt on Jack's back. He knows that Jack is in debt, that his brokerage firm is going down the toilet. He knows that Jack's own father demanded that he sell his extra cars and cut back before he bailed him out with a fifty-thousand-dollar loan. How does he know such things? Everyone does. Probably from Black Jack himself.

I watch the men circle each other, the owner and the gambler, each with his own aura of competence and suspicion.

"Is he ready to race?" Jack asks.

"He's sound enough," says Baxter, "if we can get him to concentrate. He's too damn randy."

"That'll make him a champion," says Black Jack, winking at the woman with the red ascot.

"He may be seven, but he's ready for a comeback. I can feel it. Do you still own horses, Jack?"

"Not ponies, not anymore." Jack glances up. The woman in the red ascot looks over her shoulder at Jack as she leaves. Jack twists his mustache. "Just riding horses for the girls. Speaking of . . . let me introduce you to my daughters, Jackie and Lee." Jack pushes me out in front.

"How do you do?" the owner says to me, ignoring Lee, who sits on a bale of hay near the open barn door.

Lee doesn't care about the horse, or the tenuous tango of men sizing each other up. She slips a pink ribbon from her bodice through her fingers, staring across the yard at nothing, waiting to be discovered. Rapunzel in her tower. I know she yearns to be pulled in, but I don't care right now. I want to learn from these men. As much as I can.

"I'm very well, thank you," I say, extending my hand. Baxter shakes it with mock solemnity.

"Young lady, you are looking at the cleverest horse that ever lived," the owner boasts, running his hands down the horse's neck.

"What makes him so clever?" I ask.

Baxter looks surprised at being challenged by a little girl. "You watch. When Artful Dodger races, he spots the one horse who is his challenger and ignores the others. Then he taunts him—breaks his spirit. Half of them refuse to race him ever again."

"Why does he do that?"

"So he can win."

Black Jack takes us on his rounds to all the trainers and then places his bets. At ten, the gates open. The crowds descend. The brass band plays. The jockeys mount their horses and walk them to the starting gate.

Black Jack wagers a daily double on the first and second race. He wins. There's nothing of interest to him until the eighth race—the feature race.

While Jack cashes in his bet at the ten-dollar window, Lee and I wander around the grandstand and make up stories about people. We settle down for the next race, our arms full with boxes of popcorn and soda. Black Jack tells us he'll be right back. Through the binoculars I watch him meet the woman with the red ascot and disappear.

"Let me have the glasses," demands Lee.

I deflect her interest by pointing to the starting gate. "Look, they can't get High Society into the gate." Lee is only a child, four years younger than I. She looks through the binoculars at the snorting lineup, fooled into thinking that's what interested me. Fooled because she wants to be fooled, not because she's dumb.

Everything hurts Lee more than it does me. Especially the divorce. I hate being laughed at in school, but Lee aches for the family to be together, like on a Christmas card, with dogs on our laps, a blue spruce heavy with angels, strings of popcorn and red balls, and behind us, through the windowpanes, gentle snowflakes falling. She wants it so much, it makes her stomach hurt. Divorce makes us different from the other girls—outsiders—but I know this way is better. It gives us a freedom I can't define.

Before the next race, Black Jack bounces up the stands, his face gleaming, his hair freshly combed. "Great race, huh, girls?" We don't answer, because it was a dull race, High Society leading the entire way, which everyone knew he would, the other jockeys resting their horses, merely stretching their legs. "Look what I got for you," he says brightly, whipping out from behind his back two signed photos of George Woolf.

Dubbed "Iceman" for his steel nerves, the jockey stares out at us from the glossy picture with deep-set eyes, a chiseled chin, and sensuous lips, his aquiline nose slightly flared.

We immediately forgive Black Jack for leaving us.

"He's so dreamy," says Lee, clutching her photo to her chest, as if it could give her affection. Poor Pekes.

I hold mine carefully by the corners and try to spot him on the track. "Who is he riding in the next race?"

"Artful Dodger."

"Really?"

"Sure thing." Jack grins, delighted with his surprise. "I placed a bet for both of you."

"To win?"

"Of course."

"What happened to Pickles?" asks Lee.

"He got sick," Jack says, meaning that the jockey was too drunk to get on his saddle. "Iceman is filling in."

I hear two women titter behind us and turn. They are in white dresses cinched at the waist with big straw hats. A man in a blue uniform stands beside them— their chauffeur. North Shore wives, no doubt. I recall seeing Mummy talking to them at a horse show, acquaintances of hers, rivals. They whisper to each other behind their gloved hands, cackling. I follow their gaze. They are looking at Black Jack.

My daddy, a man to be ridiculed?

For a moment, I see him from their eyes. He seems smaller, his tanned skin darkening into something unnatural, his slicked-back black hair ridiculous, his vest straining over his paunch. He looks worn-out, like a fancy dress shoe with a hole in its sole. As he sits down, he swivels his head around to see if he recognizes any-body. He pumps his leg nervously, wanting attention like a small child. Is he bored? Looking for another conquest?

Even as they mock him, I know that if either one of those North Shore women were by herself, she would be angling to follow him under the bleachers. They want something from him, something that both disgusts and attracts them.

"All men are rats," Black Jack warns Lee and me. Only after he's said this a dozen times do I realize that "all men" includes Black Jack.

"Do you ever think you'll marry again?" I ask Jack.

He looks at me, surprised, then understands that I know where he's been. He glances quickly at Lee, winks at me—*Our secret, right, Jacks?*—then says, "Your mother is the only woman I would ever marry." At first I think he's saying this for Lee's benefit, but Lee isn't paying attention. Maybe it's true, and that's why he is rutting like a spaniel. He still loves her in a way those women in the straw hats will never love, but that doesn't stop him from hurting her.

I resolve never to be like them, giggling behind gloves, so superior, pretending to be content with their dull marriages, scorning love and passion even as they dream of it.

"And they're off!"

Sixty-five thousand fans begin screaming as fourteen Thoroughbreds break from the starting gate and charge down the track toward the first turn. Hot Curry heads toward the inside for the lead. Iceman holds Artful Dodger one lane from the rail, a half length behind. The grandstand trembles. The horses streak down the backstretch, churning up dust, hooves hammering the earth. Hot Curry strains to stay ahead, clipping through the first mile in 1:35.

"He's pushing Hot Curry hard," screams Black Jack over the crowd. "That's his trick. He's wearing him out."

When the split time is announced, the crowd roars. The first mile is two seconds faster than Seabiscuit and War Admiral's match race in 1938. Up in the press box, reporters clack away on Morse wires and teletypes, fingers flying, eyes pinned to the race.

A quarter mile to go. Artful Dodger's body flattens down, his speed building, tearing up the dirt, fifty feet per second.

The jockeys, bellies to their saddles, snap their whips.

What's this? Out of nowhere, Wedding Cake surges on the inside lane, pushing Artful Dodger behind Hot Curry. A wall of hindquarter boils in front of Woolf like roiling rapids. Artful Dodger is blocked in. A very dangerous position. Wedding Cake can't sustain the speed, his ears pricked, distracted. Just as Wedding Cake loses steam, Hot Curry drifts to the outside on the turn. A narrow hole appears.

"Watch here," shouts Black Jack. "He's gonna pull up past Hot Curry, then fall back. He'll pretend to run out of gas."

Artful Dodger bursts into the lead. But instead of driving for the finish, he lets Hot Curry dog him, half a head back, teasing him, letting him slowly creep up until they are charging neck and neck down the homestretch. He lets his opponent's black nose inch ahead. Confident, Hot Curry lets up a bit.

"Look! He's making his move!" screams Black Jack.

Artful Dodger pulls ahead, then shakes free, tearing toward the finish line. Hot Curry's ears lie flat, broken. The crowd in the stands shrieks and stomps their feet.

But here comes Wedding Cake pounding on the outside, streaking past Hot Curry, pulling past Artful Dodger over the finish line. Wedding Cake wins by a nose!

The crowd goes wild. Fans leap from the grandstand onto the track, screaming. In the press box, reporters crawl all over one another like agitated bees. The winning jockey leaps off his horse into the arms of his admirers. Champagne shoots like a fire hose, dousing everyone in the winner's circle.

"Now, that's a horse race," says Black Jack exuberantly. How much did Dad lose? He doesn't seem upset, but I see disappointment around his eyes. It's not the money, but something else.

Artful Dodger spots a mare being led to the backstretch. He breaks from his handler and bolts across the track.

Black Jack claps and laughs. "Don't you worry, Jacks. He ran a great race. He'll have his comeback. You'll see."

We leave after the feature race. Dad takes us for pistachio ice cream at a roadside stand. I am careful not to let it drip, but Lee gets it on her dress and begins to cry. I quickly wipe it off with seltzer and tell her not to be afraid. I'll tell Janet that it was my fault, that I stumbled into her while she was licking her cone. Lee wipes her tears, then reaches for Black Jack's hand, jumping up and down like a five-year-old. Anything to get attention.

"Can we drive along North Shore?" begs Lee.

"Sure. Why not? We have plenty of gas."

"Can we have a picnic?"

"Sure. Whatever my princess wants."

We buy sandwiches at a deli in a small town. "No onions, no tomato, no lettuce, no mayonnaise," says Lee, causing the grocer to sigh. "We need a picnic cloth, too. Red-and-white-checkered." So Black Jack buys a red-and-white-checked picnic cloth, chips, small containers of gelatinous coleslaw and carrot salad—so he can tell Janet we ate vegetables—and three bottles of beer. "Beer isn't booze," he says. He doesn't wait for Lee to choose her picnic spot before he pops off a bottle cap.

We take the long route home on Knight's Highway along the Gold Coast. The North Shore town names ring of money—Old Westbury, Huntington Bay, Brookville, Great Neck, Port Jefferson. Black Jack points out the mansions of the robber barons, the Vanderbilts and the Carnegies. We pass Teddy Roosevelt's summer house at Sagamore Hill.

Lee gets quiet and dreamy, trying to pick out the one she likes best—the Tudor brick mansion with fifteen-foot cast-iron gates, or the Victorian with mansard roofs, widow's walks, and acres of blooming roses.

Jack gets quiet, too. His mood is changing, becoming sullen.

It starts to rain. "Can we have a picnic inside, in the living room at home?" asks

Lee. "We can pretend we're in Flushing Park. We can pretend there are picnickers all around us and it's a bright, sunny day and there's a pond and a willow tree and there are ducks eating breadcrumbs in the grass."

Lee is excited at her idea of an indoor picnic. Mummy would never allow such a thing. Jack and I look at each other, both wanting to indulge Lee because she seldom gets her way.

We drive back into the city to Dad's place, a two-bedroom apartment at 125 East Seventy-fourth street. The shades are drawn, and it smells frowsty, of whiskey, cigarettes, and bacon grease.

As soon as Black Jack closes the front door, he seems to deflate. He pours himself a whiskey and sinks into a brown leather chair. It looks like the only chair in the apartment he sits on. The others are new and uncomfortable—like something Mummy would buy. He takes off his two-tone shoes and socks. There is a large bunion on his right foot.

He appears exhausted, like an aging actor in his dressing room before taking off his makeup, the final words of his exit soliloquy, of honor and glory, settling in unhappy comparison to his offstage life.

I suddenly pity him. He seems so lonely.

I know it is hard for him to see us, to be reminded of what he's given up—his horses at Lasata, his wife, his daughters, his Park Avenue duplex, his maroon Stutz Town Car and Lincoln Zephyr, his lavish living. For what? His freedom? I try to understand, but can't.

In the hallway I call Mummy and ask her if we can stay for dinner. I am sure she'll say no, but, oddly, she tells me it's okay but to be home by ten.

"How is your mother?" Jack asks casually.

Lee and I look at each other. "She's fine," I say.

"Is she dating?"

"She goes out a lot," I say. "Dinners, cocktail parties, dances. She doesn't always tell us where or who she's with." Man hunting. Safari in Manhattan. I drew a cartoon for Lee of Mummy in jodhpurs stalking Central Park with a butterfly net. Lee and I giggle about it—"Mummy's dating her way from A to Z."

"I heard she was going out with a Davenport. I hope she doesn't get too serious with him. He's a real rat."

"She's going to remarry," blurts Lee.

Jack goes quiet for a moment, but a quiet with an echo like in a cave. He looks like someone stabbed him in the heart. "To Davenport?"

"No," I say, glaring at Lee. *It was supposed to be a secret!*

"Who then?"

"Hugh Auchincloss," I say.

Jack laughs nastily. "Auchincloss! That stuttering imbecile? What a bore! Take a loss with Auchincloss. What does she see in him? He's about as sexy as milquetoast."

I think of Hughdie's pale, soggy face, his bland conversation, his tentative speech, his limp will. Milquetoast is pretty close. "Money," I say.

"There you are. The only thing Janet cares about."

"And social position," pipes Lee, getting her lips around those grown-up words. "She says there are eighty-five Auchinclosses in the *Social Register* and only five Bouviers."

"I'm sure she counted."

"Actually . . ." I pause and glance over at Lee. Her eyes bug out hard, and she juts her chin meaningfully. She knows exactly what I'm going to say. "She's already married him. When he was on leave for a few days from the navy."

"She didn't even invite us to the wedding," says Lee, loving the scandalized sound of it and maybe a little hurt.

"She called and told us while we were at Grandpa Lee's."

Jack loses his tan. Without looking at us, he stands and goes into the bathroom. An air of grief seeps into the room.

"What did you say that for?" hisses Lee.

"You're the one who brought it up." My ears sizzle hot, as if we've misbehaved and are waiting punishment. "Anyhow, we had to tell him. Did you want him to find out from the papers?"

"I guess that would be pretty bad."

"That would be Mummy's idea of a joke. I don't want to give her the satisfaction."

Lee shrugs and lays the picnic cloth on the floor. She sets out plates, napkins, and silverware and unwraps the sandwiches, ignoring the fact that no one feels like eating. "I wish we could have a real picnic with quiche and pâté and caviar . . . and champagne. Under a willow tree. With a Victrola playing. Who's your favorite singer? I like Frank Sinatra. And Charles Trenet."

I don't respond. She sits on the rolling lawn she imagines. Then she gets it, what's happened—we have hurt the only person who's ever given us affection. Her long lashes sparkle with tears. "Jacks, can't we live with Daddy?" she asks softly.

"You know we can't."

"Why not?"

"You know why—the conditions of the divorce settlement."

"You just don't want to," says Lee, intending to be cruel. I realize she's right. I don't want to live in this dreary apartment. Not even if we can picnic on the Oriental rug and be messy.

Black Jack comes out of the bathroom half an hour later, smelling strongly of mouthwash. I wonder how many drinks he's had, then hate myself for being like Mummy.

"What about that picnic, girls?"

HAMMERSMITH FARM

*E*arly in the morning, before the mist is visible over Narragansett Bay, before the mourning doves coo, before the sky lightens from black to milky gray, before the sun glints off the white barn, and before the dew glistens on the lawn like a billion emeralds, the Hammersmith cock crows.

I jump out of bed, throw on my jeans and a man's shirt, then tiptoe into Lee's bedroom. I tickle Lee's feet until she awakens—"Jackie, stop it!"—then grab the bottom of her bedspread and flap it like a tablecloth. "Come on, Lee. We have to get our chores done before Yusha gets here."

As soon as I am sure that Lee is getting out of bed, I dash downstairs to the kitchen, let the dogs out, grab the egg baskets, snatch a cookie from the cookie jar—strictly forbidden before lunch—pull on my mucking boots, and head out the front door. I say good morning to the dusty stuffed seagull suspended in the corner of the porch—which terrifies Lee—then march across the lawn toward the chicken coop.

As I slide down the hill through the wet grass, I stop abruptly. A huge moon is setting over the mouth of the bay, illuminating a white path across the dark, rippling waves. Three naval vessels cross the beam, slipping out before dawn.

A chill raises goose bumps on my neck.

A war is on. Somewhere out there.

No breeze blows off the water. The day promises to be hot and humid. By the time I get to the coop, droplets of moisture cling to the hair on my arms.

I climb the rickety stairs into the low shed. The chickens are clucking softly. Rhode Island Red hens. I reach under a fat bird and curl my fingers around a warm egg, silently apologizing. "Everyone has to do her part," I tell the sleepy hen.

I love gathering the eggs. It is like discovering hidden treasures.

Ay caramba! Where is Lee? I turn and look up at the house, expecting to see her stumbling down the lawn, stopping to pick a flower or tie her shoe, always meandering, dreamy and distracted. But Lee is nowhere to be seen. I figure I might as well milk the cows myself.

The first thing our new stepfather, Hughdie, did when he decided to turn under the flower gardens at Hammersmith and restock the farm for the war effort— to provide fresh milk, eggs, and vegetables to the nearby navy bases—was buy two Guernsey cows. In a rare display of humor, he named them Caroline—Lee's first name—and Jacqueline. It's Lee's job to milk the cows, but Jacqueline sometimes kicks, never quite getting Lee but frightening her—"Your cow is mean to me," says Lee. I offer to trade chores, but Lee hates the chickens even more—"They'll get in my hair." Sometimes I do all the chores myself. I don't mind so much. I love animals.

I also love helping with the war effort, and when I climb up the hill back to the house after I'm done and turn to watch the naval vessels steam out the bay, I feel proud.

By the time I am finished mucking out the horse stalls and am rubbing down my horse, Danseuse, Lee shows up. She looks tired. She pulls her sweater tightly around her, her face pinched in distaste. "Do we have to s-stay here, Jacks?"

Lee stutters sometimes now, a product of the divorce. Between Lee and Hughdie, conversations around here sound like short-wave radio.

"For criminy sake, Lee! You ask me that every day. It's just until August. Then we go see Dad in East Hampton."

"Can't we go now?"

"No."

"August," Lee repeats sullenly, the corners of her mouth turning down in a pout. "Then can we stay with him forever?"

"No. Then we go to Washington. I've told you a thousand times." I love our new homes, Hammersmith in Newport and Merrywood, the winter residence, a Georgian manor on the Potomac outside of Washington. So much nicer than Dad's New York flat.

"Why did Mummy have to marry, anyhow?"

I shrug. Money—that's what Mummy said. But I figure it has something to do with the war. I don't mind our new stepfather. Hugh Auchincloss is an amiable teddy bear of a man with spectacles who wants nothing more than to be left alone with his bourbon and *Wall Street Journal*. He seems bemused to be surrounded by so many servants and children. But he is kind to us—more like a grandfather than a father. Mummy bosses him around relentlessly, teasing him for his old-man mannerisms. She torments him for not being Black Jack.

"Don't you like it here, Lee? You always dreamed of being a princess. Here you are. Your very own palace."

"Why can't things be the way they used to be? I miss Daddy. I miss New York. I miss East Hampton. I miss everything."

Poor little Pekes, scared little rabbit, shy little possum, pretty baby skunk. Lee is scared of everything. She is so sensitive, never recovering from even small hurts.

Something isn't strong enough in her—like when she got thrown by a horse and gave up riding. I try to protect her, take slaps for her from Mummy, give her advice, but nothing helps.

The war frightens Lee most of all. Every evening, after twilight but before dark, when everyone in the twenty-eight-room farmhouse—servants, children, stepchildren, parents, guests—steps to the windows to pull down the blinds lined with black cloth, Lee tugs at the edges, breathing rapidly, working herself into a tizzy, worried that light might leak out the sides, giving us away.

"Will they drop a bomb on us?" she asks.

"Don't be silly. They aren't going to fly all the way from Germany to drop a bomb on Hammersmith Farm. It's just a precaution—because of the torpedo base nearby."

"We wouldn't take a p-precaution if there wasn't a chance, would we?"

"You can also get struck by lightning. But what are the chances? A zillion to one? Don't worry about it."

Poor little Pekes.

Danseuse lifts his paint-can hoof and stomps three times—he wants his oats. He swings his head around and leers at me. I ignore him. I want to finish rubbing down Ginger before I feed them. He swings his head to the other side, where Lee is sulking on a crate. His nostrils flicker and his lips quiver, tasting the air. As I pull the grooming brush down Ginger's back, I glance up. There is a glint in his eye. Danseuse leans down to sniff Lee's head and snorts. As gentle as a kiss, he spreads wide his lips and nibbles her hair.

"Go away, Danny." Lee pushes away his face, but he holds tight.

"He must like your shampoo. Or maybe it's all that chocolate you eat."

"Get him away from me."

"You should take it as a compliment. He doesn't eat just anyone. He likes 'em young and plump."

"He won't let go. *Jackieeee!* Make him stop!" Lee's voice rises, tinged with hysteria. As she pulls away, she stumbles into horse shit. I laugh. I can't help myself.

"Jackie! Help!" Lee starts to cry.

I tap Danseuse on the shoulder and flick his ear. "I've got your breakfast over here. That's a good boy."

"I think he yanked some out. My head hurts."

"Let me look. You're fine. He just got the ends wet."

"It's sticky and yucky."

"It's good for your hair. Horse saliva has a lot of protein in it."

"My shoe is ruined. Mummy will kill me."

"Imagine. Horse shit in a barn. Why did you wear your Sunday shoes for chores, anyhow?"

"I couldn't find my muckers."

"You didn't want to wear them, I bet."

"They're ugly. I hate them. I hate it here."

"Oh, Lee. Please stop crying. I'll clean your shoe. Look, I've got an idea. We'll cut some wildflowers for Mummy. She can't get mad if we get messy picking her flowers."

Lee chews her lower lip and crosses her arms. I sense a prickly heat in my shoulders and hands, a needling desire to hurt her for being so dreamy, silly, and weak building in me like a suppressed giggle—a rage ready to unleash.

Just like Janet.

I freeze, horrified. I will never slap anyone, certainly not my children, not ever.

I spend hours alone, riding Danseuse in the woods behind Hammersmith Farm or walking along the melancholy shore of Narragansett Bay. The storms exhilarate me, the pounding surf thrills me, the fog seduces me. My senses spring alive, my heart pounds with blood. My only thoughts are what I see, feel, and smell—orange leaves, brown bark, bumpy roots, oak branches, cold salt air, warm air thermals, skunk cabbage, deer scat. I feel the boundaries of my body fall away.

And at Merrywood, I wander the shores of the Potomac as the spring snows melt, torrents of water gushing madly to the sea. I ride or hike in its steep wooded hills, smelling the earth and flowers.

In the woods I become a sly Mohican. That other world—where I am a spy, an outsider, a performer, an imposter—vanishes in the still, primeval heat of the forest. What I think of as emotions—joy, jealousy, anger, pride, embarrassment—give way to more primitive, more essential instincts: fear, courage, conquest. I experience a primal confidence, which even at a young age I recognize as who I really am—the real Jackie—a person of no gender, an animal, a survivor.

I give myself over to the power of solitude and the lure of the sea.

In the evenings, I often sit on the dock at the edge of Hammersmith Farm, smoking as I watch the navy vessels slip out of the bay. The sight is ominous and mesmerizing. Something about it has to do with my future—the sea, the buoyant ocean breeze, the ships, intimations of seacrafts that will take me away to fascinating new places—the *Liberté,* the *Queen Elizabeth,* the *Christina.*

"You come here often?" Yusha Auchincloss sits down beside me. Apart from the woods and the sea, the best thing about Mummy's new marriage is having an older brother. He is handsome and smart and funny. He is my best friend.

"As often as I can," I say. "When did you get back from Groton?"

"Just now. I stopped over at Charlie Whitehall's. He likes you, you know."

"That's nice," I say, trying to be nonchalant. "You want a cigarette?"

"Sure. You have one?"

"I hide them with Danseuse's grooming things." I've been smoking since I turned fifteen. Janet would kill me if she found out.

Another naval ship slips out of the harbor.

"Are you going to join up?" I ask.

"If the war lasts long enough. Hughdie thinks that since the Allied armored divisions have cleared most of France and Belgium of German forces the war will be over within a year. He says he's heard a rumor that the Germans are ready to surrender."

"Do you believe it?"

"No. But Hitler might not have a choice. The Soviet armies are sweeping through the Baltic States."

I love that he knows so much. "I wish I could go."

"To get away from Janet?"

"Well, yeah. All Mummy wants me to do is get married to some Newport gink with a big trust fund and ancestors who came over on the *Mayflower*. I'd rather die than live her life—worrying about bridge parties and making sure the servants don't steal the fine linens."

"Don't you want to get married?"

"At least not until I'm thirty. I want to see the world, meet interesting people, have wild affairs."

"*Vie de bohème.*"

"Exactly. Why don't we get married?" I say, exhaling a plume of smoke. "We could have an open, European kind of marriage. Best friends for life with lots of affairs on the side."

"Very modern."

"Mummy would die."

"You know, Jackie, as much as you complain about her, you know she never lies to you."

"I suppose."

"And she only wants the best for you."

"Now you're making me feel cheap. Let's go do something bad."

"How about if we cruise some Newport bars?"

"Really? Down by the docks? Oh, let's. Mummy forbids me to go there. Do you think they'll let us in?"

"I know some people."

"Oh, *do* you?"

"Let's go. Janet is shopping and Hughdie is asleep in his study."

"As usual."

"Come on. Nobody will miss us."

On weekends, Black Jack visits me at Miss Porter's School in Farmington, Connecticut, where I attend boarding school.

He screeches past the brick portals, past the stately Colonial dorms, past the white clapboard chapel, past the Tudor brick classrooms, under the majestic oaks and blossoming azalea bushes. As he careens around the rose garden, teacups rattle. The wisteria, trembling with hysteria, showers the campus with lavender blossoms. He vaults out of his black Mercury convertible without opening the door, a box of chocolates in his hands, singing up at my window in his full-throated tenor, "Jacqueline Bouvier! Jacqueline Bouvier! Where is the most beautiful young damsel in the world?"

Black Jack, dashing Black Jack, flashy and swank, a gay deceiver, wolf, stud, lecher. Womanizer. Libertine. Philanderer. How can you fault a man for loving women?

The other divorced fathers, visiting without their new trophy wives, stand nervously outside, timid about entering, mortified at the thought of being greeted by a chorus of indignant shrieks. In their Brooks Brothers camel-hair coats and three-piece suits, these titans of industry nod self-consciously at one another, until in a state of near terror they grab their daughters' hands and bolt to their waiting Rolls-Royces and Duesenbergs.

But Black Jack is a force of nature—a tidal wave of sexuality. He flirts with all the girls, making them feel pretty and grown-up. He compliments their blossoming figures and recommends colors and fashions. He remembers all their names and asks about their horses and their beaux. He gives them presents— chocolate, stockings, lipstick. He twists his mustache and winks. He courts them all.

When we play tennis on the clay courts outside Prigley Hall, girls on the sideline

flip up their tennis skirts and shake their booties at him. They tease him and promise to marry him in ten years. They call him "Lech" and "Rubber Lips" and feign
pity for me. But on Sunday afternoons many of them stick around to catch a
glimpse of him as he screeches up and bounds out of his convertible. And if one of
them is sick, or learns about a brother or father killed in the war, Black Jack makes
a special visit, to sit and listen or to bring her a book of poetry. When one of the
seniors gets pregnant, it is Black Jack who helps her find a doctor in New York. He
is godfather to all 230 girls.

"Where shall we go, Jacks? Your wish is my command."

He opens the car door for me, hurries around to the driver's side, and jumps
behind the steering wheel. He leans over and slides his fingertips down my cheek
and looks deeply into my eyes. He starts his car, waves to Phoebe and Sue and
Tucky, and screeches out of the campus.

As he turns past Parish Hall, Miss Stabler, my biology teacher, stops and lifts
her white-gloved hand with the sweetest smile on her face. As if she misses him.

"I'm sorry, Jacqueline. I did the best I could. But there's no way I can turn
Hughdie around. He says it would be unfair to his other children. He's not leaving
you anything."

I ignore Janet. I rub the currycomb over Danseuse in vigorous circular motions,
starting at his neck, working downward and back, chest, shoulder, hindquarters,
bringing dirt and old hair to the surface.

"I argued for a small trust," Janet continues, "but Hughdie says there's no reason he should divide his fortune with Bouvier progeny. You're old enough to know
about your financial future. You have nothing. You have to marry for money."

"I don't want to marry at all." I tap the currycomb on my boot, replace it on
the grooming shelf, and pick up the dandy brush.

"Don't be ridiculous. Of course you'll marry. And you'll marry rich. It's your
only choice, dear. What else can you do? Clean bathrooms for a living?"

"I'd rather do that than live with someone who's revolting."

"Don't speak of your stepfather like that."

"Who said I was?" I brush Danseuse in long, sweeping motions, conditioning
his skin. Front to back, top to bottom. His muscles flinch with pleasure and his
coat begins to gleam. "Things have changed for women since the war, Mummy.
It's not like when you were young. Women have jobs. Careers. Maybe I'll write

novels and live in Paris. Maybe I'll write cartoons for *The New Yorker*. Maybe I'll run a horse farm."

"Listen, young woman. Maybe things haven't worked out the way I hoped for you, but Hughdie is willing to pay for your debut—"

"Oh, please. Debuts are so old-fashioned. Like I'm for sale or something." I can't bear the thought of another coming-out party—dancing with pie-faced boys who blabber on about nothing but sports, school exams, who's dating whom, who only read a book if they can't borrow someone's cheat notes. They bore me stiff—I'd much rather go to dances with Yusha. "If we're short on money, why don't we save on the debut and send me to Europe? Or I could live with Dad and get a job in New York."

Simply mentioning Black Jack makes Janet's face turn waxy and gray. "You'll have a debut, and that's final. I didn't throw my life away to raise a daughter who has to work for a living like a scullery maid."

"Maybe I'll come work for you. You pay so well and treat your staff with such kindness."

The hand comes so swiftly, I don't see it coming. *Smack!* Such force from such a small woman, her arm muscles taut from horse riding, reaching up to slap her taller daughter, managing at the same time to look down her beaky nose. "Don't you dare talk to your mother like that, young lady! Go to your room. You should be grateful for all I do for you."

Yeah, like driving my father away. Like moving us so far, we hardly get to see him. Like criticizing us for everything we do. Like sending us off to boarding schools so you don't have to see us. These things I want to say, but in a newly discovered, perfectly controlled voice, one I would improve over a lifetime—soft, low, measured, almost kindly—I say, "You can slap me as much as you like, Mummy, but that won't change the truth."

I never called her Mummy again except with irony, when joking with Yusha, or later with Jack. I figured—wrongly—that the debut would be the last time Janet would force me to do something I didn't want to do, so I gave in.

I endured a dinner dance for three hundred, live music with the Meyer Davis band at the Clambake Club, just as I endured Janet's nervous criticisms—"Keep your gloves on. You don't want anyone to see those shovels." "We need a dress with puffy sleeves to hide those shoulders." "Even in dance slippers, your feet look like snowshoes." "Don't talk about books. No man wants a wife who reads. And for crying out loud, stand up straight. Nothing's worse than a tall woman who slouches."

I refused to wear the designer dress picked out by Janet, and selected the simplest dress I could find at Saks for fifty dollars. I spent most of my debut smoking near the kitchen, joking with the help, dancing with the boys' fathers, flirting in a breathy, girlish voice, a parody of everything I despised. These small rebellions made me feel cheap but also helped me feel that I was keeping something of myself.

It wasn't real. All this fuss. It had nothing to do with who I was and what I wanted out of life.

Then to be named "Debutante of the Year 1947." What a joke! Described in the local paper as having "the daintiness of Dresden porcelain." Yusha and I hooted over that one. "Hey, Dresden, you got road apples on your shoes." "Hey, Dresden, you split your pants."

I didn't want to marry a boy from Newport. I didn't want to be a housewife. I didn't want a routine of endless teas, bridge parties, horse shows, cocktails at four, wives cheating on their husbands because looking at the men they married made them sick, and all of them pretending their lives were so wonderful.

And so I hatched a plan. I would find a way to get away. As far away as possible.

PLAYBOY

Our train rattles up the Potomac River valley to Baltimore on our way back to Vassar in upstate New York.

I lean my head against the glass, my ghostly reflection superimposed over the bare black-barked trees that have shed most of their leaves. I've survived another weekend at Merrywood, made easier with my friend Phoebe. We're both exhausted, not so much from riding horses and parties as from dealing with my mother. We relax in our minor victory over her.

Phoebe's parents are Colbys, among the richest of the Newport Brahmins, the duke and duchess of the WASPs. The closest my mother gets to an orgasm is thinking about being invited to a bridge party by Mrs. Colby. They're actually very nice—casual, kooky, and fun—not like what you'd expect. Mr. Colby grows orchids and Mrs. Colby makes little clay sculptures of grotesquely deformed people. They have half a dozen dogs that roam their estate, eat at their table, and sleep in their beds. Mrs. Colby carries on conversations with them at the dining table, which she translates for her guests.

With Janet's envious nature in mind, we hatched our plot. Phoebe came home with me for the weekend—which in itself is a feather in Mummy's Balenciagia crimson-felt cap—and causally mentioned that her parents were letting her spend her junior year abroad in Paris. Then we had Mrs. Colby call Janet and say that she's so glad I'm going with Phoebe and that she'll feel so much more comfortable knowing we're together, especially because I speak French so well. If Mummy ever knew that Mrs. Colby calls her nouveau riche, she'd die. She was flattered to hell—her daughter, traveling companion to a Colby. Once she gets over that excitement, I'll tell her I'll visit all the haute couture showrooms in Paris and report back to her about the latest fashions.

In exchange, I promised Phoebe I'd do her term paper on Madame Récamier for French class.

I wish I could have a reasonable conversation with my mother and simply tell her I want to go to Paris. I know I should love Vassar—the intellectual stimulation, the rigor, the sparring—but I hate it, hate it, hate it. The Vassar approach to literature, art, and history is so analytical, so obsessed with argument, that it takes all the joy out of it. The teachers must get together in the evening and talk about nothing but Nietzsche. I really don't care about a syphilitic-addlepated madman. Nothing in the classes makes you appreciate beauty, you don't come staggering out of lectures in awe at the brilliance of man's creativity, nothing inspires you to write or paint or dance. Rather, you compare this phase with that phase, this influence with that influence, this style with that style. All this analysis sucks the sensuality out of life. I'd rather be ignorant and in awe of the world than cynical and smart.

Our professors want us to be the intellectual leaders for a new generation of women. Are they nuts? Vassar girls want to get married with an estate on the North Shore. That's it. They would be better served with classes on interior decorating and bridge.

Subterfuge is so exhausting. Janet will say we can't afford it, which means she'll have to convince Hughdie that his stepdaughter needs a year abroad to expand her horizons. He'll grumble but will cough up the dough for the sake of harmony—"Do you really think that's b-best? . . . Yes, Janet . . . Yes, I suppose you're right, Janet. I'll see what I can do."

Yusha says Janet's such a bitch because Hughdie can't get an erection. He says they had to use a spoon to conceive little Janet. It's not hard to imagine Mummy measuring Hughdie's sperm as if she were mixing a cold medicine for one of us kids.

"Do you think you'll have a marriage like your parents?" I ask Phoebe.

"I suppose. What else is there?"

"You're rich. You don't need to marry at all."

"Who would I share my life with?" She says this so simply, as if it were obvious, as if it were the only reason people married. I sense it will never be that simple for me.

The train pulls into a rural station outside of Philadelphia. We dash out to find food. An old man in a denim fishing hat sells stale-looking ham and cheese sandwiches. We don't care. We're starved. We buy a couple, a bunch of cookies, and iced tea. The train toots. We run back to the train and up the steps. Breathless, we make our way back to our compartment.

"Jackie!" Phoebe stops and tugs at my sleeve. "Look at those guys with the flags. I think they're taking our train."

Out the window, beside a vendor selling souvenirs for Veterans Day, two young men are buying hundreds of tiny American flags. The shorter one pays the vendor. They grab their bags and trot to the train, stuffing the flags in their pockets, in their shirts, under their arms, laughing like prep school pranksters. The tall, thin one with reddish-brown hair wears a rumpled suit. The other, short, stocky, and blond, is neater. They both look as if they've spent the night partying.

The whistle blows. The train begins to move. We dive into our seats, then scoot over to the inside window to peek down the corridor. As the train clunks slowly over the tracks, they walk toward us, rocking back and forth, peeking into the compartments, pretending to look for a seat. They hand out flags to the passengers, especially the women, shake hands, smile, then move on. It's obvious they're trying to spot someone they know. Or someone they'd like to know.

"Oh, my God . . . they're looking our way."

I press my face against the window. My breath fogs the glass.

"Don't look! Jeez!" Phoebe grabs my hand, yanking my shoulder back. "Act normal."

We slide across the bench seats to the outside window, praying that no one invades our compartment before they reach us. They stop and talk to a woman with a baby right outside. The tall one glances at me over the woman's shoulder. It's a glance that speaks volumes—penetrating, intelligent, unemotional—as if he's spotted something he wants to attend to but knows can wait. It's the glance of a predator, the glance that tries to assess if a woman will sleep with him, the glance I've seen Black Jack use when he arrives at a horse show to watch me jump, adjusting the blue silk handkerchief in his front pocket, his eyes roving over the mothers.

He drops his eyes back to the woman with the baby and smiles broadly—a smile for her, a smile for me.

"What do you think of the skinny one?" asks Phoebe.

Despite being disheveled and hungover, he has sparkling eyes and a naughty grin. "His head is too big for his body. Like a ventriloquist's dummy."

"I think he's dreamy."

"If you like salesmen."

"You think he's a salesman?"

"No doubt about it. Out to sell himself. Out to sell something."

"What do you think he sells?"

"Women's panties."

"Oh, Jackie," she scolds, "you're terrible. What about the other one?"

"He's Wall Street all the way. Exeter, Harvard, lives in Newport, second-generation English trash pretending to have bloodlines from the royal house of Windsor. He'll marry someone just like his mother and start having affairs the day after the wedding."

"Oooo, you are wicked," she says approvingly.

I'm just getting warmed up. "He probably sleeps with his mother's antique china dolls, and for breakfast eats—"

"They're coming in!"

"—fried kidneys because his beloved nanny always said—"

"Oh, my God. What do we do?"

"Pretend you're French. You don't speak any English."

The door slides opens. The rattling of the train deafens us.

"May we join you ladies?"

"Je vous en prie." Oh! Please do.

The men stagger in, throw their bags on the overhead rack, and sit opposite us. They look us up and down. We pretend to look out the window and whisper to each other in French. Play the game, says Black Jack.

"Are you French?" the reddish-haired one asks.

"Mais bien sûr, nous sommes étudiantes au Sorbonne." But of course. We are students from the Sorbonne.

"You're students?"

"Oui."

"Do you speak English?"

I affect a god-awful French accent. "Only a leettle beet. My friend doss not speak any."

Phoebe jabs me in the ribs. *"Jackie, ce n'est pas juste. Je veux jouer aussi."* Jackie, that's not fair. I want to play, too.

"Your name is Jackie?" Red asks.

"Zhak-LEEN," I pronounce in French. "Jacqueline Bouvier. In America, I use Jacquie. To Americans, Jacqueline sounds so"—I turn to Phoebe— *"comment est ce qu'on dit arrogant?"* How do you say *arrogant?*

"Snobby?" offers the short blond man.

"Oui. Snobby. Thees iss my friend Phoebe." I don't say her last name because Colby is so terribly English.

"Je suis heureuse de faire votre connaissance." Delighted to meet you. Phoebe extends her hand and gets it kissed. These guys are so full of shit.

"My name is Jack Kennedy. I'm a Democratic congressman from Massachusetts. This is my aide, Malcolm Pope."

"Jacquie thinks—thought—you veer loungerie salesmen." If possible, Phoebe's French accent is worse than mine—like a chicken swallowing a fork.

"Souviens-toi, tu ne parles pas l'anglais?" I whisper heatedly. You don't speak English, remember?

"J'apprends vite." I learn fast.

The aide looks at me, then at Phoebe, and says, "Do I detect an accent from the Lyon region?"

"*Oui*. My familee iss from Lyon," I say.

The one who calls himself Jack says, "I've heard it's very beautiful there. Is that the Lyon near"—he squints and tilts his chin as if trying to recall a difficult-to-pronounce foreign name—"Poughkeepsie?"

Phoebe and I look at each other and burst out laughing. The men laugh, too. They spend the rest of the trip flirting and trying to find out if we're virgins.

The skinny one is quite charming but not a serious person. I can't quite figure him out. He acts and looks younger than he must be. Don't you have to be at least thirty to run for Congress? No, that's the Senate. Twenty-five for the House. I wonder why a congressman is wasting his time with a couple of college girls. Shouldn't he be in Washington, studying political briefs or whatever congressmen do? I wonder, so I ask.

"What do you hope to accomplish for your state as congressman?"

He opens his eyes wide and hesitates. He erupts into laughter and slaps his buddy's back. "Oh, we'll think of something by the time reelection rolls around."

"I'm sure you will."

I know something about the Kennedy clan. Black Jack despises the patriarch, Joe Kennedy. He blames Kennedy for losing him millions when Roosevelt appointed Joe to the Securities and Exchange Commission in 1934 to regulate the stock market. "It takes a thief to catch a thief," Roosevelt said. Black Jack calls Joe Kennedy worse—gangster, swindler, double-crosser, bootlegger. Everything but murderer. "You can't buy class," says Black Jack. But the Kennedys *are* rich and they *are* Catholic.

As the train jiggles along, Jack lurches across the cabin to sit by me. "You don't mind, do you?"

"No. You get a better view here, if you don't mind riding backwards."

"You know, with those big brown eyes of yours, you remind me of a cow. I think I'll call you Jersey."

"How flattering. I had a cow named after me once. I milked her every morning at five. You remind me of a woodpecker. I think I'll call you Woody."

"That may be more appropriate than you know."

I refuse to blush. "I guess that's the second time you've flattered me." I glance ever so briefly below his belt.

Jack erupts laughing. "That's what they teach you at Vassar?"

"No. At Miss Hubbell's dancing school."

"You had dance classes?"

"Of course. Didn't you?"

"I pretended to be sick, so I didn't have to go."

Something in his face twitches, and I know there's more to the story. I don't pursue it. "Miss Hubbell pounded out the fox-trot with this gigantic silver staff. If she caught any young man with his hands in his pockets, she sent him to the kitchen for punch spiked with saltpeter."

"Really? Does that work?"

"How would I know? Perhaps you should try it."

"Not on your life."

Jack asks for our telephone numbers. Phoebe digs in her purse for a pen. I give her a swift kick and roll my eyes. Thankfully, the train slows, and the men grab their bags and dash off in New York.

"I think he likes you," Phoebe says as they wave from the platform.

"I think he likes anything wearing a skirt." Like Black Jack, only somehow different—more desperate.

"Don't you think he's devastating? Those eyes! And the way he looks at you. He's so charming. He's so . . . *alive*."

"He's a bounder. Besides, I don't like good-looking men. Didn't you see him with that comb? Every time he thought we weren't looking, he'd run it through his hair. He's got to be the vainest man alive." Except for Black Jack.

"Don't you want to marry someone good-looking?"

"As long as he weighs more and has bigger feet than me, I don't care."

"With eyes that melt your soul."

"Well, I suppose that wouldn't hurt." When I look sideways at her, she smirks. We burst out laughing, laughing until our ribs hurt, like overexcited children, laughing until we forget why we're laughing, so frightened that soon, so soon, we'll be expected to make a decision and we'll have to live with it the way Janet lives with Hughdie. We laugh to ward off the future, to stir the water and blur the image that frightens us.

We fall quiet, staring out the window at the rolling farmland. The train slows, waiting for the *Congressional* to pass the Newark rail exchange, thumping numbingly over the rails.

No one walks the corridor now. The air is silent and still. A strange pulsing vacuum pushes down on us. We slip to the edge of the sinkhole we later will know all too well.

"I don't want to marry. Not ever," I whisper.

"But we will, Jackie. We will."

Did I think there was something special about him? I'd like to say that I did, that I knew he would become president of the United States, that I found him charismatic, that word that stuck to him like a Homeric epithet for the rest of his life and forever more.

No. I thought he was a flirt, a cad, charming with no depth.

Nothing more than a playboy.

PARIS

Mademoiselle, est-ce que nous pouvons partager votre table? Il n'y a pas de place aux autres." Mademoiselle, may we share your table? The others are taken.

"Je vous en prie." Please do.

"Vous êtes Americaine? Vous parlez si bien. Vous êtes étudiante au Sorbonne?" You are American? Your French is so good. You are a student at the Sorbonne?

It's so easy to meet new friends in Paris.

After my morning classes I come here to Brasserie Balthazar next to the Sorbonne and do some reading, meet people, figure out what I have to study for the day, plan my evening. It is such a civilized way to live. I have a *vin blanc cassis,* a marvelous drink of white Burgundy with a splash of black currant liqueur, or, if I'm feeling extravagant, a Dubonnet for two francs.

I watch people come into the café. They all have a particular mad look, as if they've been stewing about an idea all night and can't wait to share it. Their creative embers glow, ready to burst into argument. It feels that at any moment Jean Cocteau could stroll in and sit down, or René Magritte or Paul Eluard or someone from the expatriate literary crowd—Ernest Hemingway, F. Scott Fitzgerald, or Gertrude Stein.

Everyone is excited about ideas, and books, and art. I'm not a freak here.

My new friends greet me boisterously, as if they haven't seen me in weeks. *"Elle est là, notre petite Américaine."* I love French irony. *"Bonjour,* Jacqueline. What are you drawing?"

They peek at my caricature of Emile the waiter dancing between the tables with twelve glasses and cups on a tray teetering high above the heads of three English matrons. In French, the caption reads, "What do you mean, tea?"

There is Lucien, an artist who is very popular among the women. Nimble as a monkey, he flits from table to table, handing out outrageous compliments, and tries to talk the women into modeling nude for him. He's wonderfully amusing.

Lucien is nearly always with another artist, Pierre. Pierre is said to be shy and very talented. He wears a brown beret. He lets Lucien do the talking, standing apart, watching everyone carefully, trying to read intent behind even the simplest of comments. When we see each other, he nods, knowing we share this in common.

The son of a famous novelist, John Marquand, often pops in. I call him Voltaire because he often poses ethical questions in the middle of conversations. As with the other writers, I never see him writing, or anything he's written. I suspect this insistence on being a writer is a disposition more than a profession—a terribly good excuse for doing nothing much at all.

Then there's the viscount, who takes my hand, bows over it, and whispers compliments in my ear. "I've been thinking about you all morning, sitting just like that, with the sun on your face." He is quite dreamy—tall, elegantly dressed, with shoulder-length blond hair. As he rests between cigarette puffs and sips of his pastis—a dreadful golden liquor reeking of anise—he leans his elbow on the table and regards his gracefully poised hand. He lets me sketch it if I'm in the mood.

At a certain time of day, there is only me and the writers, who appear to spend all day migrating from one café to another. The English writers wear Italian sweaters, and the French writers wear English tweeds or some idea of a Russian peasant costume. In back is a cluster of tables where the poets sit, one per table, spidery little fellows who wear black. They press their fingers to their lips and stare intensely off into space.

By midafternoon fellow students pop in like hungry coyotes, cruising several cafés until they see someone they want to talk to.

"*Bonjour,* Jacqueline. *Ça va?* Do you have any American cigarettes?"

"Yes. Chesterfields."

"What's the exchange rate?"

"Two to one."

We make our trade from the package Black Jack sends me. I get double the number of Gauloise, which keeps me in smokes all month.

"We're all going to Lola's for dinner, Jacqueline. Do you want to come?"

"Where is it?"

"In Montmartre, not far from the cemetery. You've never been there? Well, then you must come."

We meet at the Sacré Coeur basilica, then walk a few blocks to a nineteenth-century villa that has been divided up into apartments. It is worn pink stucco with red brick showing through with freshly painted lime green shutters. There is design to its shabbiness.

We climb a double spiral staircase to a room with a huge round table in the middle of it. The walls are papered with green and white stripes and are covered floor to ceiling with paintings. I recognize a Gauguin. And a Cézanne. As a joke, there is a huge gilt-framed portrait of Louis XIV in the middle of one wall, surrounded by Picasso sketches. The curtains are blue-and-white flowers, the chairs ebony carved like bamboo, the lampshades pink porcelain. A noisy parrot squawks in a large silver cage in the corner. The plates of mismatched china sit on a white linen tablecloth that is covered with smaller, colorfully patterned fabrics. The room is lit with candles. The effect is completely charming.

For a small price, Lola provides dinner at a set time every evening. Her guests bring the wine, then stay after dinner to chat about art—a kind of cross between a salon and a restaurant. She avoids the regulations of running a restaurant, makes a little money on the side, and receives the prestige of running a salon.

We are a typical collection of American and English expatriates, European artists, dancers, poets, writers, and students.

We eat *tartes salées,* a vegetable tart to begin, followed by a *tian d'agneau,* ratatouille with lamb, and a *salade mimosa.* Simple ingredients but prepared in amazing ways. The better wines are brought by the English—Côte-Rôtie and Condrieu. And of course, fruit and cheese for dessert—Camembert, chèvre, and Roquefort—followed by petit fours and coffee. We dig in as if we haven't eaten for a week.

The conversation is loud and boisterous, French, English, Italian, and Spanish in parallel crescendos like different sections of an orchestra. I feel like the last of the second violins—trying to keep up.

"Have you seen the latest ballet by Roland Petit?"

"His *Carmen*? Scandalous!" cries one of the English ladies. "And delicious."

"They say at one point the orchestra had to stop because the audience was screaming and clapping. It was a mad sexual frenzy."

"Zizi Jeanmaire is a fireball. God, the way she flies across the stage. Like she hates it."

"I like the new fellow, Nicholas, dancing in that morbid poem by Jean Cocteau. He's so earthy and brooding."

"I think they could lighten up a bit. Such violence! In one dance, two people are dying of starvation. In another, a murder, then an adolescent suicide, an artist driven mad by love."

"No, the woman represents his muse. He was driven mad by his art."

"Que Dieu nous sauve! That's even worse."

"Speaking of violence, did you hear that communist demonstrators tore up the sidewalks of the Champs-Elysées? They were pelting the anticommunist demonstrators."

"Today?"

"Yes. They brought in the police."

"I heard they had to evacuate the American embassy."

They love gossip as much as Newport debutantes. "She's having an affair with the husband of Madame du Gard." "No, no. That's ancient history. Now she's sleeping with François Gautier." "They take wine-tasting tours together." "Do they let women in the wine cellars?" "In Provence, yes." "No, they don't. Not if they have their periods. They think they will spoil the wine."

Our price for this delightful evening is ten francs—and we have to listen to Lola read her poetry. I like it, but it seems to me that it's just prose read in a strange, jilted way, with lots of word repetitions. We applaud wildly, of course.

After dinner we stagger down rue Caulaincourt to boulevard de Clichy, past Moulin Rouge, and grab the Metro to rue Montmartre. We try to get into the Folies-Bergère to see Josephine Baker, who is making a comeback, but we can't get in. We end up at some other club and watch female impersonators in bizarre costumes. Two were dressed as Josephine Baker, so we get to see her after all.

About two o'clock in the morning, I splurge on a cab that lets me off in front of my boardinghouse. I sneak through the courtyard and climb the four flights to my bedroom. I collapse on my little bed fully clothed and give in to a luscious dizziness, the lights of Paris swirling around me—deliriously happy.

I live on avenue Mozart at the end of XVI *arrondissement* with a family that takes in foreign students from the Sorbonne. They say that they are impoverished aristocrats who fought for the French resistance, but this is what all the families who take on boarders say. We call the woman who serves us meals Comtesse. At the dinner table sit her three daughters, a grandson, a son, their friends, two other exchange students from Smith, and myself. All their friends are aristocrats, too, *petite noblesse,* and I figure the whole of France could never have so much royalty. Yet, with everyone losing so much in the war and with rich Americans overrunning town, I hardly blame them for their grand pretensions.

My room is anything but grand—a tiny room at the top of a creaky staircase, which once was one of the servants' rooms. It is long and narrow with a tall window that looks out into the gray courtyard below. The wallpaper is mustard with black stripes, and a ten-inch band of roses runs around the top. Over the window are purple velvet curtains. Underneath, a radiator clanks and bangs each morning to wake me, hissing like an agitated mongoose. One of these days I expect it to walk out the door. I have a lumpy twin-size bed, an armoire, and a tiny little desk, which probably was meant to be a nightstand. A shaded bulb hangs from the middle of the ceiling. Everything is old, hideous, and supremely delightful—and so very, very French.

Outside the room is a broom closet with a makeshift *toilette*—a kitchen chair with a hole cut in it and a pail beneath, a basin on a small stand with a pitcher of water. None of us use it, so we dash down three flights to the latrine in the courtyard, which at least has a tank of water above it for flushing.

Dinner is served at a round table in the dining room off the courtyard, invariably lively affairs with extra guests who pay Comtesse a few francs for a meal. Her little poodle begs from the guests and somehow knows American girls are a soft touch. We eat terrines of decade-old pâté de foie gras crusted over with mildewed fat. We eat oysters with lemon and brown buttered bread. We eat sealed casseroles of *tripes à la mode de Caen* that hiss when opened at the table. We eat snails and stinky, runny cheeses. And always *friandises de carême,* little fried pastries and fruit for dessert.

Food never tasted like this in America.

We pay one hundred francs a month for this delightful educational experience, about twenty-five dollars, which we later learn is far more than any of the other boardinghouses. It's worth every centime for the character and ambience.

After all, we are boarding with aristocrats.

I sit in the Jardin des Tuileries, sketching some children playing, when the viscount roars up on his motorcycle.

"*Jaqueline, tu es là.* Lucien said I might find you here."

"Did you know I've been flashed twice today? Why do French men feel the need to show their privates to women in the park?"

"They air them to keep the blood moving. Here, I'll save you from the perverts. Come for a ride with me."

"On that?"

"*Mais oui.*"

We go ripping south along the Seine on quai André Citroën, down to place D'Italie, through the cobblestone streets and vine-covered town houses of the Butte aux Cailles quarter and out of Paris. I cling for dear life, petrified every time we accelerate. He leans and swerves, zipping around corners; my forearms ache from the constant strain. Gradually, I give in to the rush of air and the sexy vibration of the motorcycle. *I am free, free, free!*

We ride south through wide fields of lavender, vast carpets stretching to the mountains in various shades of mauve, purple, blue. The smell is intoxicating—like honey and pine needles. We ride over rolling hills of vineyards, past little towns tucked away. *I love France!* About halfway between Paris and Lyon, we ride down a stately *platane*-shaded road. It twists and turns up to a small medieval town of churches, fountains, and cafés that spill into the street. Belfry bells ring as we enter.

We pull up to a small castle—dozens of red flags with golden unicorns flap off its high walls and turrets. Along the ramparts are tall rows of cypress that stand like sentries.

My legs are wobbly after the long ride, badly jangled from the last bit of cobblestone. "I'm starving," I say. "Can we wait until after lunch to visit museums?"

"This isn't a museum. This is my home. The duchess has asked us to *déjeuner.*"

"Your mother?"

"*Mais oui.* Come."

"But I'm wearing slacks."

"Not to worry. She's blind."

A medieval crank groans as it slowly raises a massive iron portcullis. We walk up worn stone stairs to a courtyard of oddly shaped bushes—topiary several years from their last haircut. Above the lintel is a shield with the unicorn. "Our family coat of arms," says the viscount.

We enter a large orange-tiled salon with huge red and blue tapestries on its walls. The duchess shuffles out to greet us, a stout woman with white hair, who speaks English to me with a crystalline British accent. She escorts us to yet another salon, where I meet the town mayor, a doctor, and some relatives visiting from Switzerland. I admire beautiful antiques and paintings everywhere, but the upholstery is shabby, and the Savonnerie carpets are worn—even the mended patches are frayed and faded.

For lunch we eat paper-thin *jambon de Bayonne* with cantaloupe, a vegetable *tian*—"It looks so elegant, yet is inexpensive to make," the duchess says—and a mesclun salad over which we drizzle dark green olive oil—"We grow our own salad. Perhaps we should raise chickens. The prices the town butcher charges are outrageous."

After lunch I hear the sound of footsteps and voices coming from the front hall. "Our first tour of the day," says the duchess. "Every afternoon, we open the bottom floor to tourists. It brings in a little extra."

I get the feeling they're trying rather hard to tell me their fortunes have dwindled.

Later, the viscount gives me a guided tour through even grander rooms with gigantic life-size portraits of cavaliers and damsels, and bedrooms with square canopied beds. All the rooms are underfurnished. The library is musty-smelling and half the shelves are bare. He takes me downstairs to a room that was once the prison, full of muskets, pistols, sabers, and suits of armor. We then wander up a narrow stone staircase to a terrace with a view of the entire town and the valley beyond.

I gasp in astonishment at the beautiful vista. "I can't imagine living in a place like this."

"Why not? You'll make it a home."

I stop abruptly. Did I miss something? I'll make it a home?

The viscount continues, "With money from your family, we can restore the place, section off parts for us to live in, make them comfortable. We'll fix up the gardens. We won't have to show it to tourists unless we want to. You can spend all day sketching old men from the village and painting sunflowers. We'll have dinner up here and look out over our vineyards. *Ça sera splendide!*"

"I don't have a dowry."

"I know. Americans don't believe in such things. But your family—"

"You don't understand. I get no money from my family. Fifty dollars a month. That's it. And when I marry, not even that."

"*Tu blagues?*"

"No. I'm not joking."

"Oh. Well, then I can't marry you."

I see the viscount often at the cafés, flirting with American women, bowing and whispering as if their beauty has taken his breath away, "*A votre service.*" It must be working. I see any number of other so-called impoverished aristocrats poking around the cafés, copying his style, telling nerdy American students with heavy thighs and thick glasses how beautiful they are.

They think we're all rich. We Americans.

After my classes, I usually pick up my mail at the American Express office and take it to a café to read. Today I have a package.

"Lucien, do you have a little knife?"

"For you, darling, I always have a little knife."

"No, really. I don't want to use the silverware."

"Go ahead. It's not vermeil."

French waiters can be terrifying. I glance around, then surreptitiously use a dinner knife to rip open the brown paper wrap.

"What did you get?"

"Oh, my God! It's a Leica camera. From my father."

Lucien swipes the card out of the wrapping debris.

"What does it say?" I ask sweetly, knowing if I make a grab for it, I'll never find out. The French are such children.

"It says, 'Dear Jacks, For your class in photography. Is Europe ready for another Lee Miller?' "

"Who is Lee Miller?" I ask.

"You don't know who Lee Miller is? She's famous. She came over to Paris from America at eighteen, this gorgeous young art student. She walked up to Man Ray and said she was his new protégée. They lived together for three years. He used her as a model and taught her photography."

"Really?" I am very impressed. In my photography class, Man Ray and the surrealists are all we talk about.

"Oh, yes. She modeled for Picasso, too."

"And she starred in Jean Cocteau's surreal film *Blood of a Poet,*" adds Pierre. Even shy Pierre gets animated when discussing Lee Miller.

"Really?"

"Yes, yes. She became a huge fashion model. Then during the war, she worked as a photojournalist for *Vogue.*" Lucien lights a cigarette and sips his Pernod. "There is an exhibition over in St.-Germain-des-Prés, off rue de Rennes. Go take a look. I'd go with you, but I have a model coming at four."

"An American?"

"Yes," he says, grinning.

I nearly run to St.-Germain-des-Prés. I find the gallery tucked away behind St.-Sulpice. I walk in and look around.

The walls are covered with photos of Lee Miller by all the great fashion photographers of the day—George Hoyningen-Huene, Arnold Genthe, Edward Steichen, Nickolas Muray. She is beautiful—big sloping eyes, short blond hair, tall, small-breasted, strong legs, boyish-looking. The perfect body type for the early thirties. Like me, her best feature is her long neck and strong shoulders. I was born two decades too late.

There are photos taken by her, too, jarring images. Even in stillness and shadow, there is drama.

Her pictures of Dachau take my breath away. Emaciated bodies piled on top of one another. The daughter of the burgomaster of Leipzig, who committed suicide as the Allies marched into town, lying supine on a leather sofa, her Nazi armband above her elbow, her lips parted as if waiting for a kiss. A prison guard, dead, floating in a ditch, killed by the liberated prisoners.

She can photograph a staircase so it is menacing and evil, then take a picture of a dead body and make it beautiful.

By thirty-seven Lee Miller's beauty is gone, eyes puffy from alcohol and lack of sleep, her hair and skin flat and dull. What's left is a look of curiosity and defiance.

I nearly swoon. I want to be Lee Miller.

Inspired, I take pictures of Paris in the late afternoons—down the Champs-Elysées, across the place de la Concorde, along the quays toward Notre Dame, the bridges and monuments casting long shadows. The buildings and streets seem to come alive at twilight. They seem vulnerable and slightly sinister, baiting me to capture their secrets.

I can see why Lee's father had to come to Europe and drag her back home from her first trip to Paris. Why should I go back to the dreary snow-covered sidewalks of Vassar?

"We can never marry, you know. We're both too poor."

He echoes what my mother says in her letters. I don't care. I'm in love. He's witty, handsome, brilliant, and kind. He's the son of a famous novelist. He makes me feel beautiful and clever.

John Marquand, Jacqueline Marquand. What a beautiful name!

He's everything I love about French men.

French men are so much more refined than American men, so wonderfully put together. Even a poor student pays attention to how his shirt fits his torso. They may have only two pairs of slacks and two sweaters, but they are good quality. The sweater sets off the fleck of color in the slacks. A cravat pulls it together. Their shoes are shined and suggest, as in women's shoes, the shape of their foot. They dress, not merely wear clothes.

They walk through narrow cobblestone streets like dancers, strutting, showing off their bodies, radiating confidence. They are counts and princes and poets, every one of them.

The Frenchman sits down next to you and looks you in the eye. He delights in your presence. At that moment you are the only person in the world. When he leans forward, you smell a sensuous cologne, something spicy and mysterious that pulls you in. He makes you feel sexy and smart.

The Frenchman wants to test his soul against his female counterpart. The American man isn't even aware that he has a soul.

"Marriage is so passé," J.M. says, leaning over a café table. "We should live together."

"Like Man Ray and Lee Miller?"

"Mais oui."

How romantic it would be to live in some garret, snuggled together in bed because we have no heat, reading the poetry of Rimbaud to each other.

J.M. calls me beautiful in a hundred different ways. He is unpossessive and free. He takes joy in simple pleasures. He makes American men seem like bores. And yet . . .

"We'll have to have *some* money," I say.

"I get enough from the articles I write, book reviews, that kind of thing. One day my novel will be finished. Your French is good—you could be a translator."

We spend long afternoons wandering through the tangled forest of tombs and mausoleums of Cimetière du Montparnasse, kissing and necking, panting, clutching, joking—*so alive, so delirious*—dreaming of our future together, he a famous brilliant writer, me a famous brilliant photographer. We dash away from the perverts—*laughing, laughing, laughing*. We visit the tombs of Charles Baudelaire and Vaslav Nijinsky, and bow our heads—this is our real family, our real heritage.

We are in love, aren't we? And yet . . .

I think of my afternoons window-shopping on the rue du Faubourg St.-Honoré and the place Vendôme, down the avenues where the grand couturiers have their showrooms. Will I never be able to afford these things? "It sounds like a struggle to me. Don't you think it will wear us down?"

"Not if we don't let it. We'll have each other. Our love."

"You don't think we'll start hating each other?" I think of Black Jack and Janet fighting over money, bourbon glasses smashing against the walls.

God, I hate money. I hate not having enough. Life is too exciting to be limited by stupid money. I understand now why Janet turned into such a gold digger—money is freedom.

There is only one first time.

It wasn't the novelist's son, although it easily could have been, my back pressed against the grating of an open-cage elevator, stuck, it would seem, between the fourth and fifth floors of his cousin's penthouse, the two of us giddy with lust after an evening out at the Opéra Garnier watching the Ballets Russes de Monte Carlo from front-row seats, Frederic Franklin's sweat flying onto us from his leaping, contorted body, and afterward, a drink at the Le Boeuf sur le Toit, which led to a tipsy romantic stroll along the Seine, where we watched lovers on the benches and under the bridges, walking and walking until we were almost sober, then up the steps of a marvelous art deco apartment building with a cast-iron framework and stone friezes. "It has one of the best views in Paris," he said as the elevator cranked slowly up through a winding staircase, then stalled, his hot kisses on my neck, his hands pushing up my skirt, brushing my ears with his lips—"*Je t'adore, Jacqueline. Tu es la seule femme pour moi. Je t'aime. Je t'aimerais toujours*"—his hands pulling down my panties. *Yes, yes, make love to me, right here, as if bombs were falling on Paris and this might be our last day alive.*

Then, the sound of voices—a couple leaving their apartment two floors below—and the gears of the elevator jerking awake.

No, it wasn't him.

Nor was it the viscount, although it could've been, since he asked me out to the Ritz bar, and on romantic picnics in Bordeaux, and to St.-Jean-de-Luz on the Riviera, where we spent the night with a friend who had a château. No, it wasn't him, despite the erotic atmosphere and the gorgeous young goddesses— Swedish, French, German—scantily clad, parading along the quay, flaunting their bouncy fig-shaped breasts, and the fragrant air wafting over the water as we ate in the candlelight at a terrace café, violin music over the water, the sexy sound of voices and roulette wheels from the casino, sipping an exquisite Dom Pérignon, 1940, where he held my hand and said, "I've never met anyone like you, Jacqueline," apparently getting soft on me despite my impecunious state. Yet, when it came down to it, the viscount, concerned about not spoiling my virginity, wanted hand jobs just like American boys I've dated, which makes me feel like a thing.

Nor was it the passionate ugly artist who got me to pose naked for him, at first because he's so brilliant and famous, but really because something repulsive about him excited me, lying supine on a soiled sheet on his twin bed, up in a cold garret, the skyline of Paris out his window, sounds of people making love across the air shaft, and his outrageous pronouncements and his bold talk about sex—"You will be adored by millions one day, Jacqueline. I should rape you so I can say I was the first"—his right hand rubbing his crotch as he sketched madly with his left, then standing abruptly and storming out of his garret, leaving me alone.

No, it wasn't him.

It wasn't Lucien or Pierre, either of whom would have obliged me if I had asked. Nor any of the handsome men I danced with to the violins at Monseigneur's, clutching and rubbing, fumbling in the darkened corners.

I couldn't bear returning to the United States a virgin. There is only one first time. I didn't want it to be with a rubbery-faced Newport boy.

When the opportunity arose, I had to grab it. My art history professor asked me to house-sit his small château while he and his wife went to Italy for a holiday. He had two salukis and knew I liked dogs. I might want to use his library, he offered. It wasn't his library I was interested in.

Carefully, I plan my seduction. I would prepare a meal. Food is love, right? This is what the French have taught me. The rare truffle, the perfect cheese, the artistic arrangement of vegetables and meats—delicacies to be discovered and shared. I can't cook, so I order *escalopes de veau à la crème* from a nearby bistro to serve on fine china. We do the best we can.

I set the tone perfectly. I light candles and build a fire in the fireplace, although it is barely cool enough to need it. I pull a fur rug in front of the glowing embers.

Was his name Emile? Léon? François? I don't remember. He was a sculpture student, very handsome, muscular shoulders and arms from chipping at marble all day. He was very sexy.

When he arrives, he says he's already had dinner—at his mother's. He tastes it, and says it's very good, but doesn't eat. This puts me off. The mood is spoiled. I think about sending him home, but the fire crackles in the fireplace. I had worked so hard to make it perfect. I figure we might as well get on with it.

We take our wine to the couch and start kissing madly. "I'm a virgin," I whisper.

"There's always a first time," he says.

Half undressed, I pull him to me. But he turns me around, lifts my skirt, and tries something I never expected, something I've only read about in books that Yusha and I found under Hughdie's bed.

"What in hell are you doing?" I shout in English, slipping away. He doesn't answer, but pushes my head to his crotch, and I think, *Here we go again,* and a laugh starts in my chest because this is what I wanted to avoid by orchestrating this evening, wanting pleasure, wanting love.

Suddenly I hear the sound of tires on the gravel outside. First the voice of a woman. I've never heard the voice of my professor's wife—I guess that's who it is. Then the voice of my professor. I panic. I shove Emile, Léon, François, or whatever his name is out the balcony with his clothes. He pulls on his pants, then jumps down. I throw the rest of his clothes after. His underwear lands in the wisteria branches above his head where he can't reach them. He swears.

I laugh, imagining his underwear there in the morning when Madame Professor opens the balcony window to drink her café au lait and look out over the city. Then disappointment sets in. I sink further, reflecting that I might never know love.

Dear Jackie,

You don't want to miss this year's ball at the Dance Class. I talked to Dorothy, who's organizing it this year. All the most eligible bachelors on the East Coast will be there. Some from England, too! You've got to come back, Jacks. I already have my dress. Mummy splurged on a Chez Ninon gown for me. Can you believe it? Dances are always more fun with you. We can make fun of people and flirt with the bores so the snobs will think they're missing out on something. Remember Harold? Please come back, Jacks. We'll have so much fun.

That was from Lee. Did Janet put her up to it?

After all I've done for you, now you're neglecting your old dad. Probably you have met someone who calls himself a count and you're madly in love and your old dad looks pretty dull in comparison, but you have responsibilities at home. You'll miss out on this season's horse shows. I registered you already for the Long Island Classic in September. They're charging an arm and a leg this year. I miss you, Pumpkin. You make me laugh. Don't you ever intend to come home?

From Black Jack. There's something whiny in his tone that makes me worry. But it doesn't make me want to go back.

You must come home and finish your education. I won't have it said that I raised a daughter who never finishes anything. And you mustn't miss the Dance Class Ball. Has Lee told you about her gown? A Chez Ninon. You can have one, too.

Janet.

Everyone is putting pressure on me. J.M. wants us to run off to some small town in Italy where he can write and I can paint. The viscount wants me to marry him. My art history professor wants me to enroll in a class in London for art authenticators. Yusha is coming over to travel with me during the summer, but I suspect he's being sent to fetch me back.

Why can't they leave me alone? I love J.M., but he's beginning to expect me to behave in a certain way. He gets angry at me when I act like myself. If I had any guts, I'd simply disappear somewhere.

"It's just as easy to fall in love with a rich man as a poor one," Janet says.

I can't fight them all.

VOGUE

The *Congressional* screeches its brakes, arriving in New York at Pennsylvania Station. Suitcase in hand, I stumble out to the street, blinking up at the tall buildings as if this were my first time in the city. I am a career girl now. I hail a taxi and ride uptown to my father's apartment on East Seventy-fourth Street.

Earlier this year, at Janet's suggestion, I entered a writing contest for *Vogue* magazine, the 1951 Prix de Paris competition. Out of 1,280 entries, I won. I wrote a lot of silly highfalutin stuff about the three men in history I'd most like to meet: Charles Baudelaire, Oscar Wilde, and the Russian ballet impresario Sergey Diaghilev—all habitués of nasty sexual practices. My attempts to shock the editors at *Vogue* seem to have gone unnoticed. I won the prize—a year working as a junior editor, six months in the New York office, then six months in Paris. I get to go to Paris again!

As soon as I won, Janet changed her mind, and I had to fight with her to take the job. Any time she starts a sentence with "You're old enough to make your own decisions, but . . . ," I might as well throw in the towel. She's afraid that if I go to Paris, I'll marry the novelist's son and never return. She may be right.

"But, Mummy, I bet I'll be able to get tickets to fashion shows and discounts at top designers. You'll be the best-dressed woman in Newport."

I think I've gotten my way. It makes her batty knowing that I'll be living with Black Jack. I delight at her torment.

"Would you mind taking a loop through the park?" I ask the cabbie.

"It's your dime, lady."

Spring in New York! The maple trees are blossoming, dropping light green catkins and yellow pollen on the road. Around the Shakespeare Garden, pink crabapple trees and yellow forsythia burst into view like costumed dancers on a dark and empty stage. Through the trees I catch glimpses of the Reservoir and the bridle path where I used to ride. The air is clean and full of energy. I sway as the taxi curves around the park and up north to Harlem Meer, which is rocky and wild. My stomach flutters with excitement. It feels as if I'm coming home.

The cab leaves the park at Seventy-ninth Street. We pull up to 125 East Seventy-fourth Street.

Black Jack greets me at his door, sweating, his skin jaundiced. He is so grateful I'm here that he nearly weeps.

My first day on the job. I swish down Lexington Avenue to the Graybar Building, wearing my best outfit: a navy blue skirt with a robin's-egg blue cashmere sweater with a lace collar. On my feet, Beth Levine platform pumps. Pearls and white gloves. I think I look businesslike but feminine. I am ready.

I cram onto the elevator with others late to work. They smell freshly scrubbed; their manner is pensive. The men have taken off their hats and hold them protectively on their chests so they won't get crushed. I get off at the nineteenth floor.

My supervisor, Miss Harrison, is tall and thin with bad teeth. She gives me the rundown. I must be on time, a half-hour lunch, every two hours a ten-minute break, no personal phone calls.

My task? To alphabetize a stack of photos by designer. The stack is four feet high. The photos are covered with dust.

"We've been needing someone to organize our archives," Miss Harrison tells me. "I'm so glad you're here."

How thrilling. I can't wait to get started. I try to smile, then sit down on a wooden chair that wobbles.

The air smells of smoke even though Miss Harrison said there was no smoking in the offices. My desk faces a junior editor, Debra, an overweight nervous woman who inhales sharply as she thinks, occasionally mumbling encouragement to herself, then vigorously crossing out a paragraph with her green pencil. Her hair—a pretty chestnut color—is pulled back severely and hasn't been washed since the Roosevelt administration.

The back of my neck feels dirty, and I want to scratch it fiercely. This is what I have to look at for eight hours a day?

I look around the room. Exhaust fumes from the street waft through the windows, covering everything with soot. Telephones ring, typewriters clack, cars honk, down the hall, contentious voices rise in heated discussion. Everyone looks like a character from a Dickens novel, unkempt, unwashed, exhibiting nervous behaviors of all sorts—twitching, scratching, picking at pimples, laughing abruptly, swilling coffee. Everyone, in fact, appears to be a type that you might consider crossing the street to avoid.

I thought this was a fashion magazine!

I see my life scripted out before me. In six months I'll look like them. In a year I'll smell bad and have brown-stained teeth. The only heterosexual man I'll

meet is an editor who drinks too much and thinks excitement is an evening playing chess. The work is mind-numbingly boring. I know I've already lost the function of a million of brain cells in just the past two hours. I feel my spirit dying.
My head feels heavy, as if I'm underwater. I sense hysteria coming on, that in
three minutes I'll jump out of my chair and start screaming, "Let me out of the
box!"

Somehow I manage to talk myself into coming back after lunch. It's just the
first day, I tell myself. The excitement of fashion shows and designers and Paris
and trips to Milan is all in the future. Don't panic.

About two o'clock a tall, thin man swishes through the office with a bolt of
purple velvet brocade. He unwinds it on the floor in front of the senior editor,
then lies down on it, posing like Rita Hayworth. "Viv, darling. Isn't this color pure
orgasm?" He looks at me, the new girl, trying to shock.

"Orgasms are pink," I say pertly.

"Maybe yours are, honey, but just wait a few years."

I don't even try to guess what that means.

About nine P.M., as I am relaxing on Black Jack's sofa, stretching my toes to the
pulse of Count Basie, Hot Lips Page, and Billie Holliday, Janet calls to ask about
my first day. "Jacqueline, what are the young men like at your new job?"

"Dukes, lords, princes . . ." I stop before adding "queens." "They all have royal
blood and are fabulously wealthy. That's why they're willing to work for thirty
dollars a week."

"Don't be sarcastic, Jacqueline. It's not ladylike. Be serious, tell Mummy. Did
you meet anyone we know?"

She means, is there anyone from the *Social Register,* any eligible bachelors. "You
know how it is on the first day of work"—Mummy, of course, never has had a
job—"I was busy getting to know the office. Sharpening my pencils. That kind of
thing. I didn't have time to chat up the staff."

She falls silent, and I hear her thinking hard, her manipulation machine
whirring. "Well, dear"—her voice tightens, rising in pitch—"I'm glad you're having a good time. Be sure to call me tomorrow."

Day two. Black Jack greets me at the breakfast table in shirtsleeves and a tie, blue boxer shorts, socks, and garters. His calves are beginning to get varicose veins—old-man legs. After drinking coffee and reading the *Daily News* and *The Wall Street Journal,* he shuffles to the bathroom.

I call out, "So long, Dad, I'll see you tonight," and dash out of the house.

Today the job doesn't seem nearly as bad. I visit a photo shoot in the morning. I am hugely relieved not to be sitting at a desk, even if it is to fetch coffee and fan the models so they don't sweat. In the afternoon I help an art director lay out a nine-page photo essay on famous Washington personalities for the August edition. Two, Arthur Krock and Senator Henry Cabot Lodge, have visited Merrywood. I get points for the gossip I drop.

That evening Black Jack's maid, Esther Lindstom, tells me he has a date. Expecting him to call, I answer the phone every time it rings. It's always a different woman asking to speak to Jack. I tell them I'm his new wife, and they hang up quickly.

I make a plate of cheese and sliced pears, pour a glass of wine, and sit in the living room to sketch some fashion ideas. They quickly turn into lewd caricatures of my coworkers.

I'm as happy as can be, listening to Dad's Nat King Cole records with no intention of calling Mummy. A little past eight, my stepfather, Hughdie, calls.

"Jackie, my dear, I t-talked to William Stockton at the Red Cross here in Washington. They need a national fund-raising coordinator. It's a f-fabulous opportunity."

An opportunity for what? That's not a career—that's killing time. "I don't know anything about fund-raising."

"Jackie, you're a Vassar girl. It won't be h-hard for you to pick it up. You can live at home, ride your horses . . . and be w-with your family. What do you say?"

The next evening, a call from Mummy. "I'm so excited you'll be working in Washington. Since you'll be starting in the autumn—"

"I *have* a job, Mummy! A paying job. In New York."

"—you'll have the summer free. Hughdie and I thought we would send you and Lee to Europe for the summer. All expenses paid. And you'll be back for the high-season dances."

"But I'm *going* to Paris, Mummy! To work at *Vogue.*"

"I know you have to make your own decisions, darling, but wouldn't it be nice to be in Paris in just two weeks instead of waiting for October? You know how unpleasant New York can be in the summer."

"I like it here."

"We've booked two seats on the *Queen Elizabeth* for June seventh."

"No, Mummy."

"The seats are nonrefundable. Your sister will be very disappointed. It's such a waste of money, but obviously you don't care. How did I manage to raise such a selfish daughter?"

Then I get a call from Lee. "I can't believe you're doing this to me! Mummy wants to send me to Europe for my high school graduation and she won't let me go without you to chaperone. It isn't fair! You've been to Europe twice!"

"You can take your junior year abroad, just as I did."

"I'll never make it to my junior year."

That was probably true. As much as she's been dating, she'll have to get married soon.

"Jackie, pleeeeeease. I'll never ask you for anything again."

Thursday night, I get another call from Madame Napoléon. "I mentioned to Charlie Bartlett and his wife that you'll be in Washington over the weekend. They've invited you to dinner."

"Mummy, I have plans here in the city. Maybe next weekend."

"Oh, dear, I already accepted for you. It's too late to back out now. They will be so disappointed if you cancel."

Oh, brother! As I hang up the phone, I see Black Jack in the hallway, taking off his coat. I don't know how much he's overheard, but he marches over to the wet bar, pours himself a bourbon, and chugs it. His fingers shake. He knows he's losing. We were to go to the Metropolitan Museum over the weekend, dinner at the Russian Tea Room, and the ballet on Saturday night.

"I have to go to Washington this weekend. Janet set up a dinner engagement for me I can't break."

"It's hard to win with Mummy." He pours himself another drink and leaves the room.

Friday evening, Black Jack sees me off at the train station. His face is jaundiced, his suit wrinkled.

I take a seat by an open window. He stands alone on the platform as porters rush around him. Women bump him with their hatboxes, men jab him with their *Wall Street Journals*. His face is desolate, eyes rheumy. The world spins around him as he holds on to the past, gazing up into the train window, replacing my image with the little girl he remembers.

I see him for what he is—a broken man, a drunk, an aging playboy who, like an overripe avocado, was once exotic and sensuous but now darkens, wrinkles, and decays.

As the train pulls out from the station, Black Jack reaches up and hands me a red rose.

In Washington, Mummy greets me with "We can't believe how much we've missed you." She has never ever said anything like that to me before. Then she hugs me!

"Hughdie and I were thinking that while you and Lee are traveling around Europe this summer, you might like a little car. Of course, it'd have to be used, but you and Lee could sell it when your trip is over and buy some new clothes. How about that? You won't have to take those stinky trains filled with Italians."

"I have a job, Mummy."

Lee refuses to look at me. She stares at the scenery as we drive home, fuming silently.

Later Hughdie offers to buy me a new Buick if I move back to Washington. I don't need a car. I keep Black Jack's 1947 black Mercury convertible at Merrywood. "I w-worry about you in a convertible, Jacqueline. They're s-simply not safe." I suppose it annoys Janet every time she sees it parked in the garage—enough so she's nagged at Hughdie to get me something else. Sometimes I feel really sorry for him.

Before I take off for my dinner engagement that evening, I notice a dent in the front fender of the Mercury and a pair of underwear jammed between the cushions. Lee's? I guess I didn't need to worry about coming home to a dead battery.

As I speed over the Chain Bridge onto Reservoir Road and into Georgetown, I think about Charlie Bartlett, who now has a job as Washington correspondent for the *Chattanooga Times*. We dated a few times and remain friends, but I'm surprised that Martha, his new wife, is so eager for me to come to dinner. "But you must come, Jackie," she said when I called from New York and tried to beg out of it. "I've invited someone I want you to meet." Maybe she wants to marry off the competition.

When I enter the three-story brownstone on Q Street, Charlie introduces me to several couples, and a curvaceous blonde with the most unfortunate nickname of Hickey. We sit in the living room, sipping drinks and chatting. Everyone seems nervous, anticipating the entrance of the mystery guest.

The doorbell rings. Charlie opens it and shouts, "Jack!"

The room suddenly brightens. The men jump to their feet. The women scoot to the edge of their seats and tilt their calves at a flattering angle.

A grinning, gangly man springs into the front hallway. He pauses in front of the mirror by the umbrella stand to run his hands through his hair. I wait for him to blow himself a kiss. With the furtive energy of a twelve-year-old pickpocket, he enters the room. He is tanned and carelessly dressed, his pants ending an inch above his shoes. His cuffs are frayed. His absentminded nonchalance instantly endears him to the women in the room like a five-year-old with his shirt on backward.

Charlie introduces him to everyone, leaving me to last. "Jackie, this is Jack Kennedy."

"Pleased to meet you," he says. He catches my glance at the tie that dangles from his pocket. He winks, tucking it away, a smile playing on his lips.

"We met once before, on a train," I say.

"No, that couldn't be. I'd remember a girl like you."

"Then it must've been that other auburn-haired congressman from Massachusetts. I'm glad that wasn't you. That other congressman said I looked like a cow."

"No! I couldn't have said that!" he says with feigned indignation.

"I don't remember your exact words."

"Well, then, it wasn't me." The hint of smile breaks into a boyish grin. "People remember my exact words."

"If you plan to stay in politics, perhaps that's not such a good thing."

Charlie, monitoring our banter like a quality-control inspector, interjects, "Jackie works at *Vogue* magazine."

"Really? As a model?" asks Jack, more interested.

"No," I say. "I'm sort of a trainee. I won the Prix de Paris competition."

"You should be on the pages of *Vogue,* not editing them," he says with a roguish twinkle.

"Thank you. That's much nicer than being called a cow."

He laughs a delicious, warm laugh that stirs something deep in me. He excuses himself to see Martha. I hear her explode with joy when he enters the kitchen— "Jack! I'm so glad you could make it." When he comes back to the living room, Charlie pours him a drink. He sits next to me—too close. He talks to everyone except me.

He talks to Charlie about Senator McCarthy, to an older gentleman about Palm Beach, to Hickey about movies and tennis. He responds energetically to the conversations, yet there's a detached quality, as if his real interests lie elsewhere. Or perhaps it's me who's detached—my ears pounding, my mind barely following the conversation.

"What's this I hear about you running for Senate?" Charlie asks Jack.

"I don't know if it's the thing to do. My great accomplishment as a congressman is getting a few young ladies to read the newspaper."

"Are you kidding? You bring glamour back to politics. As a member of the press, I can tell you that covering Truman is about as thrilling as watching weeds grow."

I feel heat coming from Jack's body. I sense he's trying to attract me by his performance. When I shift my body, he shifts his as if our bodies were touching. I sense he is hyperaware of his hand on his knee, inches from mine, aroused by the proximity of our fingers. Yet he refuses to look at me.

I'm suddenly too warm and my scalp tingles. I move away to the other side of the couch. He springs away like a polar magnet.

I find him irritating. I find him attractive. I find myself wanting his attention, an almost physical need to have him to myself. I am madly jealous of his interest in anyone else.

Martha places me beside him at dinner. There are three married couples here, Jack and two single women—the blonde and me. The blonde is just the kind of girl I've heard Jack Kennedy adores. When no other men show up, I realize that the blonde is the backup girl in case he and I don't hit it off.

There's a vulnerability about him, as if some romantic sorrow has blighted his life. He tells amusing stories and has a way of looking at you as if he's fascinated. It's probably all Irish blarney.

After a game of charades, I make my excuses and good-byes. Charlie escorts me out to my car. As we walk down the driveway, Jack dashes up and takes my elbow.

"Jackie, how about going somewhere for a drink?"

"A drink? Tonight?"

"I want to hear more about your year in Paris."

A dozen ways to refuse his invitation flash through my mind. "Well, I don't really—" As I open the car door, Martha's fox terrier jumps in. Suddenly a blood-curdling scream. Inside, a body looms up from the backseat like a corpse from the grave, his face white, the terrier dangling from his wrist.

Oh, John Husted, boring John Husted with your face translucent and pink as a newborn piglet, dear John Husted, kind and good-humored, with skin that smells of uncooked turkey, bless you for saving me from a date with Jack Kennedy.

"Jackie! I was just passing by." He steps out of the car and takes my hand possessively. "I was worried about you driving home so late. So I thought I'd wait for you."

I squeeze Jack's forearm. "Maybe some other time."

"Yeah, sure." Jack turns and scampers back into the party.

When I get back to New York, a floozy opens Black Jack's apartment door and rudely asks me what I want. Behind her, Black Jack is dead drunk, passed out on his sofa, his shirt unbuttoned, his flaccid belly drooping over his belt like a dollop of butterscotch. I can't live like this. I can't afford my own place. I have no place else to go.

I hate to hand victory to Janet, but she's won big this time. She cruelly let him think I would stay with him for the summer, then tormented me until I dragged myself back to Washington, which she knew would send Black Jack off on a drinking binge. That's so like her.

Get me away from these people! I can't take it anymore.

Yes, Janet wins this round. I'll quit my job at *Vogue*. What do I care about clothes, anyhow?

ITALY

But this is the latest fashion," protests Lee. "I bought them in Milan, the fashion capital of the world. I don't understand what your problem is." She twirls on the ball of her foot, her baby-blue culottes falling just below her rump.

"This is Venice, not Milan. Besides, have you seen any Italian women walking around in them?"

"Oh, they dress so boring. They all wear the same thing like a uniform—a red or blue pleated skirt, white blouse, espadrilles, a blue V-neck sweater draped over their shoulders. And they wear the same thing day after day."

"I think they look nice."

"I'm not saying they're dowdy. It's just boring."

"So you're going to wear those outside the pensione?"

"You're jealous because I have better-looking legs than you do."

"You better wear some shoes you can run in."

She creates a riot in Piazza San Marco. As she tosses breadcrumbs into the air, a crowd of pigeons coo at her feet, attracting attention. Young men circle around Lee, trying not to get their eyes pecked out, shouting questions at her: "*Sei americana? Come ti chiami? Sei un'attrice televisiva? Ti piace Venezia? Sei sposata? Mangiamo una pizza!*" And when we try to walk away, "*Dove vai?*" They shout their names like a roll call—"*Io sono Luciano. Questo è Alberto. Lorenzo. Paolo. Giuseppe. Michelangelo.*"

Every time Lee turns a corner, men shout out and grab her butt. In every café, men descend like flies on prosciutto. *Ciao bella!* Our eyes are floating from all the cappuccinos they buy us. Up and over Ponte di Rialto they follow, down the left bank of the Grand Canal to the pink Palazzo Fontana-Rezzonico, past Chiesa di San Geremia, up and over Ponte dei Scalzi. Lee is Lady Godiva, an American star. We escape on a gondola. The men wave from the bridges, begging us not to leave.

"*Belle ragazze! Perché partite? Venite con noi.*"

"God, they're animals!" Lee squeals with delight. "They're crazy."

"*Sì, tutti pazzi.*" The gondolier nods his head dolefully as if their behavior pains him deeply. He then asks Lee if she's married. "They all ask me that! How come? Isn't that rude? They can't all be looking for a wife."

"Italian men are very vain," he says. "They don't want their nose smashed by your angry husband."

He lets us off at Chiesa di Santo Stefano to look at the frescoes. A priest in a heavy black robe waddles down the nave, flicking his hands, shooing Lee out like a farmer's wife chasing chickens from her summer pantry. "What wrong with him?" Lee asks plaintively. I leave her to fend for herself for a few minutes and dip past the altar to see the magnificent Tintoretto paintings—his *Last Supper* and his *Orazione nell'Orto (Agony in the Garden).* When I come out of the church, I see Lee, like the Pied Piper, leading a dozen men up and over Ponte dell'Accademia.

Eventually, even Lee wearies of their attention. She practices her *Va via!,* then begs to go to Harry's Bar, where all the Americans hang out—mostly East Coast college boys on summer vacation.

"Can you believe everything is so old?" says a corn-fed sophomore from Cornell. They guzzle cheap Chianti and talk about American sports and how great America is. Lee sticks to them like flypaper.

I leave her in their safe, capable hands and head out to admire the Peggy Guggenheim Collection in the Palazzo Venier dei Leoni.

Florence wakes like a surly adolescent boy who buries his head in his pillow. It dozes until the full sun hits its face, then springs alive, noisy and awkward, clanking, stomping, honking, protesting the annoyance of having to get up at all.

Whereas Venice made me feel like a Victorian psychic—feminine and opulent, melancholy and mysterious, spiritual and spooky—Florence makes me feel like Mercutio itching for a scuffle. It's noisy and busy—not like dreamy Venice at all.

I swing open the heavy dark green shutters and look out over orange-tiled rooftops. A mist rises from the Arno, giving everything a hazy blue tint. The moist summer air smells of roasting coffee beans and tanned leather. As the sun breaks over the hills, it warms the yellow-brown palazzi. The buildings begin to glow. They seem to breathe.

Behind me, I hear Lee bustling around, getting ready for the day. She's too excited to decide what to wear. This is the third outfit she's tried on. Thankfully, she finally settles on a knee-length skirt—we may make it through the morning without running for our lives.

"He's an aesthete," says Lee. "The most famous aesthete in the world."

"Is that a job? I guess I missed that listing in *The Washington Post.* Wanted: one individual especially sensitive to beauty and art. Needed to look at stuff for oohing and aahing."

"You don't have to come if you don't want to. I'll go by myself."

"Are you kidding? I'm dying to know what you aspire to be when you grow up."

"You are such a bitch sometimes."

Last year Lee read a book by Bernard Berenson in her art history class at Farmington. She wrote him a fan letter and he invited her to visit if she ever came to Florence. She's terribly proud of this, which makes it irresistible to tease her. "Does he know you're only seventeen?"

"It's not like that. He's famous."

"Famous for what?"

"For loving art. He knows more about Italian art than anyone in the world."

So we're off to see this fountainhead of culture, the sage of Settignano.

In a borrowed Cinquecento, we drive through Piazza della Signoria to Piazza della Republica, where vendors are setting up shacky little carts displaying leather purses, silk scarves, and jewelry. Vespas and impossibly small cars whiz around the narrow streets, smooshing pedestrians up against the medieval walls.

The sun climbs the sky as we drive over Ponte Vecchio. Shopkeepers hose down the streets and roll up massive grates that rattle loudly over storefronts. Pigeons take off in a mad swish.

We stop at our favorite café bar in Piazza Santo Spirito to grab a *pan dulce* and *café latte* before driving south up the hill toward the Etruscan hill town of Fiesole. Supposedly we'll run into Settignano about halfway there.

We drive out the straight, narrow streets, bumping over cobblestones until we get to Via Romana. It heads straight out the old Roman entrance of the city, then winds up into rolling hills of tangled grapevines and gnarled olive trees that flourish in the clay soil surrounding Florence. Orange-tiled farmhouses dot the landscape. Patchwork plots of tomatoes and eggplants are marked by stone walls and ancient decaying Roman ruins. Lines of cypress trees guard the orchards like a line of infantry descending a hill. The air smells of ripe apricots.

The car grinds slowly up the hills. "You're going to have to get out and walk up the hill," says Lee.

"Fat chance."

"Exactly. You're heavier than I am." Lee can't bear to say that horrible word *fat* even in jest.

"I'm driving."

Neither of us gets out. The engine gnashes and frets away in pure agony. I hope we don't start rolling backward. When we get to the top of the hill, I am exhausted and feel compelled to give the poor car a rest. I park beside a small

Romanesque church. We unfold ourselves and take a walk around the cobblestone piazza.

Florence is even more spectacular from a distance—the hard masculine lines softened by the rolling blue-green hills and the luminous haze. I think of an orange leaf fallen on a mossy forest floor.

We walk up a hill to a yellow villa that dominates the grand terraced garden leading up to it. The steps are lined with tall cypress trees that cast long shadows over the hill. Low square bushes frame marble statues of Roman gods. This is I Tatti. As we trudge up the stairs, I feel like Dorothy approaching the Emerald City.

We stand before an enormous wooden door. Lee lifts the brass ring on the knocker, which is the face of a satyr, and taps it three times. A maid in black with a frilly white organdy apron opens the door.

We step inside to a cool room with polished terra-cotta tiles, white walls, and a ceiling inlaid with various woods. While we wait, I admire a sixteenth-century Sienese triptych of Saint Francis with a magnificent gold frame. A Chinese porphyry lion watches us.

It feels tranquil and timeless.

When we sign the guest book, I flip through to see who else has been here. I'm impressed—President Truman; Bertrand Russell; famous writers like Santayana, Vernon Lee, Percy Lubbock, Edith Wharton, Carlo Levi, D'Annunzio, Walter Lippmann, Somerset Maugham, Ray Bradbury; artists like Marc Chagall and musicians like Yehudi Menuhin; royalty like the king of Sweden, the Queen Mother of Romania, the Princess Shams Pahlavi. They come to him to pay their respects—as if he were the pope.

Who is this guy?

Berenson's companion Nicky Mariano, a stocky English-looking woman who wears a long tweed skirt and sensible shoes, greets us and reads our letter of introduction. "He's in a bit of a snit today, but two young women ought to pick up his spirits." Lee's eyes get real big, as if she wonders what she's gotten us into.

Nicky Mariano suggests that we wait in the garden. We sit on a stone bench. After a few minutes a little elfin man totters toward us out of the woods from behind his villa. He is short and very thin, with a white beard and brown hat.

He sees us without expression, then slowly climbs the steps to the patio. He stops at the top, swings his cane in front, and leans on it with both hands like a vaudeville minstrel. "Have you come to worship me?" He glances briefly at Lee, then looks at me, smirking.

"I don't even know who you are," I say. I feel Lee tense, mortified.

He blinks, twice, then guffaws. "There's no reason you should. Come, dears."

Silently he leads up through the French doors into his salon, a sparsely fur-
nished room. Each piece is several centuries old. Lee and I sit on a small couch,
knees together, hands in our laps. Berenson takes off his coat and hat, and settles
down in a wingback chair. A gleaming-gold Madonna and child by Domenico
Veneziano hangs over his mantel. All around the room books and manuscripts are
piled high on intricately carved sixteenth-century tables.

He is bald with a sculpted face, long nose and high forehead and eyes that see
to your very core. He wears a gray Italian three-piece suit and a ruby ring on his
left pinkie. His hands are the most beautiful I've seen on a man—tapered and
refined without being feminine. There is something nearly translucent about
him.

"What can I do for you?" he says.

We're both taken aback. Bravely, Lee scoots to the edge of the couch and
pipes, "I studied your book in art history class. I learned so much from it that I
wanted to thank you in person."

"Which book was that?"

The Italian Painters of the Renaissance."

"Nice little book. Much is incorrect, but I didn't know that at the time. You
came all this way to tell me you liked my book?"

"Well, no. We're here on vacation and—"

"Ah, the summer abroad. And what will you do when you return from your
European tour?" He doesn't let Lee answer. "I suppose you'll get married and
never have another thought about Dosso Dossi or Domenico Fetti or Jacopo Pon-
tormo or Correggio again. Then I don't suppose I should bore you talking about
art."

"I wouldn't be bored," Lee whimpers.

He asks us personal questions, badgering poor Lee: "What do you think a husband can do for you? Why do you think you need to marry to love, to be happy, to
have a full life? I have always suspected women are better off not marrying but
having many affairs. Do you see yourself becoming your mother? Are you in love?
Are you a virgin?" Honestly! It's not as if he's particularly interested in us—rather
it's as if he is interviewing us for some survey he's putting together. But there's
something about him that makes you want to answer, his eyes scraping at the back
of your skull like an art restorer rubbing off a second-rate painting to reveal a
masterwork beneath.

At first, Lee sits enraptured, but soon I'm delighted to see her eager Sunday-
school face harden into indignation—her grand master is a horny old goat, making

love to us with words. She sits primly, muscles taut, politely attentive, until she can't take it any longer.

"Excuse me, but do you really think it's appropriate to talk about love with young women?" She sounds like Janet gearing up for a long scold.

Berenson guffaws. His teeth are remarkably white. "Have I embarrassed you, my dear?"

Of course he has, but Lee won't admit it. "No. I just don't think it's appropriate."

"Appropriate to whom? Who is listening but us three? Don't you think love is important, my dear?"

"Of course it is."

"Are you sure?"

"Yes," Lee says unsurely.

"If you don't talk about it, how will you begin to understand it? I have beautiful paintings all around me, but if I do not look at them and think about them, if I don't try to express their beauty in words, I will never know them. The same with love."

Lee shrugs, speechless.

"Sexuality is all around you—the flowers, the birds, the art. When I was young, I wondered how as an old man I could live without sex. But I have sex every day, all day. I experience the world. My senses are roused by the energy of life. I feel the excitement of creation in my loins. Do you enjoy sex, my dear?"

Lee is about to rupture. I can hardly keep from laughing, imagining what Mummy would think if she knew the Last Great Humanist, the finest intellectual of his time, was talking to us about sex.

After lunch he takes us on a walk through his gardens lined with cypress trees and along grass vistas that lead to sculptures. "You must learn to walk with your eyes," he says. He stops and frames a picture of the world with his thumbs and index fingers like a photographer or a landscape painter. "Everything in nature is a metaphor for something else. See how that shadow crosses the pavement. The world is a poem. And every day, every moment it changes with the light, the season, the passing migration of birds. I never tire of simply looking out my window."

Gradually, Berenson's words begin to make sense to me. It's as if I am learning a new language. He is talking about a way of perceiving the world that I had never imagined before. I listen carefully.

"A beautiful woman is a work of art. Take care how you present yourself. Censor the things you read, the people you meet. Make sure they are life-enhancing, that they add to your artwork. You must live your life, not merely exist."

Lee's eyes glaze over—completely tuned out. She seems to fade, and I realize Berenson is addressing me solely.

He cuts a pink rose with a small pair of scissors. He snaps off the thorns with shaky hands, takes a pin from his own lapel, and fastens it to my jacket. His stiff fingers have a hard time bending the fabric and pushing the pin. I watch him, his nose six inches from mine. I smell his elegant cologne. I feel oddly aroused. He looks up into my eyes like a lover, smiling, melting me. He steps back a foot and tilts his head as if studying a painting.

"Very lovely. You should wear pink, my dear. It highlights your hair and eyes, and brings out a subtle mauve in your skin. Yes. Wear pink, my dear."

Mauve skin? "Thank you," I say.

He pours information into us—his thoughts on love, work, and death—as if to give us a transfusion. I sense this column of golden energy between us—an electricity. His voice seems to become almost disembodied. There is an urgency to his monologue, as if he is reviewing highlights from a lifetime of thinking, skipping from one subject to another as if he doesn't have time to go into any depth but wants us to get the chapter headings. I feel smitten and strangely moved. But it's too much to take in.

After a few hours of this, he appears spent, falling into silence. He waves us a contented good-bye.

"Be sure to write me, dears." I suspect our visit won't merit even a mention in his journal.

"Jesus," says Lee as we climb back into our Cinquecento, "what a dirty old man. Can you believe it? All that silly talk when all the old lech really wanted to do was bonk us."

I don't know whether he's a dirty old man, a poet, or a genius. I feel transformed in a way I can't explain to Lee. I went to I Tatti a child. Now I am a woman. Part of me feels ashamed. I have not fully lived my life, but merely existed. I have blundered through my days unaware. He is right—I must open my eyes and see.

A month later Berenson sends me a letter responding to my thank-you note. "Please, dear, write to this old man so he can remember your beautiful young face." When I read the letter to Lee, she shoots me a look that I fully understand only years later—a mixture of hurt, jealousy, and helplessness. "How nice for you. You love to write letters," she says, then sulks off.

Berenson and I write to each other, a love affair of sorts, treading an intimacy I've never experienced before, loving a man whom I'll never see again, a man so old and rarefied that he almost seems to be a mind without a body.

Berenson becomes a voice inside my head.

INQUIRING CAMERA GIRL

*U*ntil you get m-married, you will stay at home."

Since Lee and I got back from Europe, Janet has bullied Hughdie into laying down the law. He squirms under the delivery of an ultimatum, his doughy face flushing.

"Then I guess I'll need to get another job. I can't live on the fifty dollars a month Black Jack gives me."

Hughdie wants to avoid saying that he won't contribute to my allowance. He scratches vigorously behind his cabbage-leaf ear. "I haven't discussed your getting a job with your m-mother."

"I could always get work modeling. I'd have to live in New York."

Janet doesn't approve of this idea, of course. She twists Hughdie's arm to get me a job in Washington. He calls Frank Waldrop, editor of the *Washington Times-Herald*. Not exactly intellectual fare, but lively and better than a tabloid.

I immediately like Frank, a wry old newspaperman who dresses in tweeds and wears thick glasses. He speaks in a rapid-fire monotone. "What you do is go interview a bunch of people, then snap their picture with this." He hands me an old Speed Graphic with worn decals of half-clad women on it.

"What kinds of questions?"

"Oh, like 'Do you think ladies should wear white after Labor Day?' Nothing too deep or political. You'll figure it out. Get someone in the office to help you get the form down."

Inquiring Camera Girl at twenty-five dollars a week.

I adore everything about my new job—the noisy newsroom, desks jammed on top of one another, books and papers spilling on the floor, the clackety-clack of typewriters and teletype machines, telephones ringing, reporters and editors running in opposite directions, the smell of coffee and musty books, the gurgling of continuous argument. Everyone is smart. The girls are as sassy as street urchins. The boys drop a classical reference into every sentence. They all say outrageously funny things. No time to laugh—you've got to think up a comeback.

My new friend, John White, a brilliant, very literary ex-marine feature writer, takes me to see the movie *His Girl Friday*.

"The world of journalism is nothing like that," he says.

"Yes, it is. And you're the spitting image of Cary Grant."

"In a pig's eye."

I tilt my head and squint. He actually looks more like Marlon Brando—that brooding look, muscular and meaty, with full lips and a perpetual squint. He dresses in threadbare thrift-shop clothes. His delivery is cheerless like Brando's, and he has the same disdain for everything—particularly high society and debutantes.

We have a grand time together.

They all think I'm a lightweight and call me Deb, but when it comes time for the Tuxedo Ball, the season's opening event, they beg me for tickets. Even scruffy reporters like to dress up once in a while.

John White introduced me to a fascinating guy named Bill Walton, an artist who was a war correspondent for *Time* magazine. Walton is as exuberant as White is phlegmatic. They're both friends with my old buddy Charlie Bartlett. Three wild and crazy guys. They let me hang around them, probably because I sit adoringly at their feet, begging for stories. We hit the bars after work, then go to White's book-lined basement apartment in Georgetown, smoke, and listen to jazz. I feel like an old newspaper gal already.

My column is frothy and inconsequential, the type of thing you turn to when you are exhausted and can't bear another article about Truman's incompetence in Korea. Sometimes I add my own pen-and-ink caricatures, which are a real hit.

It's the oddest thing. Ask a complete stranger a personal question and nine times out of ten, he'll try to answer honestly. If you ask people you know the same questions, you get nothing but a tissue of lies.

I love ferreting out people's secrets and exploring how a photo—an exterior exposure—can reveal their interior. A woman who says she doesn't believe in sex before marriage leans back to roll on her lipstick, mouth open, eyes half closed, focusing on her image in a compact mirror. I ask a man whether or not a contented bachelor should marry. He takes a vigorous bite of his roast beef sandwich. Behind him the Washington Monument looms out of focus.

I am in love with the newspaper world. It's the perfect way of both having a job and experiencing life. I can never go back to Newport, to people who skate on the surface of life, oblivious to the world teeming beneath them. They forget they're even skating on water, concerned only with whether the other skaters notice their new mink muffs and crinoline skirts.

God save me from becoming a Newport matron!

I go to the Capitol to ask my questions of the lunchtime crowd—aides and secretaries eating their sandwiches on the Mall.

I have two hours before I have to get back to the paper and type up my stories. It's a beautiful day for a walk—one of the first cool days after a hot, muggy summer. I feel adventurous.

There are vast sections of Washington, D.C., where a white woman is never seen taking a walk. But if Lee Miller could photograph Dachau and babies dying in Vienna's hospitals, surely I can explore my own capital city. I'm a reporter, after all.

I walk northeast, away from the Capitol. I am a little scared, yet the camera gives me a kind of protection, a passport to go where I wouldn't otherwise dare venture.

I walk down blocks of neat brick row houses, not unlike the houses in Georgetown except all the people are colored. Boys shoot marbles in the street. Women hang out laundry. Men play checkers. Old ladies sit in windows, fanning their faces. The sidewalk is their parlor, a place to socialize. There are few cars.

My heart races in my chest. I bring the camera to my eye and frame my shots. Behind the brick buildings is a narrow dirt alley of mud puddles. The Senate Building looms at the end, white, gigantic, imperial, as out of place in this landscape as an ocean liner in a mangrove. *Click.* Six little Negro boys sit on a fence. *Click.* A woman sweeps the balcony of a two-story building. *Click.* Four little girls with pigtails sticking straight out of their heads run around in circles on the sidewalk. *Click, click.* Their mothers, dressed in the same cotton shifts as their daughters, chat as they watch. An elderly woman draws water from a fire hydrant into a tin pail. Three men, one in a rocker, two in folding chairs, sit idly. They look as if they haven't moved in years. *Click, click.*

I tremble with excitement. I am Dorothea Lange documenting the Negroes from the Mississippi Delta. I am Walker Evans shooting the slums of New York City. I am Ben Shahn snapping Arkansas cotton pickers. I am Jacqueline Bouvier, photographer.

I turn at Fenton Place down another street of brick tenement houses. All the doors and windows are open with someone sitting or standing in them. Black faces look at me with curiosity.

An older gentleman asks me if I'm lost.

"My name is Jacqueline Bouvier. I write a column for the *Times-Herald.* I ask the man on the street his opinion about things, then take his picture. May I ask you a question?"

He slaps his thighs and throws back his head, laughing—his wide-open mouth reveals several missing teeth. "You gonna put my picture in the newspaper?" He stomps his feet, then shakes his head like a wet dog. "Sure, I'll answer yo' question."

I give him a dollar. Soon I have a crowd around me. By the time I'm done, I've spent my entire month's salary.

At first I ask innocuous questions like "What do you want most in life?" but I can't avoid the obvious. "What one thing should Washington do to help colored people?" "Who do you think will do more for civil rights, Adlai Stevenson or Eisenhower?" "Do you think black and white people should live in the same neighborhoods, go to the same banks and restaurants?" "Do you think black and white children should go to the same school?" "How do you think life will be different for your children?"

These men and women let me see them as they are—shining shoes, fixing bicycles, shopping. What moves me most is how they care for their children, always touching and talking to them, watching them at play. This is what it is to be a mother. This is what it's like to be part of a community.

I think of the chilly Newport picnics and wonder why wealth should inhibit affection.

I march into Frank Waldrop's office, exhilarated. This must be how Lee Miller felt when she covered the liberation of Paris.

My photos are still damp from the developer. While Waldrop blabs on the phone, I spread them out on his desk. They're the best I've ever taken. I hand him my story.

As he hangs up the phone, he raises an eyebrow. He skims my story and then tosses it on his desk. "Sorry, kid. It's a good thing it's a busy news day. We'll bump your column with a story on the autumn color."

"You won't print it?"

"Look, kid, I appreciate what you're trying to do, but your column is a fluff piece. Don't try to make it something it isn't."

"I know. But what if one day I slip in something like this? Wouldn't it wake people up?"

"It would make 'em spill their coffee. The dry cleaners of Washington will thank you. No one else will."

"But, but, but—"

"You're sounding like a motorboat, Deb."

"These are important questions."

"If you want to write about the plight of the poor Negroes, you ought to go into politics."

"Maybe I will."

"Sure, honey. You might want to register to vote first."

How did he know I've never voted? As I stomp out of his office, I hear him chuckle. "Don't forget you're a Republican."

Furious, I tear home to Merrywood to take Danseuse for a gallop. Sure, I'm a deb running home to her horses. Why bother trying to be something else?

"It will be so nice to have grandchildren." Janet stabs the air with her chin, peering down her beaky nose at me. Yes, Mummy, I understand, I'm a failure. No one wants me. "And Lee's snagged a prince. Can you image that?"

"He may be the bastard child of the duke of Kent, Mummy. We don't know for sure."

"You can see royalty in his face. He has such nice manners. His adoptive father owns a publishing house. Now that's class."

"Is he in the *Social Register?*"

"Don't use that sarcastic tone with me, young lady. But, yes, he is. At least Lee is getting married. It wouldn't hurt you to look for a few names in the *Social Register.*"

Like John White? Right.

I back down—I don't want to fight today. "He's nice and Lee loves him." I like him, too. He's funny, his humor self-effacing. But there is something dark and melancholy about Michael Canfield, as if he were happiest strolling alone in the rain, composing poems on suicide. He tries to please everyone and looks perfectly miserable most of the time.

And he drinks. A lot.

"You put me in an awkward position, Jacqueline. It's quite embarrassing for me to have to make excuses for you. Lee, four years younger, gets engaged before you. You've had your debut, you've been to Europe, you've met dozens of perfectly acceptable young men. You really must make more of an effort."

"I like working. I got a raise to forty dollars a week. I'll move on to better jobs."

"Hughdie likes that John Husted fellow. What about him? Just choose someone."

"But I don't love anyone."

"My dear, if you wait for love, you'll die an old maid."

"You loved Black Jack."

"I did not," she says vehemently. "I wanted to get away from home. He was from a good family and at the time had money."

No, you lie, Mummy dearest. You loved him and love him still, and in the dark when Hughdie fumbles with your breasts, it's Black Jack you imagine—Black Jack's coal eyes, Black Jack's gravity, Black Jack's speeding red roadster taking you away, away, away. And when you dance with him at Lee's wedding, you will lose yourself, swooning as he twirls you around the dance floor, whispering in your ear how beautiful you are and how he remembers the first time he made love to you, in a horse stall in the hay, the day before your wedding, how you looked, and how he'd like to make you look like that again—"Right now. Let's go. No one will miss us"—and you nearly go with him.

"Well, if you don't marry, at least I'll have a daughter to look after me in my old age."

She knows how to frighten me into silence.

During the wedding, Michael Canfield looks amiable but resigned, like a teenage boy forced to host his mother's tea party.

Lee's eyes sparkle as she stands above the crowd on the steps of Holy Trinity Cathedral, under the dogwood, in her gown of ivory Chinese organza, all eyes on her, imagining that she is a princess, imagining her marriage will be day after day of this giddy joy.

Poor Pekes.

From the terrace at Merrywood, Lee throws me her bridal bouquet. We both laugh as I catch it, she because this is her greatest moment of triumph, married before her sister, me because it makes her so happy, her mad rivalry momentarily appeased. She is very beautiful.

Yet sorrow tugs at my heart for what I see ahead. Lee mistakes my expression for envy, which adds to her triumph. It is all yours, Lee. I dismiss the future. I laugh and smile in her present victory. Joyously I give this to her. I wish I could give her more.

On her wedding night her besotted husband is impotent.

John Husted has asked me to marry him. He asks me once a day.

Janet springs into action, interviewing his superiors from work, fishing for gossip at the horse shows, cornering bankers at the beach clubs. "Why don't you open a detective agency, Mummy? Think of all the gossip you'd score." She decides that although he doesn't make much on Wall Street now, he has good earning potential. He's a hard worker and honest. His family is in the *Social Register*.

Oh, dear. How dreary.

Finally, I agree. By the time the announcement comes out in the *Times-Herald* in January 1952, I'm already having second thoughts.

Oblivious, John takes me to dinner at the Ashcrofts', a properly cooked meal of pork, three vegetables, and orange sherbet. Six couples: the husbands, Wall Street brokers or lawyers; the wives, seated across from their husbands, quietly agreeing to anything anyone says. Several of the women have children about to enter prep schools, and discuss the merits of Foxcroft over Farmington, St. Timothy's over St. Mark's, St. Paul's over Exeter. They all vacation in Newport and have made at least one trip to Europe, where they all stayed at the same hotels, all took the same four-hour tours of medieval cities, and all bought the same overpriced faience in Arezzo. They concur that Europe isn't sanitary and people there should take more baths.

I watch John unconsciously mimic the mannerisms of his host, sitting back in his seat after the meat course, dabbing his lips, declining, then accepting, a third glass of wine, his wholesome face slightly flushed. He implies in his conversation— "I don't think Jacqueline would mind a place on the Vineyard"—that he and I are planning a life together. Hysteria flutters below my solar plexus. A moth caught in a Chinese lantern, her wings rasping against rice paper.

I need to tell a bawdy joke, or use the fine sterling to tap out a syncopated rumba on the wineglasses, or throw off my clothes and jump in the pool. I can't breathe. I look around the table, finding fault in everyone—one wife looks like Winston Churchill, another like Minnie Mouse. They fade and flatten, becoming cartoons of themselves, their features and mannerisms exaggerated and grotesque. I begin to laugh. The hostess glances at me, at first smiling with interest, then becoming alarmed. The moth beats wildly to escape. I fan my face, sip water, then apologize—something must've caught in my throat.

Later John says not unkindly, "I suppose you were nervous. When we're married, I hope you don't act like that." He thinks I had too much to drink.

"Act like what?"

"Well . . . like you were bored. Like you couldn't wait to get out of there.

They really are very nice people, you know. I wouldn't have asked you to dine with them if I didn't think so."

"Yes. Very nice." I feel a vine slowing twisting around my body, squeezing, sapping the life out of me.

I walk alone along the shore of Narragansett Bay and watch the seagulls. Agitated, they swirl in figure eights, cawing loudly. I see an eagle dive after one and peck its tail feathers. Below, some boys have been fishing and cleaned their fish on the rocks. The birds are fighting over the heads and guts.

Watching them, I think animals never go against their instincts. If a predator attacks, they fight or flee—they do not hesitate. They don't ask themselves, "If I fly away, what will the other birds say about me?" They don't stick around, hoping things will get better. They're gone. Yet humans betray their instincts all the time. Their instincts tell them to walk out of a dinner party, to slap the person who has insulted them, to end a marriage, to strip off their clothes, to flee. But they stay. Because it's the proper thing to do.

How can civilization be a good thing if it betrays the voice that speaks loudest within us?

How can I marry into a culture where the modus operandi is artifice, phoniness, a constant betrayal of my instincts?

On a hot, steamy summer night, I arrive at yet another ball, this in a Federal mansion on the Potomac. John couldn't make it down from New York, so I am by myself. I try to muster enthusiasm, sparkle, as Janet calls it, but I feel heavy and enervated. I wonder what I'm doing with my life.

The French windows on the first floor stand open to catch any breeze. The rugs in the largest rooms have been rolled up and the furniture removed to make room for dancing. On the terrace are small round tables covered in lavender linen tablecloths. A bar attended by three Negroes in one of the smaller rooms is already crowded with mostly Yale and Harvard men. The men are dressed in dinner jackets and part their hair in the middle with fraternity pins on their waistcoats. The women wear floor-length ball gowns. I wear a strapless ivory dress I borrowed from Lee. It's a little snug and a little short, but at least I won't have to worry about tripping when I dance.

My fingers itch for a cigarette. I try to calculate how long I should wait before heading out to the terrace to light up, and then how long before I can leave.

I watch this year's debutantes sweep in on the arms of their dates, eyes dancing, filled with excitement, amazed and delighted to be the center of attention. I feel old and jaded. I don't belong here. It's hard to breathe. I step outside.

The swamp air rising from the Potomac smells primal and cloying. I watch the chauffeurs chatting serenely by the fountain, and the faint glow of their cigarettes like fireflies in the steamy night.

The Meyer Davis band strikes up a blistering version of "Blue Tango." I wave to couples I know as they enter the room or dance by, but make no effort at conversation. I sip my Americano and watch. The bitter-sage drink suits my mood.

Then I see Jack Kennedy sauntering through the garden door like an uninvited guest. He looks around, expecting to be noticed. White teeth flash from his bronzed face, his eyes blazing, hungry for fun. There is something breathtaking about his appearance, an abrupt physical impact on the entire room. Everyone looks up. Several men shout his name and wave him over. He smiles and shakes hands, making the bumblebee entrance, buzzing from table to table as he wends his way to the bar.

It's difficult for me not to watch him.

With drink in hand, he focuses in on the prettiest girls in the room, then, trying not to be too obvious, buzzes from couple to couple until he's standing next to a blonde.

He is a terrible dancer. He shuffles his feet, shoving his partner around the dance floor, his skinny limbs jangling like a marionette's. Every once in a while, I see him squeeze her arm and wince. She probably can't help stepping on his feet. He smiles hard and pulls her into his arms.

The song ends. They exchange a few words and disappear together toward the billiard room. In ten minutes he's back. Like Black Jack from under the bleachers. He spends the next twenty minutes talking to Senator Mike Mansfield. He tosses back his head in a boisterous laugh. When he lowers his chin, his eyes fall on a dainty-featured girl across the room who's chatting with a friend. She looks up and smiles. He shakes the senator's hand, then beelines across the dance floor toward her. He doesn't stalk his quarry. He doesn't need to—he plucks them from the passing water.

"Hi, Jacqueline. You look enchanting tonight, as always."

I turn and see a short, prematurely balding young man with a pie-shaped face. "Thank you, Rexford. Where's Dorothy?"

"She's over there with Milton. She sent me off to get drinks so she can talk Thoroughbred bloodlines. Hey, I read your column this morning about the Chevy Chase Ice Palace. I like your delivery. Very wry. Your stuff reminds me a bit of Oscar Wilde."

"Oh, my goodness! Oscar Wilde is my idol. I'll never live up to that comparison."

"Not that I know anything, but I think you could be a writer. I mean, like novels or plays. Have you tried your hand at something like that?"

"A little. It requires so much sitting in one place."

"Like they say, if it was easy, everyone would do it. I better go fetch Dorothy before she buys another pony. You need a dance partner? Shall I find someone for you?"

"Thank you, Rexford, but no. I don't feel much like dancing."

"Collecting material?"

"Could be."

"I'm sticking close to the doors myself. Can you believe how hot it is? Don't be a wallflower."

As Rexford waddles toward his wife, Kennedy and his new dance partner bob by like debris caught in a current. The girl looks relieved when the song ends. They stop in front of me.

Jack's nasal voice cuts through the chatter. He must know I'm eavesdropping—I'm staring right at them—but he doesn't glance up. He starts the business about how maybe she'd like to be First Lady. "I'm going to be president, you know." All in good fun, flirtatious kidding, and the girl knows it. Yet the way she looks at him, you can tell she's willing to give up something on the off chance that maybe her prince has come. Everyone in the room sees what's going on. I walk over to the girl's boyfriend, who stands glowering by the punch bowl.

"Hi, Alfred. How's the punch?"

"Hi, Jackie. Here, let me pour you some." He ladles the insipid yellow liquid into a glass cup, his eyes never leaving the awkward dancing couple.

"Thank you. Why don't you dance with your fiancée?"

"I'd rather watch Kennedy put the moves on her."

"You sound like a man in love."

"We haven't announced yet. It's a good thing I'm getting to see what she's made of. Her chances at becoming Mrs. Framingham are fading by the second."

"Don't worry about Kennedy. He's not a serious person. I haven't taken a spin yet. Let's dance."

Alfred's a fine dancer. I lean back and surrender to his lead. He begins to enjoy himself.

In the middle of the next song, Kennedy taps him on the shoulder. We exchange partners. At first, I think Alfred is going to slug him, but Kennedy works his charm. "I didn't mean to monopolize your lady, my friend, but she's simply stunning tonight. Hold on to her. She's a gem." As Alfred dances off with his fiancée, she looks over his shoulder at Kennedy, her expression slightly forlorn.

"I just spotted you, Miss Bouvier. Have you been here long?" Jack's palms are damp, and I very nearly push him away.

"I thought you were ignoring me on purpose."

"Who could ignore you?"

"You could. I'm not your type."

"Who says? I like your figure." He runs his eyes up and down my body, unclothing me. "It's athletic, not so much the Babe Didrikson type as the Helen Wills."

"Who?"

"You've never heard of the Babe? 'Thirty-two Olympics. Gold medalist in track. Woman Athlete of the Year. She's won every major professional golf championship at least once. Helen Wills won eight Wimbledon singles. A reporter like you should follow sports. At least women's sports."

"Never made much sense to me to watch sports. It's like watching the other kids play at recess while you're stuck wiping down the chalkboard."

"I bet you never had to wipe down a chalkboard."

"No, but I certainly spent time in the office of the headmistress."

"What'd you do?"

"Oh . . . the typical thing. I broke into the kitchen and stole cookies. I got caught smoking. I wore my clothes backwards. I spilled chocolate mousse in Miss Fussbuzzard's lap. What's wrong?"

"For a moment, you reminded me of my sister Kick."

"Is that a good thing?"

"Sure is. I loved Kick."

"Loved?"

For a moment the color goes out of his eyes. He blinks. "Don't you like any sports?"

"I ride."

"Oh, a horsewoman."

"What's that supposed to mean?"

"Nothing. But you're awfully pretty when you're mad. I've taken to reading that column of yours. I love your little digs at Washington society."

"I call them observations."

"I could give you an exclusive interview. What do you say?"

My ears tingle. That might win me some respect in the old newsroom. "When?"

"It's a tale that would take all night to tell. Are you available?"

I feel a burning disappointment. All he wants is sex. "How about tomorrow—during the day?"

"Tomorrow I'll be out of town. I'd like to see you again, Jackie. You're the most attractive girl I've met all summer."

"Not likely."

"But you are. All the girls here look like they've been cut from the same mold, but you're different. You've got a rare spirit." He looks deeply into my eyes, unsmiling. Something melts inside of me. I almost believe him.

"You're a good observer," he says. "You're interested in people, and that makes you interesting."

He thinks I'm different and finds me interesting!

"You sure you don't want to go for a drive?" he asks.

Not the least bit put out at being turned down, he deposits me with a mutual acquaintance, then buzzes back to another table of debutantes.

"Charlie, you're an interloper."

At another dinner party at the Bartletts', Martha places me beside Jack Kennedy. He asks me out over the second course. I agree to save my hosts from embarrassment—or so I tell myself.

"You like him, don't you?" asks Charlie.

"Don't all the girls?"

"But you *really* like him."

"He bothers me like a rash, but don't you dare tell him."

"Don't worry, I won't. He likes 'em hard to get."

A week later Jack calls me from the road, regaling me with his adventures hustling votes from the DAR. He expects me to drop everything when he calls, to make myself available. I write myself a note and leave it by the telephone—*Don't say yes to Jack Kennedy. You are busy.* My effort, valiant as it is, fails miserably.

"I'm engaged," I tell him.

"So what? I'll pick you up in twenty minutes."

He pulls up in a dented green Buick convertible. Empty coffee cups, food wrappers, books, tennis rackets, and congressional briefings litter the backseat. The dashboard looks as if it has never been cleaned. An enormous bird dropping on the windshield stares me in the face.

He drives like a maniac, draping one arm around my shoulders while steering casually with the other, his auburn hair flying in the wind. A smile plays on his lips, suddenly erupting for no reason into a boyish grin. He looks young for his age except for the crow's-feet around his eyes, and when his mood changes abruptly from exuberance to melancholy. His remoteness is alluring.

"I suppose you've been warned about me," he says. "The mothers of Washington's most attractive women conspire against me."

"I've heard a story or two. But I like rakes."

"I'm terribly misunderstood," he says lugubriously. We both laugh.

We drive along Chesapeake Bay to the coast. He leans back and lets the sea air blast in his face. As the sun sets, the ocean turns midnight blue, the sky a soft gray. He stops the car at a lookout point.

"We're the luckiest people alive, Jackie. To see the ocean like this." He squeezes my hand. I feel transported. He looks deeply into my eyes. "I'm the luckiest man alive to be with you."

I laugh nervously, a little frightened by his intensity. "You could score in a convent."

"I have. I need all the votes I can get, and nuns always vote. But I'm not trying to score. You're special, Jackie. I've never come across someone as fresh and unassuming."

I know it's a line, but I tremble, excited, waiting for his kiss. I close my eyes.

"Let's get something to eat." He claps his hands. "I'm starved." He starts up the car, and we pull off the gravel back onto the road.

We stop at a roadside stand. We carry our plastic red baskets of deep-fried clams to a picnic table. Jack winces as he sits down.

"Are you okay?" I ask.

"Fine. I hurt my back playing football with Bobby and Teddy. Wait till you meet them. You'll really like 'em."

I try to eat, swatting madly at the mosquitoes, thinking, *If Jack wants me to meet his brothers, he must like me.*

He pops a clam into his mouth. As he chews he looks at me as if I remind him of someone. "She was my best friend, you know."

"Who?"

"My sister Kick. She was the only one in the family who understood me. We were buddies. It was us against them. She married Billy Hartington, heir to the duke of Devonshire. A Protestant. The cleanest break she could've made. Rose never forgave her."

There it is again, that vulnerable, sensitive side of Jack. "You talk like you don't like your family," I say.

"You can't imagine how oppressive it is. Sometimes I feel I don't know who I am. Like I'm somehow doomed."

"You have your entire future ahead of you."

"I think my future is whatever Dad wants it to be."

"It doesn't have to be."

"It does now. I have to take Joe's place."

"Your brother?"

"First Joe died, then Kick. Both in planes."

"It's your life. You should do what you want."

"Have I told you how pretty you are today?"

Jack clenches his teeth—done with the discussion—but I don't back down. "You think I don't know anything because I'm twelve years younger than you. But I know no one can be happy living someone else's life."

"Do you have enough lemon? I'm going to get some more." Furious, he stomps back to the clam stand. I wonder if I should ask the couple in the white Cadillac convertible for a ride home.

He comes back grinning, eyes bright with enthusiasm. "Let's go skinny-dipping."

I'm relieved his mood has changed. "I'm game," I say.

"But first I have to do this." He puts his hands on my shoulders and presses his lips against mine.

"I don't like you going out with him. He's the only guy I know who can fart higher than his asshole."

John White and I eat tuna sandwiches at the Hot Shoppe. The lunchtime crowd is noisy—sizzling burgers, clattering plates, jangling silverware, slamming screen doors, boisterous greetings. I lean over the chartreuse linoleum tabletop to hear him.

"I didn't know you knew him," I say.

"We used to double-date. He and this Danish girl named Inga Arvad, me and his sister Kick. He goes through women like toilet paper. He has a great line of chatter. You think he's clever until you hear the same wisecrack the next day."

"That describes most guys out there."

"Most guys don't carry a little black book with the names and phone numbers of every woman they've ever slept with or want to sleep with. He puts check marks beside their names."

"I don't believe you."

"He showed it to me. I bet your name is in it."

"No reason to be rude."

"Listen, Jackie. He's a phony. His father does everything for him. Sure, he wrote *While England Slept,* but his father got Arthur Krock to edit it and get it published. His father bought most of the first printing to get it on the bestseller list. They say he's some big war hero for saving the crew of *PT-109.* He lost his fucking ship! Somehow people overlook that."

"I think you're jealous."

"Of course I'm jealous. He's rich. Girls are crazy for him. He's got Kennedy money behind him. But what does he really have that the rest of us don't? Answer me that."

"He has a pleasant personality."

"Are you implying I lack charm?"

"You're sarcastic, peevish, sullen, and obsessive. That's why I like you."

"I'm flattered. I betcha I read better books than he does."

"He probably doesn't sleep with *Death in Venice* under his pillow."

"No. More like, *What Makes Sammy Run?* Jackie, his father did a background check on me when I was dating Kick! He found out stuff about my family even *I* didn't know. He's probably done one on you."

"You think I'm a dope in love, but there's something there in Jack Kennedy."

"And you're going to bring it out for him?"

"Maybe."

"Do yourself a favor, kid. Forget him."

John Husted stays at Merrywood for the weekend. We do the normal things—swimming, golf, cocktails at the Polo Bar, then dinner at Merrywood. I try to be extra nice to him. He is amiable as always, but I notice he doesn't drop hints about our future together. He knows something's changed.

I find myself almost liking him again. Is there a depth I missed before? Something interesting I failed to explore? On the edge of never seeing him again, I regret that I never really gave him a chance. It's too late now. I have already cut the tethers.

When I drop him off at the air terminal to return to New York, I slip off his engagement ring and drop it into his pocket.

"I guess I saw that coming," he says.

"I'm sorry," I say, although I feel relieved. I feel like jumping out of the car and running in circles.

"We could've had a good life together, Jackie."

He leans over to kiss me. I'm repelled. Everything about him seems heavy, an anchor, as if he'll pull me down with him deep under the cold, silent sea, down to the ocean floor where the water is still and where creepy, slow-moving fish blink their bulbous eyes in the dark. I push him away. "I don't want a good life. I want an interesting life. I want to live, not merely exist."

This hurts him, and even to me my words sound hollow—a childish repetition of someone else's sentiments. He sighs hard and nods. I feel like a jerk.

"He'll never take care of you the way I would, even if he is filthy rich."

"I don't need to be taken care of, thank you."

"I hope you know what you're doing, Jacqueline," he says.

"No, I don't. That's the point."

He gets out of my car and doesn't look back.

"SENATOR KENNEDY GOES A-COURTING"

I drive my black Mercury convertible down Old King's Highway from Newport to Hyannis, past Wareham, past the seventeenth-century sea captains' houses and charming saltbox cottages of Sandwich. I pass through the rolling farmlands and salt marshes, catching glances of the sparkling ocean whenever I crest a hill. I drive under ancient trees that touch over the road, through the quaint towns of the Upper Cape that are bursting in bloom—rhododendrons, azaleas, Scotch broom, wisteria. At Barnstable I turn south to the marshes that face Nantucket Sound.

The day is warm and fragrant. I wear culottes, a linen sleeveless blouse, and sandals. A big straw hat lies on the seat beside me, weighted down with a book of poetry I've brought for Jack. The wind blows in my short hair. I've never been so happy.

Is there a specific instant when you fall in love? When you see the essence of that person? When you feel your fates are linked? For me, it was when I saw Jack swim.

He has a funny body—skinny with stick legs, one side higher than the other, shoulders pinched, and a soft, motherly chest. He jokes that he has larger breasts than I do. But when he swims, it's like music, like a knife slicing through water, like a dancer around a daisy chain, hand over hand—controlled, poised, sexy. *Chop, chop, chop.* His arms cut through the water with a steady, almost noiseless rhythm. His tanned arms barely displace a drop, slipping under a whitecap like a plane behind a cloud. He is beautiful. I can't take my eyes off of him.

The moment I saw him swim, I knew everything had changed for me. I knew, suddenly, that two people can be so much more than one, can create a world they could not even dream about by themselves. I knew my place in this world was with Jack.

"Get out of here! You can't be interested in Jack Kennedy. Not seriously. He's such a cad," says Lee. "He's a Mick and his father's a crook," says Black Jack. "He's so dreamy," say the girls at the *Times-Herald*. "He's not in the *Social Register*," says you know who. "You'll be the luckiest girl in the world." "He'll only bring you heartache."

People and their stupid opinions! I toss their comments into the air, where they blow away and snag on the thorns of wild roses by the side of the road. The sun warms my face; the wind blows my hair. I'm in love.

Slowly I pull up to the Kennedy estate at Hyannis Port, down a narrow road that divides a wide lawn with white clapboard houses on either side. At the end of the bluff stands a rambling two-story house, white with black shutters. A United States flag flaps on top of a stainless-steel flagpole in the middle of a wide lawn. The yard ends abruptly at the shoreline, where the dunes are covered with beach plum, bayberry, and marsh grasses. Nantucket Sound glistens in the distance.

Many months ago, after a dozen or so dates, Jack brought me to the Kennedy compound for a dinner with his family.

"So, you're Jack's new girlfriend," said Bobby, striding down from the house, his unbuttoned shirt flapping in the wind, grinning widely, his disheveled hair like marsh grass in a gale. He was smaller and skinnier than Jack, his voice more nasal, his tone slightly petulant.

"Is that what he told you?" I shot back.

"He told me he's in love with you."

"He's never said that to me."

"Well, Jack's not one for wild declarations of love. You'll have to get used to it."

"What about you?"

"Matters what you mean by 'wild.'"

"You're as bad a flirt as Jack."

"Perhaps, but Jack is a more successful flirt."

My skin tingled. Bobby stood close, staring deep into my eyes as if about to kiss me. *Who are these people?*

Teddy watched from the porch, a sloppy fat boy hovering in the background, watching, hungry. Waiting his turn. The sisters avoided me, suspicious, huddling on one side of the yard like a gaggle of geese impatient for the unfamiliar human to leave. I tried to keep them all straight by nicknaming them after the Seven Dwarfs. Teddy was Happy. Bobby was Grouchy. Ethel was Dopey. Eunice was Sneezy. Pat was Bashful. Jean was Sleepy. Sargent Shriver was Doc. There were so many of them.

Ethel was the only one of the women to speak to me. She barreled up to me, her masculine hand outstretched for a handshake as if we were at a fund-raiser. I soon learned that she was always like that, her muscular body coiled tight, knees slightly bent as if perpetually prepared to return a volley. "Look at you. Where did you think you were going? Buckingham Palace?" I was dressed for dinner in a strapless pink cocktail dress. She wore shorts and a T-shirt. "Jacque-leeeen, the queeeen, has come to be seeeen." She whinnied at her joke, her buck teeth chomping at the air. I pulled off my white gloves and slipped them into my purse.

Surely she didn't mean to be unkind, I thought.

The matriarch, Rose Kennedy, glowered at me with disapproval, the same look she gave all women, including her own daughters. Her smiles were reserved for her sons. She barked commands at everyone but was uniformly ignored. She pretended not to be humiliated, but I saw her hurt settling into the lines at the corners of her eyes like silt from dusty rafters. That was the first lesson I learned from this family—if a wife loses the respect of her husband, she loses the respect of her children and everyone else.

I changed into Bermuda shorts, then sat on the porch, watching them play the most pugilistic game of football I had ever seen.

"Hey, Deb! Come join us!" Ethel yelled. "With those clodhoppers of yours, you oughta be able to kick us a field goal."

Surely she didn't mean to be unkind. "Thank you, Ethel, but I'll watch first to learn the rules of the game." As far as I could tell, there *were* no rules to the game.

Soon I realized that what I first mistook for camaraderie and natural competitiveness was pure violence—full of fury and desperation. Bobby charged after Jack. The other men charged after Bobby. The sisters went after Jack or Teddy. Ethel attacked everyone, beating the air with her fists and ululating like Attila the Hun charging across the Mongolian desert. They launched themselves and tumbled onto the ground, a mass of bodies. They stood and rubbed twisted ankles and wrists. They wiped the blood from their scratched faces. Hooting and cheering, they charged again.

My instincts told me to get in my car and drive away, but instead I chatted with Joe Kennedy, who joined me.

Joe was the only one in the family with a modicum of manners, yet he vacillated between charm and cruelty with lightning-fast mood swings. No one told me to be afraid of him, so I wasn't.

"My boy is going to be president one of these days," he said.

"So everyone tells me, but I haven't heard him say he wants to be president."

"He'll do what's right for the family."

"If I were his wife, I wouldn't let him do something he didn't want to do."

Joe looked at me hard, then laughed. "You have spunk, Miss Bouvier. I like that. You just may have what it takes."

Even at dinner, the Kennedys were competitive, the men grabbing platters, dumping huge scoops of potatoes on their plates, the women interrupting conversations, shouting their opinions, banging their silverware for emphasis.

I felt like a new recruit for an elite military operation. I was razzed, tested, and humiliated. They bombarded me with questions and used anything I said as an opportunity to mock me.

Jack monitored my reactions carefully. I smiled and counted to five before reacting to anyone's jibes—it put them off their rhythm and gave me time to think.

By the end of the first evening with them, I was exhausted. I asked Jack to take me home early.

"I thought you were tough enough for them," said Jack, his voice irritated, almost angry.

I ventured cautiously. "Why do they have to be so aggressive to each other? They're your family."

"Don't take it so seriously. If you let them see you cry because Ethel made fun of your dress, you'll never hear the end of it."

I know he loves me, even if he doesn't say it in so many words. I just know it! He gets this sad yearning in his eyes, takes my hand, and kisses it. He calls me all the time, sometimes just to tell me something funny.

On our midnight drives along the Outer Cape, past the ancient seaport towns of Dennis Port and Chatham, after drinks at the Salty Dog Saloon, we park on the beach. We hold hands as we walk in the dunes, the surf lapping gently, the sand still warm from the sun. A full moon rises over the water. We build a fire on the beach and cuddle in a blanket. It is so romantic.

He tells me things that he says he's never told anyone. Holding me gently, his head resting on my shoulder, he tells me how scared and sick he was as a boy, how his brother Joe beat him up all the time, and how he had wished Joe would die, and then when Joe did die—on a pointless mission to bomb an arms munitions factory in Germany that turned out to be empty warehouses—how guilty he felt. He talks about how when Kick died, the humanity of the Kennedy family evaporated. He felt part of his soul had died. "I've been dying in bits and pieces my whole life, Jackie." He talks about how he'd really like to do something important but feels stymied in the Senate. "I spend all my time trying to look busy without actually doing anything that might antagonize some faction of the Democratic

Party. If I speak out on civil rights, I lose the South. If I succeed as a senator, I don't have a chance at the presidency, and that's what Dad wants."

I feel warm and happy. Yes, this is where I should be. I want to help this man, to stand by him. Forever.

"You're the only one I can talk to, Jackie," he tells me, and I believe him. "I can't do it on my own. I need you."

Last week he took me sailing. He was so sexy! His lean body pulling the rigging, manning the tiller, his eyes sparkling, his hair blowing. "I wish we could sail forever, Jackie," he said. And later, so I'd remember what a special day it had been, he gave me a Winslow Homer watercolor of a sailboat in rough surf. An original! Can you believe it? You don't give a gift like that if you aren't serious about someone. He must be in love! He's got to be!

At Hammersmith Farm, Janet turns to me before mounting her bay gelding. She bends her new riding crop, checking it for flexibility. "Jack is the kind of man who likes the challenge of conquest. I don't know what you were up to in France, young lady, but listen to me—no sex before your wedding."

For Janet, sex is a weapon that a woman uses to get what she wants.

"He hasn't even proposed yet, Mummy."

"What are you doing wrong?"

"I'm not doing anything wrong!"

"Do you go out with him when he calls at the last minute?"

"Yes, but if I don't, I might not see him for another week."

"Wrong. Do you give him gifts?"

"Yes, but nothing expensive. He loves little gifts."

"Wrong. Do you tell him you're in love with him?"

"I *am* in love with him. Why should I lie?"

"Because you never tell a man you're in love with him first. And certainly not before he proposes. Do you spend hours on the phone with him?"

"Yes, but sometimes he doesn't have time to see me."

"You know the rule. Ten minutes, maximum. You must make him want to see you. You don't call him, do you?"

"No. I never know where he is."

"Well . . . at least there's that. It's not doing you one speck of good, sitting around waiting for the telephone to ring. What you need is to go away and forget about him. If he sees you enjoying yourself in Europe, he'll propose or he'll start going out with someone else. But at least you'll know where you stand."

So Janet arranges for me to go to England for the coronation of Queen Elizabeth II. I get the *Times-Herald* to commit to a few stories about the trip. Just as she predicted—after my articles are published about the coronation and the celebrities, after the postcoronation ball at Londonderry House, after I stay on for another week to go to Paris, after I don't respond to his cables, which come with accelerating frequency—Jack calls and proposes. There is nothing romantic in it. "I already lost one gal to the English. I gotta get you hitched before I lose you, too." He means his sister Kick.

Instead of joy, I am filled with misgiving.

Even before our engagement, before he felt the pressure sealing him in like the lid of a canning jar, I didn't hear from Jack for weeks at a time. He had excuses, of course—favors to do for fellow politicians who helped him get elected senator, campaigning for Adlai Stevenson. Yet the closer we get to our wedding date, the more aloof Jack becomes. Our dates now all have a purpose—a function where he wants to meet someone, or a photo opportunity.

"Can't we do something just for fun?"

"I'd like to, but I don't have time, kiddo. We'll have plenty of time together after the wedding."

When Jack falls silent between jokes, he looks at me like a trapped man. Were I older, wiser, braver, I might say what he wants to hear—"If you don't want to marry me, just say so." I imagine his face relaxing, his eyes filming over in relief.

But I don't say this. I am afraid of losing him, afraid of losing our life together. Jack is the only man I've met who makes me feel challenged, expectant for life to unfold, energized to do whatever needs to be done. That is what Berenson advised—"Find a husband who is constantly stimulating." I want to be near him, touching him, smelling him, feeling the sound of his voice vibrate through my body. I'm in love.

In my vanity, I think this is the best thing for Jack, too. I sense that I am one of the few women strong enough to survive a marriage with him.

He says he loves me, but I don't feel it. Love should feel like the sun warming your bed when you wake. I don't feel that I'm essential to him, or that he would die without me, or that he thinks of me all day and can't wait to see me. But I sense something's there. I sense he wants to love me. If only I could brush aside his smiles and charm and wit like snow off a windshield to see inside.

Why can't I express what *I* need, what *I* feel, without making Jack angry? How can we be so close, our arms around each other, our fingers entwined, our hearts open and yearning, yet as far apart as two people on opposite sides of the Grand Canyon?

Jack likes and respects me. We are becoming good friends. I can only hope intimacy will follow. Am I hopelessly naive to think I can love enough for the both of us?

Why does he have to be so remote and mysterious?

Why does he make it so hard?

I pull into the Kennedy compound and park. I lean over the passenger seat to get my overnight bag, Jack's book, and a cartoon of the Kennedy clan I drew and had framed for Joe. I get out of the car, stumbling, my arms so full that I can hardly see.

"Smile, Jackie!"

When I peek over the picture frame, I am blinded by a flash. The world fades to whiteness, then to bare outlines of shapes void of color. I can make out only the most prominent lines—the horizon and the flagpole intersecting. Like a hunter's sights.

A short man in a fedora stands from a crouch and walks toward me. "Hi. I'm from *Life* magazine. Let's have a smile."

Why should I? I glance around the great lawn, befuddled. Jack sees me and sprints off the porch, shirtless. "Jackie! Just in time! *Life* wants to do a photo spread on us. You know, the gay bachelor senator finally gets hitched. Lots of pictures of us holding hands, sailing, playing football. A ripe pile of crap, but it should be good for the electorate."

Good for the electorate? "I thought we were going to spend the day on the boat?"

"We are. It'll be fun. Did you bring makeup?"

"Lipstick," I say weakly. I notice that Jack's face is lighter and even, his cheekbones reddened. Face powder and rouge?

"Don't worry. Houdini brought his box of magic. His assistant, Bunny, will do you up."

Houdini must be Jack's nickname for the photographer. And Bunny, his assistant? I'm stunned but play along. All day Houdini patters behind us with his tripods and silver reflector boards, asking us to position ourselves in the most absurd poses—Jack and I tossing a football. Jack pitching a softball to me. Jack and I walking hand in hand in the surf. Jack and I reading together, my head against his knee. Jack and I skipping stones in the surf. Jack and I barbecuing. I would think after looking at these pictures, Jack's constituents might wonder if he has time to be their senator.

"Catch you in a bit, kiddo," says Jack, heading up to the house. "Gotta make some calls." He abandons me with the photographer. Jack seems so different today. Businesslike. Did I do something wrong?

The photographer takes pictures of me alone, as if one could *ever* be alone in Hyannis Port. I hang off the porch banister over the hydrangea bushes, kicking my bare legs like a milkmaid on a hayride, my straw hat dangling from a string down my back. I contemplate Kennedy photos and graduation certificates on the library wall as if I was at the Louvre. *Please!* I chat on the lawn with the Kennedy sisters. They're hardly my confidantes—I still have problems telling them apart.

Joe Kennedy watches, arms crossed. He looks as though he's planning something. I posture and smile, knowing it amuses him. There something weirdly sexual about it.

It's fun—I guess—the continuous attention, the photographer's flattering patter. "That's perfect, sweetheart. There's a smile. Gorgeous! Beautiful! The all-American girl. You've got it, honey. This is gold. Now give me that million-dollar smile."

But where's Jack? I thought we had a date. I miss Jack.

Finally, Jack comes out of the house and walks to my car. He waves me over. It's time to leave.

"Jack!" shouts Joe from the lawn. "Bring your future wife over here before she goes. I want a picture of us together."

Jack's back stiffens. I feel him bristle. Because Joe called me his future wife? A rash of conflicting emotions flashes over Jack's face—anger, rebellion, pain. It passes in a moment. He takes my hand and smiles. "You heard the Ambassador. Let's go."

Hand in hand, we walk back toward the house.

The July issue of *Life* comes out several weeks later.

I'm filing my nails on my bed when Lee flounces in. Already tired of her husband, she makes excuses to visit Merrywood.

"Jackie! Jackie! You're a superstar." She throws a copy of *Life* magazine in front of me on the bedspread.

"Oh, that."

"Don't try to be all nonchalant. Look at it. It's so exciting."

I can't resist. I flip the magazine over.

The cover is a black-and-white photo with big red letters across the top: SENATOR KENNEDY GOES A-COURTING. It's of Jack and me sailing. I am kneeling on the pitching deck, looking off into the distance with a gleeful smile. Behind me Jack leans down to see my face, attentive, grinning as if anticipating the punch line to a joke. He looks very much in love with me. I try to remember what the photographer said to get him to look at me that way—"Jackie looks like the cat that ate the canary."

I flip to the back of the magazine in which we have a six-page spread. The girl in the pictures looks so carefree. So young and innocent. Is that me?

My picture has appeared in publications before—on the society page after winning horse shows, in *Vogue* after winning the essay contest, and in the *Times-Herald* along with my column. This is something different.

"Can you believe it? On the cover of a national magazine! Oh, Jacks, think of all the magazines you'll be in."

But this girl on the cover is not me. People will see this image of the senator's fiancée and imagine they know who I am. I find something deeply disturbing about this, something I can't quite define.

"Just think of the parties! The clothes! All the people you'll meet!"

For a moment I'm appalled. Jack's political power is part of what attracts me. I admire his force and experience, his knowledge of history. He's going to be important. But is that what I want? "Tell me about the wedding plans." Lee jumps on my bed and pulls her knees to her chin, her face eager for stories as if at slumber party the night after a prom.

"Between the Ambassador and Janet, I haven't much say." I love Lee for being excited, but her enthusiasm makes me feel rubbery and weak. I can't tell her about my doubts. I want her to imagine it's all perfect—the perfect husband, the perfect wedding. Something in me refuses to ease her jealousy, a meanness in me that I don't like.

I look again at the photo spread, with the bogus, upbeat prose beside the advertisements for cosmetics and girdles, and my stomach lurches. I fall back into my pillow, dizzy and confused. I know Jack is marrying me partly because he needs to for political reasons—a senator needs a wife. I knew we would appear in *Life*. But this?

I feel raw and exposed. I feel exploited. I feel like I've lost something I'll never recover.

AN ASSET LIKE RHODE ISLAND

I'm so sorry, Jacks," says Lee. "It was Mummy. You know her tricks. She made Michael go over to Dad's to tell him he wasn't invited to the reception. That made Dad upset, so they had a drink. You know how Dad is. He never stopped. I'm so sorry."

We never stop being pawns in their war.

Lee thinks I am crying because Black Jack is too drunk to give me away. I am. I'm also crying because Mummy made me wear this horrible dress. I'm crying because of the look on Jack's face this morning, as if he's been sentenced to prison. I'm crying because there are seven hundred guests here—five hundred more waiting at Hammersmith for the reception—and I know only a few dozen. I'm crying because I have a nauseated, trapped feeling that I've never had before. I'm crying because I am afraid.

At St. Mary's, from a small dressing room off the vestibule, I peek through the Gothic tracery of a lead-glass window. A mob jostles behind police barricades, spreading out across the churchyard and down the street for blocks. Dozens climb the iron fence or stand on each other's shoulders, pressing their faces against the church windows. Others stand on their cars, which are pulled up on the lawn as if at a county fair.

When our limousine pulled up in front of the church, people rushed our car. I was afraid we would run over someone. They pushed against our doors, so we couldn't get out, pressing their hands and faces against the windows, smearing the glass with mucus and saliva. Janet beat them back, using the long box that held my wedding veil as a battering ram. Policemen linked arms in chains on both sides of the steps, containing the crowd. Grim-faced, Hughdie took my arm and pushed ahead. Hot, bright strobes and flashes blinded me. Packs of photographers jumped the police barricades, dashing up the stairs in front and around us—crouching, scooting, lunging—shoving their lenses in my face. "Jackie, over here! Look here!" People threw rice at my face. It hurt. Someone launched a wad of spit that landed on the step as I put down my slipper. Who would do such a thing? What did I ever do to them? Yusha grabbed someone by the lapels and shoved him back into the crowd. I was afraid he was going to start a fight. I've never been so terrified in my life.

I look back into the full-length mirror. I can't bear to look at my face, afraid of what I'll see. Instead, I look at the reflection of an ivory silk taffeta wedding dress with a neckline that falls over the tops of my shoulders, tight across the bust, a full lampshade skirt with ridiculous ruffles on the bottom third and an awful rose appliqué the size of a dinner platter. It makes my neck look freakishly long and accentuates my flat chest. I look like what the maid uses to dust the piano.

"I hate my dress," I say pitifully to Lee.

"I know. I'm sorry," she says.

"You're supposed to say it's beautiful."

"But it isn't. It's hideous."

Her vehemence makes me laugh. Lee looks confused, not understanding the hysteria building in me, briefly liberated by her unintended malice.

My tears start again. I can't help it.

The girl in the mirror doesn't belong in a wedding dress. With her short curly hair, she looks like a tomboy who's raided the costume trunk. Her eyes are round with terror and regret. "I don't want to get married," I whimper.

Lee shushes me, but too late. Janet, coming from behind, hears me. "Don't be a child. Go dry your face and present yourself, young lady. There is no way in the world you're going to humiliate me in front of all these people."

I can't bear to look at her. *It's my wedding. Why isn't Black Jack here?* I want to demand. But I stand silent. I know it's a battle I can't win. I promise myself never to be a mother like her. As I put on the off-white veil of rose-point lace that she wore to her first wedding, to Black Jack, and her mother wore to wed James Thomas Lee, I wonder if it can be avoided.

I step out into the back of the nave. Hundreds of people are crammed into the pews. Who *are* all these people? Faces I've seen in magazines and in movies, of decision makers and moguls, beefy and goutish, of relatives who look vaguely familiar, of Kennedys, of bewildered non-Catholics, of ladies in furs and diamonds, perfumed in a riot of expensive scents, of men in stiff collars who look constipated, of Newport Brahmins who curl their lips at the fast Kennedy crowd—everyone straining his neck, desiring to see and be seen, all whispering to one another, "Aren't they just the most perfect couple?"

The music starts. They turn to look at me.

I feel like a British explorer feted by a jungle tribe only to realize she's being fattened for the cooking pot.

Jack waits at the altar. He glances over his shoulder, saluting his buddy Lem Billings with his chin as if he were about to climb into a bomber for a suicide mission. Lem's expression is one of sadness and unabashed love. I'm getting the feeling I've made a terrible mistake.

The music starts.

Archbishop Cushing draws out the Mass like a small-town mayor dedicating a war memorial to the town's only hero. Jack looks pale, chin tucked, shoulders pinched like a child bracing himself before gulping his spoonful of cod liver oil. I sense the tension coiled in his body. Perhaps it's back pain, from kneeling and standing and kneeling again.

Doesn't he want to marry me?

I smile hard, dizzy with fear. This can't be right. What have I gotten myself into?

I think I'm going to vomit, when the priest asks me something. "I do?" I say.

At Hammersmith Farm, Jack and I stand in a receiving line for two hours. We shake a thousand hands: senators, governors, socialites, stockbrokers, political aides, journalists, foreign royalty. Later, while I nurse my crushed fingers, I watch Joe and Jack slapping shoulders, guffawing, kissing babies, working the crowd as if at a campaign rally.

I am surprised to see unaccompanied men expensively dressed in dark suits, heavy and slow-moving with big heads and faces that look like blobs of cookie dough. They look glum, standing apart, squinting in the sun. The heavyset one with droopy jowls looks familiar. Haven't I seen his picture in the newspaper? I recall that he is from Chicago. Something to do with labor unions.

Joe greets these men with effusive embraces. They must be old friends of his.

Across the lawn Yusha glances at me, his lips pressed together, frowning. I move toward him to inquire, but he looks away.

"Jack! Jackie!" Joe calls us from opposite sides of the refreshments table. "Come take a photo with *mio fratello*." The three of us clink champagne glasses with a bulbous-nosed man who wears sunglasses and reeks of a cologne.

"Here's to the next president of the United States and his lovely young wife," says the Italian.

Is that what all these people think? Is that why they're here? Slowly it dawns on me—Joe orchestrated this entire wedding as a publicity stunt for Jack. So that's why Joe was so willing to pay for the wedding. That's why Janet allowed him control. They made a deal. Now I understand why Hughdie looks at me embarrassed, not because he let the groom's father pay for the wedding but because Hughdie, for all his dullness, has a certain integrity.

I feel as if I'm shrinking, as if everyone is talking over my head in a foreign language. Lips move, but I catch only a word here and there. I nod my head and smile—"I'm so glad you could come. How are the children?" I have to get out, out of this ridiculous dress, out of this place.

I want my father.

Teddy nudges Jack and jabs his chin in the direction of an attractive blonde who is looking at him and rubbing the rim of her champagne glass against her lower lip. Jack says something back to Teddy, and they break up laughing.

How could I be so stupid? Miserable, I glance around, looking for escape. My knees buckle. I think I'm going to faint.

Suddenly Bobby is by my side, lifting me by the elbow, leading me to a chair. He whispers in my ear, "Don't worry, Jackie. Jack can be difficult, but you can always count on me."

Bewildered, speechless, I smile. "Thank you, Bobby. I'm beginning to feel that everyone here knows something I don't."

"All you need to know is that you are now Mrs. John Fitzgerald Kennedy."

"That's all?"

"And that I'm your friend."

I think of the people I've called *friends*. Would any of them do something for me that wasn't in his best interest? I have my doubts. "I've never had a friend," I hear myself saying.

"You have one now."

My temples tingle, cold shoots up my spine, my breath quickens, I blush. His pledge feels more solid than the marriage vows I just mouthed.

"Bobby, you thief," shouts Jack from across the lawn. "You're monopolizing the bride." He slaps us both on the shoulders. "Let's get some pictures."

We line up in front of a split-rail fence, the pasture behind, me with the men—Jack, Bobby, Teddy, Sargent Shriver, Torby Macdonald, Lem Billings, George Smathers, Chuck Spalding, James Reed, Ben Smith, Yusha and Tommy Auchincloss, and Charlie Bartlett. Surrounded by his buddies, Jack relaxes for the first time today.

Jack laughs and kids around but has a strange coolness toward me. He stands apart from me, as if he hopes no one will know we're together. I've never sensed this from him before, as if he doesn't want to touch me.

Later, during his toast to us, Bobby says, "I'm glad I am already happily married. Otherwise I would've had to fight a duel with my own brother to marry Jackie." This is Kennedy charm. Everyone laughs. But his words stir something deep inside me.

The bride waits in semidarkness, sitting first on the bed, then, wanting to be seen from the best possible angle, wanting to appear both relaxed and expectant, seductive and virginal, jumps up to pose by the window, moves to a chair, and finally stands in the middle of the room.

The bride waits, perfumed and powdered, in a long, nearly transparent negligee, her body trembling with anticipation, her heart fluttering like a butterfly.

The bride waits, slightly alarmed at the sounds coming from the bathroom, sounds of a man, too familiar too soon, sounds that have a certain rhythm and will become predictable as horses at feeding time.

The bride waits, senses heightened, memorizing every detail, wondering if it was like this for her sister and her mother, wondering if this was the thing that would make her feel more like other women.

The bride waits, dazed from lack of sleep—for she hasn't slept in a week—high from just half a glass of champagne.

The bride longs to be vanquished and smothered, longs for his male gravity, longs for his demands, his strength, longs to be picked up and carried away, longs for deep kisses that lift her off into the rapids toward Niagara Falls. The bride longs for his meaty hands squeezing and touching her everywhere.

"I need you on top, baby." Jack walks in from the bathroom, lies on his back, and pulls me on top, his penis, cool and sharp, stabbing into me. He jogs my pelvis up and down like a milk shake, his eyes squeezed shut, wheezing, *ahhhhh,* squeezing my buttocks, his neck curling to his chest, his muscles tense, vibrating, then collapses.

That's it?

I am left panting, tingling all over, and deep inside, a fierce ache, an arrested compulsion to go on faster, further, harder.

Disappointment settles over me like a hunter's net.

He taps my thigh. "I'm beat, kid. Let's get some sleep."

Up in the hills in the older part of the city, our balcony looks out over Acapulco Bay. Slipping on a white gauze peignoir, I push open the living-room shutters and look out over red bougainvillea. In the distance, the ocean is light aqua, the waves crested in silver. The rising sun blushes tangerine and rose. Stucco villas, washed in pastel pinks, blues, and yellows, cluster on the hills. A steamy heat rises up over the crooked streets, laden with scents of jasmine, almond, and mango. I hear roosters, wooden wheels clacking over cobblestone, and the voices of women on their way to market.

Here I am, a married woman.

I reach out to embrace the morning, the ocean, the houses, the palm trees. My engagement ring, a square-cut diamond with emeralds, sparkles. It reminds me of early-morning light glinting off snow-covered pines. I've never liked jewelry much—it seems so matronly, and I'm always losing it. But I feel an attraction to this ring, as if it gives me some kind of power.

Joe bought it for me, not Jack—a thought I refuse to let upset my mood. I tuck away my doubts. There's no going back now.

Here I am, a married woman with a husband sleeping inside, a married woman ready to assume my duty. I do what I think young brides do. I order a breakfast tray to take in to wake my husband.

As Consuelo scurries around the kitchen preparing Jack's breakfast, she prattles on about babies and children. She insists that I drink a raw egg. It aids conception, she tells me. "After you get pregnant, everything is all right." So she has guessed my disappointment. Do all brides feel this way? She pats my hand, then pours the coffee.

I carry the tray down the Spanish-tiled hallway and rest it on an antique chair as I open the bedroom door. I pick up the tray again and back into the door. As I slowly turn into the room, I see Jack sitting on a chair, naked, bent over. He's injecting himself with a long syringe.

He glances up when I gasp. "Don't worry, babe. You haven't married a junkie. It's just medicine."

"What kind of medicine?"

"Cortisone for the Addison's. What's for breakfast?"

I have never heard of Addison's. Is it a disease? I know better than to ask. Jack obviously doesn't want to talk about it, caught sneaking his shot when I'm out of the room. I hear a door shut softly in the villa.

He's already keeping secrets from me. What's next?

I look at the six-inch scar at the base of Jack's spine. His knobby vertebrae twist down his back like the Blue Ridge Mountains under a blanket of snow. His naked shoulders are bony, crooked, and cinched.

"Hand me the orange juice, will ya, hon?" He drags himself across the room like a shipwrecked sailor crawling ashore, lurching from the bed to a wooden trunk, to a chair, to a wardrobe, then to his suitcase. He digs out four medicine bottles. He uncaps them, shakes out half a dozen small white pills, and then reaches back for the glass of orange juice. When he hands it back empty, he looks at me. "Vitamins," he says. "Nothing to make faces about."

As I serve him coffee, bacon, eggs, and toast, a chill alights upon my shoulders like a black swallowtail butterfly on a cornstalk. I wonder what kind of cripple I've married.

Since our wedding night, Jack doesn't disguise that he is in constant back pain. We try to sleep in the same bed, but the old feather mattress is far too soft for him. He moans and tosses and turns, soaking the sheets with a sweat. Finally, he sleeps on the floor with a blanket. I worry about scorpions.

Okay, I tell myself, *I can deal with this.* He won't talk to me, and he sleeps on the floor. At least he doesn't drink.

I change into a swimsuit and lie by the pool.

Mexico makes me feel luxurious, opulently female. I love the Mexican pace of life, languorous and sensual. I love their gentle sense of humor. I love the colors and music. I want to bask in the warm sun and nibble on mangoes. I want to indulge this fertile feeling, the riotous energy of sperm vying against sperm, the possibility of life already growing inside me.

But Jack is restless. He doesn't seem to know what to do with me, as if he were babysitting a neighbor's kid. We play tennis, we water-ski, we sail, we fish for marlin, we dine with Mexican politicos and their lovely mistresses—flirting and laughing and dancing. The whirlwind of activity is exciting, but I feel hollow. I beg Jack to rest. He smiles and lies back in his beach chair. In five minutes he begins to fidget.

I don't know what to make of his nervousness. We used to chat on and on about art, literature, and history. Before the honeymoon there were kisses and hugs, spirited teasing on both our parts, hours of necking and petting. Now he's glum and irritable. As if spending time alone with me is pure drudgery.

He glances away quickly when I look at him. "I'm bored," he says. "Let's go visit friends."

It's late. I pause at the top of the stairs, feeling awkward, a guest in another family's house. I'm tired of staying at the in-laws', while our own house in Georgetown is decorated. I'm tired of being abandoned here in Hyannis Port while Jack spends the week in Washington.

I want to sleep with my husband.

I hear male voices coming from the den—Joe, Bobby, and Jack.

"She needs seasoning," Joe says. I wonder if the men are talking about barbecuing or a ship or a gun or wine. "She's like a horse. You got to get her used to the crowds. They can be pretty scary to a novice."

JACK: "I don't know. Ever since the wedding, it's like she's frozen up. Why can't she be more like Ethel?"

As soon as I know they're talking about me, I turn to go back upstairs. Something keeps me there—my survival instinct.

JOE: "Give her time. Let her sit in the background for a little bit. You have at least two years before you need to start campaigning. Let her work on the supportive-wife thing. We'll get another photo spread in *Life* once you get settled in."

BOBBY: "Maybe we shouldn't use her at all. I think she'll scare off midwestern women. She's too highbrow."

JOE: "Are you kidding? They'll love her. Just like they love classy stars like Audrey Hepburn and Grace Kelly. Fantasy women. Princess women. They're dying to see how it's done."

JACK: "Maybe I should've married Hepburn."

JOE: "She isn't Catholic, and you couldn't marry an actress. You might as well marry a slut."

BOBBY: "Maybe we could start her out with a crowd that is sure to like her, like the French in Louisiana. Crowds go crazy if you say something in their native language."

JOE: "I say start her out with some women's groups, the DAR and the Rebeccas. See how they take to her."

JACK: "Are you kidding? They'll eat her alive. Besides, she's got a sarcastic wit if you get her mad, and they will, believe me."

JOE: "I know. I've been victim."

JACK: "You love it."

JOE: "So I do, but you've got to rein her in. Look at Ethel—sweet as plum pudding when she works a crowd."

JACK: "Ethel is Ethel; Jackie is Jackie."

BOBBY: "She might give you a boost in New England and California. But those are places you won't need help."

JOE: "I disagree. They're gonna love her everywhere. You wait and see. Jackie is going to be your number one asset."

BOBBY: "In the Farm Belt? Bullshit."

JACK: "I'd like to go for it in 'fifty-six. The Senate is boring me silly."

JOE: "No, too soon. They'll choose Stevenson, who's too damn liberal. He doesn't stand a chance. Johnson won't run against Eisenhower."

JACK: "How about vice president?"

JOE: "Have I ever taught you to come in second? Forget it. It's the presidency or nothing."

I'm still reeling over being called an asset when Ethel zips around the corner and sees me hovering on the steps like a gargoyle. I'm afraid she's going to give me away, but she motions for me to scoot over and sits beside me. She gives me an impish grin and presses her index finger to her lips.

The men blab on about politics. Ethel and I get restless and go to the kitchen. She pulls a bottle of vodka from a top shelf, where she's apparently hidden it, and pours herself a drink. She offers me one, but I shake my head. "I didn't think you had it in you, kid, but I guess I was wrong. You'll make it even if you don't play football. We took bets, you know."

"On whether Jack would marry me, or whether I'd survive?"

"Both. I was the only one who knew it would be you."

"How come?"

"All the obvious reasons—Catholic virgin, Joe picked you, you don't take shit. And you're so much like Kick."

"I can't imagine how any Kennedy could be like me."

"Oh, but Kick was. She was the only one who talked back to Joe. She loved art and literature. Why do you think Joe and Jack and the rest of the Kennedy males fell for you?"

"She was Jack's best friend, wasn't she?"

"Sure. But the real reason I knew Jack was going to marry you is that Jack's in love with you."

"You think?" She wouldn't think that if she had just endured the honeymoon from hell. I ache to confide in her, but I know better than to reveal myself to any of the Kennedy women.

"Not a question in the world." She doesn't smile. Something in her eyes tells me there's a very perceptive woman under all her barroom antics.

Suddenly it hits me like a sledgehammer. "You don't have sex with your sister," I blurt.

"What? God, no! What are you talking about?"

Is that why Jack seems so cool and perfunctory in bed? I'm too much like Kick?

"I'm sorry, Ethel. I was reading a Greek play earlier this evening. It kind of got to me."

"Maybe you should read something else. You don't want to ruin your good looks from lack of shut-eye."

This is the first time any of the Kennedy women have uttered anything other than thinly veiled dislike for me. I kiss her on the cheek, then head up to bed—alone.

JACK

1954–1963

SENATOR'S WIFE

*H*ave I become hideous so soon? Jack leaves me at Hyannis Port during the week when he goes to Washington. I am bored, isolated, depressed. On the weekends he comes back exhausted and in pain. He doesn't want to touch me. He has long talks with Joe and Bobby. He acts as if he's done his part by marrying me and now no longer needs to bother with me.

"Jack, are you in love with me?"

"I'm nuts about you, babe."

"You never called me *babe* before we were married."

"For crying out loud, Jackie."

He wants sex on demand, anytime during the day or night, without kisses or affection. In the bathroom I brush my hair in the mirror. He comes up from behind, lifts my nightie, and enters me. He huffs and puffs for a minute or two. My hips bang against the sink, hurting. His oozy sweat smells vaguely chemical from the drugs he takes. I study his face in the mirror—twisted and red—and try to see the man I fell in love with. I see only his anger and frustration, and an anonymous violence that alarms me. As if I weren't there at all.

He peeks through his eyelashes and sees me watching him. He lowers his head and digs his chin into the base of my neck. He groans as he ejaculates, caving us both over the sink. He hangs there for a moment, my limbs shaking from his weight. Without saying a word, he straightens and shuffles away to use the other bathroom.

I hear him draw water in the tub. Tears fall down my face.

How does a young bride twelve years younger than her husband say she doesn't like the way he has sex with her? How does she say, "No, I don't want to have sex right now—I don't like sex that way"? How does she say, "I want to be kissed and stroked and rubbed and told I am beautiful and that you love me"? How does she say, "You make me feel like a thing, sticking your penis into me"? How does she ask, "Why are you different with me now? Why do you treat me like an irritating child and dismiss me to my bedroom? Why are you so angry with me?"

Trapped in a cage of my own making, I feel humiliated and ignored.

What have I done wrong? Is this marriage?

I sit hunched over in dark shadows. Beside me, a green-shaded lamp glows over pages of medical texts. The November light is parsimonious. I push the text closer to the lamp and lean forward. It is weather for discovering secrets.

Early that morning I took the train into New York to visit Black Jack, I said, but really I was on a mission to the New York Public Library. I sat on the train alone and looked out the window, clutching my spiral notebook and pen, oddly nervous. An icy rain streaked across the window. Bare branches scratched against the sky. Remnant rust-colored leaves tore off and slammed against the train windows, sticking, sliding slowly across the glass.

Rain pelted me as I took a cab from Penn Station to Forty-second and Fifth Avenue. I climbed the slippery granite steps to the library. The lions looked haggard and grouchy.

A young man led me through the dimly lit stacks to the medical encyclopedias, dragging one foot behind him. I waited until he clomped back to the front desk, then pulled down a heavy volume. I lugged it over to a long oak table. The wood glowed, greased from millions of feverish fingers. I switched on the green-shaded lamp and opened the book.

Once I find "Addison's disease," I nearly slam shut the covers. I shiver, afraid to read. If it wasn't bad, somebody in the family would have told me about it. Anger at being deceived gives me courage to continue. I am not a child. I will not be kept ignorant.

I look at the illustration first—an outline of the male human torso with the affected organs shaded in bright colors. The pituitary in red, the kidney-shaped thyroid in ocher, and at the bottom of the duodenum above the kidneys, the adrenal glands in purple. The colors make me feel slightly squeamish, as I imagine, for a moment, that I am looking into Jack's body.

I skim the pages, too nervous to comprehend anything. I start again, slowly, dragging my finger under the words. With each sentence, I glance back at Jack's open body, his diseased parts. I learn that Addison's disease is caused by an autoimmune disorder that creates antibodies that attack the body's own organs. The hyperactive immune system attacks the adrenal cortex, which then fails to produce enough cortisol, which in turn fails to check the body's response to inflammation.

Jack's body is slowly eating away at itself.

Addison's disease shows in weight loss, muscle weakness, fatigue, low blood pressure, dizziness, and darkening of the skin, especially on the elbows, knees, and lips.

That doesn't seem so bad.

Addison's disease can cause a craving for salty foods.

Big deal.

Addison's disease can cause irritability and depression.

Yeah . . . so can politics.

Addison's disease is a chronic condition. Daily replacement hormones can never be stopped.

At least there's a treatment.

Under stress, someone with Addison's disease can have an addisonian crisis. Symptoms include a penetrating pain in the lower back, abdomen, or legs, vomiting, and diarrhea, followed by dehydration, low blood pressure, and loss of consciousness. Left untreated, an addisonian crisis can be fatal.

Jack is always under stress.
I close the volume. Slowly it sinks in. I have married a very sick man.

I massage his neck and shoulders. His shoulders are bony, and his skin is loose from weight loss. Dark patches of skin color his elbows and knees. A purple circle appears at the bottom of his spine just above the crack of his butt. His thighs, covered with angry red stings from his daily cortisone injections, are soft from lack of exercise—he can't even swim now.

I don't even think of him as a husband anymore, but as an old man I've been hired to care for. Massages are the only way he accepts affection from me. If I try to initiate sex, he waves me away like a pesky fly.

If only I could get pregnant.

Jack uses his crutches all the time now. If he drops something, he asks me to pick it up for him. He has stopped going to his speed-reading classes in Baltimore because he can't tolerate the long drive. He sits in his Senate seat all day so he doesn't have to walk back to his office, or he stays in his office all day and hobbles to the Senate chamber only if there is something to vote on. He's begun canceling speaking engagements.

Sometimes the pain makes him impotent. He punishes me for that as well, refusing to engage in any conversation other than basic pleasantries. When the pain is at its worst, he refuses to talk altogether, sinking deep into himself.

He grinds his teeth at night, tossing and turning. I move to the guest bedroom and sleep with Gaullie, Lem Billings's poodle, who's staying with us.

I watch helplessly as Jack suffers.

I see myself quoted in a women's magazine. "I'm an old-fashioned wife. House-keeping is a joy to me. When everything is clean and neat, organized and running smoothly, flowers fresh in the vases, the good food on the table, I find such satis-faction."

What's happened to me? I look in my high school yearbook and under "life am-bitions" are my words: "Never to be a housewife." I've become what I vowed I'd never be—servant, nurse, and maid to an absent husband.

We should listen to our younger selves.

We live in suitcases—a few nights at Merrywood, a few nights at the Mayflower in Washington, a few nights at the Carlyle in New York City, a few nights at Hyannis Port. We are sad Gypsies.

Finally, I find a house to rent at 3321 Dent Place in Georgetown. I want to be the perfect wife. I do what I think I am supposed to. I decorate, I buy him clothes, I make him lunches and take them down to the Senate Building. I take a class in American history at Georgetown—a dreadful recital of war that I've always avoided. I translate French texts, the speeches of de Gaulle, the writ-ings of Voltaire, Rousseau, and Talleyrand. As long as I am of service to him, he seems to tolerate me. I feel as if I am trying to befriend a wolf with small tokens of food, a wild animal who trusts me only so far as he can get something out of me.

He is here, and then he's gone.

I find myself lonely for the first time in my life. The men I dated, dear friends still, don't dare call the newly wed bride. My women friends are all busy with their own husbands and children. Lee lives in London.

For stimulus, I fall back to my old friends—books. I read for hours a day. I smoke too much. I feel useless. I can't spend my life this way.

I lay out the linen napkins and the silver, the cucumber sandwiches, the quiches, the pâté de fois gras, the blackberry tarts with crème brûlée, the baked Camembert, the strawberries dunked in Swiss dark chocolate. I hire my neighbor's maid to pour coffee. I play Mendelssohn on our new RCA record player, a wedding gift from Joe.

I'm supposed to make friends with the other senators' wives. I invite them to tea, as I am expected to do. They trickle into the house, their perfectly coifed heads swiveling on their necks, sharply scrutinizing, taking in the curtains, the rugs, the paintings. Like spies, they look for crucifixes on the walls, a prie-dieu in the corner, a painting of the Virgin Mary, a photograph of the pope. Their faces appear eager and pleasant, until I see criticism threatening to crack their crusts and spew out like molten lava. They search for something gracious to say. "You've made the place so nice and homey," but their eyes say something else—"How pretentious! The curtains must've cost a fortune." "What is that hideous caricature hanging over the fireplace? Something she did herself, no doubt." "The idea of serving Camembert! I thought she had a problem with her plumbing. Why serve something like that when gingersnaps would do?"

They all dress like Mamie Eisenhower, even the younger ones—floral dresses cinched at the waist, properly buttoned to the neck, thick stockings, and sensible shoes. They even smell the same—like grandmothers, of potpourri, cinnamon, and mothballs.

Soon I discover these women are completely consumed by their husbands' careers and children's bowel movements. I have no interest in politics and have no children. I have nothing to say to them. Their greatest thrill in life has been moving to Washington. They don't expect life to be particularly interesting or challenging. They have become their modest expectations—wives.

Theirs is the kind of niceness that says "I can be moderately polite to you, but don't ask for any favors." Such niceness stuns me into stupidity. My voice disappears into a whisper. I act shy. I barely manage to utter the requisite inanities.

"Would you like to join us to fold bandages at the Red Cross next Thursday?" one asks. Or a bake sale for the Democratic Party. A tea for the DAR. Visits to children's hospitals and the Braille Institute? Old-age homes!!

I sit on the edge of my chair, back straight, and sip my tea. I blink twice and set my teacup down on my saucer. I am dying for a cigarette. "Yes, yes," I say, "please, do call me. I would be delighted to help." My head feels light, and I sense something inside me sinking, as if my heart were cut adrift.

I cannot do this.

Thankfully, the women understand I have no interest. They understand the difference between "Please, do call me" and "Please call me." The placement of the *do* means everything.

I know what they think of me—a spoiled snob, too immature to accept my responsibilities as a politician's wife. They effect an effort to make me part of their club, but I see in the set of their jaws that they hold no hope for me.

Gaullie meanders into the living room to check out what's going on. He sniffs one lady's knees. The woman beside her stands up indignantly. Another says, "I can't believe you let your dog in the house." Averting social calamity, I quickly shoo Gaullie upstairs.

"Forgive me," I say when I return. "He escaped from the doggie dungeon, where we normally keep him." I say this softly with a smile. The women giggle, but more than one isn't fooled. They hear my sarcasm and already hate me.

"Learn to play bridge," Janet advises me. "Bridge and shopping. What else does a wife need?"

I find myself at Mrs. R's house with a royal flush in my hand. It is a stupid game of stupid deceptions. The only trick is to look as bored as you feel, and you win every time. The women think I'm a natural and, to my surprise, invite me back. "I'll check my husband's schedule," I say. "He's so busy. I want to be available whenever he's free. You know politicians." They nod and smile and pretend to excuse me but, on their invisible scorecard, smudge out my name.

I feel imprisoned. I am losing myself. I am smoking too much.

The more I try to be what I think Jack expects of me, the further he slips away. We have a routine of banter and sex, but I no longer feel his heat, the core of him that desires the core of me. We're drifting down the same river without touching. How can I reach him?

If only I could get pregnant.

I bolt up in bed, my heart pounding. The alarm clock reads 1:12 A.M. I hear boisterous male voices downstairs, cupboards slamming, toilets flushing, glasses crashing. Cigarette smoke wafts up the stairs and under my door. I hear a *thunk,*

thunk, thunk and can't imagine what it is. When the last voice says good-bye and the front door slams, I slip on a white peignoir and head downstairs.

Jack is lying on the couch, his right hand across his heart.

"Are you all right, Jack?"

"Hi ya, babe." He grins and rubs his crotch. "Come here."

Pizza boxes, napkins, and beer bottles litter the floor and mantel. I survey the damage—overflowing ashtrays, spilled drinks, a cigarette burn on a Louis IV chintz-covered chair, water stains on my teak table. Tacked on the wall, a picture of Adlai Stevenson is quilled with darts. The wallpaper is peppered with holes— the *thunk*ing. I try to act cool. "I thought Adlai was your friend?"

"No, I said he wasn't my enemy. A good politician can't afford enemies. They're too unpredictable."

I see shards of a lead-glass heirloom in the fireplace. "Oh, Jack, how could you?"

"What do you mean?"

"Our home isn't some fraternity house. Look at it. The wall is destroyed, the chair . . . I just finished re-covering that."

"For Christ's sake, don't cry! It's a fucking chair and fucking uncomfortable as hell."

"That glass belonged to my great-grandfather."

"I'll buy you another glass."

"Jack! You can't live like a pig and be a senator."

"It's the way I live. I got elected. People must like it. Don't try to control me."

"I'm not trying to control you. I'm not Rose; I'm not your father. I'm your wife."

Our fight covers what six months into our marriage is already old territory— my need to control, his irresponsibility and thoughtlessness. As usual, I go to bed feeling humiliated.

The next morning I wake up late, oddly invigorated after our row. I need only to try harder, to be more understanding. I skip down to the kitchen and pull out my new French cookbook from the class I'm taking. I will prepare for Jack what I learned to make last week, a timbale—a savory custard with vegetables. I line up everything I need—eggs, Parmesan cheese, zucchini, cauliflower, cream, scallions, Madeira, and nutmeg—like paints on a canvas. I chop the vegetables and mix the custard, then pour it all into molds and bake them in water. I cross my fingers, smoke, and watch the clock. I pull them out when they're lightly browned on top. Baked to perfection.

As the timbale cools, I dress and think of what I can do to entertain Jack. I pull out my pen-and-ink set and a sheet of heavy, finely textured paper. I draw a caricature of Jack and his cronies sprawled over my living room, take-out boxes hang-ing from the chandelier, Red Fay tap-dancing on the piano, and Kenny O'Donnell throwing darts at the *Mona Lisa,* saying, "You don't think Jackie will mind, do ya?"

In a basket, I pack the timbale, the sketch, and a thermos of coffee. I kiss Gaullie and tell him I'll be back soon to walk him, then drive down Pennsylvania Avenue to the Senate Building.

Cherry trees are blossoming on the Mall. The air feels clean. Tulips and daf-fodils toss their heads in a light breeze.

I am filled with optimism—we can make it work, I know we can. They say the first year of marriage is the hardest.

It's lunchtime. The Senate hallways and offices are empty. I walk past his sec-retary's desk and open the door to Jack's office.

Jack is leaning back in a leather chair by the window. A woman kneels in front of him, her skirt rumpled around her waist, her breasts spilling out of an unbut-toned cashmere cardigan, her mouth running up and down Jack's left-leaning erection. She doesn't hear me and continues bobbing up and down. My first thought is that she made a dreadful choice in wearing magenta cashmere with a green tartan skirt. My second thought is she's putting an awful lot of effort into it. I'm certain she'll get a crick in her neck.

Jack says the only thing he can say in such a circumstance. "Hello there, Jackie."

The girl freezes, then scoots beneath the desk without looking at me. I hear her elbows and knees knocking under the desk as she tries to pull on her clothes.

Jack sits with his shirt unbuttoned, his baby-blue back brace like a bandage around his middle. I wait for him to say something more, but he watches me closely as if this were a test.

"Hi, darling. I brought you some lunch. I packed extra napkins, which you might find useful. Enjoy." When I place the basket on his desk, the rustling under-neath abruptly halts. I hang there a moment, enjoying her terror, then, with a star turn, saunter out.

I cheerfully greet Evelyn Lincoln, Jack's secretary, who's back from lunch, tucking her purse in her desk drawer. I make a point to chat and ask her about her cat and her mother. Her eyes widen, surprised at my sudden interest in her per-sonal life. I'm just trying to make Jack sweat a little. When I'm done with her, I wave to the Senate minority leader, who's walking down the corridor.

"Mrs. Kennedy, good to see you. Have you seen Jack? I have something I need to talk to him about."

"He's in his office getting boffed by his new receptionist." I wave and stroll out. "Ta-ta."

The fight comes later.

"I am not your mother. I will not allow myself to be humiliated in public."

"That wasn't in public. That was my office."

"When there are witnesses, it is public."

"You were the one to call attention to the situation, not me."

"You were fucking your receptionist!"

"It's called a blow job."

"She wasn't blowing."

"I will not let you tell me what I can and cannot do. It was a condition of our marriage."

"What condition? I never agreed to adultery."

"You knew what I was before you married me. Did you expect me to change? Did you?"

"No."

"Give me a break. Besides, it doesn't mean anything. It's an itch that needs to be scratched."

"For us, too?"

"Oh, for crying out loud, Jackie."

Ironically, timbale becomes Jack's favorite dish. He requests it often. He frames my sketch and hangs it in his office. He points it out to visitors. "Isn't my wife talented?" I interpret this as a declaration of love—we take what we can get.

Today Jack addresses the Senate. I sit in the gallery. I've heard this speech over and over as Jack honed certain passages. I suggested the part he's giving now. When he speaks my words, my skin chills. I feel like giving someone a long passionate kiss. It thrills me the way he tenses his body, his vocal cords taut as harp strings, each word vibrating with emotion.

I glance at the other wives. One looks intently across several rows, eyebrows lifted, as if she's spotted her husband's mistress and is trying to see if the brooch she's wearing is similar to one he gave her. Another fingers her tennis bracelet and glares at someone who's coughing. One smiles wistfully as if recalling a passage from a romance novel she's reading. Another looks down over the railing with a disgusted, superior face as if she's spotted a woman wearing white shoes after Labor Day. Yet another is fast asleep. Only one wife appears to be actually listening—the wife of the British ambassador.

Apparently I'm not the only one to feign interest in politics.

Jack will be amused. I can't wait to tell him.

I begin to understand why the congressional wives resent me. Not simply because I refuse to play the game—the bridge parties and teas, the visits to hospitals and retarded children, the speeches to the Girl Scouts and the DAR—but because they play the game and hate it. Perhaps the only time they have for themselves is during political addresses, when they can fix a smile on their faces and drift off into their own worlds.

I see longing on their faces, longing to escape, to live a life for themselves. I feel them wanting to bust out of their suits and gloves and hats, wanting to run naked and shout profanities.

I am filled with both compassion and rebelliousness—compassion because I realize we are more alike than different, rebelliousness because I refuse to become one of them.

My sense of duty is not so great that I will accept misery.

Of all of the senators' wives, I thought Mrs. Q might possibly become a friend.

Mrs. Q is a youngish woman, educated at Bryn Mawr College, lively and attractive. She invited me for tea.

I enjoyed the walk from Georgetown to her home in Dumbarton Oaks. The sky was blue. Hot-pink azaleas and cherry-red rhododendron were blossoming everywhere. The air was filled with the scent of honeysuckle. I arrived at her stately Georgian house feeling hale and happy. She has an interest in eighteenth-century porcelain, particularly polychrome enamel and grisaille pieces from the Sèvres manufactory in France. While we viewed her collection, we giggled about the pomposity of the Embassy Row cocktail parties. We shared our experiences in Paris. We commiserated about our enslavement to our husbands' careers. She told me where to sell my gowns: "All of us sell our used clothing to Encore for extra cash. You can't be seen in the same gown too many times or everyone will think your husband has you on a budget."

"We can't have that."

"Oh my, no."

I slipped into a girlish chatter I usually risk only with Lee. It felt so liberating, spontaneous, and unguarded. A great weight lifted from my chest. I realized how little I had laughed these past few months. Perhaps all I needed was a good friend.

We settled down to tea. "I looked everywhere for madeleines. I wanted something French for you."

"How thoughtful. They're absolutely perfect. Where did you find them?"

Then I discovered why I had been invited.

"I hate to spring this on you," she said, sighing deeply, "but the other senators' wives thought it important. They selected me to talk to you because I'm closest to your age."

"If I'm to be reprimanded in some way, I'm glad they chose you. I've enjoyed myself this afternoon."

"Me, too." Her face brightened, but only for a moment. "No, I'm not going to reprimand you. It's about your husband."

"Jack?"

"Yes. I don't know exactly how to say this. . . . Jack has been seen at various clubs in the company of a variety of young women. Some were professionals, if you know what I mean. Others work on the Hill. Some, actresses. We all hoped he would settle down after he was married, but . . . oh, my dear . . . I see how awful this must be for you. . . . You didn't know."

"Women find Jack attractive," I said lamely.

"There's a suite he keeps in the Mayflower Hotel."

"Oh, that . . . He's had it for years. After we moved to Georgetown, he decided to keep it for nights when he has to work late at the Senate."

"Well, that's not all he uses it for. He sets a bad example and makes such a spectacle of himself at every function. It's embarrassing. He seems to think Washington is Las Vegas or Miami."

"What do you want me to do about it?"

"As his wife, surely you can do something. A scandal would severely hurt the Democratic Party, and the party is anxious to win back the Senate in the next election. We won't have any chance at Eisenhower in 'fifty-six if this hits the papers."

"Do the other wives talk about this with their husbands?"

"Some, I'm sure. I think a number of the husbands seem to admire his . . ."

"Promiscuity?"

"I'm so sorry. . . . I see how upset you are."

Jack's behavior I knew about. Being subjected to gossip upsets me. If his behavior really threatened the party, the senators would not leave it to their wives to deal with. Then something occurred to me. "Has Jack ever propositioned you?"

This time she was the one to blush. I suppose I have to assume any pretty woman is fair game to Jack.

I don't remember how the tea ended. All I remember is my face burning and my body shaking in humiliation and anger.

Damn him! Damn him! Damn him! I'm furious that he puts me in these situations.

I'm furious at Mrs. Q for interfering. I'm furious that I am made an outsider once again.

A memory comes back to me.

I am changing into my swimsuit in the cabana at the Maidstone Club. I am ten and self-conscious about my breasts. I insist on changing by myself. Janet charges in, dangling a wet silver-blue bathing suit from her middle finger. "What is this?" She snaps it at my face and I gasp. A red welt like Indian paint splashes across my cheek. Black Jack stumbles into the cabana, sun-baked and groggy. He sees me with my hand to my cheek, tears in my eyes. Alarmed, he glares at Janet. "What's going on?"

"You bastard. How dare you! In our own cabana!" "What are you talking about?" "I found this suit in the ladies' shower room." "Michelle must've forgotten it." "It doesn't belong to your sister. I know damn well who it belongs to, you pig." Janet's neck muscles strain, her fingers curl, her arms stiff like a scarecrow, her voice shrill. "You bastard! Where'd you fuck her? Here?" She grabs my arm, swinging me away, pointing at the ground where I stood. "Here? Right where your precious daughter is standing?" "You bitch! Don't you touch her like that." "You devil! I'll cut it off!" She flies at him with her fists. I hear something crash.

I run from the cabana, topless, arms over my breasts, onto the beach, into the water, ashamed, frightened, tears streaming down my face, thinking, *Why is she so mean to Daddy?* The other club members see me and laugh—"Punch and Judy are at it again"—the cousins, the stewards, the neighborhood boys—"What you trying to hide, Jackie?"—the women in white dresses and big hats sipping lime daiquiris, the men with cigars, who scratch their hairy bellies, the toddlers who think it's a game, they all laugh as shrieks rise from our cabana, laugh as the striped tent bulges with elbows and feet, laugh as my parents flay each other with their hate.

I refuse to repeat my parents' marriage. I won't allow it!

I ride Byron up the hill behind Merrywood on a rough path. He is the jet-black stallion Black Jack gave me for a wedding present. Each hoof beats the ground: *da-DUM, da-DUM, da-DUM, da-DUM.* Right hind foot, right fore, left hind, left fore.

The ground is spongy from snowmelt and early spring rains, and slippery with wet decaying leaves. Here, spring is weeks behind the city. Deep in the forest, hidden from the sun, snow piles remain. The air feels vibrant, moist, and cool.

When we get to the fire road that runs between two estates, we speed up into a two-beat trot, his diagonal feet falling in pairs: *DUM, DUM, DUM, DUM.*

Byron is feisty today, eager to run. His ears are alert and forward. He tosses his head and neighs. He'll never be sensitive to my moods the way Danseuse was, but he knows anger and he knows when I have to ride mine out.

I try to keep my mind clear, but my ordeal with Mrs. Q looms loud, our conversation running over and over in my head, the sound of her voice soaring over the *DUM, DUM, DUM, DUM* like a descant—*As his wife, surely you can do something.*

I shake it out. They can't touch you here, Jacks.

We come to a meadow where my neighbor let me build post-and-rail jumps. Byron sees the walls of fieldstone and surges. I hold him at a trot, then slowly squeeze my thighs and loosen the reins. *Ba-da-Dum, ba-da-Dum.* The three-beat gait thunders into a canter. I stand on the stirrups, lifting out of the saddle.

You must dominate your horse completely. I hear Janet's voice in my mind. *Keep your head up, eyes forward.*

He senses my fury; my fury fuels him. I am fearless on the brink of abandon.

Elbows in, Jacqueline! Don't flap your arms like a chicken!

He lifts his head and forehand, his hindquarters spring him into the air. We take off, his muscles hot and steamy, his massive bulk airborne, his head stretched forward, his back rounding beneath me like a porpoise surfing the waves. For these seconds of suspension, I have no control. I cling to this rocket of power, without will, without self-awareness.

I am anonymous, I am one with the horse. I am not Jackie Bouvier, I am not Jacqueline Kennedy.

His forehooves land, pounding the earth. His head comes up, then stretches forward. In seconds, he charges down the stretch, back into rhythm: *ba-da-Dum, ba-da-Dum.* I lift out of the seat.

Byron clears the jumps cleanly. I rejoice at his glistening coat, his meaty shoulders, his impertinent ears. I throw my arms around his neck and hang there, letting him cool down at his own pace, wishing he would carry me like this forever. Take me away, Byron, take me away.

I should've stuck with horses.

NURSE

*Y*ou don't get points for being sick in this household. I need you to come with me to a rally in Malden."

"Oh, Jack. I can't."

"Sure, you can. I'll be back to pick you up at seven. Be sure to look great." He grabs his crutches and hobbles downstairs.

That's the sympathy I get for my miscarriage. I lie in bed, weary and depressed. It feels as if I have granite boulders grinding against each other inside me. I'm bleeding heavily and my back hurts. I feel like such a failure. What is wrong with me? The women in our family have never had problems with their pregnancies. "It's your smoking," says Rose. "It's stress," says the doctor. "It's the Bouvier blood," says Janet. Joe stares at me as if I'm a prize racehorse that's developed swelling knees—an expensive disappointment. To the perpetually pregnant Kennedy women, it is one more thing that sets me apart. They shake their heads grimly as if to say, "Well, what did you expect? She can't even throw a football."

Jack can't stand to be around me, as if my failure were contagious. I disgust him.

By five o'clock I drag myself out of bed. I put on a black gown that comes to the throat in front but is cut out in back. A costume from Givenchy to assume my character. Jack's eyes twinkle when he sees me. "We better keep you facing the audience."

We head to Boston's North End. Muggsy O'Leary driving, me in front in the passenger seat, Jack lying in back. Jack talks nonstop, warding off the pain, I assume, or maybe he's taken a pill. "I owe him that, at least, a buddy from *PT-109*. . . . If we could just get another Democratic seat from Massachusetts . . . He's a bosom buddy of Johnson, and that could help in 'fifty-six. . . . Hey! Watch it over those potholes, Muggsy."

As he rambles, I wonder about the bottle of Benzedrine I found in the medicine cabinet—prescribed for a woman. I wonder if he stole it from her bathroom cabinet after they had sex. Was she one of those women who wake up with Benzedrine and go to sleep with Nembutal? Was this what was in store for Jack? For me?

The high school parking lot is crammed with cars, the sidewalk packed. "Not bad, huh, Jackie? I asked Joe to get the word out. Gotta have a good showing for my war buddy."

As soon as we climb out of the car, a pack of photographers surrounds us, assaulting us with their Cyclops eyes. *Pop, pop, pop.* Teenagers dive under the photographers' elbows to get close, their faces grim and determined, like children vying for candy. What do they want from us?

"Smile, Jackie," Jack reminds me.

Four men in gray suits hustle us backstage. We catch our breath by dusty maroon curtains and wait for our cue.

"How's my hair?" Jack asks, handing me his crutches.

He strides to the podium, waving and smiling to his clapping, stomping, screaming fans. *Pop, pop, pop.* Cameras flash like a swamp of fireflies. He dazzles them with his flawless white smile, his tanned face, his sparkling eyes. But the pinch of his shoulders tells me he's in pain.

As the applause peaks, I tremble, knowing this is the precise moment to make an entrance. I lean into it, momentum carrying me through momentary paralysis. Flashbulbs blind me, and the heat from the stage lights nearly knocks me over. A fresh burst of applause and stomping. A small chorus from the balcony chants, "Jackie, Jackie, Jackie." I wave, and wonder why they are calling my name. Do they know me? Jack laughs, as astonished as I am. He gestures with his hand—"My wife, Jacqueline Kennedy"—his eyes drinking me in, proud, beaming.

Suddenly a cramp stabs me in the gut—a wave of nausea. The bottom half of my body seems to want to break off. I worry about bleeding through my Tampax.

My feet carry me forward. I smile broadly, first in pain, then in absolute terror. But then I feel this glowing warmth from the audience. I am astonished and thrilled. I realize they're not clapping only for Jack—they're clapping for me.

When I'm close enough, Jack takes my hand. I lean toward the microphone: *"Grazie tante. Jack e io siamo multo felici di essere qui. Ho girato l'Italia quando ero ragazza. Non c'è posto più bello tutto il mondo. Non c'é una cultura piu artistice. Non c'è gente piu simpatica."*

The audience explodes with mad stomping and cheering. I look back at Jack, who throws back his head, laughing. I love it when I can surprise him.

Tomorrow we'll read in the *Boston Herald:* "The couple radiates youth and vitality." Even now as I listen to Jack's speech, the irony makes me giddy. I fold my hands, tilt my head, and smile. "Look how attentive she is to her husband," I imagine them saying. But my head is spinning with apprehension. I think about what the doctors at the New York Hospital for Special Surgery said yesterday. "Your husband needs a back operation. A lumbar fusion. It might kill him." I think of the bloody eggplant mess dripping down my legs as I sat bare-bottomed on the edge of the bathroom tub, rocking in pain, terrified, alone, Jack off campaigning for someone but mostly for himself, feeling like a failure as a mother and wife, doubting I'd live through the pain, much less conceive again. As the audience applauds us—the perfect couple, the picture of health—we prop ourselves up like paper dolls. Sick and frightened, we hardly dare think of the future.

"You see before you a man who not only will give you the shirt off his back but will give you his tuxedo—I speak from experience"—Jack's fingers clench the podium—"who will work hard to restore integrity to political office"—he leans nonchalantly on his elbows, twisting his lower spine in a way that looks casual but eases his pain—"so get out there and let's get our candidate elected."

We should get Academy Awards.

After all the thank-yous and speeches and songs, Jack takes my arm and hustles off the stage. "You were great, Jackie."

I bask in his praise. I don't trust the feeling. "Your crutches," I remind him.

"Forget 'em. Too many cameras. I'll have someone pick them up later." We shake hands all around. An older Italian kisses the top of my hand. I feel like the pope. Then the reporters, waving microphones in my face, yap questions: "Does your husband speak Italian, too, Mrs. Kennedy?" "Only in his sleep." "Does that make you more intelligent than your husband?" "There are those who are clever without being intelligent, and those who are intelligent without being clever. Jack is one, I'm the other, but I'm afraid I can't tell you which." "Will you be campaigning with your husband, Mrs. Kennedy?" "Oh, yes. I love politics."

Jack places his hand on the small of my back and pushes me out of the school and through the crowd on the sidewalk. We can't open the door to our car. Too many people. Muggsy pulls up ten feet, and Jack and I quickly dive in.

"Go slow, Muggsy," says Jack. "It wouldn't do to run over anybody." He groans and stretches his leg diagonally over my feet. "Not a bad showing, huh, Jackie?"

"Is it like this wherever you go?"

"Pretty much. I must say, you sure fired 'em up with that Italian stuff. Gotta take you more often."

"Everything's negotiable."

"That's my Jackie."

Gradually the crowd lets us go, dispersing like a mob beneath a dirigible. The lights fade quickly as we enter a heavy mist drifting in from the ocean.

Halfway down the street, Jack collapses on my shoulder and passes out.

Jack's hospital room looks like a kid's room. Books and papers are piled every-where. Football pennants and posters of sailboats plaster the walls. Pink plastic wa-ter pistols, balls of various sizes, magazine photos of politicos pinned to the wall with darts. A human-size Howdy Doody doll sits in the corner reading the *Con-gressional Record.*

When I close the door for privacy, bright red shoes with three-inch heels stare me in the face. A life-size poster of Marilyn Monroe in navy blue shorts hangs up-side down over the door. Her lips, glossy with red lipstick, are parted invitingly, her legs splayed wide, ready for entry, her mammoth breasts straining against a white cotton T-shirt. Yellow-feathered darts cluster like honeybees in all her erogenous zones.

"You moved Marilyn," I say casually. She first appeared several days ago on the ceiling above Jack's bed.

"The nurses made me take her down. They were afraid the darts would fall and stab me. I had Teddy hang it on the back of the door in case Rose shows up."

"She might spank you."

"She'll have one of the nurses do it."

"One of the pretty ones, I hope."

"Mom makes sure they're all crones." Even when joking, there's bitterness in Jack's voice when he speaks of Rose.

Every morning, I find myself trying to ascertain his condition. Sometimes he's almost incoherent from the pain, other times the drugs make him silly.

Last night was not bad. I kiss his forehead and can tell the fever is about the same. I feared worse. For hours I rub his buttocks and lower back, which seems to be the only thing that relieves him. Jack begs me not to go: "Just one more story, one more game, please don't leave me." He clings to me like a child refusing to go to kindergarten.

For his friends, he controls his pain, his face stiff with forced jocularity. As soon as the others leave, he cracks. He clutches me and sobs.

Jack is terrified of surgery but sees it as the only possible end to his pain. Joe begs him not to have the operation, begs me to insist. I agree with Joe but see the trap and say it is Jack's decision. I won't set myself up to be blamed. The doctors give him less than a 50 percent chance of surviving. "Death is better than a fuck-ing wheelchair for the rest of my life," Jack tells me. That I may soon be a widow seems both impossible and inevitable.

During the past year Jack has looked at me as if I had forced him into marriage. Now, behind his eyes, I see the resentment fading, replaced by a glimmer of grat-itude. When he's close to delirious, he tells me he loves me. I find this a little frightening, as if he's saying good-bye. At the same time, I see our love growing, becoming something solid and irrefutable. I see for a moment what our marriage could be.

The doctors remove the metal disc placed in Jack's spine by navy surgeons in 1944, then fuse the vertebrae of the lower spine. A staph infection of the urinary tract sets in after three days.

I curse the doctors and their arrogance, curse myself for not standing up to Jack and telling him not to have surgery.

I go to the hospital chapel to pray but feel ridiculous. I have mouthed meaningless verses for so many years. I don't know where to start. *Please, God, don't let Jack die.*

The Kennedy clan leaves for the night. I stay beside Jack's bed. I recite poetry, I plump his pillows, I read his pain, then summon the nurse for a shot of morphine. When he rallies, I put pieces of chopped ice between his lips to suck on. Later I spoon-feed him broth and tell him the dirtiest joke I can think of. In the morning I call the worst gossips in Washington for the most salacious morsels I can find. That which isn't about Jack, I use to entertain him.

If he can manage the pain enough to relax, he may have a chance at healing.

The priest's assistant unpacks a Communion box. He lays a white napkin over the night table by Jack's bed and sets out two candles, a crucifix, holy water, and a spoon. He asks me to cover my hair.

Silently the priest comes in with the Host. I kneel on the floor with him, Bobby, Teddy, and Eunice. He adores the crucifix in Latin, sprinkles holy water on us, and sends us out. The door closes on Jack's last confession.

I have often wondered about Jack's confessions. When the priest's assistant calls us back in, the priest's face looks ashen. Jack must've told him plenty.

We kneel again beside the hospital bed. We murmur the Confiteor—I have sinned exceedingly in thought, word, and deed. The priest stands before the crucifix and elevates the wafer, the body of our Savior. When Teddy and I help Jack sit upright, Jack cries out in agony. The priest intones three times the Domine non sum dignus—I am not worthy—and lays the wafer on Jack's tongue. Jack tries to swallow but gags. The priest retrieves it, gives Jack a spoonful of holy water, then tries again. Jack chews it twice, swallows, then collapses back on his pillow. He turns to me. "Thank you, Jackie, for everything."

The priest invokes the archangels against the power of the devil over him, but I hear only Jack's gratitude, and I think that if he dies, I will be able to bear it. I heard in his voice the love I always hoped for. I feel my soul flutter. *Please, God, give us a second chance.*

The priest moistens his thumb in holy oil, makes the sign of the cross, anointing Jack's eyelids, praying for forgiveness of the wrong he has done by the use of his sight, his ears for the wrong he has done by use of his hearing, his nose, his mouth, his heart, his palms, his feet. The priest then kneels with us and we mutter the Kyrie Eleison and the Pater Noster.

As Bobby leads the priest out and pays him, Jack slips into a coma.

I sit in a chair by his bed and watch Jack sleep. Time moves in fits and starts. I think an hour has passed, when it's been only a few minutes, then nod off for a moment and find thirty minutes have flown by.

Jack's face is a grayish white, his cheeks sunken like a cadaver's. As a child, I tried to will things to happen simply by desiring hard enough. I try to will Jack to live, to will his fever down. I see no difference. It merely exhausts me.

Depleted, I stagger into the hallway. It is two o'clock in the morning. I want a cigarette, but what I need is sleep. The wall feels so good to lean against. I don't want to sit down, just lean there until dawn. I should go to the hotel and change, but I haven't the energy. I close my eyes.

The hallway is cool and quiet. The air pressure seems a bit off, as if I were ascending in a plane. Fatigue? I hear night nurses chatting, someone moaning softly in his sleep, voices in the visitors' lounge. The hum of electricity. Someone setting a Pyrex coffeepot back on a burner. The clatter of an empty stretcher being rolled down the hall—perhaps a nurse getting ready to take someone to surgery in the morning. Or to the morgue. Then footsteps walking quickly toward me. I recognize a familiar rattle from my Inquiring Camera Girl days—lenses, light meters, spare cameras jangling against each other. My eyes spring open in alarm.

"Mrs. Kennedy, is it true your husband is dying?"

A flash blinds me, the camera lens jabbing in my face. My ankle turns as I try to scoot away. I cry out and fall back against the wall. The camera shutter clicks. And again. *Flash, flash, flash.* "We saw the priest leave. Has Mr. Kennedy received his last rites?"

From the lounge, Bobby, disheveled and red-faced, swoops down the hallway like a falcon spotting a rat. He grabs the photographer by the elbow and slams him against the wall.

"What the hell are you doing?" Bobby yanks the camera out of the photographer's hands and smashes it on the floor.

"Hey, you can't do that! That's my property!"

"To hell, I can't. How did you get in here? This floor is off-limits. Got that?"

"The public has a right to know."

"You fucking parasite! Get out!"

"Fuck you!"

"Fuck you!" Bobby slugs the photographer in the nose. He shoves him, blood dribbling down the hall, and kicks his ruined camera after. "Jack Kennedy is *fine.* You got that? Now get the fuck out of here before I call the cops."

The blood on the white linoleum makes everything seems so much more horrible. Grateful, weeping, I lean against Bobby's chest. He puts his arms around me—wiry fighter arms, so different from Jack, who seems soft and mossy even when he's skin and bones. "It's okay, Jackie. Jack is too stubborn to die." I'm embarrassed. Kennedys aren't supposed to cry. But no one is around except us. I let go, soaking Bobby's flannel jacket. "I'm here, Jackie. Don't worry about a thing. I'll take care of you."

Jack hobbles around the pool in his swim trunks, his wound exposed. There is something surreal about the oozing hole in his back, like the melting watches of Salvador Dalí.

After Jack had been in the hospital for two months, Joe hired a private jet to fly him down to Palm Beach. The doctors say they think the sunny climate will encourage him to heal. I think they've given up on him and are sending him home to die.

It's nearly impossible for Jack and me to talk anymore except right after an injection, when he's almost human. The doctor gives him Novocain in the spine and a shot in the hands, probably adrenaline. He seems to have shrunk, not simply his weight—which has dropped from 170 to 120—but his height as well.

After months of relentless cheerfulness, I am quite sick of myself and suspect he is, too. But I know I am his only tether to sanity. "I would die without you, Jackie," he says.

Even the Kennedy brutes seem to sense we're working on something and leave us alone. With others, they are ruthless at any sign of weakness. Within their family, they are unbelieving, helpless, and scared. Joe hides in his cabana. The others all find some important errand to do.

Every time Jack falls into a drug-induced sleep, I think he may never wake. Part of me hopes he will die to put him out of his misery. I try not to think of the future.

His nightly bouts of pain are horrible. Irritably he orders me out: "I don't want you sitting around my deathbed." I don't know how much more either of us can take. It takes all my courage not to collapse in a trembling heap. What I find hardest is Jack's general withdrawal from life, his spirit losing color like November leaves. He sees right through me. I know what he is doing. He is trying to save all his strength to fight the pain, to keep from giving in to hysteria.

I've never seen him this despondent. He lies for hours with an open book on his lap. Occasionally he turns a page, but he reads nothing. I see him watching the clock, waiting for his next shot. It's the only thing that interests him.

He has full-time nurses, but he wants me to give him enemas and massages. He turns over to have me change his dressing, moaning and cursing if we are alone. I use forceps to carefully pick off the gauze, which is saturated with pus. He howls when I have to yank off the pieces where the pus has dried to his skin. I uncover an eight-inch incision from his coccyx up his spine. It gapes open, the size of a nectarine, smelling and looking like an overripe brie. The edges are red and inflamed. Shiny white vertebrae are clearly visible. I clean the wound with iodine and some antibiotic jelly.

I have to shut myself off from the horror of it all. I close off my emotions, like a captain shutting off torpedoed sections of his submarine. It's the only way I'll survive.

"You know what I hate most about being sick, Jackie?"

"No floozies?"

"It's such a waste of time."

The only thing keeping Jack alive is his mind, but he needs something more than diversion and jokes. "Why don't you write a book?" I ask. "You claim to want to be a writer. When else are you going to have the time?"

I see a spark in his eyes for the first time in weeks. He presses the tips of his fingertips together and rubs them over his lower lip. "How long does it take to write a book?"

"About a year, more or less, I suppose."

"I'll do it in six months. I'll be well by then. What do you think I should write about?"

"What do you care about?"

"I'll think of something." I wonder if he means he'll think of something to care about or something to write about.

The next day he starts what will become *Profiles in Courage*. I call a political science professor at Georgetown to get names of senators who have shown great acts of moral courage in the face of opposition—John Quincy Adams, George W. Norris, Daniel Webster, Robert Taft—spend a fortune at Rizzoli Bookstore, and read to Jack for hours on end. He interjects with comments, ideas, and speculations that I scribble down on legal pads. Slowly an idea forms for a book. He attacks the work like a particularly rigorous penance, as if he's seeking to remedy a lack he sees in himself.

He hands me scribbles he's written on napkins and in the margins of newspapers, along with chapters written by others. "Put this together, Jackie. You're good at stuff like that." I marvel how he manages to demean my ability to organize even while praising me, as if succinct prose were of lesser value than his jumbled insights. He dictates. I edit and coach. "What are you trying to say, Jack?"

For months we work on the book. There is something fresh and marvelous in how we work as a team. On the morning after a sleepless night of torment, he greets me excited and full of ideas. I am so grateful for this time we spend together. As the work mends his spirit and his body, it mends us—it gives us a forum to get to know each other in a way that seemed barred before. It seems we are finally working on our marriage—something Jack refused to do before, because he couldn't admit he actually *was* married.

Jack looks at me with new eyes. "If I die before it's done, you'll finish it, won't you, Jackie?"

"Sure, and I'll add your life story," I say flippantly. It's been a particularly long day, and my patience wears thin with his death talk.

"I don't have much time, Jackie."

I kiss his hand. "Time enough for what counts."

"You think so?" He stares off through the window, down to the ocean. The palm trees and sand so close, yet so far. His eyes harden, seeing into a place of private torment I cannot enter.

As he heals and returns to my bed, Jack pulls me in tight and wants to cuddle. This feels warm and good, but I sense part of him is experimenting, seeing how far he dares go. He is newly considerate when we make love. Yet he has not climaxed. He fears his physical limits.

Cynically, I can't help think that he is merely practicing on me. Failure with the wife is tolerable, but with someone else it would be humiliating. I chase away these thoughts and try to enjoy it. How can so much be so good and yet be so unsettled and unsettling?

ARABELLA

*H*ow will it look to her, lying here in her crib? They say babies first see black, white, and red. How will blue, white, and pink look to her?

I sit where the crib will be—against an interior wall, looking out the window into the woods. Suspended over her, a mobile of monkeys and elephants. She can see the door, so I won't surprise her when I come in. The wallpaper is blue-and-white-striped alternating with a narrow band of dusty-pink roses. Along the top is a lighter pink frieze of frolicking rabbits, geese, and frogs. Out her window, swaying tree branches will give her a sense of rocking and put her to sleep. In the spring she'll see the dogwood trees in their pink tutus around the fish pond. The morning sun pours through the windows, which will help her get up and go to school. Rubbing her sleepy eyes, she will stagger to the window and watch me as I head down to the barns to feed the horses. Perhaps she will get an idea—a prank to pull on Mommy—or maybe she'll want to surprise me by being dressed and feeding herself breakfast, or maybe she'll run after me to see her new pony, or maybe she'll sit in bed and read until I come to get her up.

And if it's a boy? I'll quickly paper over the frieze with a design of sailboats or toy soldiers and I'll change the curtains from white chiffon to blue broadcloth. But I so much want a girl. Not because I want to dress her up with ribbons in her hair—I'll do only as much of that as she wants. I won't have her feeling precious, like Lee, thinking she's oh so dainty and pretty but nothing else. No, I want her to know she's smart and capable and can do anything she wants.

"How about a rocking horse in the corner?" I ask my belly. I feel a swift kick and laugh—she'll be a horsewoman, no doubt about that.

The room still smells of wheat paste and paint. Tomorrow the floor will be varnished and I won't be able to sit here, imagining. I hear workmen pounding down the hallway, finishing the cabinetry in Jack's walk-in closet. I designed shoe racks and drawers at waist level so Jack won't need to bend down. The doorways were widened to accommodate a wheelchair if necessary. When I told Jack that I widened doorways to give a more gracious feel to the rooms, he was grateful for the lie. Slowly we are learning to live with each other. Small kindnesses do much to heal our wounds.

We both fell in love with Hickory Hill as soon as we saw it. Jack loves its history, a Civil War command post for General George B. McClellan, and its feeling of stately majesty, sitting on top of a hill above the Potomac. It is modest, comfortable, and friendly. I love it for all those reasons and because of the miles of woods behind us, and the view of the Blue Ridge Mountains in the distance. It reminds me of places I've loved. It has the light elegance of Lasata, the ivy-clad Bouvier estate in East Hampton, the vistas of Hammersmith, and the woods of Merrywood. It fills me with joy and expectation.

Already there is more tranquillity between Jack and me. I love being pregnant. Jack is deferential, careful not to upset me. Had I known that a home was so important, I would've insisted on it when we first married, but I was too shy and diffident. I was aware that people said I married Jack for money and didn't want to start off demanding things. Jack was reluctant to make a commitment to marriage, thinking that if he could still live like a bachelor, maybe he would still be one. A house was not on Jack's agenda. Perhaps because Rose never gave the Kennedy kids their own rooms, Jack's sense of home is skewed. He says he feels at home only on a boat. But I should've insisted.

Perhaps with a real home, Jack won't feel so restless.

Jack hands me a copy of his book, face beaming. "Here, Jackie. Hot off the presses!"

The book smells of ink, fresh paper, and glue. The dust jacket is blue with the word *Profiles* in white, and *in Courage* in bright red. I turn to his picture. "What's going on with your hair?" I tease. He doesn't fall for it—I supposed he's memorized his author's photo by now.

"For cryin' out loud! Just open it!"

I fancy tormenting him some more, but am curious.

I flip to the title page: *Profiles in Courage* by John F. Kennedy. I turn to the next page and nearly drop the book. *To My Wife.* My eyes begin to burn. "Keep going. No, not there!" He grabs the book from me and flips to the last paragraph of the preface and hands it back to me, drumming his finger on the page. "Go on. Read it!" he begs. So I do.

> This book would not have been possible without the encouragement, assistance, and criticisms offered from the very beginning by my wife, Jacqueline, whose help during all the days of my convalescence I cannot ever adequately acknowledge.

I break into sobs.

"For Pete's sake, Jackie! I wouldn't have dedicated it to you if I thought you'd cry."

I can't begin to tell him how I feel. He could've dedicated it to his father, who's done more for him than anyone else. Or to the people of Massachusetts, who made him a senator. But he dedicated it to me. He took the risk of reminding his readers that he had been sick. He almost gives away that it was my idea—from the *very beginning*. But he doesn't mention anything about love, his love for me or my love for him. Even the dedication itself, *To My Wife,* not using my name, strikes me as impersonal. He says he can never "adequately acknowledge" my help, not that he's grateful beyond words. Rather than expressing emotion, he states his own inadequacy to express feeling. I try to understand—does he mean he can never love me enough, even though he feels he ought to?

I cry both for what he says and for what he doesn't say.

In my mind I revise and edit. He would've been more honest to simply write, *To my wife, Jacqueline,* and left it at that. But he rambles on, trying to express something, trying to break out. He was so proud and excited to show me the book. Perhaps it is, after all, an expression of his affection.

I process all these thoughts while Jack is still looking at me like a startled moose, ready to plunge across a swamp. Why do my tears frighten him so?

I decide to believe the dedication is his sincere attempt to express love.

"That fucking prick! I could kill him."

"But Jack. It's an honor. Adlai could've chosen anyone to nominate him. He chose you."

"Fucking right he chose me. Fucking asshole."

August 1956, two blocks from the Chicago amphitheater and the Democratic National Convention. Jack stomps back and forth in his hotel room, slamming doors, kicking chairs. By the window Bobby stands guard like a guy watching his buddy at a bar getting drunk and loud, prepared to tackle him if necessary. Other aides shrink in the corners. One by one they escape, slinking out the door.

"I don't understand," I say, trying to make sense of it.

Jack places his hands at the base of his spine and leans back—as if simply having me around aggravates his pain. "If I nominate Adlai, I'm taking myself out of the running for the VP nomination. And I can't tell him no, because I've already officially endorsed him. Fucking bastard."

"I thought Joe didn't want you to—"

"Fuck Joe. He's the one who started the machine to get me nominated in the first place."

"But that was when he thought Johnson would get the nomination. Now the delegates are going for Adlai."

"Jackie's right," interjects Bobby, shooting me a look that tells me, for my own sake, I'd better stay out of it. "No one's going to win against Eisenhower. With Johnson, you'd lose with dignity. But with Stevenson you'll get clobbered, and they'll blame it on your being Catholic. You'll never be able to—"

"You're telling me about politics?" Jack rocks back and forth like a bantam rooster. I've never seen him so angry.

"I didn't think you wanted to be vice president," I venture.

Jack glares at me. "Who says? How do you know what I want? How do any of you know what I want? What if I don't live long enough to become president? Did you ever think of that?"

The room crackles with hostility. No one says a word. Jack is so vital that we forget how sick he is. Jack never forgets. He stomps to the credenza by the window and pops a few pills.

Ted Sorensen, who's been cowering on the couch, advises meekly, "You have only a few hours to write your nomination speech."

Jack whips around and stares angrily at me, his face red and puffy. "Have Jackie write it. She's so in love with him. She wants so damn much to be helpful. I'm taking a bath. My back is killing me."

Jack hobbles into the bathroom, slams the door, and turns on the faucet. Water thunders into the bathtub. My face stings with embarrassment. We all look at one another. There's nothing to say. Bobby gets up and follows Jack into the bathroom. "For Christ's sake, can't a man take a shit around here without being harassed?" Bobby carefully closes the door, then walks into the hall. I hear the elevator bell.

Sorensen shrugs, hands me a legal pad, and follows Bobby. He needs a breather, too.

Humiliation is not a friend to creative writing. All I can think of is what a mistake it was to come to Chicago. Why did I risk something happening to my baby to be ignored and abused? I look around the abandoned room. Piles of garbage lie everywhere—newspapers, campaign literature, half-eaten sandwiches, empty coffee cups, dirty laundry, pizza boxes, half-empty bottles of booze, puddles of melted ice. The Stockyards Inn. The name seems appropriate.

I swallow my fury and do as Jack asks.

I write a few sentences, scratch them out, write again. Words begin to flow. It is oddly liberating to write in someone else's voice, but I soon realize that in praising Adlai, I can't help but criticize Jack. After a few minutes Bobby and Sorensen lumber back with coffee and doughnuts. They sit quietly on the balcony, summoning energy for the next round.

Jack stumbles out of the bathroom wrapped in a white towel. "You'd think the fucking hotel could give you a decent-size towel." His penis dangles where the ends meet at a V. "What do you have for me, Jackie?"

Water continues to fill the tub. I hand him the legal pad.

Jack puts on his glasses, mumbles the first part, then reads aloud. " 'Adlai Stevenson was my choice for the presidency in 1952. . . . His intelligence, farsightedness, and reasonableness have neither diminished nor been matched by any other potential nominee.' " Jack looks up from the page, gives me a long look, then smiles. "You think I lack farsightedness and reasonableness?"

"I thought those were qualities you could admire in him without praising him too highly."

"Kind of awkward, don't you think? Farsightedness? Reasonableness?"

"You're the writer," I say sweetly.

Momentarily appeased, he reads on. "Blah, blah, blah. 'But Adlai Stevenson is beholden to no man and to no section—only to the welfare of our nation at home and abroad.' Ouch, Jackie."

"I thought you could use the opportunity to answer your critics."

"Not bad. What do you think, Ted?"

"I think it'll do the trick."

"Let me get dressed. I want to make the rounds on the convention floor before nominations start. Maybe he can be pressured to open up the vice presidential nomination to the floor. Take himself out of it."

I watch as the carpeting outside the bathroom door darkens.

"That would be politic," says Bobby.

"That would save him from choosing Kefauver and antagonizing the South."

"And save him from antagonizing you."

"Too late for that. But it'd give me a chance."

"Don't you think you might want to turn off the water?" I ask.

He glances at the water-soaked carpeting as he tucks in his shirt. "You take care of that, Jackie. Come on, Bobby. Let's go."

Jack swims across the floor of the Chicago convention, shaking hands, then lifting his arms aloft as if to flip off seaweed that impedes his stroke. After three
days of nonstop campaigning, his eyes are red with exhaustion. He's fired up,
running on sheer willpower, his charm and confidence on automatic pilot. He
struts, swinging his legs straight out. He is the Jack of old, the Sammy Glick
Jack, the Jack who wants to win for the sake of winning. He cuts through the
frenzied crowd like a broker who bought low on a stock that's shooting for the
moon. The delegates look at one another, wondering what they have missed.
"Who is this fellow, anyhow?" "He narrated the presentation film." "Really?
Why him?"

On the other side of the hall, Kennedys rush around with invisible crowns on
their heads, everyone excited, high, as if the hall were filled with helium, passing
out KENNEDY FOR VP buttons that mysteriously appear. Bobby must've had them
made up weeks ago. Just in case.

For the first time I see Jack has made this run for the White House his own, not
Joe's. For the first time I see that he wants it. He *really* wants it.

I am tucked away with the Kennedy wives, eight months pregnant and extremely uncomfortable in a mezzanine box above the convention floor. It must be
close to one hundred degrees in here. Ethel, as pregnant as I, jabbers on a mile a
minute. "Isn't this the most exciting thing that every happened? They're going to
nominate Jack for vice president. Our Jack! Can you believe it? Oh, this is too exciting. I hope I don't go into labor. Wouldn't that just be ripping?"

I see no reason to be excited. Jack won't win. Joe is right. It would be a terrible mistake to accept the nomination. Stevenson will lose to Eisenhower. Why be
remembered as a loser in 1960? Even Jack knows this, or did before he got here,
but now he's caught up in the hype.

I feel detached, sitting here with a smile screwed on my face, a dummy, a plac-
ard displayed by the Kennedy clan.

Jack waves to me from across the crowded hall like a football star to his
mother in the stands.

I should never have come.

"And the state of Missouri casts its votes for . . . John Fitgerald Kennedy."

The Massachusetts delegation screams like delirious cheerleaders.

"And the state of Georgia casts its votes for . . . John Fitzgerald Kennedy."

Bobby trots after Jack like a secretary taking dictation. Occasionally he glances
in my direction—is he making sure I'm behaving, or is there something slightly
apologetic in his eyes? He has never expressed to me any criticism of the way Jack
treats me, but the look has always been there. Is it concern? Love? Even as I stood

poised to cut our five-tiered wedding cake—my white-gloved hand clutching the
handle of a sterling-silver cake knife, Jack's hand over mine, both of us smiling
like giddy stand-ins—Bobby wore this expression I've never been able to read but
seems to be reserved for me.

Johnson stands in front of the delegation from Texas, looking as though he's
just swallowed a horse fly. "Texas proudly casts its fifty-six votes for the fighting
sailor who wears the scars of battle . . . Senator John F. Kennedy!"

I feel faint. Could it really happen? I clutch Ethel's hand. She mistakes my gesture for excitement and grasps my bicep with her other hand—"Oh, Jackie! He's
going to win! I think I'm going to tinkle."

But he doesn't win.

Back at the Stockyards Inn, Jack stands on his bed in the crowded motel room,
his most loyal followers gathered around. The men are on their way to a serious
drunk. It feels like a wake.

Jack doesn't even try to make jokes. He lost. Kennedys don't lose. He thanks
everyone for their help and asks them to leave.

Jack never wants to be alone.

Bobby, the better strategist, insists he won. He sticks around, dancing on his
toes, like a sprinter itching for another race. "Don't you see? It's the best fucking
thing that could happen. Everyone thinks you're hot shit. And you won't go
down as a loser with Stevenson. Don't you see you've really won? Big-time. Look
at all the exposure you got. I counted how much time you got on TV. Two hours!
Just on you! Everyone knows who you are now. You've got it in the can for
1960."

"It's never in the can."

"You know what I mean. You're hot."

Jack won't have any of it. He sinks into a chair, his face in his hands. I try to
comfort him, but he shakes me off, violently, nearly throwing me off balance.
Alarmed, Bobby catches me, his face terrified, full of concern for my unborn
baby. Jack doesn't even look up. "I'll take you to Eunice's," Bobby says.

Silently, we leave him.

The day after the convention, Jack and I fly back to New York. We spend the night at a hotel near La Guardia. The next morning Jack boards a flight for France. My connection is to Newport.

Jack is ragged with nervous exhaustion. He is hideous to me, as if the loss is my fault. He wants to get away from everything—me, Joe, politics, America.

As I help him pack, I know I can't keep him from going—it would only make him hate me more—but I try. "Please, Jack. Can't you wait until after the baby comes? It's only a month away."

"I'll be back in three weeks."

"What if she comes early?"

"Didn't you say you were six weeks late at birth? The baby will wait for me."

I give it my best shot. "Please, Jack. I need you."

"What do you need me for? All I can do is hold your hand."

"That's exactly what I need you for—to hold my hand."

"For cryin' out loud, Jackie. I always go to Cap d'Antibes in August. I deserve it after all I went through." He doesn't even pretend to hide that his trip is anything but a babes-and-booze blowout.

"Of course you deserve a rest, but can't it wait a few weeks? Maybe you could go to Florida or Jamaica instead? Some place closer."

"You know where my swim trunks are?"

Then I think, do I really want him around, resenting me like a grounded teenager? Better he screw himself into oblivion under the hot Mediterranean sun.

I could say that I'm frightened to be by myself, that I'm frightened of losing our child, that I'm afraid of giving birth. I could say that he'll be cheating himself out of the first few moments of his daughter's life. I could say many things. But I let him go.

I slip a box of condoms in between his white cotton shirts and swim trunks.

At Hammersmith Farm, I go to sleep in the bedroom of my childhood. It is the same—yellow with white caned furniture, a large window with a view of the lawn spreading out to the ocean. It feels smaller—familiar yet strange. I recall the lonely girl who read late into the night in this room, who wrote poetry and drew pictures, but the girl I remember doesn't feel like me.

I try to sleep on my back, the moonlight streaming through the window blocked by my enormous belly. I dream that my baby is floating in a basket like baby Moses in the Nile, then I am the baby, and the river runs faster and faster, the basket vaulting over boulders until it dumps me on the shore, naked, the shawl my mother wrapped me in tumbling off my body into the mud. I can't breathe. Did I fall into the river? Am I underwater?

I wake as if drugged—hot, sweaty, and nauseated. I look out the window. The watercolor sunrise is lightly overcast, gray and violet with Swiss cheese holes of pale orange. I stumble downstairs for a cigarette, not caring that Janet will scold me for not brushing my hair. I pour myself coffee and look across the lawn, wondering if I dare ride Byron—maybe if I only trotted around the corral a few times.

Suddenly I double over in pain, grabbing the edge of the kitchen counter to keep from falling. Half a dozen men in work boots are kicking my stomach. I feel warm liquid squirt down my leg. I look down—a red puddle of blood forms around my right foot. "Help," I manage to utter, so softly that I'm sure no one hears. I groan in agony. *The pain!* I'm in rapids above a waterfall, slammed against boulders, dumped over a precipice, the falls pounding down on my smashed body. If I just hold on, I think, I'll make it, just hold on and the baby will come out.

Finally a maid wanders in, carrying a tray with coffee and half-eaten toast. "Oh, my God," she cries, dropping the tray, porcelain crashing on the floor. She shouts for Janet, who calls an ambulance to take me to Newport Hospital.

Where's all this blood coming from? There can't be that much in my entire body. I grip the edge of the sink, watching as blood seeps around my feet, feeling a weird sense of accomplishment as it reaches the edge of the tile I'm standing on. My head lifts like a hot-air balloon. I feel a warm sleepiness flow over my body, then pass out.

I wake up hours later. I don't open my eyes at first. The moist antiseptic odor tells me that I'm in a hospital. My first thought is surprise that I'm not dead. I feel a little disappointed.

My body feels like lead. I lift my head and a horrible pain stabs my gut. Someone is holding my hand. "Jack," I call, pulling the hand to my lips and kissing it. It feels different, finer, smoother. I drop the hand and open my eyes.

Bobby is looking down at me, his forehead crinkled, his eyes watery. He regards me like a lover, and I realize something has changed between us, like two strangers who have survived a hurricane together. Something binds us together now.

"It's Bobby," he says. "Don't worry, Jackie. I'm here."

"Is it a girl?"

"Yes. A beautiful little girl. She was born dead." Bobby is never one to mince words. "I'm sorry," he says. "You need to relax and concentrate on getting well.

You lost a lot of blood. They had to give you a transfusion. I don't want you to worry about a thing. If you need something, I'll be here."

"Where's Jack?" I ask. Bobby doesn't answer immediately. I sense something is wrong. "Has something happened to him?"

"No, no. Nothing to worry about. We're still trying to reach him. He's probably in some part of the Mediterranean with poor radio transmission. I'm sure he'll catch the next plane as soon as he hears."

Bobby is a hopeless liar. Later I find out that Jack's secretary, Evelyn Lincoln, told Jack of the news while he was aboard a charter boat in the Mediterranean and was instructed to say that she couldn't get ahold of him. This I sense now from the look on Bobby's face.

I fall back on my pillow, feeling completely abandoned. All my effort has been wasted. The years, the suffering, the love. I shouldn't have bothered.

"I'm never going back." I realize I've spoken aloud.

"I know he's not an easy man to live with, Jackie. But he's a good man and he loves you. He doesn't mean to be cruel."

"Don't apologize for Jack," I say angrily. The effort sends stabbing pains to my gut.

"I'm not. I'm merely explaining what Jack can't say for himself."

If I didn't have tubes in my nose, I'd snort in disgust. "How much am I supposed to forgive?"

"He's Jack," Bobby says, as if that were an answer.

Barely awake, I hear someone come into the room, a doctor I don't recognize. He is handsome, young with blond hair, a round angel face with red cherub cheeks. For some reason I'm filled with hope—maybe this doctor will tell me that Arabella lived.

"How are you doing, Mrs. Kennedy? I'm Dr. Jenkins. Your doctor asked me to cover his rounds this morning."

"I hurt like hell."

"You'll have to stay in bed for a few weeks, but I don't see any reason not to release you from the hospital tomorrow."

I don't care. I don't want to live. I'll stay in bed until I die.

"We'll put you on some antibiotics. Your doctor ran some postoperative tests. The condition of the fetus must've alerted him. Did you know that you have chlamydia?"

The strange word wakens me. "Chlamydia?"

"It's a bacteria that is passed along in the transmission of reproductive fluids."

It takes me a few moments to focus on what he's saying. "You mean a venereal disease?"

"Well, yes. It's very difficult to detect in women. It tends to lurk unnoticed in the uterus. But it can cause problems in childbearing."

"Problems?" He stands with his clipboard, so proud of his superior knowledge. I'm beginning to hate him.

"Yes. The bacteria can spread from the cervix to the fallopian tubes, which can become blocked with scar tissue. It could easily have caused your miscarriage and your stillbirth. If you plan to try to have children again with your husband—"

"Of course we'll try again."

"Well . . . it may prove difficult. Chlamydia can eventually cause sterility. I suspect that since you had a miscarriage in the first year of your marriage, you've been carrying the bacteria for a couple of years."

"Who are you, again?" I feel an indignant rage breaking through my stupor.

"Dr. Jenkins. I am an intern under your physician. I was asked to—"

"You can only catch a venereal disease through sex, isn't that correct?"

"Well, yes . . . through the transmission of sexual fluids—"

"Which means my husband gave me this venereal disease."

"Presuming he is your only sex partner, I would say—"

"Which means my husband killed my baby."

Flustered, the intern stumbles. "No, I wouldn't necessarily say that. . . . There could be other factors. . . . Really, Mrs. Kennedy, I wouldn't—"

Another doctor I don't recognize pops his head in my room and waves his clipboard at Jenkins. "Excuse me, Mrs. Kennedy. Dr. Jenkins, may I have a word with you?" His tone is severe.

"Certainly. I'll be right back, Mrs. Kennedy."

They talk in tense, hushed tones, in the hallway. I suspect Dr. Jenkins told me something he wasn't supposed to and is getting the scold of his life. He doesn't come back.

All I hear are the words over and over again in my head—Jack killed my babies.

NOTHING CURES THE BLUES
LIKE COLD CASH

'm surprised you bothered coming back at all," I quip. "Joe must've given the orders. Did he say you didn't have a chance at the White House if you didn't hurry back?"

Jack blushes, itching the back of his neck furiously. This, I realize, is exactly what Joe told him. "I'm here now," he says lamely. "What can I do for you?"

What can I do for you? As if I was one of his constituents he's kept waiting in the lobby, a generous but tiresome contributor, someone he can't avoid. Furious, heartbroken, I want to rail at him for our child's death. I don't have the energy. Softly I say, "You draw up the divorce papers; I'll sign."

Jack nods and agrees to a divorce.

"I'll stay at Hammersmith Farm. I refuse to be bullied anymore."

Jack looks at me with bedroom eyes. If he had looked at me once in the past six months with those eyes, I wouldn't be threatening to leave him, I wouldn't have lost my baby, I wouldn't have killed her with my anger.

"Whatever you want, Jackie."

As he leaves the room, Janet marches past, giving him the evil eye. For the first time in my life, I feel as if she's on my side.

Three days later, up in my old room at Hammersmith Farm, I realize the nurses never showed me my baby. They whisked her away like some nasty bodily fluid.

I never got to hold her or to touch her little fingers. I never got to tell her I loved her.

The doctors sliced me open, scooped out everything I loved, and sewed me up like a Cornish game hen. A neatly stitched seam stretches between my hip bones—a constant reminder of my inadequacy.

As if I needed one.

I lie in bed. A foul, black-leafed vetch twists around my body, sucking the strength out of my limbs. It blocks the sun with its greedy leaves. It sucks the moisture out of me. I can't weep, I can't cry out. My parched lips have forgotten how to make words. I try to sit up. I can't move.

My own thoughts bore me. I find pleasure in nothing. The idea of eating makes me want to weep, but all my tears are used up.

I surrender to darkness. I lie on my side, knees to my chest like a fetus. I am crushed and depleted. I want to die.

There's no fight left in me. Whatever hope I had when I left the hospital has dissipated. I haven't the energy to kill myself. I can't even roll over. Every second alive hurts, a pain without the pleasure of sensation, a pain of nothingness, a pain with no hope of ending.

I try to talk myself into doing something simple, like take a shower, but a heavy weight lies on my chest. My limbs feel rubbery and I am too feeble to move. I'm terrified of having to look at anyone ever again. It's an effort to breathe.

So many people have something real to despair about in their lives—poverty, illness, violence. Many women lose children. They go on to live happy lives and have more babies. But I cannot face my life. Everyone expects so much from me. I can't go on.

Jack is off campaigning for Stevenson and Kefauver as if the race were his, charming party activists, making them love him, particularly the young ladies. Everyone wants him for a rally—the witty, handsome young senator. He receives a hundred invitations a week to speak around the country. Even as he chooses carefully—the states where he'll need the most help in 1960—he takes on more than he can physically handle, purging himself for his loss, for his failed marriage. He knows Stevenson won't win. He's only putting time in for the party. And for himself.

I can't bear going back to Hickory Hill, the hallways echoing with baby cries that aren't there, her perfect room, empty, her crib, empty. When I suggested to Jack that we sell it to Bobby, he jumped at the idea with the exuberance of a skipper setting sail. Bobby has signed the sales contract and has it in escrow.

Staying at Hammersmith makes me feel as if I've reverted back to my childhood, feeling as I always have—a guest in my mother's house. Jack stops in for obligatory visits on his way to Hyannis Port. He mustn't appear unconcerned for his poor, sick wife.

The doctor gave me pills for depression. The medication brings its own set of problems. My mouth and throat feel dry and parched. My vision is blurry and I feel drowsy. There is a tingling tension in my head—along the sides from the temples back—as if I'm wearing an electrified halo. This morning my body set up a strange trembling, my hands and knees vibrating uncontrollably.

I hate myself for having to take the drugs. I hate that this is the best the doctors can do. One brilliant doctor suggested electric-shock therapy!

Whenever I see Jack, we resurrect all of the frustrations that we have ever had with each other, hurling them back and forth like javelins. I feel completely over-powered by Jack. As he pours out his dissatisfactions, I begin to hate myself.

My life has no purpose, no meaning. There is no reason to go on. There is nothing I want to do. I have no place to give my passion and love and caring. All my energy goes to nervous tension that eats away at my heart. It is destroying me slowly.

I receive a letter from Bernard Berenson.

> Carina Jacqueline:
>
> I am so sorry to hear you lost your daughter, Arabella. Were I not such a tottery old man, I would come to you and fold you in my arms. I have outlived most of the people I have loved and held them as they took their last breaths. I never had children, but I know intuitively that the pain is deeper to lose a child who has never had the chance to rejoice in life's bounty. I am so sorry.
>
> Do not despair. Have courage to take your life into your own hands. Your life is your artwork—no one else's. As I near my final days, my advice remains: make sure your life is constantly stimulating and challenging.
>
> I am an old man, so I can tell people I love them in a way I couldn't when I was younger—by simply saying the words. I love you, Jacqueline.
>
> With eternal affection,
> Bernard

The letter makes me weep deep, cleansing tears. I completely give in to the physicality of it. For a second I forget why I'm crying, overcome with curiosity at the sound.

Quickly the crying runs its course like an electrical charge. I fall asleep, comforted.

Janet bursts into my room and sweeps back the curtains. Sun pours through my windows.

"It's time for you to stop feeling sorry for yourself and get out of bed. I'm going to stand here until you do."

Her voice seems so far away. She glares at me like an angry crow, eyes narrowed, her arms across her chest. I give up hoping she'll go away and summon the energy to answer. "I can't."

"The doctor says nothing is wrong with you that a little exercise won't cure. Up, up, up!" She claps her hands and marches around my bed.

"Let me sleep a little longer. I'll get up, I promise."

"You've slept enough. Just because you failed in your marriage doesn't mean you can spend the rest of your life in bed."

I notice how she implies the fault is mine.

A servant brings in a breakfast tray of coffee, orange juice, toast, and marmalade. I feel nauseated. "I don't want breakfast."

"You're going to eat it. Sit up. And don't expect breakfast in bed again. I asked Clara to bring it up to you today only because I wanted to talk to you alone."

"Oh, Mummy."

"Don't 'Oh, Mummy' me, Jacqueline. You're making everyone in the house depressed. Especially the children. The chickens have stopped laying eggs. You haven't ridden Byron in weeks, and he's kicking his stall and nipping at the groom."

I squint against the sun and gingerly pick at a slice of dry toast. It doesn't even look like food to me. "I'll ride him this afternoon," I say feebly, knowing I couldn't possibly pull myself up on a horse.

"I've had enough of your childish behavior. You have a husband and a home. It's time to either patch things up or divorce him."

"Jack doesn't want to patch things up, and he's afraid to talk to Joe about divorce."

"Well, let him make the first move, if you will, but not here. Hughdie and I are sending you to Europe. It worked once with Jack—it may work again. If not, you can look for a job. Lee has a number of connections in the fashion industry in Europe. There may be something for you there."

I crumble at the thought. "Why would they want me?"

"We're putting you on a plane next week. We've bought you a ticket. I'm going shopping at ten. You may come with me to pick up whatever you need for your trip."

With that, Janet spins on her toes and marches out of my room. She purposely leaves the door open so I'll have to get up to close it.

I sigh heavily but feel relieved she has made a decision for me. I try a bite of toast and chew it for a long time until it tastes sweet. I smear on some marmalade, then take another bite.

I lie in a bikini on a white sandy beach in Ravello, Italy. Around me jagged mountains plunge into the surf. The sea is turquoise blue. The hot sun soaks into my skin. Inside, the bones and cartilage are becoming soft. My blood flows as slowly as the Tiber.

As soon as I stepped off the plane in Rome, I felt my senses returning. Sounds and colors came alive—almost too vivid, almost painful. The smells of coffee and pizza filled me with happiness. The stress of the past few years slipped off me like a winter fur.

I begin to recall the girl who first came to Europe, a girl of enthusiasm, intellectual curiosity, and passion. I must find that girl again. I will let her come to me in her own time, softly, shyly like the morning dew.

Europe feels like home. I've had it with the United States. The culture is violent and crass—bigger and louder is always better. Americans care nothing for art or literature. The only history they're interested in is the past one hundred years, and that doesn't interest many. The finer aspects of the human soul—sensitivity, compassion, aesthetics—are pushed aside by their greed and bumbling stupidity. As soon as an American family gets their house and yard, they aspire to nothing more. They oppose anything and anybody who's different.

I will never return.

I plan my escape, my future. I should get something from the divorce, but that will take time. Until then, I have a few jewels to sell. Not much, but enough to keep me going until I get a job. Princess Bedoni has offered me her apartment in Paris for as long as I want. Lee thinks I could get a job with a consortium of French designers to represent them in America. I can do freelance translations from French into English.

My body tingles with excitement. My life is my own again.

I see a boat rowing toward the beach. I think it must be a fisherman and put on my top. He rests the oars inside the boat, then jumps into the water and tugs the boat to the sand. Something about the way he moves is familiar. He drags the boat out of the water, brushes off his hands, and walks toward me. He pulls his shirttail out of his pants and unbuttons it. I see the back brace.

I panic. There's no place to run. I think of swimming away but know that would be foolish. I've been betrayed. Only Lee and my host knew where I was this morning. Someone told him.

I stand and place my legs wide apart. I wait for him to approach.

"I was just rowing by and I spotted this beautiful woman on the beach all by herself."

"How dare you track me down!"

"I wanted to see my wife."

"I'm not your wife anymore. You're free, Jack. I lost our baby. I won't tie you down. Go fuck every bimbo on the Riviera. Let's separate before we destroy each other."

"You look like a goddess." He takes off his brace, then the rest of his clothes, his eager penis wagging back and forth. He stops and extends his hands.

"Don't do this to me, Jack." Rooted, my feet won't obey my command to back up. I want to touch him, his face, his shoulders, his hips.

He sees my spine soften, desire taking hold of me. He draws me toward him, his penis hard on my belly. He pulls off my sunglasses and unhooks my top, his hands diving into my suit, his fingers probing between my legs. He pulls me to the sand. As he enters me, he says, "Come back with me, Jackie. Give us another chance."

His words are far away. I want the physical release. I whine and grab his buttocks and pull him to me.

He holds back. "Will you come back?" Frenzied, I refuse to say yes, but I can't say no. I groan and force his mouth to mine.

He kisses me hard, then pulls out. I cry out in protest. "Say yes," he says.

I reach for him, but he resists. Slowly he pushes himself deep inside me. I relax and moan. He pulls back, teasing. I'm teetering on a cliff, a breeze lifting my arms. "Say you'll come back. Say yes." He thrusts deep inside me.

I lose my will. "Yes," I say, pulling him to me. "Yes," my feet digging into the sand, my pelvis arching, pulling him deep inside me. "No," I say, my contractions pulling him deeper and deeper. "No," I say as I feel a future grief press down on my chest, grabbing hold of my soul, ripping my heart from my chest. I surrender.

Jack collapses on me and in moments is fast asleep. I'm aware of the hot stillness, the sand flies buzzing at our feet. I roll him off, then continue rolling, grinding sand in my eyes and mouth, sticking on his semen. I stand, mummified in sand.

I walk to the water's edge and dive in. I swim out several hundred yards, then float faceup in the tepid water. I can't go back to him, I can't not go back to him. If only I could float here forever.

Jack sits up, dazed like a waking drunk. He spots me and waves, grinning. I swim to shore. He hands me his shirt to use to dry off. He lifts my chin and kisses me. "You'll come back with me?"

"I don't know, Jack. I can't take the humiliation. You're sucking the life out of me."

"It'll be different this time."

"You'll never stop with the women."

This he doesn't bother to deny. "At least see me through my senatorial reelection. Then you can decide. I promise."

"You won't let me go until you're president."

"Then you won't want to go." He laughs, and I feel weak and trapped. "I need you, Jackie. I can't run for president as a divorced Catholic."

"Why should I care if you run?"

"I need you beside me. You are strong. I need your keen sense of people. I need you to keep me focused."

"I don't care about your damn politics. I don't care about the great Kennedy dynasty. I've lost two babies. Do you have any idea what that means to a woman?"

"It means we'll have to try again."

"What's in it for me?"

"Think of it this way, Jackie. I'm not going to live that long. Two terms, tops. That should pretty well use me up. Then you'll get everything I have and your freedom."

I give up. You can't outtalk a Kennedy. We dress and climb into the rowboat. "At least let me row," I say. "I don't want to look like a runaway slave you've recaptured."

"Oh, Jackie. You make such a big deal about everything."

Jack drags me back to the States, but I refuse to go back to living with him. I will stay at Hammersmith Farm until I can figure out what to do. Janet pretty much leaves me alone. She knows I have my strength back. I've talked to a lawyer.

I go to New York to visit Lee and her new husband, Prince Stas Radziwill, who bought a place on Fifth Avenue. I avoid seeing Black Jack. I can't bear his recriminations. Not now. "You girls love no one but yourselves. All the trips and horses and presents. You never call. You don't care one twit about your father." His apartment is dirty, smelling of poorly washed women, the only kind that will have anything to do with him. His breath is rancid—his clothes worn and out of fashion. He is never sober.

It's too depressing for words.

Lee and I go shopping. She is obsessed with clothes and decorating, and is glad to have a husband who can afford them. She introduces me to all the latest designers, and I have to hand it to her, she has taste and a real sense of design.

In weak moments I think of Jack. I miss his flippant anecdotes that make me roar with laughter. I miss his ironic comments that pull me out of my fussy fits. I miss trying to make him laugh. I miss the twinkle in his eyes and his smile. I miss hearing him yell, "Oh, Jackie, for cryin' out loud!"

One weekend Joe Kennedy calls me at Lee's and asks me to meet him in the city. Only after lunch at the Russian Tea Room and a walk in Central Park do I wonder how he knew I was in New York—I haven't spoken to Jack in weeks.

Joe doesn't look well, still recovering from an operation to remove his prostate. I've heard that makes a man impotent. That must be awful for a man like Joe. He must feel as if his time is running out. His face is white, his hands shake. Under his dousing of expensive cologne, he smells like an old man. He hangs on my arm as we walk through the zoo. We stop by the penguins.

Then he offers me a deal.

At first I am furious. I'm not some peasant without options. I can work. I have friends and family.

"You're the only woman for him, Jackie. You know that. You are his wife."

"How much is a wife supposed to put up with? I deserve a life of my own. I want my freedom."

"Do you really? A divorced Catholic woman?"

In an instant, the reality of separating hits me. I envision myself living in a garret, working as a secretary at a job I hate, too exhausted to enjoy life, a penniless woman in her late twenties, her looks fading, a Catholic who can't remarry or have a family with children. These are dim prospects.

"You are a bright woman, Jackie. Do you understand the ramifications of divorce? You'll ruin his career."

"It's always Jack's career! What about his happiness? Do you think he's happy in our marriage?"

"He needs you. Not just for politics. You can work on happiness. That's a wife's job."

The penguins frolic in the cold, plunging into the icy pool. I consider Joe's offer. A million dollars would give me a little security when the time comes for me to strike out on my own.

"Think of it as a dowry," Joe says.

"How long do I have to stay with him?"

"Through his second term in office."

We both know he's talking about the presidency. "What if he doesn't win the election?"

"He will. But if he doesn't, you're free. And you can keep the million."

If I thought Jack didn't love me on some level, I wouldn't have even considered Joe's offer. Some deep female instinct stronger than reason makes me believe that one day I will open his heart and he will cherish me. But can I really take money to stay with Jack?

I decide to deal. I am, after all, my mother's daughter. "One million now, put in trust for my first child. If I don't get pregnant by the second term, the money is mine. For every additional child, I want a million-dollar trust set up."

Joe laughs. "You got spunk, kid. I wish you were a man. I'd run you for president. I bet you've already decided to go back to him, haven't you? Otherwise, you wouldn't be so cocky."

"I'm sure you don't want to count on that."

"No, you're right there."

"Why is it so important that he become president?"

"Because he's my son."

I plunge forward to close the deal. "Deposit the first million in a Swiss account and I'll come back to Washington."

Joe laughs, delighted. "You've got to stand by him—the perfect little politician's wife."

I assume Joe means that I must agree not to take lovers. "I'll be the perfect wife." A thought makes me hesitate. "You won't tell Jack, will you?"

"Hell, no. If he doesn't know half the votes I buy for him, he sure isn't gonna know I bought him his wife." That slices right through me. Of course, I deserve it. "We understand the world, you and I, Jackie. We've gotta keep the boys idealistic. Can't let them know too much."

I begin to understand why his children dislike him. It's not his control they resent so much—there is, after all, a kind of freedom in not having to make one's own decisions—but his arrogance. "Let me know when you've cabled the money," I say.

"We have a deal. You get back to Jack and make up. He loves you, Jackie."

"How can you say that?"

"Because I know my boys better than they do. I'm their father."

I step into a taxi, shaking. What did I just do? I may now have some security for the future, but I sense I negotiated away something valuable—a belief in the possibility of a simple, loving marriage.

A belief in myself.

CAMPAIGNING

*F*rom the moment he laid eyes on her, Jack has been besotted by Caroline. At the mention of her name, he becomes soft. A glow appears in his eyes, a twinkle on his lips. Caroline has unlocked his heart.

Part of the glow he reserves for Caroline shines on me. He looks at me more tenderly. He is more solicitous to my physical pain, always concerned for my comfort. As if he now values me in a new way.

He loves to nap with Caroline sprawled like a crab on his chest. He cradles her in his arm like a football and asks her opinion on international diplomacy. Seeing him so in love with her makes me love him more.

But I am my mother's daughter, and as much as Jack's joy with Caroline moves me, I am not beyond taking advantage of the good humor she induces. If I need a large expenditure for the house, it always helps to have Caroline on my lap when I mention it to Jack. He had precious little interest in the home I planned at Hickory Hill, but now he wants a perfect home for Caroline. He even offers decorating suggestions. Do I need help with the baby? Let's hire a full-time nurse and maid. Do I need an additional allowance for clothes and toys? He is even more willing to spend money on his own clothes—Caroline must have a well-dressed father. I wonder if other women see their stingy husbands open their wallets wide when they have a child together. Perhaps in some primal way, men don't take their wives completely seriously until they have a child, as if they want to see a dividend on their initial investment before committing further.

I know Jack will never love me with the same immutable and inexhaustible love he has for Caroline, but I also know he will never love another woman with this kind of love. This gives me, as mother of his daughter, a certain sense of power.

For a moment I'm struck with horror that I might resent Caroline for her hold over Jack, just as Janet resented me for Black Jack's love. I search deep inside and gratefully find no such feelings.

I find myself weeping when I look at her. She is so beautiful. A miracle. An absolute joy. Jack leaves me alone again, back on the campaign trail, but I no longer mind. I perch beside her bassinet to watch her breathe. Nothing seems important except her smile. I kiss her all over. I nibble her pudgy knees and teensy toes. I smack my lips on her belly. I let her chomp on my fingers to ease her teething. I know when her cry is for food, when she has gas, and when she wants a new diaper. I call her Buttons and Pumpkin and Little Bug. I kiss her all the time, and flutter my eyelashes on her cheeks to make her laugh.

I can't believe how she fills my heart.

I have never felt love like this, a bliss that fills the room with a golden light—until she starts screaming. She communicates so clearly without words—a violent burst of crying, a glance, a frown—that I wonder if she'll ever learn to talk. Her little will delights me, screeching up a scale to see if I come running, then laughing, laughing, laughing. And the way she clings to my neck with her fierce little grippers. You can't imagine the strength in those tiny fingers. She throws her body into my arms with such ferocity, trusting me completely.

Nothing Jack does bothers me now.

Jack and I ride in a white convertible down Main Street, an unpaved road in Logan County, West Virginia. Ted Sorensen, the town mayor, and the local chieftain of the Democratic Party ride with us. There is no high school band to march behind us—the town's schools have no money for trumpets and drums. Instead, a handful of tattered World War I veterans limp behind us, playing off-key. The newest car parked on the street is fifteen years old. The storefronts are grimy with dirt. Above the windows swing crooked signs full of spelling errors: PENI CANDY, HAM SANWITCHES, SAM'S HARDWEAR. Townsfolk stare sullenly at us from porches. Men in overalls, brogans, and miner's helmets stand on corners in front of pool halls. Women breastfeed their babies in rusty trucks. Children dart around corners, excited, as if we were gun-slinging strangers riding into a dusty pioneer town looking for trouble. The mayor, who drives our car, honks the horn. Jack waves to the townsfolk.

They don't wave back.

We park at the head of the empty square where Jack is supposed to give a speech. "Some fuckin' rally," curses Jack. In a few minutes groups of men are hustled out of the bars, each man pocketing ten bucks, his mouth watering, already looking forward to a good drunk.

Jack gives a short speech, which ends to feeble applause. "This is crap," snarls Jack. "We're wasting our time here. What's our next stop?"

"The Silverback coal mines," says Ted.

"At least there will be people there. Next time, don't forget the free hot dogs and soda. C'mon, Jackie. Let's get this over with."

"It be cold down there, Mrs. Kennedy. You'd better wear this."

The miners stare at me curiously, white eyes in faces black with coal dust. They are fine-boned men with narrow noses, broad shoulders, and huge hands. They look incredibly strong. They know nothing of haute couture or of Givenchy, the designer of the simple sleeveless dress I'm wearing. They see only a lady in white who wants to go into a coal mine. They offer me boots, a hard hat, and a man's shirt to wear over my dress.

Apparently women are never allowed in the coal mines. They appear to wonder if I'll drop dead. "I'm ready," I say.

Beside the black square entrance to the mine, a slag heap two stories high smokes in the damp air. I step into the coal car that will take us half a mile down into the mountain. Fifteen miners in hard hats with headlights, picks, and shovels get in the car with me. The foreman orders the other miners to step back. He is nervous and worried. I called his bluff. "You wouldn't wanna see the mine shaft, would ya, Mrs. Kennedy?" he said, laughing, making a joke, annoyed at being stuck with the wife while the big boss tours the loading dock with the senator who might become president, sure that I'd decline in mock horror. But I said, "Yes, I'd love to." Now he's trapped into taking me into the mines, and all he can think is that if his boss finds out, he'll lose his job, and what if something should happen, but he can't take back the offer in front of his men without looking foolish. Resigned, he starts to climb onto the coal car.

"Would you please get my sweater?" I ask. "I left it in the convertible." He looks astonished and annoyed, just wanting this ordeal to be over. "Sure, Mrs. Kennedy." He turns and walks toward the parking lot. The coal car begins to descend. He dashes back, frantic. "You can't go down there by yourself!" I call back sweetly, "I'm sure your men will take good care of me."

We sink out of view. The miners laugh and relax. They know what I did, that I wanted to be alone with them, that I trust them, that I tricked their foreman because he tried to belittle me because I was a woman, just as they as uneducated miners are belittled every day. They don't care that the foreman will probably find a way to punish them. They've endured worse. Much worse.

The coal car descends, clacking and screeching over the tracks. A string of lightbulbs blinks along the limestone ceiling, which is pinned with steel rods set every two feet. Dank air hits my face. It feels as if we're entering something alive. It gets colder and colder.

These are not men who feel comfortable around an unescorted female. They push back against one another to give me room. They watch one another, suspicious, denying the bad thoughts that come to them, because they know only one thing to do when there's a pack of men and one woman. Some chew tobacco; others stare off down the shaft. The air sizzles with male sexuality. I ask them questions to tame them and because I'm curious: "How long is your shift? How many years have you worked here? How many days a week? If you get sick, does the company pay for you? Are there many accidents? How much are you paid? What is the number one thing you'd do to make your work safer?"

At first they answer tentatively, but soon they open up and tell me stories of blowouts and cave-ins, of poorly ventilated tunnels and gas explosions that incinerated whole crews. How a man missed one day after ten years and got fired. How they all expect to get silicosis and are all in debt to the company store and don't ever expect to be free of it.

The coal wagon jolts when we get to the bottom. We step out. It's very still, but somehow vibrantly alive. I hear the trickle of a stream, the buzz of the electric lights, the scraping of the men's shoes.

"Could we turn out the lights for a second?"

The men look at one another, then one walks to a circuit box fifteen feet down the tunnel and throws a switch. It is thick with blackness—cool, velvet-soft blackness. It is blackness with a life of its own, a seductive, predatory blackness. The men stand completely silent. I sense their tension. This is what they all fear more than anything—being trapped in a tunnel without light.

We stand in silence for two minutes, which seems like fifteen. "Dear God," I say softly, "please keep these men safe in their work. Give them health and health for their families. May they always return to the light." My voice echoes down the mine shaft. After a moment, one man says, "Amen," then the others. In the brief moment between the "Amen" and when the man by the circuit box flips on the lights, I feel this incredible sense of oneness with the men. As my eyes adjust once again to illumination, I see they felt it, too. Their faces are moved. We have shared a benediction. "Thank you, gentlemen," I say.

Silently, we head back to the surface of the earth.

When we reach the top, the men on the ground crew break into cheers—as if we had been saved from a cave-in, as if the men above sensed what we had experienced, that in plunging deep into the earth together, we transcended our different religions and backgrounds, that we had brought hope to their lives and renewed pride in their work. They clap and hoot as if we were heroes, and I, Joan of Arc, have led them into battle, led them to do more than they ever expected of themselves.

Then I see Jack. At first he looks annoyed, then bemused, and then, as the men continue to cheer—"Jackie! Jackie!"—he breaks into a beaming smile. He affectionately rubs some coal dust on my nose with his thumb, and the coal miners cheer again, "Kennedy for president!"

It seemed like a small thing, thirty minutes in a coal shaft with fifteen coal miners, but news of it travels around the state like wildfire. Where there was wariness and reticence before, now people show up in the streets to greet us. They all know about the wife of the presidential candidate who entered the mines. Because I trusted the miners, they now trust us. They show us their homes and schools and tell us of their worries and troubles. They show us their shacks of crates, cardboard, and tar paper, their yards of wrecked cars, rusty bedsprings, and garbage, their dead squirrels and coonskins hanging from clotheslines, their outhouses, their unpaved roads, their children with mucus-crusted faces, cleft palates, and clubfeet, and their one and only clinic, a lopsided trailer on cinder blocks. When we ask for their vote and tell them how to register, they don't back away, frightened and suspicious, but bravely sign up. Later, when I address a group of women and take off my shoes because I see a young woman in the front row without shoes, they open their hearts. "It's important for women to vote," I say. "It's the only way to change things for the better. Women can change the world. If Jack Kennedy becomes president, he will create a food-stamp program in your state within sixty days. He believes the people in this state deserve a helping hand. So, please, vote for my husband for president. Vote for Jack Kennedy."

Afterward, I hear them chat among themselves, unaware that their voices carry. Or perhaps they want me to hear but are too shy to address me directly. "Ain't she pretty. Not a snob at all. Her dress is so plain. Looks homemade. Poor thing, husband won't buy her dress an' she has ta make 'em herself. She ain't wearing stockings even."

In their faded cotton shifts, scarves, and men's shoes, they reach to touch me. I do not shrink back. These women know nothing about me, yet they look at me with hope. I am overcome with the awesome responsibility and wonder how politicians can routinely betray such trust.

As we drive through towns of cheering coal miners and their barefoot wives and children, Jack, too, is moved. "This is what politics should be about, Jackie. Not Embassy Row cocktail parties. Not conventions and rallies. Not reporters and photographers. This is it—the real thing."

For the first time, I begin to understand why Jack wants to run for president. I feel that we could really do something for these people. There is such abundance in this world. Surely we can find some way to relieve their suffering, to improve their lives. They ask for so little.

It is a scene that will be repeated a hundred times.

When Jack and I enter the ballroom to a Democratic Party fund-raiser, we stop at the top of the stairs. I can almost hear a trumpet fanfare. All eyes are on us, the hot new couple. We pose, our heads moving slowly, left to right, showing our faces like royalty, smiling hard, but at nothing in particular—a generalized smile of triumph. Jack clenches my hand too hard. He resents having to show up with me. It's part of the script he wants to revise. He quickly hands me off to an assistant, as if I were a matador's cape, and surveys the arena. His face is a mask, his smile eager and rapacious.

On the other side of the crowded room, I see Peter Lawford talking to a local party official, then to a lovely young woman. He makes a barely visible gesture to Jack, jabbing the air with his chin at the girl.

Jack pretends not to notice. He looks around, smiling, then abandons me to make his bumblebee rounds. He works his way around the room, efficiently shaking hands, then disappears with the girl.

I am mortified, too humiliated to take the fake smile off my face. No one dares approach me. They simply stare.

So I stand alone. In a pink satin Balenciaga gown with a bodice of sewn-on pearls with over-the-elbow white kid gloves. Jack may humiliate me, but at least I'll be well dressed.

I soon realize that a distant gaze, a fixed smile, a posture of rapt attention will keep people away. I practice it. Behind the mask, I slip away into my own thoughts.

Jack waves a Bloomingdale's bill in front of my face. "For Christ's sake, Jackie! You're killing me. I could make a dress like that for fifty bucks."

I laugh. The image of Jack hunched over a sewing machine with pins sticking out of his mouth is too vivid.

"What's so funny?"

"Oh, nothing. I'd like to see you give it a try."

"What?"

"Make me a dress for fifty dollars."

"If it'll keep you from breaking my balls, I'll do it."

"I'm sure one of Rose's maids has a sewing machine someplace in the house."

Jack has never so much as sewed on a button, and his patience for reading directions is nonexistent. The results promise to be interesting.

That weekend we visit Hyannis Port. Jack acts very mysterious, sneaking past the laundry and utility room with a large package. No one sees him all day, but a low hum resonates throughout the house, mixed with cursing and "ouches." He comes in for dinner, ebullient, his face alive. "I've been thinking. We ought to do something about how much garment workers are paid. I'm going to introduce a bill in Congress. I'm going to get the minimum wage raised from seventy-five cents to one dollar an hour." He says nothing about the dress.

A week later he presents me with a simple pink dress made from a *Vogue* pattern. I'm flabbergasted. It's beautiful.

"You made this for fifty dollars?"

"Hell, no. The fabric itself was twenty bucks a yard, at six yards, plus the lining at five bucks a yard, zipper, buttons, thread. Had to hire Dad's tailor to tear out my stitching and sew up the damn thing. All in, I guess we're over four hundred."

"It's beautiful, Jack."

"Go, put it on."

When Jack complains about the cost of my clothes, of redecorating our house, of entertaining, of his clothes, I know it's the price of ambition he's griping about. He's paid with his health. He's paid with his freedom. He's paid with his buried children. Our marriage was included in that price. As was this house, which he thinks he doesn't need. He'd rather be entertained than entertain, but grudgingly he pays for dinners and booze.

When you really want something, the price is never too high. A few more suits from Givenchy will not make it much higher.

Up at six. Yesterday, visited seven small towns in Wisconsin and a farm-equipment auction in South Dakota. Tomorrow, a tea in Oregon. My hand aches from shaking hands, my cheeks numb from smiling. I'm so tired, I don't even know what I'm doing. I tilt my head, listening, then say, "Oh, yes, Jack has always supported farmers."

Today, a grocery store.

I wear a black-and-white houndstooth wool tweed suit. I extend my hand

and smile. "I know just what you mean. As a girl, I gathered eggs and milked cows as part of my chores. Our farm provided provisions for a nearby military base."

I stand behind a table with a red, white, and blue poster with Jack's grinning face on it.

KENNEDY FOR PRESIDENT.
LEADERSHIP FOR THE 60S.

Jack doesn't like the poster—"It makes me look fat. Look at those cheeks! I have to go on a diet."

It's the cortisone injections that do it to him. His ferret face is softer now, less carnivorous. He looks more honest. More likable. "It makes you look more mature," I say.

The shoppers make a point of avoiding me. One woman, loaded down with diapers and cereal boxes, backs up her shopping cart, knocks down a pyramid of canned corn, and makes a beeline for the cashier who's farthest away from me. "I don't vote." "I vote the way my husband does, and he's a Republican." "I can't chat right now. I have a baby in the car." "I have ice cream. So, sorry." They say anything to evade me.

I see obese ladies with huge white cakes in their baskets, skinny ladies with a dozen cans of cat food, men missing teeth buying six-packs of beer, teenagers with fists full of candy, and young mothers who spend half their time replacing items their children grab from the shelf.

My feet ache. Only teenagers too young to vote drift by my table. "Thank you for the doughnut, Mrs. Kennedy. I'll tell my parents, but I think they're Republicans."

A middle-aged cashier peers suspiciously over half-glasses. I wave a few fingers at her and smile.

Where in hell is Jack? Why does he put me in these positions? He's probably off bonking the local librarian, expecting me to do his job.

The store manager, a man in his early thirties with a buzz cut, struts to the front of the store, picks up a microphone, and turns it on. He taps the mike, then leans over it, nearly touching it with his lips. He lifts his sleepy-cow eyes and gazes down aisle number four. "Attention, shoppers. Welcome to Gipel's Groceries. Our specials this week are canned corn, five cans for fifty cents, and in our meat department, shoulder ham at nineteen cents a pound. For the kids, look down aisle three for new cereals from Post . . . and don't forget bread. . . . Wonder bread builds strong bodies twelve ways." This guy loves the sound of his own voice, imagining, no doubt, that he's headed for a job in television, host of a variety show, introducing the next Ritchie Valens between advertising plugs for Brylcreem.

I shake my head awake. He's hypnotizing me. Soon I'll be wandering the aisles, filling my arms with peanut butter and Ovaltine. What am I doing here? I can't believe I'm standing in a grocery store in flat, treeless, cow country where everyone drives a truck, where one bagboy is retarded and the other is ninety. This is how you get votes? This is politics? "For those in your family with a sweet tooth, Gipel's Groceries is offering Knox flavored gelatin at . . ."

I get an idea. I couldn't feel any more ridiculous than I already do. The store manager looks astonished when I ask to borrow his microphone. "Good morning, shoppers. My name is Jacqueline Kennedy and my husband, Jack Kennedy, is running for president. While you enjoy your shopping, let me tell you about my husband. . . ." Everyone stops. One woman stands frozen with her hand gripping a box of Saltines on a high shelf. "Jack Kennedy was a hero in the Second World War; now he wants to use that leadership to lead our country. . . ." No one moves until I stop my pitch.

I'm a little charged now, so I help bag groceries while chatting with the customers. I sign Jack's name on the bags, then start signing my own name. I stuff a flier into each bag. "Please, vote for my husband, Jack Kennedy."

I forget to worry about Jack.

Two o'clock in the morning. I wake when I hear Caroline stir. She has bad dreams sometimes, but I'm told that's normal for a three-year-old. I hold her hand and tell her a story until she falls asleep.

As I head back to my bedroom, I stop and listen to the voices downstairs. Jack and his cronies. Plotting.

"So, what do we have so far?" asks Jack.

"We got these numbers yesterday," reports Teddy. "When asked, 'Who will do more for the country?' fifty-three percent said Nixon, and forty-seven percent said Kennedy. 'Who is more experienced?' Nixon sixty-nine percent, Kennedy thirty-one percent."

"That's not so bad, is it?" Jack believes in polls like a farmer believes that squirrels burying nuts early means a long, hard winter. Lots of Joe's money goes into polls.

"That's just Democrats. Nationally, on the issue of experience, we're getting around eight percent."

"Ouch. People don't think I'm experienced? I've been preparing for this half my life."

"They think you're young."

"How do you beat that? It brings out the kids, though."

"Most of them are too young to vote."

"On sex appeal, you get ninety-five percent."

"Well, that's something! What's Tricky Dick's strategy? We got any clues?"

"He knows he hasn't a chance in New England, and he's weak in the South, so he'll probably try to establish himself in California, Colorado, Illinois, and Michigan. Then he'll hammer the big mid-Atlantic states—Pennsylvania and Ohio."

"How we doing on dough?"

"We got some fund-raisers lined up in Massachusetts—thirty-dollar-a-plate dinners, ten-dollar cocktail parties. You'd better tell Jackie she's gotta face some rubber-chicken dinners."

"Do I have to? She makes such a fuss."

"You get a fifty percent greater turnout. The wallets of those horny old geezers swing open when she whispers the secret words. We gotta get her back to Wisconsin. Maybe she'll pull a West Virginia."

"I wonder how much that'll cost me. A new spring wardrobe?"

"Don't give her such a hard time. The reason you're getting the big bucks is because of that wardrobe and her in it. Out in California, we got Lawford setting up some Hollywood parties."

"Now you're talking." His voice suddenly sounds eager and strong. It's the bimbos he's thinking of.

"Sinatra agreed to do some fund-raising."

"Fabulous."

I nearly fall asleep eavesdropping. I shuffle back to bed, sweeping my hand over my rounded belly, grateful I don't have to campaign anymore.

Today I see a man destroyed.

Me and 80 million Americans who tune in on millions of black-and-white Admiral and General Electric televisions to get their first real look at Nixon and Kennedy. The debate.

As Nixon gets out of his car at Channel 2, he sees me smoking outside the studio door. He waves. Suddenly a soundman stumbles into him, jabbing his knee,

the very knee that has recently been operated on. I see by his scowl that he wonders if it was an accident or a dirty trick.

He enters the studio, glaring at the cameramen. Perhaps he senses how eager
they are to film the candidate with the healthy tan and good looks. Or maybe he
suspects that Jack came earlier, bringing doughnuts, bantering and joking, making
friends with the network president, the news division head, patting each camera-
man on the back like their best buddy, saying, "I know it's a challenge, but make
me look good, will ya?" then scooted out to make a second, more dramatic appearance.

When Jack returns, the photographers swarm like swooning teenage girls
around a matinee idol. He greets Nixon with a banal pleasantry that must feel like
a snub—"How're you doing?"—then looks away to smile for a camera. Jack
doesn't offer to shake hands. He hardly looks at him.

I thought we were friends, Nixon's expression says.

"You want makeup?" asks a production assistant. Jack, with his own makeup
artist busy laying out combs and subtle shades of rouge in his dressing room, says
nonchalantly, "No. Let the American public see me as I am."

The production assistant asks Nixon the same question. In that moment, I see a
man open wide the door to his humiliation. "No, thanks," Nixon says. "I'll have a
quick shave. That'll do it for me." He sounds confident, but his eyes give him away.

Jack disappears into his dressing room. Within minutes, a young woman is de-
livered to his door. She is not a production assistant.

Nixon wanders the studio, appearing uneasy, tripping on camera cords, bumping into grips, so he takes his position at the podium. His knee is obviously bothering him. He swallows his pain with the tired, doughy expression of a man who
expects a bad day to get worse.

Two minutes to airtime. Nixon's eyes dart around the studio and at Jack's
dressing-room door in near panic. *Where's Jack? What's his game? Damn him!*

He has more time for more self-doubt, time to remember a humiliating interview with Walter Cronkite earlier this week. A veil of self-pity, lethal and
radioactive, covers his face.

The dressing-room door bangs open. Thirty seconds before airtime, Jack saunters onstage behind his podium, zipping up his pants. Smiling, relaxed, confident.
And so very handsome. He doesn't even glance at his opponent.

Nixon—sweating, pale, and suspicious—hovers over his podium like a vulture.

The debate begins. They spar and joust. Jack attacks like a prince. Nixon jabs
and scrambles like a street fighter.

The whole country sees these two images—victor and loser, aristocrat and schlemiel, gallant and whiner. In this moment, I know Jack will win. I hear America turning off their television sets. They have seen enough.

Then Jack plays a trick. Jack attacks the Eisenhower administration for not getting tough with Cuba. Nixon can't defend himself by saying that the administration is putting up millions to arm anti-Castro Cubans without breaching national security. His face becomes pinched. He turns defensive like a caged wolverine, hissing and gnashing at the boy who torments him with a stick.

He frightens me. He frightens the country.

Feebly he offers to impose economic sanctions.

Jack's duplicity destroys him. For the rest of his life, something will be broken in Nixon. He'll be a man America will delight in hating.

Perched on the backseat of a blue Cadillac convertible, we ride through the Canyon of Heroes, a cold October wind tearing between the Manhattan skyscrapers, American flags flapping overhead, ticker tape falling like snow, Jack's grinning mug bobbing on sticks above the crowds, flashbulbs popping, blinding us. Two million people scream from Broadway to Yonkers, businessmen, secretaries, bellhops, ladies out shopping, children on recess, leaning out windows, jumping in the streets, faces weaving back and forth, trying to catch a glimpse. Girls in packs, hysterical, flapping their hands, wave photos of Jack to be autographed, reaching out to touch the shiny car with KENNEDY FOR PRESIDENT posters taped to its hood. A man runs beside us, dodging pedestrians, shouting up to a small boy bouncing on his shoulders, "Look, son. There they are!" as if telling the boy to remember this day for the rest of his life, the day he saw Jack Kennedy, the day his life began.

I hold on to my white felt pillbox hat and smile.

Twelve bodyguards in dark blue suits march on either side of the car like pallbearers. Each rests a hand on the car, unsmiling, eyes probing deep into the crowd, gently prying off the women who throw themselves on the hood.

"The world is changing. The old era is ending. We stand on the edge of a new frontier. A frontier of unknown opportunities."

Sitting on the back of the rear seat, I feel like Humpty Dumpty. Under my voluminous white wool Givenchy coat, our baby is kicking, wanting to be part of it all. I lift my elbow waist-high and rock my white-gloved hand from side to side. They welcome you, little one. The world will always love you.

Young men and women crash through a police barricade, running to the car, hoisting themselves on either side of the Cadillac, rocking it back and forth, screaming, "Jack and Jackie! Jackie and Jack!" We'll be crushed in their rapture, I'm sure.

The bodyguards shove them back into the crowd. They knock down other people, which starts scuffles and flying fists.

"Let's get the hell out of here!" the New York mayor shouts from the front seat. "They're going crazy."

"They love us," says Jack, waving to the crowd, unfazed.

The Cadillac speeds up, jolting Jack and me into the seat. Even as he grabs his back in pain, Jack waves and grins. "It'd be a great time for someone to take a shot at me," he says, laughing as if it were the funniest thing anyone has said all day.

THE MEN IN BLUE SUITS

ommy, who's that man in our yard?" Caroline stands looking out the kitchen window while eating a bowl of cornflakes.

"Come sit at the table to eat, honey." She obeys only when she sees me get up. Filled with apprehension, I cross the room. I glance at the clock: 7:14 A.M. I pull aside the blue gingham curtain.

Thirty feet in front of our house, dressed in a dark blue overcoat, you stand—arms crossed, looking away from our house, your steady gaze slowly moving from side to side like the steady swipe of a lawn sprinkler.

"He's a friend of your daddy's," I say. "Why don't you take Miss Shaw upstairs and wake him up. Say to him, 'Good morning, Mr. President.'"

Caroline scampers upstairs, excited.

I look again out the window. The sky is clear. The sun glints off the water and sparkles on the frosted lawn. You must be cold out there. You take your gloves out of your coat pocket and put them on. You must feel me watching you, because you glance back at the house. It's your first day on the job. You must be nervous. This must mean a promotion for you. You're not sure if you can handle it—the intensity, the responsibility. You're worried that something will happen on your watch.

So you have come into my life to stay. Forever in my face, lurking like a ghost on my peripheral vision, disappearing as soon as I turn my head fast for a decent look. Here you are, to protect us. For the sake of national security.

You will be there every time I leave the house, noting in your little book what time I lock the door. Every time I take the children to the park, or take a walk, or run an errand. You'll drive the anonymous Mercury sedan, glancing at me in the backseat in your rearview window, never chatting, addressing me only to ask if this is where I want to go, and you will note the time I enter the hair salon, what time I leave, if I talked to people, and who they appeared to be. If I leave something behind, if I change my mind, I let you know so you won't become alarmed.

You will always be there, with a revolver holstered to your side. Every phone call will be cited, every visitor logged, every trip chronicled.

You will know secrets about Jack that I will never know, noting what time he disappears into a bedroom with a bimbo. You'll note what time she arrives, what time she leaves. You may open the door for her and take her coat. Perhaps she says something to make you blush as you pat her down for weapons. Perhaps she'll offer to service you, too.

You will observe Jack's guilty glances when he sees me again. You will notice how I flinch when I smell sex on him.

Will you admire his sexual appetite the way his friends seem to, like an Italian mother watching her son dig into a huge plate of pasta? Will you pity me?

Every time I go for a walk at night with the dogs, you will be there.

Every time Jack bends down to kiss my ear, you will be there.

Every time Jack humiliates me in front of a group of friends, you will be there. You will know all the details, with whom, when, for how long.

You will read our moods when we smile and eat breakfast together. You will know when we've quarreled and why. You will know how long we sleep, how often we have sex. You will know when I have my period.

You are not our servants. We didn't hire you; we can't fire you. You are our keepers. We are like exotic animals being studied in a zoo by animal behaviorists, our every bowel movement weighed, the time, consistency, and texture dutifully noted in a little black book.

You will know us better than we know each other. You know our sins more thoroughly than our priest.

What do you do with your notebooks? At the end of the day, do you lay them on your nightstands to read before you sleep? Do you pass them back and forth to other Secret Service agents? At the end of the month, do you hand them to someone to review?

As you lie in bed at night, do you fantasize about selling what you know to *Confidential* magazine? With the money you would make, you could retire to some tropical island. Do these temptations keep you awake?

Do you ever let one of these secrets slip to your wife when she teases, "Just tell me something, honey, and I'll do it the way you like." When you visit your relatives who say how lucky you are to work for such a dear family and how they seem to love each other and how sweet and perfect it must all be, do you itch like crazy to say just one thing to enlighten them?

You will know everything about us, but do you care? When Caroline falls down, will you pick her up? Or will you stand apart, watching, because that's what you're trained to do? When she cries, will you feel it in your heart? Do you have children of your own? When I am rushed off to the hospital, hemorrhaging blood, my unborn baby's heart beating frantically like a finch in a snare, will your stomach churn with worry?

You are here to protect me, but will you protect me from rapacious reporters and the long lens of the Cyclops? Will you protect Jack from a clever assassin or a lone lunatic? Will you protect me from humiliation?

They say it's the price of fame. But a price can be negotiated. This cannot.

A sense of dread lies heavy on my skin like a thick sweat. It's a frightening thing to lose your privacy at thirty-one.

FIRST LADY

*W*hen I try to sit up, the seam above my pelvis, cut and stitched for a third time, scar upon scar, smirks at me with malicious lips. Pain stabs into my gut like fresh razor cuts. Something else deep inside isn't right, angry and pounding in my uterus.

I can't do it. I can't face them. I can barely lift my head.

I dread all the people waiting for me downstairs, the relatives, Kennedys and Auchinclosses, all characters in this play, crushing in on me, expecting my lines to be perfect. I want to find a corner and hide.

A princess has her whole life to prepare to be queen. How does one learn to be First Lady? I am thrust into the role like an understudy who's been backstage reading comic books for so long, she's forgotten her lines.

Can't I stay in bed?

My lower back hurts so much that I'm nauseated. Even a cigarette doesn't help. I think how funny it would be for Jack and me to show up at the inaugural gala both on crutches. My laugh stabs my gut. I cry tears of weakness, and bile seeps into my mouth.

There's a knock on the door. In comes Max Jacobson, Dr. Feelgood, Miracle Max, Dr. Dreamer, Dr. Fix-it, with his black bag, his greasy hair combed over his balding tortoise head, his bulging eyes behind thick glasses, his thin-lipped mouth clamped tight.

Jack bursts in behind the doctor. "Jackie, I think we need to give you a boost, or else we'll never get you out of bed."

I can tell Jack has had his shot. His face is flushed, his eyes glazed, the whites full of mucus, the pupils enlarged and fixed. "It's great, Jackie. Try it. I've never felt so good."

"What's in it?" I ask.

Before the doctor can answer, Jack says, "Just vitamins. It's healthy, right, Doctor?"

Vitamins and what else? Steroids, amphetamines?

Depression is a chemical thing, right? A chemical thing should be handled with chemicals, right? I have to get up. For Jack. For the country. "Maybe just this once," I say.

Dr. Feelgood sits beside me and takes my pulse. His fingernails are black crescents. He inhales through his nose in spurts. His touch repulses me, yet I close my eyes and give him my arm. I don't care—just get me through this.

Jack scampers in and out of my room like a boy on the way to a ball game. "C'mon, Jackie. We got half an hour. Get dressed." He takes a cigarette out of my hand. "I don't want you smelling like smoke. Last thing we need is someone sniffing you and yelling fire at one of these things."

I slip on my white satin Cassini gown, careful of the hair and the borrowed Tiffany diamonds. I look in the mirror.

She is there, ready for her entrance.

The First Lady of the United States of America.

As I step over the threshold and lift the hem of my shimmering white gown, big fat snowflakes float over me like rice at a wedding. The toe of my slipper touches the pavement and I look up, smiling at the cameras. *Pop, pop, pop.* A sea of flashes blinds me. I am Cinderella off to the ball, the penniless stepdaughter made good. I am the Snow Queen. I am the Sugar Plum Fairy. I smile, feeling slightly dizzy, slightly ridiculous. Jack in his top hat, me in my gown—we are as self-conscious as children playing dress-up, pretending to be king and queen.

I am reborn as the nation's bride, emerging like a white woolly moth into the night. I leave me to become her.

Invigorated by the cold air, I laugh. Alarmed by the applause from reporters and Secret Service agents, I reach for Jack's arm for support. I need a fairy godmother to tell me how it's done, but no one is there to guide me.

Where is my carriage? My horses? I step into the limousine, snowflakes swirling around me, and, though giddy with terror at my future, think how perfect it would be to arrive at the inaugural gala in a horse and carriage.

"Keep the interior light on," says Jack as the chauffeur pulls away from the curb. "I want people to see her."

He is showing off his political asset, waving out the window as if he's still campaigning. Jack will never stop campaigning.

He looks at me proudly.

Isn't it enough that he's grateful? Why do I need love?

The next morning Jack and I walk hand in hand down the White House drive solely to let the photographers take our picture. Last night's snow clings to the trees and buildings, frozen in the predawn chill. The Mall before the Capitol is blanketed in dazzling white, and in the distance the Washington Monument sports a jaunty white beret.

The sun is blinding. The midwinter midday light is a pale violet, making the snow whiter than white. I would kill for a pair of sunglasses, but I've been told First Ladies don't wear sunglasses.

I shiver in a beige Oleg Cassini coat with a fur collar and muff, wishing for my mink, the only sensible thing to wear in a Washington winter. Yet I know that amid the dowagers in their furs, the effect will be perfect—an image of youth and accessibility, a woman well-off but not rich, stylish but not snobbish, not so very different from the average American woman.

But I am frozen to the core.

After Cardinal Cushing short-circuits the wiring with his endless invocation, and after Robert Frost recites a poem, Jack strides to the podium and begins.

I sense the excitement in the crowd. Their faces are surprised, exhilarated, rapt. His beautiful words mean little, yet they ignite something behind their listeners' eyes, even in his enemies. "Let the word go forth from this time and place, to friend and foe alike, that the torch has been passed to a new generation of Americans. . . ."

The crowd watches his words written in the air in vapor. Reporters lift their pencils, still as charmed cobras. Cameramen raise their eyes from their lenses, transfixed. Cynical old-time politicos sit up in their seats, chins jutting, pensive. Senators' wives, jaded from years of campaign smiling, grip their husbands' forearms with their fingertips. Even the Secret Service cock their heads.

"Now the trumpet summons us again—not as a call to bear arms, though arms we need, not as a call to battle, though embattled we are—but a call to bear the burden of a long twilight struggle year in and year out. . . ."

The still air sizzles. The crowd is mesmerized.

A breeze flips a piece of his hair. He stands coatless, defying the cold, not to demonstrate his vigor, but to numb his pain, to force him beyond the pain, to break open his spirit like ice over a pond.

This is what the crowd responds to—his raw spirit.

"And so, my fellow Americans, ask not what your country can do for you, ask what you can do for your country. . . ."

It's not the words. It's beyond the words, a shaman's invocation, waking us up to a magic we know exists but have forgotten. I feel the world change, a subtle shift, like the moment a fine wine changes from good to sublime. The world will never be the same. I nearly shout with joy.

Jack appears as I have always imagined him, a perfect idea of a man, valiant and brave. Aroused, nearly swooning, I feel the blood pumping in my neck. I forgive him everything.

Then I remember. He is my husband. A pride infuses me like something I've never felt before, inflating me with courage.

Yes, together we can do this. We can make a difference.

"Is that her? In white. Is that her? Is that her?"

Men's voices, women's voices, whorl in tight eddies. Heads bob back and forth on the other side of the ballroom, necks straining, hands pushing, shoving.

"Look at her dress! She looks like a queen." "She's so beautiful." "She's so young." "All alone? Where's the president?" "Where's the president?"

Jack is off at a dinner with Frank Sinatra, getting his walking stick polished. He promised to be back to take me to the second ball at the armory, then the third, the fourth, and the fifth. I'll never make it.

I smile and move my head from side to side, paralyzed with fear. I smile until my cheeks hurt. No one knows that knives stab at my gut, their points nicking the base of my spine. No one knows my knees are buckling, that vomit lodged beneath my sternum is preparing to spew. I smile harder.

If only I could have a cigarette.

Mrs. Johnson, wattle-necked and pale, stands beside me, cool as a cucumber, cool as Mamie Eisenhower and Pat Nixon were this morning in the Blue Room, exchanging meaningful glances over coffee and cake. *Imagine her marching in here, saying she's going to change the place. The first thing out of her patrician little mouth—— "Wouldn't it be lovely to have some early American antiques in the White House?" Wait until she tries to use that flirty voice to get money out of Congress. Good luck, Missy. That'll take the starch out of her Parisian knockoffs.*

Women are sore losers. Men run a mean race only to cross the finish line and embrace their rivals, but women never forgive an opponent's victory. For women, victory should be awarded for intrinsic worth, not for a particular performance. Yet, it is I, not Jack, who is deemed unworthy.

It's clear they don't like me.

Pat held her teacup tightly, her fingers white, her lips pressed tightly together, scooting to one end of the couch, staring out the window—*All this was supposed to be mine! My couch, my Blue Room, my view of the Washington Mall.* And Mamie, hands in her lap, grieving for her younger friend whom she groomed for the White House, chatted politely, smiling, continuing her silent critique—*Obviously, she's too young for the responsibility. She thinks she can handle First Lady? She'll find out what's coming to her.*

Imagine Mamie's horror at seeing the army of painters and carpenters who will arrive tomorrow, marching up to the second floor to do battle with her bubble-gum pink and vomit green. I laugh, delighted. Out with the old, in with the new.

And what is Nixon doing now? I imagine him drunk with self-pity, roaming the snow-covered streets of Washington in the car he'll have to surrender at midnight. Or stalking the empty corridors of the Capitol one last time, past the Senate Chamber to the Rotunda, the soles of his cheap shoes slapping against the marble like a flagellant's whips. "This all should be mine!" Perhaps he huddles on the Rotunda balcony, looking across the Mall blanketed in snow, envious of the parties he can almost hear, parties to which he wasn't invited.

Mrs. Johnson taps me on the forearm. There's a roar outside. Jack saunters into the ballroom to raucous clapping and cheers. At the top of the stairs, he flashes an uneasy smile, fearing he might be trapped by bores, already planning his escape route. He shakes hands as he comes toward me.

His eyes are charged, his body radiating energy. Something has changed about him, an authority, as if the oath of office, like the coronation of a medieval king, magically bequeathed him power.

"Looks like everyone is waiting for me to get the party started. C'mon, Jackie. Let's get 'em dancing, then make our getaway."

He pushes me along the dance floor. I feel a pulse of pain jerking through his body with every step, giving me courage to resist my own pain. He smiles, I smile, we circle the room until other couples join us, and the floor is crowded.

Then Jack takes my hand and pulls me toward the exit.

I wake in the Queen's Bedroom to hammering, pounding, ladders being dropped, workmen shouting to one another. I hope they finish the children's rooms today. They are staying with their grandparents until some of the confusion dies down. They have a nanny and a nurse—they'll be fine—but I miss them so much that it hurts.

My body doesn't want to move. I'm exhausted. I start crying for no reason I can think of. There's so much to do: thank-you notes to write, remodeling of our second-floor living quarters, the selection of art from the National Gallery, the swearing-in ceremony in the East Room for members of the cabinet, a thank-you dinner for the Roosevelts.

Jack isn't helping at all—"It's your territory, kiddo." He acts like a giddy debutante, flitting from room to room, traipsing in with all his friends, campaign workers, anyone who asks, leading them around the workmen, the ladders, the buckets of paint, showing off color swatches, which he carries off someplace where I can't find them.

My bed is covered with to-do lists on yellow legal pads. Charlie, one of the terriers, lies on the pad I want—I yank it out from under him. He sneezes from being so rudely awakened, stretches his hind legs, and jumps to the floor. His foot rips the top sheet of paper. I smooth it out and puzzle the torn edges together. *Oh, that list.* I wad it up and throw it across the room.

Notepads lie everywhere, on my dresser, in the bathroom, on the television. Lists of whom to invite, what to serve, whom to call for tablecloths, what flowers are in season, lists for Mr. West, for secretaries and maids, for cooks and butlers, for military aides and musicians. I need lists of lists. Nothing must be forgotten. I'm too tired to read them.

I have to get up. Someone has to look in control. I roll over and pull the covers over my head.

Someone knocks on the door. I can't bear to face anyone. He knocks again. "Jackie, it's Robert. May I come in?"

I don't answer. Jack has sent the big guns to get me out of bed.

Bobby opens the door and peeks around the edge—like a fox sniffing the air for dogs before making a mad dash from his den. He pulls a chair up to my bed and takes my hand. For a moment I relax. Bobby has an air of competence and reliability. He's so small and wiry, but there's something solid about him, as if he were made of steel.

"How are you doing, Jackie?"

If only Jack would look at me with such concern. Tears spring to my eyes. I start blubbering. "It's all too much. I don't even know what I'm doing. Jack is bouncing off the walls."

"Don't worry. I'll keep Jack in line. He's been running for so long, he doesn't know what to do now that he has the prize. But he's got a job to do. He'll get down to business."

"I don't think he knows how."

"He can't do it without you, Jackie. He needs you."

I groan and say I can't, but I feel a slight spark of energy, and my mind begins to organize what I have to do today. I pull Bobby's hand to my cheek. He isn't bothered by my tears. He watches me with a steady gaze. For some reason this makes me feel better.

"Okay," I say. "I'll get up. Will you hand me my robe?" As I swing my legs off the side of the bed, Bobby glances at my thighs. Our eyes meet. We both freeze. I'm not embarrassed. So much passes in that glance. He feels it, too. He brushes my forearm with two fingers, then stands and fetches my robe.

How am I going to make this place a home?

Naval spittoons sit in the corners of all the rooms, gleaming brass, exposed and vulgar like glistening genitalia. Behind the doors, wilted brown-fringed palms hide, dry and forgotten—probably left over from the Victorian jungle salons of Presidents Arthur and McKinley.

The whole place is freezing and drafty. No wonder Andrew Jackson got tuberculosis and William Henry Harrison died of pneumonia and Zachary Taylor got typhoid. Theodore Roosevelt called the White House "a peril to health and even to life itself." He wasn't kidding. It doesn't look as though the fireplaces have been used since the Truman administration.

The furniture is mostly hideous nineteenth-century reproductions, as bad as hotel furniture, arms and legs chipped to show the cheap veneer, the cushions stained, rank with cigar smoke. The lamps are straight out of Sears Roebuck, rust poking through the bronze paint, with dusty paper lampshades. The third-floor guest quarters have white linoleum floors and water fountains in the halls like a sanitarium. The only kitchen is downstairs, so your food is cold by the time it's brought upstairs. There are no toilets downstairs, so every time you have to tinkle, you have to dash upstairs, where half the toilets don't flush. There's no hot water.

Caroline follows hesitantly as I show her around. "Are we going to live here, Mommy?"

"Yes. For as long as Daddy has this job."

"Can we sit on the sofas?"

"Yes. You can even jump on them."

She looks at me in disbelief. In my opinion, that's all they're good for. She thinks I'm joking. I choose a particularly awful love seat. I flip off my shoes and help Caroline up. Tentatively, I jump, then higher, clapping my hands. Caroline jumps, giggling, clapping. We're making it ours—our home.

The sofa surrenders a loud crack just as J. B. West, the White House chief usher, walks into the room. He arches an eyebrow. "I don't believe I ever saw Mrs. Eisenhower enjoy her fine furniture with so much gusto." His wry smile lets me know he's on my side.

"I thought the couch needed to get broken in."

"Well, yes, things are a bit . . . shabby. You may find something you like better in the basement, or in the warehouses."

"Warehouses?"

"With each new administration, most of the furniture is either thrown out or sent to a warehouse."

"Any treasures?"

"I don't know. You'll have to take a look."

"There's nothing I love more than a treasure hunt."

Caroline stops jumping, catching something the grown-ups are talking about that interests her. She opens her eyes wide. "A treasure hunt? Like gold and diamonds?"

"We'll have to see, honey."

The next morning I pull on old capri pants, one of Jack's old shirts he refuses to throw out, and a scarf around my head.

I descend the staircase by the East Room to the ground floor. I walk past the China Room and the Diplomatic Reception Room to where the rug stops and naked cement begins—at the utility and housekeeping rooms. It feels like a basement in every way—dank, naked lightbulbs hanging from the ceiling, the smell of boilers, rusty pipes, and mildew.

I open the door to the carpentry shop, which is dimly lit with low ceilings and barrel arches. The floor is old brick, there since Mrs. Benjamin Harrison tore up the soggy planks that had rotted from the marsh beneath. An old fan stands in the corner.

A black man works behind a table, not young, tall with a wide, flat nose and glasses, with mashed potatoes around his middle. He appears to be working on a birdhouse.

"You are Mr. Frank Wilson?" I recall that he is a carpenter from J. B. West's introduction to the household staff several days ago. "Would I bother you if I look around?"

"Go ahead, Mrs. Kennedy."

He watches me out of the corner of his eye as I poke around. Newspapers, paint cans, various pieces of furniture without upholstery or with broken legs. Close to the wall I spot a tall sideboard covered with paint, varnish cans, brushes, and jars filled with turpentine. It is eight feet long by eighteen inches wide, with a slab of white marble on top. The marble is textured with globs of dried paint and wood glue. Each leg is shaped like two bowling pins standing end to end with stylized acanthus leaves like a bandage where they meet. Around the top is a design of acorn leaves. It is painted black.

I trace my fingers over the exquisite carving and imagine the master carver rubbing his calloused thumb over the curves as he worked. Frank looks alarmed. "It's called a pier table," I explain. "I recognize it from some etchings I've been studying of the White House from the time of Monroe. He refurnished the White House after the fire of 1814."

"A pier table?"

"You know the space between two floor-length windows? In architecture, it's call a pier. These tables were designed to stand between the windows."

"What's the mirror fo'? Never could figure that."

Between the two far legs sits a long mirror—eight feet by three feet—designed to be set against the wall. "What I've read is that it was for women to check to see if their hems and trains were straight."

"Or check the shine on their shoes."

"Maybe it was for the husbands to look up the ladies' dresses."

Frank laughs behind his fingers like a geisha. The feminine gesture on such a huge man makes me think of Peter Lorre.

"Do you have a flashlight and something sharp?"

He hands me a flashlight and a screwdriver. I kneel and gently scrape the top layer of black paint on one of the legs. Underneath is gold. "It must be gilded in gold paint. Is there any way to take off just the top layer of black?"

"Paint an' varnish remover will take it down to the wood."

"What do restorers use to clean varnish off paintings?"

"They use a mixture of solvent an' linseed oil."

"Could we try that?"

"I reckon. But what am I gonna use for a workbench if you furnish the White House with all my tools?" He smiles broadly.

Frank finds a bottle of cleaning solution. I dab some on a cloth and wipe the pier table leg, rubbing in circles until the black paint breaks apart in tiny flakes.

"That stuff is murder on yo' hands," says Frank too late. He pours kerosene on a rag and I wipe my fingers. They turn raw and red, and sting terribly.

"I have to shake the hand of the president of Tunisia tonight. He'll think the First Lady has leprosy."

"Gloves," he says.

"Yes, gloves."

Frank becomes my partner in crime. He tells me about the three chandeliers held hostage in the Capitol since 1902. (I use LBJ's personal influence to get one back for the Treaty Room upstairs.) He finds a charming white marble bust of George Washington in the bathroom behind the toilet brushes. He helps repair antiques that come from donors, and shows me how to reupholster, make picture frames, and use gold leaf.

It takes two months for Frank to refinish the pier table, much of that time waiting for a piece of Carrara marble for the top. When he's done, he leaves a note with J. B. West letting me know I can take a look at it whenever I want. Dressed in a Chez Ninon evening gown, a black silk velvet bodice with a Chinese yellow silk satin skirt and a gigantic yellow bow at the waistline, for a state dinner honoring President Mañuel Prado of Peru, I fly downstairs.

"Oh, Mr. Wilson. It's beautiful. You are an artist." I grab his hand, which is stiff with dried varnish and covered with sawdust, and kiss it.

Frank looks at me as if I've lost my mind, then gives me the smallest of smiles. He is very proud.

"We can do it, Mr. Wilson. People will come to the White House and will be proud to be American."

When I find a piece of slave art in one of the congressional warehouses, I take it to Frank. I ask him how he would feel if I hung it in the White House. "Would you find it embarrassing or hurtful? Washington owned slaves. So did Jefferson."

"I know that, Mrs. Kennedy."

"It's part of our past, but it's shameful. Do you think it's right to display it in the White House?"

"Don't do nobody no good to hide the truth."

"If you were taking a tour of the White House and you saw this painting hanging on the wall, would it make you angry?"

"Expect so. Maybe that's not such a bad thing. Shows where we been an' where we's goin'."

"What if we showed it next to a portrait of Frederick Douglass?"

Frank spun around, and I was afraid I'd offended him. He rummaged behind a bookshelf and pulled out a framed letter from Frederick Douglass.

"Oh, Frank. It's so right. We'll hang them together."

And so they went into the Blue Room.

"Are you trying to get me fired?"

"Presidents are impeached, not fired. And if you don't stop chasing tail, you'll manage that on your own."

As Jack flips his hand dismissively—his usual response when I mention his relentless pursuit of poon. "Americans love their White House. They don't want any changes."

"Most Americans have never seen the inside of the White House. What they imagine it to be is how I want to make it."

"You just want an excuse to purchase all those antiques that I never let you buy."

"Possibly."

"Oh, Jackie, can't you be a good girl? Truman got blasted for building the second-floor balcony, and he didn't spring it on the public in his first month in office."

"I'm not springing anything on anyone. It's a project for me. You know what you're supposed to do as president. What am I supposed to do? I'm not spending my days pouring coffee for a bunch of ladies from the DAR. I want to help you. I want to help the country. The White House needs to be restored. The United States can't go on forever pretending to be a nation of cowboys. How can we be the superpower of the world without a minister of culture, without a budget for the arts, without a cultural center in Washington, without a White House we can be proud of? These things can be done, and I can do them."

Jack looks completely baffled. He doesn't even try to come up with an argument. He sends me to his lawyer.

"I feel like a fucking prisoner," Jack rants, restless and irritable. He stalks through the halls at night, then drags me on a walk with him. As we stroll around the Mall, the Blue Suits trail us, twenty feet behind, stomping through snow and slush. They're not happy about it.

Tonight he snuck out with Red Fay to see *Spartacus* in a movie theater. When Security suggested he use the White House screening room, he blew up at them. "Goddammit, I'm president. I don't need to ask your permission to see a goddamn movie."

I see his tension building, and it frightens me. He verges on being out of control. He's distracted—completely unfocused. I'm glad he doesn't have any big diplomatic decision to make right now.

I never knew sex was such an addiction for him. It was always something he did when he was away from me. Now that he can't get away, his mad promiscuity stares me in the face. I can't even attempt to accommodate him—I haven't recovered from John's birth, and the doctor says it will be months before I should have sex. The more tense Jack gets, the more withdrawn he is toward me. He blames me. I am his jailer. He doesn't know how much he can get away with in the White House, but he knows for sure he can't fuck someone with me in the next room. At least he doesn't have the courage to try. Not yet, anyhow.

I can't think of any way to keep us both from going insane except to leave.

The next morning I wake the children and help pack their bags. We will spend a long weekend at Glen Ora, the retreat we have rented in the Virginia countryside. As we climb into the helicopter on the South Grounds, Jack runs out from a meeting in the West Wing and ducks inside the cabin. He shows Caroline how to use the seat belt, and makes sure Maud Shaw and the baby are secure. He doesn't want us to leave, but he can't wait for us to go. As Jack puts a blanket over my knees, he pauses and looks at me with gratitude. He knows I am giving him his freedom.

"Be careful," I say.

He nods, kisses Caroline's forehead, and limps back into the White House.

As soon as I return to the White House, I sense something different. I send the children up to our private quarters and set off to find Jack. I want to see him. I want to thank him for renting Glen Ora for me. Buried in ten feet of snow in the rolling Virginia country, it was as romantic and secluded as an aristocrat's hunting lodge in a Russian winter landscape. It's perfect for us.

The halls of the White House are unusually quiet, yet there is the sense of people being here, in the shadows, slipping silently from room to room. There is something ominous, spooky, and queer.

Panic jolts me. More than ever, I want to see Jack.

As I dash down the hallway, I see a Blue Suit disappear into the room with the swimming pool. I slow to a walk. I stand quietly outside the door. I hear water splashing, the quick slap of bare feet on tile, and the hum of the elevator. As soon as the sounds stop, I open the door.

The pool is empty. Running the length of the far wall is a mural of St. Croix at sunset, dimly illuminated in orange and yellow light. Music is playing, a wistful bossa nova with a male voice whispering a love poem in Portuguese. Two glasses— one with lipstick on it—sit at the edge of the pool. Four wet footprints lead to the elevator, two large, two small with high insteps and narrow heels. Fiddle and Fad- dle, Jack's special assistants, have big feet—I assume this is a special guest.

So this is the way it's going to be?

It's my fault, of course. I should have telephoned before I came home. I should know better than dare risk a spontaneous impulse to see my husband. I am not al- lowed such luxuries.

I asked him not to humiliate me, to be discreet. "Change the sheets anytime someone sleeps in them," I told the White House maids, so I won't be surprised. But I was surprised, a pair of black silk panties fallen between the mattress and the headboard. "Not my size," I said as I tossed the panties into Jack's lap. "Try to find out who they belong to."

A lingering naughtiness hangs in the air above the pool just as when a mother, hearing giggles, opens the bedroom door to faked snores, and sees a pillow feather, recently liberated, floating across a streak of light.

At one corner of the pool, a lot of water has splashed out. I wonder if that's where they had sex. What is it like to have sex underwater? Why has Jack never tried it with me?

A Blue Suit enters the pool room, looks around, then leaves without speaking. I figure he was sent to retrieve the evidence and discovered he was too late.

The bossa nova tickles something deep inside me. I take off my clothes and dive into the pool. I swim across the entire length of the pool underwater. Music from underwater speakers pulses against my body, the voice pressing its tongue and lips into my stomach and thighs.

I race back and forth, chopping the water with my hands, anger hardening my muscles, my heart beating fast. The water is too warm for swimming, sapping my energy. I rest for a moment, hanging on the edge of the pool to catch my breath, then push off, this time swimming faster. Ten laps. I come up for air, my lungs raw from the chlorine fumes.

The music ends. The room is still. Water slaps gently against the sides of the pool.

The exercise tames my anger, but I feel it becoming part of me, like a disease that lingers, not killing you but not letting you feel well.

I must pretend it doesn't exist.

I towel off and put my clothes back on, ready to become First Lady again.

I handle everything during the day. But at night deep feelings swell up in my dreams, tossing me about in a half-asleep stupor. I wake feeling depressed and worthless. My chest is tight, my stomach constricted. I think about suicide.

The constant humiliation is too much for me to handle. I prepare madly for a lovely state dinner, then face a room full of people tittering away. "Does she know? How could she not? Doesn't she care?"

I hear them whispering behind my back, comparing scorecards, the secretaries, the female members of the Capitol Hill press corps, the wives of his friends, many who have slept with him or want to. There are no secrets in the White House.

I hear them speculating on our marriage. "She wanted money." "She wanted to show up Lee." "She's always been ambitious." "The fool thought she could change him." "It must be her fault. She must be frigid." "How can you blame him?" "How does she put up with it?" "She must be made of ice." "Yes, she's an Ice Queen." "She's cold." "She's a phony." "There's not a single emotion in her entire body."

They watch me keenly, waiting for me to crack.

I'd rather have their jealousy than their pity. I'd rather have them think I'm cold than know my rage and shame.

I can't bear to face them. I feel mercilessly exposed and exhausted. This is a twenty-four-hour job that I don't get paid for. It's too much.

I retreat. I cancel engagements. I get Mrs. Johnson to fill in for me at teas and press briefings.

I want to disappear.

Jack is more eager than concerned when the White House doctor, Janet Travell, recommends that I go to Palm Beach for a few weeks to rest.

Our good friends the Wrightsmans invite me to stay at their home. I am too listless to tend to the children. I leave them with Maud Shaw at the White House. Little John is so little, so sick. There's nothing I can do for him. I can't entertain Caroline. I'm good for nothing.

The Wrightsmans give me a lovely room, but I keep the shutters closed. I feel as if I'm in a tomb. Like Juliet, waking from her drugged stupor to discover she has sacrificed everything for her lover who is dead.

I imagine Jack's gay friend Lem Billings playing hostess, filling in for me at the

White House, a white apron around his waist as he arranges the dinner table for Jack, his brothers, his war buddies, his many pimps, Frank Sinatra and other scum, plus any number of bimbos. Lem, like a discreet hostess, will retire to the kitchen as Jack and his buddies make off to the White House bedrooms with the girls.

I imagine the girls running naked through my bedroom, orgies on my couches, in my bed, fucking madly under framed photographs of Caroline and John.

I imagine them trying on my clothes and my wigs, gyrating in erotic dances, teasing Jack's bobbing erection.

I imagine them laughing at me, squealing with delight. "If Jackie could see us now! On her precious Louis Quinze divan!"

I imagine the Secret Service watching all this, appalled, pitying me, or perhaps joining in on the fun.

An antique clock chimes in the living room. Time ticks on, but my world has stopped.

I slip a black satin eye mask over my eyes and pull the covers over me. I will stay here in this dark room forever.

Until I die.

When I see Jack again, he is not wearing the satyr grin he usually wears after a week of debauchery. His back pain is worse again, but that's not it. He actually seems relieved to see me.

This almost jolts me out of my self-pitying mood.

We celebrate Easter at Joe's house in Palm Beach. Jack huddles by the pool with Bobby and Joe, and takes walks on the beach with his advisers. When he comes to bed, he holds me tight. "It's Cuba. I've got to make a decision. I've got to make the right decision."

Joe and Bobby are for invading and overthrowing Fidel Castro. Several advisers are against it. Jack thinks he loses either way.

I have seen Jack so depressed only once before—after his back operation, when he lay with an open wound oozing pus like a volcano, betrayed by his body, tormented as his flesh and spirit wasted away. This is a greater betrayal.

He sits with his face in his hands, utterly defeated. "Jackie, how could I have been so stupid?"

He approved the Cuba invasion, the Zapata Plan. The Zapata fiasco. He ordered eight B-26s to bomb Havana, San Antonio de los Baños, and Santiago de Cuba. He approved sending Cuban exiles trained by the CIA to storm the Bay of Pigs. He sent eight U.S. ships and the aircraft carrier *Essex* outside Cuban waters. He sent six brigade planes to bomb Castro's principal airbase.

It was a complete failure. Only five of the Cuban air force planes were destroyed. Two exile ships were sunk. The invading brigade planes were chased off by the Cuban air force, stranding the exiles, who were captured by Castro. Oblivious of the time difference, the air cover showed up an hour late. There was no popular uprising to support the exiles.

He looked like a fool. "The biggest mistake I've ever made," he says, weeping in my arms.

He followed his father's counsel—he owed Joe, didn't he? He followed his trusted advisers—they were more experienced than he, weren't they? He carried out Eisenhower's plan—Eisenhower was a general and wise about such things, wasn't he?

Now he feels betrayed. The greatest betrayal of all was that Jack doubted his own instincts. While trying to show he was not his father's puppet, an isolationist, he jumped into the arms of his advisers mad for war. He denied U.S. involvement when it was obvious.

The son pays for the sins of his father.

After Jack exhausts himself raging and blaming, he falls asleep beside me in our newly painted bedroom. I lie awake, feeling a vague but urgent need to stand guard, like a sentry outside the tent of a defeated general. My mind is oddly blank of the concerns that normally keep me awake—the hundreds of details for the state luncheon tomorrow for Prime Minister Karamanlis of Greece. I'm in shock. How has it all come to this?

My eyes travel over the shapes and shadows in the room, taking in the eighteenth-century French bust of a child on the mantelpiece dimly illuminated by a night-light, the French etchings on the walls, the blue-and-white Sèvres vases, the cream walls that took two paint jobs to get right, the crystal chandelier, the daisy drapes, the silk canopy over our heads, the piles of art books. Perfect as a painting. Yet, now so unimportant, merely bibelots that require dusting.

What if we died right now? In each other's arms. In this perfect room.

Morning comes and the disgrace continues, Jack's failure compounded by scathing headlines and reprimands from international heads of state. He has yet to meet with

a contingent of furious Cuban exiles, the fathers of the brigadiers who were abandoned and are now Castro's prisoners. He has yet to speak to Adlai Stevenson, U.S.
ambassador to the United Nations, whom Jack, not untouched by revenge, left out
of the loop. He has yet to meet with Eisenhower, who will upbraid him like a child.
He has yet to meet with Khrushchev, who will gloat at his failure.

"How could I have been so stupid, Jackie?"

The hope for his administration—something new and vibrant—has collapsed.
The world sees Americans as self-righteous, gunslinging boobs. And it's Jack's fault.

As Jack slips into depression, my mood begins to lift.

I lie in bed, listening to Jack in the bathroom—a rustling newspaper, running
water, the *whoosh* of shaving cream, a razor tapping against the sink, the sudden
thunder of hot, steaming water, the clinking of shower curtain rings pulled back,
then pulled forward. The sounds of any husband getting ready to go to work.

He comes out of the bathroom, a towel around his waist, smelling of shaving
lotion. He winces as a bolt of pain tears up his spine. His eyes widen and glass
over. He reaches out and stumbles toward me, catching himself on the edge of the
bed and kneeling. He grabs my leg, pulls himself up on the bed, gasping. He
buries his head in my crotch, driving his forehead against my pelvic bone until it
hurts, as if he's trying to crawl back into someplace safe.

"Don't let me ever get like that, Jackie. Seeing him like that . . . drooling . . .
it's horrible."

We've just returned from an arduous weekend at Palm Beach. Joe isn't getting
any better from the stroke he had while playing golf at the Palm Beach Country
Club. He's paralyzed on the right side and can grunt only "No" and "Shit." He's furious, spitting and making incoherent shrill noises most of the time, unless I'm
there to coo and smooth his brow. For some reason, his stroke doesn't bother me,
but it terrifies Jack.

"God, it's awful." Jack's body trembles with revulsion. "I don't think I can do
it without him. He's the one who wanted the presidency to begin with."

"You have Bobby."

"Bobby's a kid." Jack groans and rolls onto his back. "I feel like the world is collapsing on top of me. Sometimes I think I can't drive myself anymore. I don't
want to end up like Dad. You've been at the White House only ten days over the
past six weeks, Jackie. You don't know how lonely it is."

I laugh. "With all your bimbos? How can you be lonely?"

"I can't make it without you, Jackie. Will you come to Paris with me? Please, Jackie. I need you."

Here it begins to happen, my despair lifting like a dirigible off the ground. He needs me. Not simply as a wife. No, he means something more. In France I can help take the pressure off his fiasco. "Yes," I say with a vigor I haven't felt in months. "I'll go with you to Paris."

MRS. PRESIDENT

ave you come to make Cinderella into a princess?"

"You have no need to become a princess, Mrs. Kennedy. The French already love you."

His unctuous voice drips like melted cheese. He smells of cigarettes and formaldehyde. He is loathsome. Yet, as I lie beneath clouds of jasmine-scented bubbles in a marble tub in the sumptuous quarters provided to us by Charles de Gaulle in the Quai d'Orsay, I extend my arm over the gold-plated rim to offer him the white belly of my arm.

Who is my fairy godmother for this magical evening? None other than the troll, Dr. Feelgood, slipping into our suite with his bag of magic potions, needles, and pills.

The squat, hulking figure peers at me through thick glasses, his eyes darting back and forth. He points to a light sconce above a mirror and presses his index finger to his lips. They are listening. He drags a gilded Louis Quinze chair across the floor, sits on its red velvet seat, and opens his bag.

"You are wearing a sleeveless gown tonight?"

"Yes, of course."

"Then perhaps you would like the shot in your thigh?"

He is right. It wouldn't do to have the First Lady show up at Versailles with track marks on her arms. I wrap a towel around my breasts and stand in the tub. Quasimodo leans over. His dirty nails tap an alarmingly large syringe. After he stabs my thigh, I sink back into the tub.

"I will be back later this evening to help you sleep, *mon trésor*." He slips out of my bathroom into the *chambre du roi* to give an injection to Jack.

Repulsed by his endearment, my spine shudders. I relax when the door closes and the troll is gone.

As I lie under the hot water, a fire springs from my groin, suffusing through my spine into the muscles in my thighs and shoulders, and out my fingertips. I am lit from within. I let the energy grow inside until I can no longer lie still. I climb out of the tub, dry off, and put on a robe.

A halo of light burns around me. My head is light; my body glows, warm and powerful. I feel capable of anything. Nothing I do can go wrong.

I sit in the *chambre de la reine* as the famous Parisian coiffeur Alexandre styles my hair. Through walls, I hear Jack yelling over the phone at Bobby. The dictator Rafael Trujillo has been assassinated in the Dominican Republic. Jack is furious, apparently afraid of being blamed for another international debacle.

His voice fades—it's not my problem. I give in to the sensuous pulling of Alexandre's comb. Deer and unicorn spring alive from the tapestries around me. Faces of obscure French aristocrats smile at me from elaborate gold frames. I feel the red damask walls around me flow with my blood. I am part of everything; everything is part of me.

I am a princess. I have no fear.

As in many fairy tales, this one starts with a dress. A costume for diplomacy and seduction.

The dress is a Givenchy evening gown of ivory silk zibeline with a bodice embroidered with silk floss and seed pearls and a white bell-shaped skirt. I wear long white gloves up to my shoulders and, in my hair, diamond hair clips that resemble a tiara.

My coach, the first limousine in an eleven-car motorcade, snakes through the vast avenues of trees and formal gardens of Versailles. Jack, still frayed from Bobby's emergency calls, looks sullenly out the window. As we pull up and step out before the dramatically lit château, forty trumpeters in full eighteenth-century regalia announce our arrival.

Charles de Gaulle greets us from the pink marble staircase that leads to the Queen's Bedroom. He is over six feet, with a stiff military bearing. Dour and stone-faced, he looks down his enormous nose, his eyes half closed and skeptical. He is not a man, one would think, accustomed to flirting.

"*Vous m'eblouissez, Madame Kennedy.* You take my breath away. Yesterday morning you were Madeline in a yellow dress and yellow straw hat. Tonight, you are queen of Versailles."

"*C'est trop gentil de votre part.*" You are too kind.

"*Pas du tout.* The French never underestimate the woman behind the throne."

"I am merely an American housewife."

De Gaulle guffaws loudly and takes my arm. "One day I hope an American housewife becomes U.S. ambassador to France."

"Anything is possible," I say.

I float through the halls of Versailles on the arm of President de Gaulle, my chin raised, smiling. I am Mme. de Pompadour, the beloved mistress of Louis XV. We stroll through the bedrooms of red damask and gilded pilasters, by tapestries of royal hunts, through the library and chapel. Trompe l'oeil murals extend the endless train of rooms to even greater expanses and vistas. My brain grows giddy.

We pause in front of a portrait of Louis XIV's mistress, the Mme. de Maintenon, a sour-looking, pudgy-faced woman, clutching a Bible in one hand and her breast in the other. Louis XIV eventually married her and made her queen.

"Some say she wielded more power than the king himself," de Gaulle says.

As we visit the chapel, the Salon d'Hercule, the Grand Appartement, and the elegant library added by Louis XVI, I feel oddly unconcerned about Jack. All this walking must be painful for him. He shuffles along behind, smiling uncomfortably at Mrs. de Gaulle, who looks like a blind pygmy shrew in black sequins. She speaks no English, Jack no French. I can tell he's trying to think of something to say to her that is worth bothering the translator for. He exclaims over and over, *"C'est magnifique!"* I get a small vindictive pleasure from letting fend for himself.

Later we dine in the Hall of Mirrors, an enormous room extending along the west facade of Versailles. The inside wall is lined with mirrors, which reflect the arched windows and the gardens beyond. A long table with 150 guests runs down the middle. I sit between General de Gaulle and Jack.

Flames dance on top of long tapered candles in elaborate vermeil candelabra. The newly restored ceiling frescoes come alive in pink, peach, and cyan. A pantheon of mythological creatures swoops down around us.

It is dark outside. The fountains sparkle. Illuminated white marble statues appear to frolic between the boxwood hedges. Reflected in the windows and in the mirrors behind me, I see myself amid gardens, fountains, gods and goddesses, candles, diamonds, flowers, and faces all glimmering in different shades of brightness. I am dazzled.

The translator who dodges back and forth behind me gives me the jitters and has bad breath. He's mangling Jack's wit, making Jack's self-effacing humor sound either insulting or feeble. I turn and pull the sleeve of his tuxedo. When he leans down, his cheek almost touching mine, I dismiss him. He steps back, alarmed and insulted. He looks to de Gaulle, then to André Malraux, the minister of state for cultural affairs.

"It is all right, isn't it, Monsieur President? Your translator deserves to enjoy such an elegant meal, and it would give me such pleasure to translate for you. I promise not to start a war."

De Gaulle is pleased. He flicks his long imperious fingers, and the translator

withdraws. Down the long table, French diplomats gasp at this breach of protocol. Several cabinet ministers exchange glances—should they intervene? De
Gaulle ignores them.

So I sit between the president of France and the president of the United States,
flirting with both, leaning first to one, then the other, my hand alighting briefly on
their forearms for emphasis. As translator, I can make Jack appear more knowl-
edgeable about French culture, and I can make de Gaulle appear kinder.

We dine on six courses, three wines and champagne, the waiters appearing and
disappearing behind painted screens like magic hands serving us.

In the flickering candlelight, Jack's eyes come alive, no longer wearing the
mask he wore when he stepped off the plane, his back in spasm, his ego flattened
by his Cuba debacle, humiliated by his own administration, dreading the whole
damn trip, because if his own staff could treat him so shabbily, why should de
Gaulle or Khrushchev treat him any better?

Now Jack smiles, not his radiant smile but the cautious smile of a rascal peeking around a door, unsure if he has been forgiven for a prank gone awry. As he sips
from a crystal goblet, he looks at me as if for the first time, his eyes bewitched,
sparkling, exploring: Who is this beguiling woman? Why is a whole country on
their feet, cheering her? What did I miss?

The fates have charmed our visit. The day before our arrival, Paris television
broadcasted an interview with me in which I spoke in French about how I love
French culture. De Gaulle made the day a holiday so people could watch as we
were escorted by the Republican Guard with their red plumed helmets on gigantic snorting black horses. When our motorcade entered Paris Porte d'Orléans, we
met with a 101-gun salute, and as we circled the place de la Concorde and over the
bridge to the Left Bank, thousands of Parisians screamed and waved flags, shouting, "Jacqu-ie! Jacqu-ie!" Above it all, fighter jets roared through the sky in formation. "Vive l'Amérique!" Jack waved to the ecstatic crowd with an astonished
General de Gaulle seated beside him. He looked at me in disbelief—he never
imagined that the French would love us and that their love would save us.

After dinner, musicians, dressed in eighteenth-century costumes, serenade us
as liveried footmen carrying candelabras light the way down long dark hallways to
a theater. We watch a ballet commissioned for Louis XV performed in candlelight.
The performance is enchanting. Even Jack, teetering in discomfort on a tiny
eighteenth-century chair, squeezes my hand in rapture.

I have a sudden insight that nearly makes me giddy. In a country whose power
has been declining for a century, de Gaulle creates an image of power with lavish
spectacle. I can do this for Jack—in the world's eyes, he looks weak, but I can

create an image of power by bringing high culture to the White House. Great governments support great artists and musicians—the White House will glow with their brilliance.

Well after midnight, we climb back into our limousines and the motorcade winds its way slowly through the Versailles gardens. An illuminated fountain sparkles like a thousand jewels. The splashing water calls to us. We ask the driver to stop, and we get out. The motorcade waits.

We walk to the fountain, a magnificent sculpture of Apollo in a horse-drawn chariot as he breaks from the ocean depths into the sky, his massive muscled arm steady on the reins, the horses laboring, heads thrown back, nostrils flared, struggling as they defy gravity. Porpoises leap, water gods trumpet, water spews.

Music wafts over the gardens. A light mists falls, catching the light. We turn and look back at Versailles.

The moment is magical. No other Americans will ever experience this. Ever.

I find myself helpless to express my euphoria. I squeeze Jack's hand and hope he senses some of what I feel.

"You are the only woman I could be standing here with, Jackie. Without you, I would never be here."

Every fairy tale has the moment when one's dreams come true. When the scullery maid dances with her prince, when the knight saves the princess from the dragon and carts her off into the night. She suffers for her prince. She endures humiliation for her prince. But always the princess wins her prince.

"No matter what happens, I love you, Jackie."

Jack has told me before that he loves me, but I have never believed it. For the first time, I do. My heart feels as if it is filling the entire garden, the entire night, and all the apartments and farmhouses in France.

I hear gravel slipping under shoes. Jack senses the chauffeur's impatience and the motorcade of mystified diplomats halted behind us. Silently, he leads me back to the limousine.

"Did we lose the Harpies?" That's my name for the troop of vicious female journalists who pursue me wherever I go, asking the most amazing questions: "What does Caroline eat for breakfast?" "Do you believe in naps?" "Where do you buy your lipstick? Where do you buy your clothes?" "How do you keep so thin?" "Do you dye your hair?"

I refuse to answer.

"But, Mrs. Kennedy, American women want to know these things. They want to model themselves after you."

The Harpies watch me through binoculars whenever I leave the White House. With wily subterfuge we manage to lose them.

For the moment we appear to go unnoticed, mingling with the tourists as we stroll over the lawn at Mount Vernon. Tish Baldrige, my tall social secretary, walks beside me, her long, heavy arms swinging back and forth like tree trunks. She looks a bit like Charles de Gaulle in drag. No matter, she is brilliant—she would've made a fabulous general. She ran the American embassies in Paris and Rome like clockwork, bossing everyone from diplomats and local politicos to maids and local wine merchants. Even though she has a tendency to think I work for her, I couldn't manage without her.

"I think, Jacqueline," she says somberly, "that an invasion of Cuba would be easier."

"For Pete's sake, don't mention Cuba in front of Jack."

"I really don't see how we can host a state dinner at Mount Vernon. There's nothing here. No heat, hardly any electricity, a couple of little toilets downstairs, a totally inadequate kitchen, inadequate parking. We'd have to truck everything in."

"Can that be done?"

"Well, yes. I suppose we could enlist the army field kitchen trucks."

"Do you think René can cook without wine? We'll be entertaining General Ayub Khan, president of Pakistan, and his daughter, who are Muslim and don't drink."

"He will, but he'll grumble. Perhaps we could have the state dinner at the White House, and the after-dinner entertainment here?" Tish suggests boisterously, trying to sell me.

"Oh, yes. Dinner *and* entertainment. Do you think we could arrange fireworks?"

She sighs heavily.

A month later a convoy of army trucks grinds up the hill from Memorial Parkway to Mount Vernon, lugging refrigerators, warming ovens, electrical generators, eight-holers, tables and chairs for 132 guests, linen, crystal, food, and twenty-two butlers. A huge canopy—dusty blue on the outside, buttercup yellow on the inside—sits on the lawn beside the mansion overlooking the Potomac. Tish and I run around with our checklists, handling last-minutes crises.

"We sprayed the lawns for mosquitoes, but the pesticide is drifting toward the kitchen tent. Shall I test the food?"

"No. I can't lose you. Get one of the Secret Service agents to try it."

"Someone's going to kill themselves on the canopy cables. Shall we cover them in ivy garlands?"

"Yes, that will look pretty. Isn't the National Symphony Orchestra supposed to be having their dress rehearsal?"

"They're playing now. Can't you see them?"

"Yes, but why can't we hear them?" We run down the hill to the natural grotto behind the mansion until we're close enough to count strings on the cellos. The violins saw away, the cheeks of the brass section are inflated, trumpets to the sky, the arms of the timpanists thrash away on their drums. Still, we hear nothing.

The orchestra conductor leaps off his podium and strides toward us. "I'm sorry, Mrs. Kennedy. It's no use. The wooded ravine sucks up all the sound."

"Oh, Jacqueline, what can we do?"

"We could have a sing-along. We would have the luxury of not hearing the Kennedy brothers."

"Seriously."

"Maybe . . . if we could get a band shell," suggests the conductor.

"We have six hours. Call the army, Tish. Have them construct something. Maybe their pounding will drive away the mosquitoes, too."

Dark storm clouds hover near the horizon. *Please don't rain.* We walk up from the loading dock to imagine what our guests will first see. What we see are trucks, crates, and toilets.

"Oh, my God. It looks like a garage sale."

"We'll get everything moved behind the hedges and trees."

We check out the ominous-looking eight-holers and spray them with our best perfume. It's no use. They stink. "What do we feed those army boys, Tish?"

"If the DDT doesn't get them, the honey wagon will."

"Oh dear. I have to get back to the White House. Don't let anything happen."

The weather holds. As the heat of the day fades, a light breeze picks up on the Potomac. Four boats—a PT boat, two presidential yachts, and a navy yacht—chug up the river from downtown Washington to the dock at Mount Vernon. All of the dinner guests disembark, many with cocktails in hand; several ladies step lively to the bands on board, Ethel and Bobby dance on the lawn. Like a scene from a Luis Buñuel film.

After we sip mint juleps—George Washington's own recipe—and wander around the mansion, the army's Old Guard Fife and Drum Corps in powdered wigs and tricornered hats performs a Revolutionary military drill, shooting their muskets over the heads of the press corps. A nice touch, I think.

As the sun sets, we dine under the canopy, eight guests per table. Yellow tablecloths with small bouquets in low vermeil cachepots. Candles dancing under hurricane lamps, sparkling on the crystal and silver.

And what we do eat? Avocado, crabmeat, and watercress salad; *poulet chasseur* (chicken with mushrooms and tomatoes); rice à la clamart with vegetables and Parmesan cheese; raspberries and cream with chocolate petits fours. Three violinists meander around the canopy playing folk tunes that sound distant and mysterious, as if drifting over the hills from a nearby village.

I glance at the table where Jack and Franklin D. Roosevelt Jr. amuse Ayub Khan's daughter. At another table Bobby appears relaxed. Beside me, Ayub Khan tells tales of the wonders of Kashmir. The feeling is light; the diners are happy.

After dinner the guests float down a path lit by citronella candles, listen to the orchestra play Debussy and Gershwin, and sip champagne. We watch the dancing fireflies and the stars above, the lights shimmering on the Potomac like a million golden minnows, and on the hill, Mount Vernon blazing white with floodlights.

As the guests depart in limousines, Jack takes my hand and we gaze at Mount Vernon.

"So, Jackie, what do you have planned for next week?"

What do you think about when the cameras roll? You try not to worry that 80 million Americans will watch this show. You try not to worry about whether your skirt makes you look bowlegged. Or whether red is the right color to wear. You try not to worry about the crew of fifty-four men in suits and ties staring at you. Or if your hair looks okay. You try not to worry about the hot lights melting your makeup. *Why do they need so many lights?*

Over the weekend the White House has been transformed into something resembling a tunnel under construction. Thick cables run down the hallways, men scurry round with electrical cords, other men with coffee-stained scripts dash in opposite directions. Parked outside are huge trucks, the CBS videotape mobile units. The crew has been filming for two days—the cutaway shots, they tell me. They are waiting for me.

I'm terrified. I know what they're thinking—*Look how clumsy she is. How stiff. How tentative. What are we going to do with that voice? A rank amateur.* I try to speak louder, but the sound gets stuck in my throat. I am paralyzed with fear. What if I can't do it? I'll make a fool of myself and the president. It'll be so bad that they won't be able to broadcast it and we'll never raise any donations for the White House restoration.

I squint beneath the blinding lights to see who's talking to me. I make out a dark blob squatting beside the camera. "Mrs. Kennedy. I want you to enter the room, make your mark, then turn to Mr. Collingwood."

He's not talking to me. He's talking to the First Lady. She is always elegant and charming. She knows not to look at the camera. She speaks with knowledge and authority. But not too smart. No one wants a lady too smart. Don't go reciting dates and historical periods.

Her foot lands on the green tape where it's supposed to. She swivels and points to the mural behind her. "This is wallpaper that was printed in France about 1834. It's all scenes of America—Indians, Niagara Falls, New York Harbor, West Point, Boston Harbor, and Natural Bridge." Her words are absorbed by the room, as if spoken into black velvet. Her face feels flushed, her ears hum. Undaunted, she smiles and continues. "These chairs are sometimes called 'Martha Washington,' but that's the name given to a style of Federal furniture rather than indicating that Mrs. Washington owned them."

The First Lady repeats the take, flawlessly, then moves to the next room, the upholstery shop, then upstairs, taping the sequence of the rooms backward, but that doesn't throw her. The State Dining Room, the Green Room, the Blue Room, the Red Room, the East Room, the Entrance Hall. Then the second floor, to the Treaty Room and the Lincoln Suite. When she points out the Lincoln Bed, nine feet of solid rosewood, erotic and voluptuous with its carvings of pendulous grapes, she doesn't think about Jack and the Blonde or the Brunette in that bed, the scrambling and giggling she's heard behind the door in the middle of the afternoon when Jack thought she was at Glen Ora. "Mrs. Lincoln bought this bed along with the dressing bureaus and the chair and this table. She made her husband rather cross because he thought she spent too much money. Theodore Roosevelt slept in it. So did Calvin Coolidge."

She smiles and doesn't think about that at all.

The mainstream press calls me glamorous, dignified, and intelligent. The Harpies call me affected, superficial, and cold. My staff calls me witty, sarcastic, and fun. I realize you can say just about anything about anyone, and it always seems to fit.

"For Christ's sake, Bobby," shouts Jack, "you stirred up enough trouble with the McClellan Committee. Give it a rest!"

I don't intend to eavesdrop, but it's impossible not to in this house. Diplomacy takes place in any room at any time of the day. But I don't walk in the other direction, either.

"You didn't mind the McClellan Committee when it got your face in the papers every day," Bobby quips. "Look, we've got the mob on the run, Jack. It's time to clean them up. I've read through Hoover's files and made up a hit list. I got Marcello kicked out of the country. I want to open up on the Chicago Mafia. I got bugs all over Sam Giancana's office."

"Jesus! When Dad wanted you to be attorney general, he didn't think you'd do something as stupid as this. You're gonna get yourself killed."

"The Ambassador was wrong on this."

"Damn, you're headstrong."

I hear silence. All of a sudden Jack grabs my hand and yanks me into the Treaty Room. "Ha! I caught a spy!"

I can tell Jack's not really mad. "I'm sorry," I say, "I just came to tell you that the children and I are going to Glen Ora now."

"How should I punish her?"

"Send her to talk to Khrushchev," Bobby suggests. Jack has been fuming the past few days over his latest crisis. Khrushchev is building a barbed-wire wall between East and West Berlin.

"Let's send her to India and Pakistan," says Jack.

"You just want to use me as a diversion," I say.

"You guessed it. A tried-and-true military tactic."

"Do I get any say in this?"

He and Bobby look at each other. Jack grins. "Nope. Why don't you stop and see the pope? I got to show those Catholics who voted for me that I haven't forgotten about them."

So that's it. The press will follow me around as I ride elephants and give Jack some breathing room to figure out what to do about Khrushchev.

"I haven't a thing to wear," I say.

"Well then, you'd better get busy."

J.K.

I walk down the halls of the Vatican wearing a full-length dress in black silk-and-wool Alaskine, as sleek and shiny as a missile. I wear a black mantilla over my head. My escorts, portly cardinals in black and red, line the hall. Frightened, I grin nervously.

I meet Pope John XXIII in his library. He dismisses the interpreters. Alone, we speak in French.

I give him a copy of Jack's collected speeches and a velvet-lined vermeil box. He puts these aside without interest.

Later, reporters would marvel at how long my private audience was with the pope. They speculated on what we talked about. Outside, the cardinals were beginning to worry. Little did they know that it was the pope's kindness that extended our session. He didn't want me to have to reappear with a tear-streaked face.

"Don't speak to me as the wife of a president," he says. "Speak to me as my child. Tell me, how are you?"

His compassionate concern undoes me. After the stress of anticipation—my sleepless night, my terror at saying or doing the wrong thing—I meet this gentle old man, who asks about me like a loving uncle. I completely lose my composure. I begin to weep, as if he were the first person in the world ever to ask.

I tell him I'm afraid of the poverty I'm going to see in India.

I tell him I'm afraid I can't handle this image I've become.

I tell him I'm afraid of Jack's infidelity, what it will do to us, to the country.

I tell him I'm afraid Jack will die.

I tell him it's too much. I'm afraid I can't go on.

"God doesn't plant a rose tuber and expect an ear of corn. Nothing you expect of yourself cannot be done. If a fat bald man can represent God's church, you, my child, can represent a woman's love for her husband, her children, and her country."

I feel chastened yet comforted. Strong enough to go on.

Dressed in saffron Cassini day dresses in shimmering zibeline, white gloves, and pearls, Lee and I float on a barge down the Ganges. Marigolds and pink parasols decorate the barge. Thousands wade into the water and wave. Others kneel on the shore and bow their heads. They chant, "Jac-kie, Jac-kie, Raja Americana," blowing deafening blasts on conch shells and banging triangles.

It's thrilling and embarrassing. What could I possibly mean to these people, a lady in pink strolling through the silk market, the lady in yellow perched on top of an elephant?

I am on a goodwill tour to India and Pakistan, smiling, laughing, making small talk, asking questions about their art and culture. But it's so much more than that. It's almost as if the U.S. president and the American people have made a gift of me to them. I embrace the role, because it is my job; but, honestly, what good can I do?

My hosts carefully steer me away from the naked, emaciated children who line the streets, from the man whose face is riddled with leprosy, his skin rotting, with maggots crawling out of his eyes. But they cannot hide it. Smoke from a million cow-dung fires hangs over the city. The stench of feces fills the air. When I breathe in, the smell of urine burns my throat. There are so many skinny, barefoot people. It's hard to believe the world has so many people.

Lee and I climb onto a magnificent elephant. His ears and trunk are painted with white tracery that is colored in with blue and yellow. A gold and red tapestry hangs over his forehead between his eyes like an altar cloth. His body is covered in a red blanket, and golden medallions hang around his neck. We rock back and forth in a golden seat that sits on top like a teacup. Straddling the elephant's neck, the driver in a red coat and a red tasseled hat urges the beast on. The rocking motion feels like a small boat—we float over the crowds.

Leprous beggars beat their stumps in the air. "Jackie, Raja Americana!" A sacred cow lies dying in the street. "Jackie, Raja Americana!" A teenage girl lifts her withered baby. "Jackie, Raja Americana!" Pilgrims, standing naked on one leg for hours, bare their decaying teeth. "Jackie, Raja Americana."

Death is everywhere. Everywhere people are sick from cholera and malnutrition—diseases easy to cure.

Yet there is so much life amid the death. After we travel through a maze of dust and poverty, we see a market that springs alive like a flowering cactus in a desert—sandals, sitars, and gorgeous silks, peacocks, incense, and exotic fruits. A woman in an iridescent pink and orange sari glides beneath a crumbling tenement. Children splash in muddy green pools in front of great crumbling Victorian Gothic mansions. Six men jog up and down over the crowded sidewalks carrying a charpoy, a funeral bed with the corpse of a holy man covered in flowers, his sunken face bouncing and rocking side to side as the men run. A street performer balances a monkey on the top of a pole, amusing hungry children who suck the edges of their shirts. Beggars and cripples drop to the ground and reach out to touch our feet.

Everywhere hang giant posters of Indian movie stars, the red *bindis* on their foreheads like flaming suns sinking behind a dung-fire haze. Below the billboards, naked children use sticks to pick through piles of garbage.

Lee is shocked, but I am amazed. These are the people of the world—a sea of beautiful, fascinating faces.

What am I, rich woman from the West, expected to do? If I gave all my money to them—and all my husband's money—it would do them little good. Instead, they give me gifts.

In a hospital I hold a small girl on my lap. Skinny, with a bloated belly, her eyes wide and black, she fingers my pearls and laughs. On her thumb she wears a plastic ring with red glass. She takes it off and puts it on my finger.

An elderly woman on the street runs up to me, her back hunched from years of malnutrition. She gives me a beautiful fuchsia sari. She says she was married in it.

Children wearing nothing but dirty T-shirts run up to me and hand me candies of rice and honey.

These gifts overwhelm me. How is it they love me? What can I give them in return? My terrified joy?

I look at Lee. She sits pensively behind me, on the barge, on the elephant, on the camel. She sucks in her cheeks and flares her nostrils. There are tears in her eyes. I, too, feel every discomfort, the heat, the bugs, the stench. I, too, feel her horror, but I want to shake her by the shoulders and say, *Feel it, Lee, this is life. This is love.*

For the first time in my life, I understand that I am part of humanity—this shakes me to the core.

The sun sets, turning the sky tangerine, then fuchsia, then red. The café au lait water deepens to plum. These are the colors of the clothing and art of India, tying everything into their ideas of eternity. And who am I to them, standing on this barge in my orange dress, amid the marigolds, beneath the pink awnings? Hope for the future, queen of America, a reincarnation of an ancient priestess? I wave back. My performance is not painless. They crack open my chest and yank out my heart.

Along the edges, holy men, gaunt with long beards and deep wells for eyes, sit folded in the lotus position. A jumble of white stone ashrams crowd along the east bank, their turrets like red artichokes. Pilgrims bathe in the muddy water.

To my Western eyes, the Ganges is a stinky open sewer, yet my host recites a hundred names for the river—Giver of Delight to the Eye, Eternally Pure, Destroyer of the Poison of Illusion, Water Mine of Nectar, Destroyer of Sorrow, Bestower of Happiness, Emancipator, Light amid the Darkness of Ignorance. I tell my host that I have another name for the river—Revelation. This pleases him, and tomorrow I read myself quoted in the New Delhi English-language newspaper.

In my own country, reporters will criticize me for prancing around the world in my haute couture. Yet the people of India understand. When they see my paisley sleeveless dress based on an Indian design, or what John Kenneth Galbraith calls my radioactive pink *rajah* coat, or the saffron satin dress the same color as their monks' robes, the people of India know I honor them.

WHITE HOUSE GUEST LIST

*J*ackie's White House guest list:

Luncheon for Princess Grace and Prince Rainier; dinner on the lawn of Mount Vernon for 150 to honor the president of Pakistan, General Ayub Khan, and his daughter; concert dinner with Pablo Casals for Governor and Señora Muñoz Marín of Puerto Rico; musical program for youth concert with the Metropolitan Opera Studio performing Mozart's *Così fan Tutte*; state dinner and performance of Jerome Robbins's ballet for the Shah of Iran and Farah Diba; dinner and dance for 175 people to honor Nobel laureates Pearl Buck, Lester B. Pearson, Ernest Hemingway, and scientist Dr. Linus C. Pauling; dinner honoring France's minister of state for cultural affairs, André Malraux, including leading artists Thornton Wilder, Arthur Miller, Tennessee Williams, Paddy Chayefsky, Saul Bellow, Lee Strasberg, Archibald MacLeish, Robert Lowell Jr., Elia Kazan, Andrew Wyeth, Julie Harris, George Balanchine, and Charles Lindbergh, among others, all entertained by Isaac Stern (violin), Eugene Istomin (piano), Leonard Rose (cello) in the East Room; Washington Opera Society's performance of *The Magic Flute* for President Radhakrishnan of India; recital by mezzo-soprano Grace Bumbry; recital by pianist Eugene List; *Brigadoon* for the king of Morocco; *Hamlet* enacted by members of the American Shakespeare Festival.

Among others. A cast of thousands.

Jack's White House guest list:

Judith Campbell, Mafia moll of San Giancana; Mary Meyer; movie stars Marlene Dietrich, Jayne Mansfield, Angie Dickinson, Gene Tierney, Arlene Dahl; the Princess Elizabeth of Yugoslavia; Odile Rodin, wife of Porfirio Rubirosa; Hjordis Niven, wife of actor David Niven; several female members of the White House press corps; ex-girlfriend Flo Smith; suspected spy Ellen Rometsch; and many, many other women, professional and not, ushered through security by Jack's Irish pimps, their names never recorded, never remembered by Jack or anyone else. As well as the in-house crowd of secretaries and aides, including my own press secretary. Did I forget my sister, Lee Radziwill? Yes, that's the rumor, so I hear.

And Marilyn Monroe.

Among others. A cast of thousands.

MARILYN

She calls me when Jack isn't home. At first I don't recognize her voice, thinking a crank has somehow gotten ahold of our telephone number and is mimicking me, her voice like willows in the wind: "Is Jack there?"

I ask who is calling.

"This is Marilyn."

I pause to think. Oh, *that* Marilyn. Of course Jack would want her. I know what they say about her, that she is a manic depressive addicted to prescription drugs, insecure, mentally ill. Pity washes over me—briefly—followed by a pleasurable twinge of malevolence. I decide to have some fun. "This is Jackie," I say sweetly.

"Oh." She sounds like Caroline when Jack gives her a complicated explanation for a simple question, resting her thumbnail on her lower lip, listening hard, then uttering, "Oh," before skipping off into the next room.

"May I help you with something?" I ask.

She hesitates, then whispers, "Well, I guess I should talk to you."

"What about, Marilyn?" I rasp back, the two of us whispering like stage mothers during their children's performance.

She speaks slowly, slurring her words. "I guess Jack hasn't told you, but he's going to ask for a divorce. He loves me, and we're going to get married."

My lip trembles with fury and laughter. Yet my heart aches for her, poor creature, drugged and deluded, even more lost than I was when I agreed to marry Jack. But I'm not so awash in empathy that I don't want to torment her a bit.

"Well, in that case, Marilyn, you should drop by the White House so I can help you with all your future duties—running the White House staff and completing the restoration. Next week you'll need to organize the state dinner for the Shah of Iran, host a diplomatic reception on May second, christen the nuclear submarine *Lafayette* in Groton, Connecticut, then plan a White House event for André Malraux. Of course, André will be most offended if you haven't read his books. It's important to Jack that you speak to foreign dignitaries in their native tongue, so you'll have to learn French and Spanish. Then there's taking care of Jack and his back, knowing what he needs when the pain is too much, helping him with his injections."

"Oh," she says.

"I have to warn you, fidelity is not Jack's strongest character attribute, but, unlike me, you probably are woman enough for him."

"I'm not a lollipop," she says, her voice suddenly querulous.

"A lollipop?" For a moment I'm horrified. No doubt, that's what Jack calls the women he sleeps with.

"He says he loves me," she says, her voice more slurred. I hear her snuffling back tears.

"I'm sure he does. Tell me, Marilyn, how *do* you manage to satisfy him?"

She giggles through her sniffles. "You know what he says. He isn't done with a woman until he's had her three different ways."

I try not to sound shocked. "Really? Tell me more. How do you do it with him?"

She giggles again. "Oh, he likes it in a bathtub full of water. I get on top of him. Sometimes he gets someone to take photos of us."

"It was nice chatting with you, Marilyn. I'll be sure to tell Jack you called." I slam down the receiver.

That evening I root through a pile of magazines. I find what I'm looking for, last month's *Vogue,* in it a photo of Marilyn dressed like me in a short brunette wig. She wears black palazzo pants and a white silk blouse slipped off one shoulder. She kneels with her knees apart, her hands hovering over her breasts, her fingers fondling the heap of pearls around her neck as if negotiating her price. She has a dreamy drug-induced expression.

The parody cuts me to the quick. I assume the photographer is drawing a parallel between us, the actress/whore and the First Lady, both of us trying desperately to please, both dressed in costume, both selling ourselves for pearls.

A wild idea comes to me.

That evening, as Jack sits in bed with a heating pad, naked except for white boxer shorts, reading a briefing paper on Mexico for our three-day trip next month, I enter his bedroom and posture by the doorjamb. He doesn't look up.

"Jackie, what do you think of President Adolfo López Mateos? Do you think he'd be open to free trade?"

I don't answer.

Impatient, he looks up at me and freezes. "Oh, for Christ's sake, Jackie! What in hell's name——?"

I'm wearing a blond wig, false eyelashes, a beauty spot, a bra stuffed with tissue, and bright red lipstick. I wear a pink peignoir with a white boa.

"Jesus, Jackie. Would you take that shit off?" He throws his papers across the bed in disgust.

I saunter across the room and sit on the bed. "Tell me, Jack, what does she do that I don't?" I run my hand down his foot and up his bare leg.

"Jackie! Stop it! You're acting crazy."

"She tells me you're not done with a woman until you have her three ways. What ways, Jack?"

"You talked to her?" His voice aghast.

"She called me. She thinks you're going to get a divorce and marry her."

"Oh, for Christ's sake, Jackie! I don't have time for this."

"Do with me what you do with her." I straddle his feet and move my hands up his thighs.

"Jackie! Cut it out!" He jerks away, then yelps, grimacing in pain. He holds his breath, then gasps for air.

I'm out of sympathy. I dive in, relentless. "Why do you need them, Jack?"

"Damn you, Jackie. I don't want to talk about it."

Furious, Jack yanks off my wig and pulls off my robe. I'm naked except for the stuffed bra. I feel ridiculous. "Isn't it enough that you humiliate me in public? Do you have to humiliate me in private, too?"

We both know what I'm talking about—the Blonde singing a sultry "Happy Birthday" to him at Madison Square Garden, stitched into a sequin gown, her aching, desperate, heaving movements, her sexual longing for the president apparent to everyone. Like a glistening clitoris, ripe and tremulous, she sang, her lips red, her hair white, her breasts and hips as rounded as a fertility fetish, her voice quivering, struggling to remember the words, running her hands over her hips, teetering at the edge. And Jack in the balcony watching, his jaw slack with lust.

Exasperated, Jack sighs heavily. He gently pulls me onto his bed, curling my hair behind my ears. "Jackie, I'm sorry. Christ, Jackie. Why do I have to explain it to you?"

Furious, I pull away. "Why did you let her do that? In front of twenty thousand people? It's political suicide. They're going to come after you, Jack. You know they're ready."

He nods and presses his palm over his mouth. He sighs, then drops his hand. "I don't plan on seeing her again." He goes back to reading his briefing papers.

"Don't you ever think about what you're doing to these women?"

Jack gives me a bewildered look. "What do you mean?"

"Screwing them, then kicking them in the teeth."

"I've never asked a woman to do something she doesn't want to do. I don't want to discuss this anymore, Jackie."

I feel ashamed, for Jack, for myself. I've won the battle, but not the war. Why can't I accept his philandering as some kind of cortisone-induced stress relief? I think of what they say about the Blonde, how she's slept with hundreds of men, not for money but out of a pitiful desperation for love. Is that it for Jack? No. Is it power? Sadism? I want to pound his chest, to demand to understand. What drives him? Why take such risks? Why does he hurt his family? Why can't he love me?

How does he have the time?

He loves me, he'll say. The other women don't have anything to do with us. The reporters are his friends, he'll say. It'll never get in the papers.

"It only takes one lady to talk, Jack, and your political future is over."

"It's not over till it's over."

Defeated, I retreat to my room.

"For Christ's sake, Bobby! I asked you to take care of it, and you end up fucking her? Dammit! What a fucking nightmare."

I pause in the hallway, eavesdropping on Jack and Bobby.

"Next time, you dump your own women, Jack. You should've seen her face—like a kicked puppy."

"She's been calling Jackie, for Christ's sake!"

"Whose fault is that? She got the number from you! Look, Jack, she's threatening to talk to the press. She's totally out of control. We've got to handle her carefully."

"Get Lawford to talk to her. And for God's sake, don't offer her money. That would send her over the edge. Have you talked to her shrink, Greenson?"

"You want me to get him to commit her, or something?"

"Do whatever you need to do. Jackie's all over me on this. Take care of it. And keep your fucking dick in your pants."

"You want me to—"

"Dammit! I don't care what you do, Bobby. Just fucking take care of it!"

I hear Jack throw something across the room. Bobby leaves through the Treaty Room. In a moment, he'll see me when he crosses the room to the hallway. My first instinct is to flee. Instead, I pull myself up and walk calmly into the Yellow Oval Room.

Jack looks up, wondering how much I've heard. He guesses I've heard enough. He kicks the chair and swears to himself.

He straightens, then looks pensively out the window. Most of the cherry blossoms have fallen from the trees, and the young leaves are tinged with maroon. He turns his head and, as if nothing has transpired, says to me, "Jackie, do you think we could have René whip up some clam chowder for lunch?"

After an informal dinner with Lee, Stas, the Bradlees, Franklin D. Roosevelt Jr., and his wife, Suzanne, in the upstairs dining room, we call the children to join us to watch a movie in the East Wing.

Still angry at Jack, I choose *Some Like It Hot*.

He gives me dagger eyes. "You know I only like Westerns. How about *The Man Who Shot Liberty Valance*? We haven't seen that yet."

He refers to this year's blockbuster from Paramount. "John Wayne is so dreary. Besides, I thought you might like a change. The critics are raving about this movie. I thought you should keep up with popular culture."

Lee shoots me a warning, afraid that I plan to make a scene.

Jack shrugs as if one movie is as good as another. He slouches in his seat, his knees jiggling impatiently, shifting positions every two minutes, pulling his knee up to his chest, then crossing his legs, switching weight from one hip to the other. He taps his teeth with the nail on his index finger, then rakes his hand through his hair. The movie doesn't engage him enough to stop the pain. He gets up and leaves after twenty minutes, comes back, then leaves again.

I wanted to humiliate Jack, but I'm the one who's embarrassed. The Blonde jiggles and wiggles and giggles. Her big hair and boobs, her red lips like candy, her aspic ass nearly popping out of her backless gown. There's something ripped-open and raw about her. She is too vivid to look at without discomfort, like examining an incision, the blood and muscles throbbing beneath, your eyes incapable of looking away, both fascinated and horrified.

Whereas you might catch a glimpse of your lover's soul glinting across his eyes at sunset, Marilyn wears her soul on her face in broad daylight. You sense how difficult it is for her. Her body trembles with the effort. She teases mortality like a moth over a flame.

She makes me feel prudish, safe, and cowardly. My instinct for self-preservation is too strong to expose myself like that. My soul is my own.

The children watch, enraptured, Caroline's big blue eyes taking it all in, and later, when I ask how she liked the film, she says, "She's so pretty, like you, Mommy, only different." John is quiet, not like he is after a Western or cartoons, when he runs around squealing and giggling so hard that I worry. He crawls into my lap and wants to be held, as if his two-year old heart has been touched by something magic.

When Lee asks me what I'm going to do about the "Marilyn situation," I say, "Life is too short for Marilyn Monroe." I mean that my life is too short to worry about Marilyn, but a few weeks later I discover with alarm that my comment was unknowingly prescient.

We both needed an escape. I chose Ravello, Italy. Her escape is permanent.

In New York, before my flight, I return to the Carlyle after a shopping trip with presents for Lee and our Italian host. I set the bags on the second double bed and turn on the television while I change. I switch to the news to see if there's a story on Jack.

There is only one news story today. Every newscaster calls it a tragedy, as if this were the only word they knew for death. I would say it's a waste or a pity.

This morning they found her, the Blonde, dead from an overdose of sleeping pills, Nembutal and chloral hydrate.

At first I'm overcome with terrible guilt. I forced Jack's hand to stop seeing her. "I'm not going down with you, Jack. If scandals come out and you lose the election, you can count on my filing for divorce." Did his rejection push her over the edge? Maybe I should've met her, talked to her. Instead, I arranged for a trip to Ravello. I imagine her desperate, breathless phone calls, receivers slammed down in her ear, followed by cruel dissembling from Peter Lawford and Bobby, washing their hands of her as if she were a toothless hag. And from Jack, not a word of explanation.

Her only sin was wanting to be loved.

The Kennedys hate weakness of all kinds, particularly tender weaknesses like needing to be loved.

My heart breaks for her as it breaks for Teddy's wife, Joan, women too innocent, too good for Kennedy abuse. Women like Ethel and me can survive them, but not the Marilyns of this world.

Yet was she so unlike me? I wonder. She got herself into a situation that she couldn't get out of. Beneath the carefully constructed image was the woman ignored, pitied, unloved. Pushed and exploited by men, dying penniless and alone.

They find her sprawled naked in bed, her hand on the telephone receiver. I imagine her watching the phone as her eyes fluttered shut, waiting for her prince to call, then giving up, begging the pills to work their magic.

There is no magic—only Death.

There is no prince—only the Prince of Darkness.

Furious, I call Jack in Washington. Evelyn tells me he's on another line. I imagine him hunched over his desk in crisis mode, cursing and yelling. I imagine him saying the words *audiotape* and *FBI,* ordering someone over to her house to make sure there's nothing there to incriminate him.

Finally I get him on the phone. He acts as if he doesn't already know. "Marilyn's dead? Imagine that."

"That poor girl. How could you be so heartless?" I hang up before he can answer.

Furious, I finish packing my bags for my trip to Ravello. Caroline and I will go for two weeks, maybe more. If a scandal breaks out, I do not want to be in the country. Let him fend off the jackals himself.

I see clearly how an image without money behind it self-destructs. Men say they admire beauty, but in the end they have no respect for it. They respect power and money. Everything else is dispensable.

As I pack, I promise that I will never let myself be driven to suicide. I have my children to take care of.

Briefly, the thought alights on my brain—what if it wasn't suicide? "I don't care what you do, Bobby. Just fucking take care of it!" The way Jack yelled at Bobby like a double-crossed mobster. Mobsters take care of things in the simplest way possible. If Marilyn wasn't a woman you could buy off, if she wasn't a woman you could reason with, how else would you take care of her?

My skin tingles with cold—I sink into a chair. Outside, Manhattan is moist and gray.

No. The idea is too horrible to entertain. Could Bobby do such a thing? To protect Jack's reputation? To protect the family? To protect his own future presidency?

I try to purge the thought. Swimsuits, sunglasses, presents, sandals. What else is on my list? I flick off my tears with the back of my hand. Suntan oil, cocktail dress, costume jewelry.

I don't want to know.

THE PISSING CONTEST

Friday morning, October 19, 1962. I dash barefoot out of the South Portico without a coat or makeup, not caring if the Harpies see me. Jack turns and hobbles down the helicopter steps. When he spreads his arms and hugs me, it's like a roaring fire in a cozy winter cabin. I forgive him everything.

At this moment Strategic Air Command is deploying bomber fleets to civilian airfields across the country. On bases in Spain, Morocco, and England, bombers are being loaded with nuclear weapons, each with assigned targets in the Soviet Union. Polaris missile submarines are leaving their bases in Scotland to patrol the North Atlantic.

It's a kaleidoscope of events—a twist of the lens and reality changes all over the world. If we go to sleep, tomorrow everything may be different, the kaleidoscope shifted.

"I didn't want to worry you, darling," he whispered to me three days after he found out. Now worry is all there is.

Three days ago was a Tuesday morning like any other morning. Jack left his bedroom window open all night to catch the October smells—the bark of fruit trees, wet earth, burning leaves, and, wafting up from the Rose Garden, the lingering perfume of the late-blooming Lady Hillingdon rose. He found a red maple leaf on the floor by his bed. He laid it on his breakfast tray.

As Jack ate his toast and eggs and read *The Washington Post* and *The New York Times,* McGeorge Bundy knocked on his door. He walked in and spread a dozen black-and-white photos on Jack's unmade bed. "What's this?" Jack asked. Bundy stood silently, waiting for him to take a look.

Jack pulled his robe together and walked to his bed. The photos were grainy, but he could make out roads, palm trees, one-story buildings, and what appeared to be jungle huts, but which he knew were silos. "Cuba?" he guessed.

"Our U-2 spy planes spotted eight launchers for medium-range ballistic missiles in Cuba. They're nearly operational."

Jack didn't want us to alter our schedules. He will go to Chicago and Cleveland over the weekend. I will go to Glen Ora with the children. As if nothing has changed.

The helicopter rotor whirls over us, trying to blow us apart. Jack kisses me hard on the lips, and we cling to each other. He feels clean, his shirt collar freshly ironed and smelling of starch, the texture of his suit, finely spun Italian wool, almost as soft as silk. His shoulders feel broad and strong.

"If I were ever to lose you and the kids, I couldn't live." He says this not in the charming Jack voice, or the persuasive Jack voice, or joking Jack voice, but the raw, raspy voice he uses only when he is desperate. I want to say I'm sorry for every mean thing I've ever said to him, every nasty little trick, every wildly extravagant purchase, every sarcastic comment. For all the bitterness. But I cannot speak.

Behind us, the helicopter whines, its engine hot, smelling of fuel. "I've got to go," he says, and pulls away. I step back and glance around. Eight Blue Suits watch us intently; the White House staff press their noses against the windows. The nanny holds her palm over her heart.

Sunday, October 21. We nap together in my bedroom. Jack lies quietly on his back in boxer shorts, unable to sleep. Lying beside him, I feel the tension in his muscles, and he smells musty the way he does when he's nervous.

Late Friday evening, Bobby telephoned Jack in Chicago. Twenty Soviet ships are moving from Soviet ports toward Cuba, seven big enough to carry intermediate-range ballistic missiles. Jack dashed back to Washington.

The next morning Jack called me and the children back from Glen Ora. He wants us together.

In bed, at dinner, or playing with the children, we suffer the endless, drawn-out waiting, every minute an hour, every hour a lifetime. Time is not going forward but sideways—underwater time, space time, dream time.

"I feel used up, Jackie." Jack rolls onto his stomach, offering me his back.

I run my fingers lightly over his spine—he says it takes away the pain.

"McNamara wants a seven-day aerial offensive, followed by an invasion. The CIA wants war. The Joint Chiefs want war. Hell, my whole fucking cabinet wants war."

I have never seen war. Jack has. I can't imagine it. "I don't understand why the Soviets would want to set up missiles in Cuba in the first place."

"Khrushchev sees it as a way to even out the balance of power. We have around five thousand nuclear warheads. The Soviets have around three hundred strategic weapons, total. All of their weapons are primitive and unreliable. If they launched one of those babies from the Soviet Union, its chances of hitting us would be like you pitching a softball over home plate. But with intermediate-range ballistic missiles in Cuba, they would cover ninety percent of the continental United States."

I could've done without his reference to my athletic prowess, but I get the point. "Khrushchev knows you won't tolerate missiles in Cuba. Why does he try?"

"I guess after the Bay of Pigs, he figures we're not as tough as we look."

"Does he think we might invade Cuba?"

Jack turns over and sits up abruptly, cinching his back, his face flushed. "How did you know that?" he demands.

I look at him, surprised. "Know what?" I hadn't meant to guess state secrets, but I have talked to Khrushchev and know he is not irrational. He is more concerned about keeping things together at home than threatening the United States. He would make such a move only under extreme pressure—like a threat to Cuba.

I then realize this crisis, like the others, is Jack's doing.

Jack continues to stare at me furiously, wanting an answer—*How do you know that?* My own fury is frozen with shock, my lips numb. I want to scream at him that his stupid pride has gotten us into this mess: "So you were humiliated by the Bay of Pigs fiasco. What good could it possibly do us to invade Cuba?" I want to tell him of the children I saw skipping down the streets of New Delhi, and how the children in Cuba must be like that, full of joy even in a world of fear and poverty. I want to tell him of the desert islands of Greece, once dense with forest, burned in war to naked rock—that will be Cuba, that will be Hyannis Port. But it's too late for arguing, even if I could find the words.

I can tell by the way he straightens his arms and lifts his hips that he is in terrible pain. I go to his bureau, open the top drawer, and take out a box the size and shape of a revolver case. Inside lie a dozen hypodermic needles filled with Dr. Feelgood's special formula. Silently, Jack rolls back over and yanks down his boxer shorts. I tap the needle and, not without some pleasure, stab his butt. "Our little bunny has gotten himself into big trouble, hasn't he?"

My flippancy falls flat—I immediately regret it. I don't want to hurt Jack—not now. It's all too frightening.

Jack's anger dissipates. He reaches out for me and pulls me down beside him. He sweeps the hair from my face and kisses my brow. He holds his lips there for several moments, then drops his head to the pillow, as if the kiss took all his strength. He speaks softly into my ear.

"Our U-2 spy planes will know the second they launch a missile at the United States. McNamara will get word first. He'll tell the Secret Service. You will have twenty minutes to get to the air-raid shelter in Virginia. Grab the children and

Ethel if she's here and go immediately by helicopter. Bobby and I will follow in a separate chopper." He opens the drawer of his nightstand and hands me the pink slips I need for entry to the Defense Department's emergency shelter.

They look like opera tickets and I almost laugh. "Did you get us box seats?" Then it hits me—box seats to the annihilation of the East Coast. I count the tickets. "What about Joan and Ted? And Lee and Stas?"

"The bunker is only big enough for cabinet members and their immediate families."

"You could lose half your family."

"I know." He holds me tight. "You are all I need."

His sudden tenderness washes over me, and I want to ask why the two of us wait for crises to bring us together. I wonder how he can so easily separate his needs from the needs of his family, how easily he accepts that some will live, others will die. But the moment is too dear to waste. I hold him gently.

Tomorrow we may be dead.

Monday, October 22. Life doesn't stop. We cancel a dinner dance for the Maharajah and Maharani of Jaipur and hold a private dinner for them upstairs in the dining room—as if they were neighbors stopping over for a bite to eat. They are obviously disappointed.

I have my picture taken with them in front of the South Portico. My hair is messy. I wear my pink Channel suit, which I probably wear too often, but I can't think of anything else to put on. The Maharani in her stunning white silk sari looks strangely at me as if she doesn't believe I am the same woman who flew through India on a magic carpet. The Maharajah wears the sour expression of a man who's gone to a lot of expense and bother for nothing. Doubtless, they have heard of the Mount Vernon dinner we threw for General Ayub Khan, and I don't blame them for feeling slighted, particularly after the extravagant dinner the Maharajah held for Lee and me in the Amber Palace.

I feel incredibly embarrassed—an American bumpkin with no manners. Everyone is running around acting oddly, so I beg Jack to level with him. The Maharajah turns pale and immediately makes plans to leave Washington.

Tuesday, October 23. The day after Jack announced to the nation on television that a fleet of Soviet missile-bearing ships is facing down an American blockade of Cuba, the White House feels deserted. The ground floor is open for tourists, but the rooms are empty of the familiar shuffle of footsteps and the echo of the tour guide's voice. The stress of sitting around upstairs is too much for me.

Blue Suit and I take a walk.

The streets of Washington are empty. No Harpies dog us. No photographers blind us with their flashes. No tourists stand in huddles, gathering courage to ask for an autograph. No crazies eye the Secret Service, waiting for their chance to rush the First Lady. This is the first time since before the election that I can walk unnoticed, unencumbered down the streets. Free and anonymous.

Perhaps I should send Khrushchev a thank-you note.

The air is damp and cool, the thinly overcast sky magenta-gray, the color of faded tulips. Over the past few days, the foliage has faded to gold and reddish brown. Piles of leaves collect at the curbs. The Mall is our private park, the lawns green from recent rains, the cherry trees bare, their black branches ramulose and twisted. In the distance, the granite monuments glisten with frost.

Contrary to protocol, Blue Suit walks beside me. Perhaps, like me, he needs the personal contact.

There is an odd sense of dread and apprehension in the air. We both feel it. I try to imagine how the city would look after a nuclear bomb—collapsed buildings burning for days, crumbled rooftops covered in gray ash, trees stripped and lifeless, the sky white with poisonous smoke, the streets crackled and melted, huge slabs upended, the White House and government buildings smoking rubble.

"We'll never be the same again, will we?" I say.

"The same?" he asks.

"We'll never feel safe in the same way. We'll never be able to pretend the rest of the world doesn't matter."

Blue Suit doesn't answer. He bows his head for a moment before taking my elbow and leading me on.

Thursday, October 25. "This may be it," Jack tells me.

Khrushchev has sent him a cable saying that since the blockade is illegal, he plans to send his ships right on through the quarantine line. The U-2 spy planes show that work on the IRBM sites in Cuba has accelerated around the clock. Medium-range missiles will be operational within a few days.

John's fever is 104. I can't even tell Jack. He has enough to worry about. I'm concerned if we have to move John to the air-raid shelter.

I sit by his crib and watch his little chest rise up and down, his disturbed, rapid breathing, his face flushed, his lips dry and parted, the gap between his front teeth whistling softly.

"Children get these high fevers, Mrs. Kennedy," says Maud Shaw. "John will be fine."

I know, but he's my baby. His favorite doll is a nun. I tuck her under the covers beside him, her black wimple cascading over his chest. "He looks like such an angel when he's asleep," I say.

"Make the most of it. By Sunday, he'll be a holy terror again."

Will he? I know Miss Shaw is trying to make me laugh, but nothing tears your heart out like a sick child. Will he see Sunday? What if they launch a bomb tomorrow, and I never see his impish grin again, his hands clapping and missing, racing his toy car around his cereal bowl, his scamper, his waddle, his march, all to entertain his dad, his lilting soprano singing, "Daddy's a foo-foo head"?

I massage Vicks VapoRub into the soles of his feet. His heels are as soft as a newborn's tummy.

He groans slightly, not a groan of pain but a groan to let his mommy know he deserves sympathy. I kiss his temple. The fever has fallen a bit, I think. "Mommy," he says, half asleep. If he were well, he would demand a story or a song or a toy, but now all he wants is to know I'm there—"I love you. Try to sleep. I'll be here. I love you"—and he wraps his hand around my finger and groans again in case I missed the first one.

"You'll make yourself crazy watching him, Mrs. Kennedy. I'll take care of him."

She's right, of course. There's nothing I can do, but when I sit here beside him, I touch him with my heart. I would not be a mother if I didn't believe it helped.

Miss Shaw stands at my shoulder, not daring to tap it, to ask me to leave, to tell me my anxiety, my emotional indulgence, will encourage the boy to sickness. I understand. I leave her to put compresses on his head, and go downstairs.

I never knew I could love like this.

The heartache is worth the pain.

"Halloween is next week, Mommy. We need jack-o'-lanterns."

Caroline wants to carve pumpkins. This is an issue of utmost importance. Nothing else matters—not Daddy's pensive meetings behind closed doors, not Mommy's dancing around the edges, trying to keep up Daddy's spirits with a note, a limerick, or a visit from the White House school. Caroline is right, of course. What is more important than carving pumpkins—creating a leering grimace to scare away our fears, to scare away Castro and Khrushchev—as good as a defense as any against nuclear war—to scare the restless evil spirits back into their graves? We'll set them on the Truman Balcony above the South Portico, their faces seeming to change as the candles flicker inside. The solitary walker standing on the Washington Mall, looking up toward the White House, will see their ghastly ghostly grins.

"Without a face, it's a pumpkin. With a face, it's a jack-o'-lantern," Caroline explains to me.

"Jack-o'-lantern? Like Daddy?" I tease.

"Yes, like Daddy." She squeals with laughter. "I'm going to carve Daddy's face like when he thinks I'm eating candy."

"Don't you want to carve a Caroline-o'-lantern?"

"Nooooo," she says. "I'm too pretty."

René has cleaned out the seeds from several huge pumpkins now ready for carving. The biggest sits eighteen inches high. When Caroline hugs it, her fingers barely meet. She draws a face with a black marker pen. Two triangles for eyes, squiggles for eyebrows, a triangle for a nose, an eel for a mouth.

"Be careful, honey. The knife is sharp."

"I am careful, Mommy."

She's almost five. I watch, trying not to grab the knife out of her hand, reminding myself, as I do ten times a day, you can go only so far to protect your children.

With little grunts of effort, her tongue peeking between her lips in concentration, she saws through the smooth orange skin to the slippery yellow pulp within. She then leans into the pumpkin, her entire arm disappearing into the squash, her chin pressed against the top for leverage, and pops out a triangle for an eye. She squeals in victory, then sets aside the knife to go hunt down someone to help her.

Jack charges out of the presidential bedroom into the West Hall as if he's heard someone yell, "Fire!" When he sees Caroline dragging a reluctant usher toward the pumpkin, he offers to help.

"Your boyfriend's got only one eye," he says.

"I tried, but it's too hard and all slimy inside."

"Let's see what we got here." Jack crouches by the pumpkin, knife in hand, his entire concentration on carving the pumpkin as if it were a matter of national defense. Caroline sits beside him, drawing on a white pad of paper the faces for the other pumpkins exactly as she wants them, just as she's seen her mother draw sketches of rooms and outfits. As I watch Jack check with her, trying to follow her directions precisely, making jokes with her, I think we would never have a chance at love without the children and think maybe that's what children are for, not simply to perpetuate the species but to teach us how to love.

Jack receives two letters from Khrushchev. In the first one, received on Friday evening, Khrushchev offers to withdraw ships if we promise not to invade Cuba. In his Saturday-morning missive, he demands that the United States get its Jupiter missiles out of Turkey.

Jack does both. Officially, he responds to the first letter, while negotiating secretly with the Soviet ambassador Anatoly Dobrynin to withdraw the Jupiters out of Turkey within five months.

On Sunday, October 28, Khrushchev tells members of the Soviet Presidium, "In order to save the world, we must retreat."

Khrushchev is a hero. Jack is a hero. All the men are heroes.

I wonder what all the fuss was about.

In a flash, my relief turns to fury. So much energy, so much money, so much emotion, wasted on nothing. Stupid male egos risking the lives of children.

It was all a damn pissing contest.

PATRICK

*H*e was our love child. I knew the very moment I conceived, during a break in the cold weather in early December.

I felt it, I'm sure, the moment one brave sperm broke through the wall of my egg, a pinch of pain, a flash of energy, like a small orgasm, an hour after we made love, then a flood of warmth poured through my body. Jack knew, too, I think, deep inside—he touched me gently the way he does when he knows I'm pregnant—and slept the night with me, with his head on my stomach.

On the bitter cold evening in mid-January when I told Jack, he kissed my forehead and whispered, "After all we've been through and now we're pregnant," as if we'd survived some terrible rite of passage and were now rewarded with a baby.

Since the crisis with Cuba, Jack touches me differently, as if I am precious, our life together precious. Before, if I ran my hand over his chest or played with his hair, he'd jerk away—"For Christ's sake, Jackie, don't pet me! That's what you have dogs for"—but now my touch seems to relax him.

We shouldn't have made Patrick a symbol. A covenant. But we couldn't help it. Every time Jack touched my stomach, we were there again, united beneath the whopping of the helicopter rotors, clinging to each other at the edge of the world, on the brink of apocalypse. We survived the crisis. God had mercy and gave us Patrick, and as Patrick grew inside me, I could feel a solid bond growing between Jack and me, as if every day we were adding bricks to a dream house.

We came from opposite sides of the universe and met in Patrick.

Jack and I adored our other children, but Patrick was different. With all the wisdom of the unborn, he instructed us, reached out with his peanut-size hands to grab our hearts. "I am here," he said. "I am all that is, all that you are. I am the future and the past, I am laughter and despair. Cherish me."

He was our love child, conceived in love. He gave us another chance.

"Miss Mary Meyer," announces the butler.

Mortified, I look at the petite blond woman at the entrance to our private

quarters. She vigorously removes her hat and gloves, as if a whole room of important people were waiting for her. She jabs a hatpin into the brim of her felt pillbox
and says to me, "I guess that voice of yours has finally faded to nothing. Aren't you
going to invite me in?"

My eyes dart to the Blue Suit who stands behind her. "Her name was on the
guest list," he says, giving me a look I can't quite interpret. There's a spark, as if
he's willing me to make a scene. Other dinner guests are sipping cocktails in the
Yellow Oval Room, listening.

She's back. The vixen. Jack didn't give her up after all.

Miss Mary Meyer, who pretends to be wild and unconventional, who fancies
herself a beatnik artist, a cohort of Timothy Leary and Allen Ginsberg, who dis-
dains morality and kindness of any kind and who dares call herself Jack's mistress,
is back. She is the most vicious and calculating woman I know. She will do, or say,
anything to get attention.

She postures before me, one hand on her hip, oozing sass. Even her dress is impertinent, a knockoff of a dress I wore to India. Unfortunately, she also looks
stunning—her little snub nose, her pixie blond hair, her petite little figure.

"Don't you look nice," I say. "You remind me of the Marquise de Montespan."

"Dropping references no one gets. How like you, Jackie. I assume it isn't flattering."

I get momentary pleasure from comparing her with Louis XIV's mistress who
attempted, but failed, to poison nearly half his court, impregnating her rivals'
clothes with arsenic and red sulfur. The king tired of her. She grew grotesquely fat
and was banished from the court. "Please, come in," I say. The words feel like broken glass in my mouth.

Smiling like a crocodile, Miss Meyer swishes past me into the Yellow Oval
Room. She makes much noise as she greets the other guests. "Hello, hello! Isn't it
sooo exciting? I heard Martin Luther King sent him a message. He did? Isn't it wonderful? I've been telling Jack for years . . ."

I stagger, overwhelmed by her gall. Her exuberance over Jack's speech deflates
all my joy and pride. I begged Jack to take a stand on civil rights when he was a
senator. Now, feeling politically strong after his Cuba victory, he does. How
proud I was. How hopeful. Now I feel sick to my stomach.

"Are you all right, Mrs. Kennedy?"

"Thank you, Mr. West. I'm fine. The little one is reminding me of his presence." Thank goodness a pregnant woman has an excuse for sudden mood swings.
"I think I'll see how the hors d'oeuvres are coming." I nearly break into a run
down the hallway to the kitchen and collapse on the chair the chef uses to rest his

feet. The kitchen hums around me—waiters whizzing by with trays of glasses and plates, chef's assistants whipping egg whites and sautéing scallions, the butler popping in for fresh ice. No one bothers Mrs. Kennedy in the corner.

Why did Jack invite her? After all we've been through. Why did he let that viper slither back into our lives? When I'm so close to my due date? After he promised to end it? After his nearly catastrophic exposure when Phil Graham, publisher of *The Washington Post,* gave a mad, ranting speech before an Associated Press convention in Phoenix, announcing to the entire room of reporters that Jack Kennedy was having an affair with Mary Meyer? After the huge fight we had before the dinner dance I held for Lee?

"Jack, you've got to end it," I demanded. "It's public now. Reporters may look the other way when you screw around, but they're not going to let you flaunt it."

"Graham's gone off the deep end. He's in a nut house. No one will believe him."

"They all believe him, Jack. Please. You're getting enough power to do some good for this country, things you dreamed of doing. Why throw it all away?"

"I don't see why I should give her up. I find her amusing."

"She makes you cynical and cruel. I can tell in a moment when you've seen her."

"I don't understand why you don't like her, Jackie. She's refreshing and fun."

"She is *not* fun. She wants to destroy you, Jack. She only married Cord Meyer because she thought he was on the short list for the White House. She drove him to drink when she discovered he didn't have what it takes, then divorced the poor guy. She wants to destroy everything she thinks she's entitled to. She hates me. She hates you. She hates this country. She's Medea."

"You have no right to ask. That was part of our deal."

"She's beyond the deal, Jack. It's not just us. We're talking about the stability of the country. Think of the children, how humiliating it will be for them."

"I hate it when you're so conventional. You remind me of your mother."

Behind his words, I heard Mary's voice, the work of her poison. I imagined them lying naked in my bed, smoking reefers, giggling and making fun of the conventional First Lady.

I used my number one weapon. "Please, Jack. I can't take the stress. I am afraid of losing our baby."

Jack's face paled. After half a minute of silence, he nodded. He promised to end the affair that night.

Later that evening, during Lee's party, I saw a distraught Miss Meyer staggering alone in the garden, dragging her dress in the snow, the diamond hairpin that she wore to mock me slipped to one side, her face numb with disbelief. I admit to having felt a flutter of victory when Jack, right in front of her, slipped off to the pool room with a young model. As a Blue Suit helped her into her car, Jack and I held hands and wished her good night. I could not suppress a gloating smile.

But now she's back. Jack isn't even here to deal with her, expecting me to entertain her. How long can I hide out in the kitchen? No longer, I realize.

The butler is leaving the kitchen with a tray of mixed drinks. I ask to take it in to the guests.

I play the perfect hostess—I know the role—but I begin to feel frenzied and crazy inside. The harder I try to contain my rage, the more out of control I become. I become excessively gay. I laugh wildly at everyone's jokes. I flatter Mary. When Jack finally arrives, I kiss and pinch him. After dinner I play a song on the record player, a silly homage to Jack's *PT-109* heroism, over and over I play it, singing and dancing around the room, improvising gestures to the lyrics, "The biggest hero of them all."

Jack leaves to go to bed. The party breaks up soon after.

I have embarrassed Jack and myself. It leaves me feeling cheap and vulgar.

I read about the suicide on an early August morning. The sun is rising over the water at Brambletyde, our little hideaway we rent on Squaw Island not far from Hyannis Port. Completely serene, I sip coffee and nibble toast with honey. I feel happy to be expectant. Expectantly happy. Then I read the headline.

PHIL GRAHAM, PUBLISHER OF *THE WASHINGTON POST,* COMMITS SUICIDE. I am shocked, horrified that the whole Mary Meyer issue will get talked about again. Only later, while I watch Caroline ride her pony at Osterville, do the coincidences hit me full force: Marilyn committed suicide. Phil Graham committed suicide. Both threatened to expose Jack. Were they really suicides?

I feel sick and cling to the gate to the corral. Wasn't it Jack who ordered Phil Graham out of Phoenix—paid Graham's own physicians to drug him and drag him back on a government plane? Wasn't it Jack who got him committed to Chestnut Lodge, a private psychiatric hospital? Could he have gone further? Did he do the same to Marilyn?

Suddenly pain stabs my gut. I cry out and fall to my knees. *No! Please, no!*

Blue Suit calls Dr. Walsh, my obstetrician, who rushes me from Squaw Island to a makeshift hospital room at Otis Air Force Base.

"We need to perform an emergency cesarean," he says.

"It's nothing," I say, "really. I know he's not ready. Let me rest. We'll be fine."

I *must* be fine. I won't let Jack's womanizing kill another baby. I *won't* let it happen.

A doctor I don't know gives me anesthesia. "No, not yet! No!" I scream, even though the labor pains slice through me like the scalpel that will soon cut me, slicing so deep that I am sure they have gone clear through my body, like a buzz saw out of control. *No, not yet!* They wheel me into surgery, and I hear someone counting back from one hundred, and I feel myself fading, yet I fight it, struggling for consciousness, grabbing for a tree root or a rock or anything that will keep me from sinking, and cry, "Don't take my baby," until all I know is a thick blackness.

I go to a frightening purgatory where disembodied voices swirl around me, hot lights roast me, and cold instruments prod my body. I push aside the darkness as through murky water, reaching for my baby. I catch glimpses, little fingers, an eye, his lady's slipper bottom, obscured by seaweed, appearing, disappearing as the ocean respires. The water pitches and tosses me, and I become conscious of its rhythm, its breathing labored and tired. I know breathing is the problem, breathing is the danger. A wave picks me up and throws me against the ocean floor, knocking me out.

As soon as I wake from anesthesia, I call for him: "Where's my baby?"

"You had a boy, Mrs. Kennedy, four pounds, ten ounces. He has respiratory problems. We had to send him to Boston Children's Hospital. He's getting the very best care."

"No, he must be with me." I push the sheet off my body and try to lift my head. "I must go to him."

"You mustn't get out of bed, Mrs. Kennedy."

"Please call me a plane. I'm going. My baby needs me." I know they are wrong, but they don't listen to me. They give me a shot to put me to sleep.

They put him in a plastic box and took him away.

It might as well have been a coffin.

He was our love child, but I never saw him.

Jack grieves, too. Later—it seems like weeks—when I am out of the hospital and trying to recover at Brambletyde, Jack tells me his part of the story.

At 11:40 A.M. a Secret Service agent charged into Evelyn Lincoln's office, pale-faced and stammering like the boy who reports that someone has fallen through the ice on the pond. She got up from her desk and, instead of using the intercom, knocked on the door to the Oval Office and told Jack that an ambulance had taken me to Otis Air Force Base Hospital. Jack asked her to cancel his meetings for the rest of the day. He called the helicopter pilot himself and told him to be ready to leave in ten minutes. "Nothing must happen to the baby," he said.

He, Pam Turnure, and Nancy Tuckerman, my press secretary and new social secretary, flew to Andrews Air Force Base, where a Jet Star plane, engines running, prepared to leave at 12:10 P.M. As they climbed the stairs leading up to the plane, Jack suddenly felt, so he told me, that it was the beginning of the end and that it was too soon and that he was going to fight it with everything he had.

He stared out the window for the hour flight. The sky was hazy, whitish gray. He noticed that the fields were tinted brown from the August heat. As they flew over towns and lakes and roads and hills, he became conscious of seeking out water—snakes of blue, tortoiseshells of olive. He noticed all the little houses crowded around the rims of the lakes. He thought how feminine the rivers were, the hills and ponds, all round and curvy, and how brutally straight, how male, the roads and railroads seemed.

He thought how ten years ago, he would have never thought of such things— the world divided between female and male, the natural and artificial, the curved and straight. He realized that I had taught him to see the world as art and that he was a different man, a better man, because of me. Because of me, he was a father, an experience far beyond anything he had ever imagined.

He thought of my giving birth, the blood and embryonic fluid flowing, and of holding in his arms another infant son.

He prayed as a child prays—"If you let the baby live, I'll give up poon, I'll give up . . ." He couldn't think what else he could give up that meant anything to him. He thought of all the bargains with God he had made as a child, sick in bed, fighting for breath. "I promise I'll give up sweets, I'll stop picking on Bobby, I'll do my homework, I'll listen at church, I'll be good, I'll try harder, yes, I will. Just let me breathe." He always got better. He always broke his promises. Every one of them. And he kept on getting sick.

"If you let the baby live, I won't run for another four-year term."

Even as Jack made his deal with God, he knew it wasn't adequate, because he wasn't sure he even wanted a second term. His popularity rating was at 82 percent, but his reelection was not assured. The Republicans were busy digging up scandals that could sink him. He couldn't count on a code of silence among reporters. Not anymore. Before he took office, a president's private life was private, yet he had opened the door to television, used it to his advantage, displayed his family, his wife, his children, and it was only a matter of time before reporters felt entitled to report on things that were none of anybody's business.

No, the presidency wasn't enough. What else could he give up?

Jack decided that if God would let Patrick live, he would give up everything—the presidency, the power, the women, the dirty jokes. He would teach history, and he would be faithful to his wife. He would study every day with sage theologians and try, try, try to understand a religion he cynically dismissed. He would love God. He promised.

At 1:25 P.M., when Jack arrived at Otis, he jumped into the waiting car and raced to the air force base hospital. He forgot about Pam and Nancy—even his Secret Service agents had to get their own car.

He rushed past the doctors, into my room. I was still unconscious. Patrick had been born while Jack was in flight. "Where's the baby?" he demanded as he tracked down the tiny infant being rolled in a Plexiglas incubator to a helicopter ambulance. Something was wrong. Why were they taking away his baby? The doctors explained that Patrick needed special facilities at Boston Children's Hospital, that he had been born with underdeveloped lungs, so he couldn't breathe. Jack sensed something was slipping away from him, his baby, his power, his life.

He ordered the helicopter to prepare to follow. He dashed back into my room. He wanted me to know he had been there, that he would stay if he could, but he had to look after Patrick. He took out the Saint Christopher money clip that I had given him at our wedding and laid it in my hand. He glanced around the bare hospital room—the shiny blue linoleum floors, the blank white walls, the blue enamel bedstand, the naked Venetian blinds, the lone hospital bed in a large empty room—and he felt an eerie aloneness, as if he'd run into a station just after the train had pulled out.

"Find something for Jackie to look at when she wakes," he asked of Nancy, "a Monet or van Gogh print or something." Satisfied that Pam and Nancy would stay to watch over me, he rushed out to the helicopter.

He spent the night beside Patrick, watching his little chest squeeze for breath. "If you let Patrick live, I'll become a priest after he graduates from college. I'll give all my money to the children in Cuba. I'll take a vow of chastity."

The next morning Jack flew back to Otis to see me. I was groggy and in pain. Patrick was getting better, he said. We both knew it was a lie, but just as a high-wire acrobat will hold on to her umbrella even while tumbling to her death, we clung to this precious fiction.

We kissed and parted.

Jack flew back to Boston, where he spent a second night holding Patrick's tiny hand through a hole in the breathing chamber.

He stopped making deals with God and pleaded with the baby.

Hang in there, Champ.

You're a good boy. You've got the best mommy in the world. Wait until you get a look at her.

You can do it, Champ. I came back four times and I'm not half the man you are. Come back for Mommy. She'll die without you.

He nodded off to sleep—someone touched his shoulder. Startled, Jack looked up at the nurse beside him. She told him that the baby's heart had stopped. The doctors couldn't revive him.

He stumbled out of the intensive-care unit and found a utility room halfway down the hall. He stepped inside, closed the door, fell to his knees, and cried.

He cried as he had never cried in his life.

He cried because every means known to medical science was used to save his child—but it wasn't enough. His money, his power, his love. Nothing was enough.

He cried for a life unrealized, then understood it was his own life he was crying over—crying because his mother never loved him; crying because he lost two men from *PT-109;* crying because he didn't save his sister Rosemary; crying because he hated his father for letting them ice-pick her brain; crying because he didn't deserve back pain or Addison's disease, but feeling in some way he did; crying because he didn't love me when he first married me, didn't know how to love, and had lost years to misunderstanding; crying because the doctors told him my child-bearing problems were caused by his venereal disease, chlamydia, passed on to me; crying because he cared about all those women he had fucked but they would never know; crying for all the suffering he'd caused when he never meant to hurt anyone; crying because he didn't believe in God, because the only God he knew was his mother's God; crying because now that he felt he had something to contribute to the world, he was running out of time and he'd never be able to do what he knew he could do; crying because he realized, above all things, he was a coward.

Beside the hot steam pipes, the rumbling furnace, the mouse traps, the buckets and mops, the paint cans, and cleaning solvents, in the dark room with the small, dirty window high above, he cried until his throat felt raked with glass, his stomach on fire, his very soul turned inside out. He cried as he had never cried, calling out from the steamy dark room, calling out for comfort in a black empty universe.

He cried in shame.

The president cried and didn't care who knew it.

Jack doesn't have to tell me. I know. Patrick is dead.

I know it as soon as Blue Suit starts to shut the hospital-room door for our privacy: his face, framed by the closing gap between the jamb and the door, shows his grief as if it were his own child, his eyes despairing that he, who is trained to take a bullet for the president, can't trade his own life for that of the president's baby. He looks as if he's failed us.

Jack stands there, arms hanging limp, face inscrutable. He doesn't say a word—he understands that I know. He can't look at me. He lies down beside me, clinging to my shoulders.

We tumble, the two of us, down a deep tunnel—we have only each other, falling, falling, no bottom in sight.

It's as if we had expected this wonderful, unnamable thing for all our lives, and as soon as we touched it with our fingertips, it vanished.

We grieve, not only for Patrick but for ourselves, our foolish hubris. Our hopes were too grand. Mortal love cannot save us. Two people can never be one. For this, not for our petty cruelties, we must forgive each other.

Oh, Patrick, did you have to die for us to open our hearts?

Oh, Patrick, wise, darling Patrick. Did you have to deny us your chubby embraces, your laughter? Oh, Patrick, you are a severe taskmaster.

We celebrate our tenth wedding anniversary today on Squaw Island. Just the four of us—Jack, Caroline, John, and me. Jack gives me flowers he's picked from the White House gardens. Actually, Blue Suit picked them, but, Jack tells me, laughing, he supervised.

Jack also brings us a cocker spaniel puppy, which Caroline names Shannon for a river in Ireland. That gives us seven dogs: Wolfie, Shannon, Clipper, Charlie, Pushinka, and two puppies.

Jack and I sit on the deck overlooking Nantucket Sound, the same view that we looked at when we were engaged. We are not the same people we were then, and even though I think we like ourselves more now, I wonder if I would have started on this journey if I had known all it would be. I know Jack feels the same. I think he would've been happier as a college professor and I as an expatriate writer living in Paris, a lovely, lonely life of wild and devastating affairs. Yet we have come together, two weary warriors tired of fighting. Wounded, we collapse into each other's arms. In grief, we surrender.

We lay beside each other, trying to nap, not daring to make love. I feel shy and frightened. Jack slips off my clothes delicately, as if I were wounded. He touches my body as if for the first time, as if mine were a body he long desired but never thought he'd possess. He is gentle, smelling my skin, tasting it, brushing his fingers lightly over my breasts, my arms, my legs. He draws his finger across the red scar above my pubic hair as if it hurt him, too.

Jack's passion has always been white-hot, a virulent itch, a desperate hunger, an antidote to pain—quick, hard, and shallow. He has never been tender. I feel love in his touch.

After dinner we walk on the beach. The fog is coming in, and in the distance, a foghorn. Jack turns to me and quotes his favorite poem—"I have a rendezvous with Death . . . At midnight in some flaming town." He recites the words thoughtfully, pressing the side of my face to his chest, kissing my hair. I feel a flash of anger—why has he withheld his tenderness for so many years? Why did we have to lose a child to discover this?

Jack feels me resist and lets me pull away. He kneels in front of me and hugs my knees. I feel ridiculous and kneel. There we are, kneeling together, as if exchanging vows.

Then we sit, staring out at the sea. Jack lays his face in my lap, reaching under my skirt, up my leg, squeezing my inner thigh, holding me tight. He trembles and I feel his pain shoot up from the base of his spine. After a moment he relaxes and kisses my knee.

"Do you think we earn our deaths, Jackie?"

"No. That payday comes even to the indolent."

"Thank you, Jackie."

"You're welcome, Jack."

"I mean for everything."

"I know."

"I don't want to go to Greece, Jack. I want to be with you. I don't want to leave the children."

"No, you should go. It will be good for you. Two weeks on the *Christina* with nothing to worry about except cruising around the Mediterranean."

"Think of the bad publicity."

"Fuck the publicity. I insist you go."

Lee told her part-time lover, the Greek shipping tycoon Aristotle Onassis, about Patrick's death and my depression. He has invited me to recuperate on his lavish yacht—all very proper, with Lee, Stas, Franklin D. Rockefeller Jr., and his wife Suzanne, Princess Irene Galitzine, and Onassis himself as host. Jack wants me to go, but I feel odd, as if I'm being sent away.

Jack is healthy but nervous and agitated. He acts like a warrior preparing for battle who sends his wife away so she won't see the blood and gore. He never sits still, jumping up, abruptly ending conversations, his fingers in and out of his pockets, through his hair, tapping his teeth, drumming his knees. Even when playing with the children, he seems agitated.

I worry that all the drugs are finally taking their toll.

I agree to go even though I fear that Jack is distancing himself again. But I sense there's more to it.

I sense he's trying to protect me from something, but I don't know what.

I lie baking under the Greek sun. There is something about this land that calms and heals me. That transports my soul.

I remember what Bernard Berenson wrote me in his last letter before he died—always teaching me something. He discussed synesthesia, a sensation produced in one modality that evokes another, as when hearing a certain sound induces the visualization of a certain color.

Here the water of the Ionian Sea is wine-colored, and I smell roses. The sky is bright blue, and I taste madeleines. The buoyant perfumed air smells of salt air and wild herbs, and I hear Stravinsky's *Rite of Spring*. The light is magical—it seems to illuminate objects from within. It has taste and texture, a playfulness— it is light with a sense of humor.

I relax and feel the *Christina* rocking beneath me. I hear waves splashing against the bow, and gulls screeching overhead. It is otherworldly, austere and serene, a landscape of the mind.

Onassis's 315-foot yacht is amazing—decorated in a hodgepodge of images and styles. Like a dream, it is both fantastic and hideous—the lapis lazuli fireplace, the two El Grecos, the jade Buddha, the main bar decorated with scenes from the *Odyssey,* and barstools covered in whale scrotum—or so Onassis claims. The playroom is hung with fairy-tale tapestries. There is a movie theater, a swimming pool. There are nine guest suites named after Greek islands, each with marble bathrooms and gold fittings. It is not a work of art as I have tried to create in the White House, but rather a scrapbook of visions. It's like being in someone's imagination—a Greek imagination. It puts me in a state of creative reverie.

Onassis is a most interesting man. We met once before when Jack was a sena-tor, we had cocktails with Winston Churchill on the *Christina*. For some reason, Onassis didn't make much of an impression on me at the time.

He is a funny-looking creature, short and stocky with long, powerful arms. He wears a short-sleeve shirt and baggy pants, smokes a huge cigar, and always has a glass of ouzo close by. He has an eggplant nose and small black eyes so far apart that they seem to be slipping off his face. His mouth is wide, with almost no lips. He has huge cabbage ears with tufts of hair growing out of them. He parts his thinning salt-and-pepper hair on his right side and combs it back from his face. His neck is as wrinkled as a turtle's. When he wears his darkened glasses, which he al-most always does, he looks like a gangster.

His reputation is one of a ruthless tycoon, yet to me he appears sweet, gra-cious, and poetic. He reminds me of that part of me that I have neglected, the part of me that loves nature, that soars when it hears a beautiful line of poetry, that yearns for beauty.

As we sail to Istanbul, stopping at Lesbos, Crete, Ithaca, Skorpios, and Smyrna, Onassis stays out of sight of the paparazzi. But when we land at Smyrna, his birthplace, he takes us on a tour.

As we walk through the cobblestone streets and the ancient ruins, he thrills me with tales of his grand escape as a youth from Smyrna, the invading Turkish army hot on his heels, how he learned to dance the tango in Argentina from an opera star, how he made his first fortune importing Turkish tobacco, and how he bought his first six tankers for a bargain—twenty thousand dollars apiece—stranded in the St. Lawrence Seaway, and decided then and there to become a shipping tycoon even though he knew nothing about the business.

I love his stories.

Late one night, as the *Christina* drifts in the Mediterranean, Onassis and I lie on deck in lounge chairs, our faces upturned to the impossibly brilliant stars. The night is moonless. The Milky Way, a wide, white band, arches across the heavens. While the others dance in the ballroom below, Onassis says to me, "You have a Greek soul, Jacqueline. A tragic soul."

I am getting accustomed to his dogmatic pronouncements and don't take of-fense. "Why do you say that?"

"A tragic soul is capable of great feeling."

I laugh. "Do you know what some of the White House staff call me?"

"No, what?"

"The Ice Queen. They say I don't have any feelings at all."

"Don't worry about petty, jealous people. They have no souls."

"I thought everyone had a soul."

"Perhaps. But the only true aristocracy is that of passionate souls. Like you and me. Everyone has feelings. It binds us together as humans. But the great soul, the tragic soul, feels deeply and arouses in others compassion and respect, pity and awe."

I think about Patrick, and how the country seemed to grieve with me. "I don't want to share my feelings."

"You don't have to. We see your pain—your soul—etched in your being. That's why the world is crazy about you."

"I think they envy my clothes."

"No. It's your soul they're wild about. It's your soul that attracts me."

I ignore his last comment, the kind of silly talk flurried about by European men like fly swatters. We go on to talk about other things—Plato and Greek myths.

I find myself seduced by this land. I never want to leave. It makes me love Jack more. It reminds me that there was a reason we were drawn together—a meeting of our souls. I know we can work it out.

I return to my cabin and write a long love letter to Jack, astonished that after all these years, I have never really tried to express to him how much I love him.

Greece frees the poet in me.

When I get back to Washington, I find that my trip has created an uproar. I am accused of demeaning the presidency by hobnobbing with a jet-setting mobster. Of neglecting my duties as wife and mother. The tabloids even accuse us of having an affair. Rubbish. The lavish gifts he doled out mean nothing to him. I try hard to hold on to that special feeling I had in Greece.

I expect Jack to be furious, but he isn't. I think my letters moved him. Onassis has brought us closer, putting our lives into perspective. Our tenure in the White House is short, the history of our country short, our lives short. The only thing of true importance is our love for each other and the children.

Jack asks me to go on a campaign trip to Dallas with him. Right now I would do anything for him that he asked.

LOVE FIELD

wake before dawn with a slow throbbing above my pelvis. I sense dampness, reach between my thighs, and feel the slippery wetness of menstrual blood.

So that's what made me sneak into Jack's bedroom last night under the pink neon lights that flashed across the parking lot and through the hotel windows—TEXAS RIBS, TEXAS RIBS—slipping under the sheets, arousing him with feathery kisses as I massaged him, Jack croaking awake with tender concern: "Is it too soon? Don't hurt yourself." That's what lured me with such force despite physical exhaustion from three days of campaigning. That's why I took command, straddling him, my lust engorged by the garish lights, his skull and bones nearly glowing through his skin between the bursts of neon.

And to wake with such joy! My first period since Patrick's birth. The pump is primed! We can try for another child. My blood is a baptism for our new life together. I vow to campaign with Jack until I'm pregnant again. How perfect to start our second term with a new baby!

I kick off the sheets and run to shower. As the hot water reddens my skin, I think what a miracle it is when all the pieces fall into place, when despite compromise and frustration and disappointment, things work out just as you dreamed. My joy erupts in a tremendous geyser of energy! I can't wait to smile and shake hands. I'll campaign for Jack until I drop.

I rub myself hard with a fluffy white towel with the dark blue letters: Hotel Texas, Forth Worth. I wrap another towel around me and hurry into the bedroom.

As I pat-dry my hair, I sit down on one of two double beds, the one I slept in. On the other bed, carefully laid out, is a navy blouse, handbag, shoes, pink Chanel suit, and pillbox hat. The suit is his favorite—he chose it for this trip.

Jack barges into my bedroom; he, too, is euphoric. He pushes aside the curtains and surveys the view. "Just look at the crowd! Damn, they love us."

As I walk up to hug him, I peek around his shoulder at the crowd below, mostly men wearing cream-colored ten-gallon hats. I flash on a graveyard of white marble stones. The image, so contrary to my giddy mood, vanishes in a blink. I look again. Men, drinking coffee, rocking placards on their toes, wait patiently for the president to speak.

While I showered, Mary Gallagher left a tray with breakfast and the paper. I pick up *The Dallas Morning News* and open to a full-page political ad, laid out like a funeral notice, a thinly veiled threat from the John Birch Society accusing Jack of everything from selling food to communist soldiers to imprisoning and starving thousands of Cubans. My fingers begin to tremble. Of course I knew Jack had enemies in Texas. But this? "Where does such hatred come from?" I ask.

Jack looks shy, as if he's been caught in a lie. "We're headed into nut country today, Jackie. But don't worry. With you beside me, they'll melt like snowmen."

"Did you know it was going to be this bad?" I try to keep the sound of accusation out of my voice.

"A few people warned me," he says reluctantly.

"Who? Please tell me, Jack."

He taps his front teeth with his fingernail. "Byron Skelton from the Democratic National Committee in Texas. He wrote Bobby and told us not to come to Dallas."

"Who else?"

"Well . . . Walter Jenkins—he's from Texas, Johnson's right-hand man. Adlai Stevenson. Governor Connally. Senator Fulbright from Arkansas. Billy Graham had a premonition and warned us not to come. Even the Dallas chief of police."

"Oh, Jack!" My legs weaken; I sink onto a chair.

"I'm surrounded by Chicken Littles. You can't spend your life worrying about other people's fears."

Shivers shoot up my spine. I recall sailing in shark-infested waters, and Jack throwing off his clothes and jumping in, daring his buddies to join him. "Why didn't you tell me?" I ask.

"Don't worry. They loved us in Houston and San Antonio. Remember last night when we arrived? They were wild. Don't worry. They'll love us in Dallas, too."

That was his third "don't worry." It doesn't reassure me. Supposedly we're here to heal the rift in the Democratic Party between conservative Governor Connally and liberal Senator Yarborourgh. "Why did we really come, Jack?" I ask.

"I don't mind being hated for good reason, but I can't stand being hated out of ignorance. We've got to win them over." He then beams at me. "*You've* got to win them over."

"I'll do my best," I say without much enthusiasm.

"They'll give you another standing ovation. You'll see." He puts his arms around me and kisses me. "I couldn't do it without you, Jackie. You know that?"

Warily, I nod my head.

"Now, be a good girl and get dressed."

11:37 A.M. *Air Force One* touches down at Dallas's Love Field. Before I step out of the plane, Jack whispers, "It's showtime, Jackie," his lips softly brushing the edge of my ear, arousing me. I flare my nostrils—a promise for later. We both laugh. I step onto the mobile stairs. The crowd chants, "Jackie! Jackie! Jackie!" Someone hands me an armful of red roses. Not yellow roses, the flower of Texas, but red, the color of love.

I laugh, delighted. I can do this. I really can. I can stand by Jack as he campaigns. I can open my heart to a crowd without fear. I can do this for them. I can do it for Jack.

It is our destiny.

Main Street, Dallas. The sun is hot. The glaring light glints off the windows and off the Cadillac's shiny chrome, blinding me. My pink suit itches, perspiration seeping between the silk lining and my skin, and I think I'm glad I've tired of the suit, because it will never be the same. People line the street, six deep, dressed in their Sunday best, babies on their shoulders, cheering and waving—"Look, there they are! Jack and Jackie!"

I wonder what makes them come out to see the president and his wife, the limousines, the Secret Service, even though they know they will catch only a glimpse, a flicker of pink between the bodies like a flamingo in the mangroves. They smile and cheer, capturing memory snapshots as they crane their necks around the heads in front of them. Women and men reach out, tears running down their faces. For a moment it frightens me. If they can wave and cheer, they can hate and jeer.

I play the part, queen for a day. I wave and smile and forget for a moment that they know nothing of who I am or who we are, but only what they think we are, an image, perhaps, of what they would like to be. Then I realize a truth—it doesn't matter that what they see and what I am are not the same. Their love is real.

I give in to it, a kind of rapture. I let the cheers flow over my body like a warm tsunami. It is beyond my greatest joy, this erotic surge, beyond the joy of riding a horse early in the morning, beyond the joy of seeing patchwork farms and forests from an airplane window between white puffy clouds, beyond the joy of watching my children play with furball puppies.

The Cadillac turns right for a block, then left. I see an underpass before us and yearn to slip under the cool earth, away from the sun. I anticipate the brief relief, like the closing of the stage curtains between curtain calls, a respite from the lights and the applause.

Jack slides his hand over the backseat and squeezes my fingers. I turn to look at him. He's smiling, radiant. He says something to me, but I can't hear over the roar of the police escort motorcycles on both sides and the cheering crowd. I see it in his eyes, apology, joy, love, as if he were saying, *See, this is what it's supposed to be, for us and forever, you and I.* I suddenly realize this is the look I'd been waiting for, on my wedding day, after sex, together on the beach with our sleepy-headed children snuggled in our bare arms.

His beauty breaks my heart, his hazel eyes, his square chin, the wrinkles at the corners of his eyes, his perfect forehead.

This is my husband.

The crowd cheers us on as if they, too, are part of this forever, part of Jack and me and our dream for the country.

Suddenly a car backfires. Red paint sprays over my eyes. Two more blasts. Jack jerks into the air like a marionette, then slams back against the seat. His brains fly into my lap. Blood cascades over me with tiny bits of bone and tissue.

He looks at me, lifting a hand to his forehead with a quizzical look on his face as if he has a slight headache.

Horror crashes over me. *They will kill us all.* This is the end. The mob will tear us apart with their hands. They will eat us alive. I hold a chunk of Jack's brains in my hand. He's gone. I shove it back on his head and throw my body over the seat onto the trunk, crawling, grabbing frantically on the slick hood. I must get out. They will kill us all. I must save myself.

The car suddenly jerks, accelerating.

My face slams against the hot metal, burning my skin. Arms grab my shoulders and toss me back into the car. A Blue Suit throws himself over me. I smell his aftershave and wonder why Secret Service agents always wear too much cologne. I can't breathe. I don't want his protection. I struggle, kicking, pushing him away. I pull Jack into my arms.

It is the end, I think over and over, and blame myself for daring to want love, knowing I could have lived without it, but I wanted it more than anything, and now Jack is dead.

I knew it was coming, swerving madly toward us, pulling us to its gray magnet mass. I knew it was coming, and I couldn't stop it. Jack knew it was coming, too, baiting it with his jokes that weren't jokes, but little prayers to quell his fear, because he felt the earth tremble under Death's approach.

I press together pieces of Jack's pulpy head and rock him gently. I am here, Jack. From the corner of my eye I see figures running around us until they become a blur. We gave them everything, and they have done this to us. I hold him to my chest, and I think if I hold him softly, I will make it easier for him. *The end has come, but I am with you. I love you, Jack.*

As I gently wipe his face with my white gloves, I notice his blood seeping into my skirt. The oddest thought comes to me—at least I'll never have to wear pink again.

But it is not the end. We arrive at a hospital. Men in white surround me, pulling at my arms. "You will not take him from me!" I scream. I rush after the gurney as it bumps over the asphalt, over the smooth linoleum, excited voices engulfing us, echoing down the corridor. I feel a cord between Jack and me—I almost see it, a yard long, white and shiny like an umbilical cord. It keeps me by his side as the doctors roll him into emergency surgery. I will let nothing take him away from me. I must be there.

Doctors jump around him, frenzied, trying to revive his heart. I want to tell them to stop but I know they need to do this, not for Jack but for themselves. It is part of the sacrifice. Part of the ritual.

The cord is strong between us, then begins to fade. I let him go.

Part of me feels relief. It's over, our exhausting larger-than-life existence. The dream and pace were unsustainable—for us, for our country—our emotions and expectations stretched like rubber bands, now broken. The sense of relief passes, and I tremble with grief.

They pull a sheet over his body. His naked feet, bloodless and white, poke out below. I kiss his feet, then pull back the sheet. I have never seen him so naked, so still, and I realize that movement itself is a costume, a distraction against the absolute nakedness that is death. I kiss his mouth, his eyes, his chest, his forehead, and a sexual urge pulses through me as I kiss him again and again, wanting to make love one more time, for maybe if we make love, he'll come back to me. I slip my hand under his penis, soft, gray, and warm, like a chick fallen from its nest, and gently close my fingers around it.

I hear Jack's voice—*For Christ's sake, Jackie, I'm dead.*

A Blue Suit places his hand on my shoulder, a heavy hand of warning, taming my hysteria.

I step back and straighten my spine. Jack's staring eyes seem filled with compassion, as if he's trying to tell me something. Compassion? For whom, Jack? A

horrible fury embeds itself in my groin. I want to rip down these curtains that stu-
pidly try to hide death. I want to scream and scratch the faces of the dumbfounded
nurses and doctors and aides.

Compassion? Not now, Jack. Not for a long time.

Blue Suit feels my rage growing inside me like a demon fetus. He stands behind
me, afraid to touch. "Mrs. Kennedy, they want to prepare the president for trans-
port. Would you please wait outside?" How do they learn to make questions sound
like orders? I look at him with pure hate, wanting to fly at him, rip at his live skin
smelling of cheap cologne, his solid, muscular body full of life and blood and sex
and vigor.

Instead, I reach for Jack, my hand hovering over his chest, not touching, sensing it hurts him. Jack tells me to think of our children.

I slip my wedding band onto his little finger and kiss his palm. Blue Suit
touches my elbow, leading me away, and I let him. Jack is gone. There is nothing
here but this hunk of flesh that I don't recognize. It has nothing to do with Jack.

I go sit in the hall and wait. I am oblivious to the reporters and doctors and
White House staff running around as if there were still a crisis. They fade into a
fog around me, their voices distant, down by the beach near the water.

I am alone, invisible. I begin to shake all over as if an electrical current were
coursing through me. Water pours from my eyes, but I am not sobbing. My breath
is oddly regular.

Suddenly I'm outside my body, looking down at this woman in a blood-
spattered suit who stares blankly at the door, water falling down her face. *I'm free,*
I think. *I can go, too.* I look around to see if anyone notices I'm not in my body.
They're busy doing what they think they're supposed to do. Why not go? But
something holds me back. Take care of the children, says Jack.

I slam back into my flesh, the loss, the pain excruciating as if my limbs are being
pulled apart. *I can't take it,* I think, *my body can't take it. My mind is going to explode.*

Something snaps in my chest. *How did I crack a rib?* I wonder, remembering how
a cracked rib felt after a tumble from Sagebrush. I realize it is my heart breaking.

Then I feel nothing.

I see faces but recognize no one. They take my elbow and lead me away and ask
me questions I don't hear. "Thank you," I say. "You're so kind." I stop and freshen my
lipstick. I am ready to go on. I lay my hand on the bronze casket and follow down the
corridor.

At Love Field men take charge, or try to take charge, like boys stepping into their dead father's shoes to go to war. They argue about the body, whether to wait for the Dallas medical examiner or take the body to Washington immediately. They argue about when and where to swear in the new president. The Kennedy camp versus the Johnson camp—the old guard versus the new.

They are all terrified of more snipers, more gunshots, armies of assassins— they shout orders at one another, panicked, frenzied, frightened.

As if anything mattered anymore.

I say nothing and let them pretend to take charge. I know they need to do this, like the doctors who madly pumped blood into Jack's dead body.

Johnson walks back through *Air Force One* and asks me to stand by him as he receives the oath of office. I stand to his left as a federal judge swears him in on Jack's Bible, which someone found on the plane. It is oppressively hot. Thirty people squeeze into a cabin designed for eight. I can't breathe. Like a drunk feigning sobriety, I concentrate hard not to sway.

Johnson repeats the oath in his inimitable drawl: "I do solemnly swear that I will faithfully execute the office of president of the . . ."

A jet flies overhead, and I think the world hasn't stopped after all, and soon that plane will open its doors and passengers will get off, not knowing what has happened, greeting their loved ones, going on with their lives.

". . . so help me God." Bizarrely, Johnson kisses and hugs his wife, then turns to hug me. Repulsed, I press my palms to his chest and discreetly push him away. Hugging is more than I can tolerate.

As I turn, I hear Johnson say, "Now, let's get airborne."

Alone, I stumble back to the rear compartment, back to Jack, where I belong.

The airplane roars, the air temperature cooling as it reaches higher altitude.

With me in the aft galley, Ken O'Donnell, Dave Powers, Larry O'Brien, and Godfrey McHugh—Jack's closest buddies—drink whiskey and reminisce about Jack, already beginning an Irish wake. I hear them, but don't hear them.

I lean against the coffin. The surface is cool against my face. My eyes rest on its elaborate molding, which reminds me of a church pew. I suddenly feel as if I'm in a church, the whispering of the men, the dim lights, the cool air, the engine noise like the drone of city traffic outside St. Patrick's.

Where are you, Jack? How could he be here one moment, then gone? I press my ear to the side of the coffin. Is he whispering to me? I listen hard but can't make out the words. I must be imagining it.

Suddenly we're on a vast green lawn stretching down to the ocean, Jack and I, Caroline and John. Jack wears a white shirt, unbuttoned. He lies on his side and tells John he can hear the grass grow. Excited, both children press their ears to the ground, Caroline's face crinkled in concentration, John's eyes sparkling with mischief. "I hear it! I hear it!" John squeals. Caroline looks skeptical, then yells, "I hear it, too," and we all break out laughing, because no one really hears anything. I am moved at their desire to share the experience, to make us one, a family.

Where are you, Jack? I keep thinking that we almost made it, that I was almost able to break through the isolation and find you on the other side, waiting. But it didn't happen. Perhaps we were too much alike. Perhaps it isn't possible for two people ever to really know each other. I thought after Patrick that we might find each other, and for a moment we did, feeling in our palms the weight of each other's hearts. A glimpse was all, and then it was gone.

Perhaps it's like knowing God—we are allowed only glimpses in this lifetime.

Where are you, Jack? Since I first met you, this is the question I have asked, the question that drove me to agree to marry you, the question that made me stay with you. I always felt I would find you someday. But now you're gone.

The plane drones. I sink against the side of the casket, wondering how I can possibly go on.

My leg, red with blood, dries and begins to itch furiously. Lady Bird wanders back from the front of the plane, where the Johnson people are. She asks me if I want to change clothes. "No," I say, "I want them to see what they have done to Jack."

Lady Bird stares down at me, her beady eyes over her hooked nose, her lips pressed together—the disapproving look of a mother at her headstrong daughter who's too old to be told what to do.

She touches my shoulder, then returns to the front of the plane. She is already looking to the future, to the prize she'd always hoped for and had given up on. Her opportunism doesn't make me angry. I pity her—the prize she thinks she wants is a purse of vipers.

6.00 P.M. The plane lands at Andrews Air Force Base.

As soon as the doors open, Bobby rushes on board, pushing past the shoulders of Johnson's men, shouting my name like a child lost in a train station. "Jackie!

Where's Jackie?" He grabs me by the shoulders, looks down at my suit, and makes a sound as if he's been slugged in the gut.

I see in an instant that Bobby will never recover.

I had always thought of Bobby as Charlie Chaplin's little dictator who shouts orders that no one pays any attention to, and now it's as if he realizes no one will ever pay attention to him, not ever, because his small hold on authority has died with Jack.

He squeezes my hand too hard, unaware that he's hurting me. He leads me to the exit of the plane, thinking, I'm sure, that he is my rescuer. Beneath his sense of mission, beneath his stiff-legged walk and pushy hands, I see him quiver in terror. He clings to me.

I cannot save him. I can only save myself and my children.

I step off the plane. You are there with your camera. I dare you to take a photo, and you do. This is what you have always wanted, my body spattered with blood. The virgin sacrifice. But it is not my blood.

The skin on my face is stiff with tears. Numb, I look at you as if this were a game gone out of control, a game where all the rules have been broken, which now becomes the point of a new game. Greedy and sensing victory, you take my picture.

You look up for a moment to check your light meter. Our eyes meet. I need to see horror in your eyes. Even a glimmer would be enough. I need you to feel what I feel, to understand what has been destroyed. I need you to see that what could have been now will never be, where there was light will only be darkness. I need you to acknowledge that it is over.

I lose. Your only concern is framing the shot.

SWING LOW, SWEET CHARIOT

*F*inally I am alone in my bathroom, free from people clinging to me, those afraid to leave me alone, afraid for themselves, afraid that I, too, might disappear.

I take off the bloody suit. The blood-caked stockings stick to my legs, tearing the skin as I peel them off. I let the garments fall to the floor—streaks of maroon over a mound of pink. It reminds me of the arteries and veins covering Jack's brain.

I wonder what to do with the clothes. I'm afraid to give the suit to the maids, afraid that instead of burning it, they'll sell it years later at Sotheby's for a small fortune. I'd like to bury it, but where? In the Rose Garden? I envision myself sneaking out at night past the Secret Service—shovel in hand, the bloody suit in a shopping bag—and kneeling in the dirt between the rosebushes, thorns biting my skin as I dig a hole for the suit. Like a murderer. The idea is absurd.

As I step into the tub, the water turns pink. The rising heat weakens my muscles. I sit in the water, feeling numb, feeling as if someone else's hands were washing my arms, my legs, my breasts. I realize this is the last time I will touch something of Jack's body—his blood. The hot water begins to relax me. I sense this is some kind of perverse Communion. My body, Jack's blood. *Taste my blood, and with it remember me.*

I recall bathing Jack when he was in the hospital, sponging down his feverish neck and arms, then changing the oozing bandages on his back. I wonder if he was washed before he was laid in his coffin. I see an image of a small Irish cottage, women, old and young, sponging down one of their husbands on the kitchen table as the men drink in the living room. I wish I could have washed Jack's corpse.

As I soap my body, I imagine that I am washing Jack, his legs, his arms, his chest, that his hands are running over my body. I realize we'll never make love again.

You can let go now, I tell myself, but tears don't come, and I recall that when Black Jack died I couldn't cry. I think of Black Jack lying in a hospital bed, asking a doctor to call me. I didn't know his liver was riddled with cancer. I didn't go to him but spent my birthday with Janet, she, too, thinking it was Black Jack just using his poor health to get attention. Then I got the call that he was dead, his last words calling for me—"Jackie!" I wasn't there for him. I didn't help him die. I ignored him in his old age, in his bitter drunkenness, his recriminations, his bad smells—booze, urine, sweat—and the stench of something rotting, which must have been the cancer eating him alive.

Dry-eyed, I planned his funeral at St. Patrick's. Dry-eyed, I chose bouquets of yellow daisies and bachelor's buttons to surround his casket. Dry-eyed, I visited his last mistress to ask for a photo, amazed that with all my scrapbooks, the only pictures I had of Black Jack were pictures with me—as if his only importance was in his relationship to me. Dry-eyed, I cringed at my own self-centeredness.

I think of Black Jack careening past the brick portals of Farmington, singing up at my dorm window, "Jacqueline Bouvier!" I think of him taking me dancing at the Rainbow Room, and on carriage rides through Central Park—courting me like a lover.

He died wanting me by his side, while I ate cucumber sandwiches with my mother. I wanted to remember the old Black Jack, the dapper playboy, the gay deceiver who was full of fun. So I stayed away. I'll never be able to forgive myself.

I think of Dallas, of Jack's death mask, his blank, staring eyes. *Compassion, Jackie*—his last admonishment to me. Where had been my compassion for Black Jack?

Finally I give in to tears, keening as they fall down my face into the bloody water. I didn't love enough. Not my father, not my husband. Not when I had the chance.

I begin to tremble all over. I cannot go on. This is far more than I ever bargained for.

I hear a knock on the bathroom door. "Mommy?"

It's Caroline. I can't let her see me like this. "Just a minute, honey." Quickly, I drain the water, throw a towel over the pink suit, and put on a white terry-cloth robe.

I open the door. Caroline stands, sleepy-eyed in her nightgown. She carries a stuffed kangaroo, John's favorite toy, and I realize that it must be her favorite toy, too, and in the sweetness of her nature, she'd given it to John but, now needing it, had borrowed it for the night.

I squat down and she takes my face between her two small palms the way Jack used to, her eyes determined, "Don't cry, Mommy, I'll take care of you."

I try to sleep in Jack's bed, mad at myself for insisting that the sheets be changed after every use. Now I can't find his scent. The gravity, the shadow, the warmth that should be Jack's body, there in the dark beside me, is absent.

I toss and turn—I can't sleep. I get out of bed and walk down the hall to my dressing room. I set candles around the room and light them. I lie down on my blue satin fainting couch and pull a leopard-skin throw over my legs. My eyes roam over the light blue walls, the white lintels and woodwork, the baby-blue drapery. I look at the photos of our family that hang on the wall above my feet—riding horses, sailing, wrestling with the dogs under a Christmas tree. The flickering candlelight seems to give the images the possibility of life.

It has been thirty-six hours since Jack left me, and I begin to sense a crushing and painful obligation: My life will continue. Alone.

I take a pen and blue stationery to write a letter to Jack. At first, I can think of nothing to say. Then I begin.

Venom and recriminations spew out of me. Angry tears pour down my face. "Coward!" I accuse him of bringing this down on our family, of preferring martyrdom rather than facing scandal. I accuse him of stupidity. "How could you ignore all the warnings!" I accuse him of cruelty. "How dare you leave me! How dare you leave the children!" My hand cramps. I rant and rave until I am purged. Ten years of anger and hurt.

I tear it up and burn it with a cigarette. I take another sheet of paper, and write:

> My Darling Jack,
>
>   I will never love again as I loved you. I will never feel the same joy as when we sat with our children on Squaw Island, looking out to sea, embraced by the fullness of our love—for each other, our children, the sea, the beach, and the sunset. I felt whole.
>
>   You taught me many things over the years—patience, duty, humor in the face of adversity—but above all, you taught me to love humanity. Now I fear all love I had for my fellow man has died with you, Jack. My heart festers with hate—I fear it will never heal.
>
>   Watch over us, Jack—especially your children, John and Caroline.
>
> With love forever,
Jackie

Sunday morning at dawn, Bobby and I take my letter and a letter from Caroline and John, and sneak down into the East Room. An honor guard stands watch over the casket. They say nothing as we fold back the flag, open the coffin, and place the letters inside. On his chest, I lay a pair of Jack's favorite cuff links and a piece of scrimshaw that he loved. Bobby adds his *PT-109* tiepin and a silver rosary.

They say that hair and nails continue to grow after death. My fingers find their way to his head and stroke his hair. I sense part of him is still living. One of the honor guard leaves the room and returns with a pair of scissors—he hands them to Bobby. When Bobby cuts a lock and gives it to me, I feel something fall away from me, as if Jack's spirit tethered by a thread were now snipped free.

I caress his face with my left hand, running my fingers over the cold, waxy surface, his nose, his lips, his forehead. A cold dark flame consumes my body. My swollen lips are too numb to utter the dark pain inside.

I glance up—one of the honor guard looks worried, as if he's afraid he'll have to restrain me. I withdraw my hand and see his relief. Bobby closes the casket.

Jack's spirit feels very far away. For the first time I feel that Jack is really gone.

I pull aside the edge of Caroline's bedroom curtains and look down at the mob in Lafayette Park across the street. Hundreds stand quietly. I recognize faces—judges, members of Congress, friends, all simply standing there.

Gradually it sinks in that I am not the only one mourning his loss.

Grief comes in waves. As soon as I think I'm strong enough to go on, it crashes over me, threatening to drown me.

Decisions and details anchor me to sanity—planning the funeral, the grave site, where to hold the Mass, what to print on the Mass card, guest lists, flowers, the Bible readings, who will deliver them, who will give the graveside eulogies, the grave marker.

I spend all morning making calls. My lack of sleep is catching up with me, and I need to rest. The Amytal injections that the doctor gave me do nothing to sedate me. I go to my bedroom to lie down—only fifteen minutes, I tell myself—but my mind is so cluttered with things I need to do, I can't sleep, my brain whirring. I don't want to stop—if I do, I'll start feeling, and then I know I'll fall apart.

I need to decide on flower arrangements. I look around my white bedroom and think white chrysanthemums, daisies, and stephanotis. I'll ask Bunny Mellon to order flowers and act as flower police—I can't have everyone's wreaths cluttering up the church and grave site like some kind of floral compost heap.

I pick up the phone to call Bunny and drop the receiver on the bedstand. When I pick it up again, the mouthpiece falls into my lap. I screw the plastic back on, then lift the entire phone onto the bed so I don't have to tug at the cord. After I make my call, I replace the phone. Glancing down at the baseboard, I notice that the wallpaper is curled up at the edge and, underneath, a dark line. It looks like a cord has been removed. There's fresh plaster dust on the edge of the baseboard.

I think of calling Traphes Bryant, our electrician, to ask if we've had any work done lately on our telephones, but a numbness spreads through my shoulders and I sink into the pillows. I lay exhausted. A nagging back pain tells me I have reason to fear.

I rock my head back and forth in the pillow. *No, no, no.* I don't want to know. I refuse to speculate or give in to terror.

I spring out of bed, remembering that I told Ralph Dungan I'd get back to him about my choice of grave site, Arlington, not Brookline with the rest of the Kennedy family. There is much to do—guests to be served, a performance to be planned, a nation to appease.

No time for helplessness.

Nights on the second floor of the White House have always been quiet. Now that the rooms are filled with guests, there's a restless silence to the place. I hear voices whispering, toilets flushing, a cough, ice dropping in crystal glasses. There is a pent-up hysteria to the silence, as if everyone is trying too hard to be quiet.

I shuffle into Jack's room. I want to handle things of his, as if his warmth might linger there. I sit on his bed and look at the dark gleaming wood of his four-poster bed draped with blue-and-white toile covered with cherubs from a Victorian print. Three years ago, when Sister Parish showed him material samples, he chose the angel pattern without hesitation—he could be so childlike sometimes. I imagine him lying on his back, awake in pain, his eyes roving over the faces and wings, then slowly closing to sleep under the guard of angels.

My eyes drift over his dark walnut chest of drawers, eighteenth-century American, his bedstand, the coffee tables. I notice that personal items are missing—his comb, pills, cuff links, books. The staff and relatives have been busy. I recall the reporter who walked off with Jack's Bible after Johnson was sworn in on *Air Force One*—how strong the scavenger instinct is, how quickly it takes over, even before the dead are buried.

The scavenger instinct. The survival instinct.

Hope is dead, but the will to live surges on.

I collect small items from Jack's bedroom—a cigarette case, a cigar box, a pen, a tie clip, a paperweight. I will hand them out to his staff and friends, telling them that Jack would've wanted each of them to have a remembrance. I will get a small vindictive charge out of seeing the faces of those guilty of pilfering, their eyes mortified as they finger Jack's reading glasses in their pockets. How Jack would laugh.

Then I notice that something else is missing. Jack's bottles of pills. Curious, I get up and go to the bathroom and open the medicine cabinet. All of his medicines are gone, the pills from his doctors, the pills he had the Secret Service procure for him—Lomotil, Cytomel, phenobarbital, testosterone, Trasentine, fluorinef, Tuinal, Benzedrine, Dexedrine, Dexamyl, Seconal, Nembutal, Demerol. All gone, even the aspirin.

The extra back brace that Jack hung on the chair in the corner is also gone. I suddenly recall seeing Jack's bloody clothes in a pile in Parkland Hospital in Trauma Room One, and wonder what happened to the brace he was wearing.

Surely, nobody stole these things as keepsakes.

Frantic, I look in his closet—his crutches are missing. I open the top drawer of Jack's bureau, where he kept a case of hypodermic needles prepared by Dr. Jacobson and his needles for his cortisone shots, which he took every day. They're all gone.

Either we have a drug fiend in the house or someone doesn't want any of the guests reading Jack's prescription labels. What frightens me is the thought that someone thinks this information may be exposed, passed on to a nosy reporter.

Deposed and powerless, I fear our lives will become an open book.

Sunday morning. I walk up the steps of the Capitol.

I tread into the underworld. John and Caroline hold my hands and guard me as I visit the land of the dead, standing by to bring me back when I am ready.

I follow as nine pallbearers carry his casket up the stairs. A double row of servicemen stand on either side. On my left, John, concentrating hard, takes each step one at a time, pulling himself up, making sure his shoes come together, then kicking out again, looking up at me after every few steps, so proud, his entire little being wrapped up in making it to the top of the stairs. On my right, Caroline squeezes my hand and looks up at me to make sure I'm not crying. I smile gratefully.

The cool air inside the Rotunda seems to have a life of its own, like the mouth of a cave where deep inside sleep a thousand bats. Hundreds of people circle the edges behind red velvet ropes. As the pallbearers lower the casket onto Lincoln's catafalque, great squares of light shine down from a circle of windows above. I hear the gentle susurrus of prayers.

I am watched and scrutinized.

Kennedys herd around me in a solid block. I feel the brothers—their heat and maleness. Bobby radiates rage, his core burning hot and bitter. Teddy, cooler, looks as bewildered as a puppy staggering out of a mud puddle. I feel the Kennedy women hating me, blaming me, because I was the first to take Jack away from them. In their minds, Death and I are in collusion.

My legs feel as if they are going to give out. Caroline squeezes my hand, keeping me steady.

The eulogies begin. I know the first speaker. His white hair and aristocratic face are familiar, but I can't remember his name. His words start something vibrating inside of me—"She took a ring from her finger and placed it in his hands." He repeats this after every paragraph, driving a stake into my heart.

As the next two speakers drone on, I bend down and tell Caroline their names and what they do and how they knew her father. Then I close my ears until they're done. I won't tolerate their futile attempts to make sense of this tragedy. I won't have them cheapen it with their words, however honorably intended.

When they're done, I smile a thank-you. Then Caroline and I step forward and kneel before the catafalque. I kiss the red-and-white-striped flag draped over the top. Caroline slips her hand under the flag to feel the coffin beneath.

Her bravery amazes me, and I think for a moment that children understand death better than adults. Perhaps being so young, they are closer to that other world we came from, its memory lingering in their imaginations. When I say, "Daddy's in heaven," they have no doubt he is there, watching over us. We spend the rest of our lives trying to regain that faith.

Caroline and I stand, turn, and walk out of the Rotunda, where John, rescued from the boring speeches by a navy aide, returns to my side, eager to try the steps again.

Scores of people descend on the White House, extending condolences. I don't know whom I'll run into when I turn the corner. It makes the Secret Service nervous—they charge about in a frenzy as if they expect a coup d'état.

I want all the guests to sign the usher's log so I can send them thank-you notes afterward. I enter the Red Room and walk to a seventeenth-century writing desk. I open the rolltop. The usher's log isn't there. With so much confusion, nothing is where it should be. Maybe someone has set it out already. I look in the logical places—the Lannuier table in the Red Room, the French Empire pier table in the hallway. I look for J. B. West but can't find him anywhere.

I track down Sargent Shriver, who's overseeing the task of making the guest lists. He's already taken care of deciding the thirty hymns for the marine band, tracked down a charger for the riderless horse, and negotiated with the Roman Catholic clergy for a simple Mass. When he sees me coming, his eyes widen apprehensively, as if he's afraid I'll assign him another task.

"Sarge, have you seen the usher's log?"

"No. I need it for the guest list but couldn't find it." Then he adds, "Evelyn Lincoln is helping me pull together friends' names, and I'm getting family names from Rose. I have two men handling the diplomatic corps, two for Congress, one for clergymen, and one for the press. Sandy has already started inscribing the invitations. By the way, where do you want the Mass? We have the choice of St. Matthew's or the Shrine of the Immaculate Conception. I need to know today to arrange seating charts."

"St. Matthew's would be lovely," I say. He flinches, and I know he's already started arrangements for Immaculate Conception. "I just know St. Matthew's is right." I rest my hand lightly on his forearm. I know his nerves are frayed. "Why don't we call in the Flying Wallendas," I heard him yelling down the hall yesterday. "I can't thank you enough for all your work. I couldn't manage without you." He rolls his lips inward, itches his nose, then looks away. No tears in front of the widow.

Next I go downstairs to look for Evelyn Lincoln. She hasn't seen the log. I finally find J. B. West in the State Dining Room speaking with the maître d'.

"Mr. West, have you seen the usher's log? I'd like to set it out for our guests."

"The attorney general asked for it, ma'am. I haven't seen it since."

"When did you give it to him?"

"Friday afternoon. By the way, Prince Philip, Duke of Edinburgh, has just arrived from England, and Stanislas and Lee Radziwill are waiting for you in the Red Room."

"Thank you, Mr. West." I hurry to greet the guests, knowing they'll stumble in, shaken as if they just missed being in a terrible car accident, oddly needing reassurance from me.

I rely on a memorized script and a well-practiced smile—"Thank you. Jack always spoke so fondly of you. You're so kind. It would mean so much to Jack that you came"—but I feel a pinprick below my rib cage, a slow leak. Why would Bobby need the usher's log? Why hasn't he returned it? Doesn't he know I need it?

I shake myself into the present. "You must be thirsty from your trip. What can I get you to drink?" Half the time I don't know what I'm saying.

I think how good manners protect you from so many things. Good manners come without thinking, giving you time to censor yourself and to plan an appropriate response. They protect you from revealing suspicion and fear. I rely on these false graces like a soldier on his military training.

I would like to say nothing can hurt me anymore, but it isn't true. It hurts more and more every day. Small violations hurt far beyond their import. I am embarrassed that they pierce so easily through my fragile armor.

I look out a second-floor window above the White House executive offices to see if the weather is clearing. It's still drizzling. I see a portly black man wheeling Jack's rocking chair, upside down, on a dolly across the parking lot, moving it to storage. The chair keeps slipping, and I wonder why the janitor has it upside down, if this is a sign of respect, to keep its seat dry even though no one will be sitting in it.

Johnson bustles around the West Wing. I can't blame him—he has much work to do—but his eagerness and efficiency hurts me.

Later I see Aristotle Onassis escorted down a hallway near the Green Room. Lee invited him to the funeral, or rather, he called her and asked to be invited. Lee fantasizes that he'll ask her to marry him. "There's something revolting about him that really turns me on," she once said. I think he looks like an ancient toad that suffers from stomach ulcers.

I blame him for my believing in Jack again, our future life together—and now he's gone, along with all my hope, forever. I am irritated at Onassis's insinuating himself in my family, as if his previous hospitality has given him certain rights.

My anger melts when I see tears in his eyes.

He offers his arm, and we walk together into the Rose Garden. "I came as soon as I could. I want to do anything I can to help."

"The Greeks understand tragedy," I say, barely smiling.

He pats my hand. "I'm sorry, Jackie, for that conversation. Now, it seems so . . ."

"Prescient?" He doesn't know the word but understands my meaning.

Was it only a month ago that Lee and I rocked on board the *Christina*—my soul awakened?

Onassis snaps off a white rose and hands it to me. Red drips down his fingers—a thorn has drawn blood, which he licks from his pudgy fingers. He does this carelessly, like a peasant without a handkerchief. There is something disturbingly sensual about it.

"I don't take back what I said, Jacqueline. You do have a tragic soul. When the tragic soul suffers, her pain exalts, transforming pain and death, giving us meaning beyond our puny lives. A tragic soul gains dignity by what it suffers."

"I have no interest in either dignity or suffering," I say hotly.

"Perhaps not. But, you play the role beautifully."

Blast his soul talk! What arrogance! How dare he? All I can think of is Jack's brains in my lap. I turn to him angrily. "I think, Mr. Onassis, this is not an appropriate time for such talk. Would you please excuse me?"

I escape inside, wondering what in the world Lee sees in this ugly, presumptuous man.

9:00 P.M., Sunday night. Bobby left dinner early to make some telephone calls, or so he said.

Later, as I pass down the hallway by Jack's bedroom, I hear him crying inside. I knock. "Bobby? It's Jackie. May I come in?"

I push open the door. Bobby sits on the edge of Jack's bed, his ferret face creased from pillow weeping. A lost little boy. "Let's go visit Jack," I say.

Bobby nods, and we get a couple of Blue Suits to go with us in a limousine to the Capitol.

The streets are dark and quiet. The air, still moist from the afternoon rain, chills us through our clothing. As we drive by the Mall, we see a line of yellow light, three miles long, snaking out of the east end of the Capitol, down the steps, around to the front, hundreds of thousands of people, holding candles, bundled up in winter coats and hats, huddled together for warmth, resolved to spend the night in line, even though they must know that once they reach the Rotunda there will be little to see, a flag over a casket flanked by an honor guard, an image many probably saw earlier that day on television.

Closer to the Capitol, the line dims, and I realize that after six hours of waiting in line, they've run out of candles.

We get out of the limousine and stroll down the Mall. I fear snipers—anyone could take a shot at us. Yet I want to see the people's faces. In the dark, they don't appear to recognize us.

We walk in silence until I hear a baritone singing alone, a Negro's voice, rich and deep as a slow-moving river, "Swing low, sweet chariot, comin' for to carry me home/Swing low, sweet chariot, comin' for to carry me home."

There may be people out there who want to kill us, but for a moment, I feel safe, wrapped in a blanket of collective grief.

We climb the steps around the queue, hand in hand like Hansel and Gretel in the forest. Both agents come with us.

The Rotunda is cold and dark. A golden glow encircles the room where picture lights beam down on the huge varnished historical landscapes that hang on the walls. The people queuing around the catafalque seem to be stepping out of the crowded paintings.

Bobby and I kneel in front of the casket. He recites a Catholic prayer that I know but seems only vaguely familiar. He stops in the middle and I look over at him. He's not crying, just staring in front of him at the flag.

"You'll never leave me, will you, Jackie?"

He grips my hand like a desperate lover, or an old crone clinging to her youngest daughter, refusing to let her marry. I'm filled with panic, sensing a trap, a burden greater than I want to carry. I feel the small window of hope that keeps me from despair—the possibility of escape, from politics, from the Kennedys, from public view—slam shut in my face.

What would Jack want me to say? Would he have me protect his children, or stand by his brother? Would he want me to live my own life, or sacrifice myself for the sake of his family's ambition?

Then I hear his voice clearly, *For Christ's sake, Jackie! Why do you make such a big deal about everything?* Jack never understood the malignant manipulation of his family, never credited much meaning to the sidelong glances, the smirks, the unkind jokes.

My instinct to save myself and our children is strong, but I know what Jack would want me to say.

I squeeze Bobby's hand. "No, Bobby," I say. "I will never leave you."

FUNERAL

I walk down Pennsylvania Avenue, Bobby on my right, Teddy on my left.

Drums beat the death march. The wheels of the caisson roll in muted clatter. Horses' hooves clomp. The soles of our shoes clack on the pavement, tap, tap, tap. In a crowd of thousands, I hear a single woman weeping.

I do not collapse. I do not cry.

Beneath my numbed mask, I feel like screaming, like flying at the people who line the streets, digging out their eyes with my fingers, shouting, "You killed him! You all killed him!" ripping off my clothes, biting my wrists until my blood squirts over them, raking my thighs and my breasts with my nails until I bleed, screaming, screaming until all the blood drains from me and I mercifully die.

This is what I fantasize about as I walk in solemn dignity.

A whirling dervish of hate gnashes at my insides. The devil tries to sweet-talk his way out, tries to seduce me, mimicking Jack's whispery voice—*It's all over, anyhow. Your life is over. What does it matter? Give in, Jackie, let it out.* As I listen to him, hysteria climbs up my spine and yanks at the roots of my hair. Rage wants to leap from my body, spewing venom.

Bobby squeezes my hand hard, warning me. In the photos, this will look like a gesture of sympathy, not the threat that it is. Kennedys surround me. They will make sure that I complete this farce. That I behave. For my children, I walk on.

My shoes—not designed for walking—rub against my heels. I feel blisters, raw skin, and then blood seeping into the bottoms of my shoes. I am thankful for the pain. Only the pain keeps me from screaming.

My swollen eyes create blurry halos around everything, the casket, the trees, the dignitaries.

The marine band plays Chopin's funeral dirge. The drums roll. Our footsteps fall in time, one foot in front of the other.

The riderless horse with boots backward in the empty stirrups swishes his tail angrily. His name is Black Jack. Like my father, the horse wants nothing to do with the Kennedys, or protocol, or ceremony and, as if in concert with my father's spirit, bucks and kicks, refusing to obey his handler. The horse, like my father, is terrified of death.

I have a strong desire to run up behind him and jump on his back, to break from the procession and gallop far away into the Virginia countryside.

Bobby senses my impulse and squeezes my hand—*Don't even think about it.*

If this death ceremony is so important to the people, why do I feel as if I am betraying them? Don't they deserve rage? Don't they deserve to see me rake my nails across my face? Don't they deserve to see my blood?

I hold on. Barely. If Bobby weren't clenching my hand so tightly, my demons would surely pop out.

My mind wanders to the face of the man they say killed my husband—his oversize egg-shaped head with a small chin, his sly expression. How can one man kill the hope of a nation? I realize that Lee Harvey Oswald did not kill Jack alone. The details don't make sense. Then Oswald was murdered, no doubt to shut him up.

The truth blinds and deafens me. I gasp with terror and nearly collapse. If not Oswald, then who?

I suspect everyone. I imagine assassins taking aim—at Johnson, at the Kennedys, at me. I feel them out there, watching, waiting for the right moment.

I panic. I must get away. I must see my children.

Bobby takes my elbow, his fingers digging into my arm. "John and Caroline are in the limousine," he says. "They are both safe."

I realize I must've spoken aloud. Hearing the names of my children eases my panic. We can't escape now. Later. We will flee this country of murderers.

My performance is over. Like an opera diva who's given every last ounce of energy, when the curtain falls, I collapse.

I have earned my grief—I let it engulf me.

I feel the weight of the air around me. I feel pressure against my eardrums, and my ears buzz. Everything is wobbly. Something is happening to my senses, my vision, my sense of touch. Everything seems to be fading—people's faces, sounds, music, voices. Nothing seems to carry any meaning.

Unable to sleep, I wander the halls of this empty house. It's not a house anymore, but a huge coffin. All that's left is a huge bloodless wound in a cold, lifeless body.

In my rational mind, I know Jack's spirit is gone, but as I walk through the rooms, I wonder, does it linger? In the corners? In that sudden cool draft? I remember how when he entered the ballroom, his spirit was so bright, so grand that it seemed to spin people to the edges. I sense him here but know it's only my own desire for his body, his gravity.

I let my body be propelled forward by its own momentum, the East Room, the Green Room, the Blue Room. I pause at the South Portico and look out to see moonlight across the lawn, the Washington Monument, bright and cold.

I wander into the West Wing and find myself in front of the Oval Office. I have an enormous desire to sit in his chair behind his desk, to feel, if not Jack's presence, how he must have felt those nights when, in too much pain to sleep, he wandered down to his office to work.

A security guard stands outside. He looks at me blankly, as if he's not sure if I'm real. "I want to be with Jack for a while," I say, knowing I wound him just enough to let me in.

The office still smells of Jack—a musty old-man smell mixed with expensive cologne, stale cigar smoke, and camphor lotion. I sit in his chair and think of those rare moments when Jack pulled me onto his lap, his chin in my neck, folding me into him, and I wonder why it was so seldom he held me like that, his physical displays of affection spontaneous and sporadic.

Johnson arrives tomorrow to take over. I think to gather more relics for the staff. I take the in-box on Jack's desk and begin to fill it with little things—a piece of scrimshaw, a miniature sailboat in a bottle, a picture of his *PT-109* crew, a polished piece of petrified redwood.

I walk to his file drawers against the wall. Inside, Jack hid an ugly little knick-knack he picked up in the Caribbean—a seashell with a copulating couple hidden beneath. He would take it out to amuse his friends. Ben Bradlee would like it. Jack kept other joke gadgets in there, ancient sex aides from India and Japan—he liked to see if people could guess what they were. The Irish Mafia will like those.

Remembering the combination from when Jack asked me to get a contraband Cuban cigar for him last week, I spin the lock to the top file drawer. It doesn't open. I'm tired and rattled—I must've made a mistake. I dial the combination again. No luck. I try the combination on the other drawers. They do not open.

I walk outside the office to the security guard. "I'm sorry to bother you. All of Jack's combinations seem to have been changed."

"Yes, Mrs. Kennedy. The attorney general had them changed."

"Really? When?"

"Friday."

"This past Friday?"

"Yes, ma'am."

A chill shoots up my spine. While I was holding Jack's hand in the emergency room, his blood wet on my body, Bobby was busy changing combinations, rushing around the White House like a maître d' on a restaurant's opening night. I think of the usher's log he commandeered, the broken telephone and removed wires, and the missing medicines.

"They're empty anyhow," the guard adds.

"The file drawers?"

"Yes. We took them to the executive offices, third floor."

I feel as if the ground has become pudding beneath me. The third floor of the Executive Office Building is the most secure area of the White House complex, patrolled twenty-four hours a day by armed guards. It is where Jack housed the Special Group for Counterinsurgency, a task force to fight communism in Latin America and Southeast Asia. It is Bobby's territory.

I leave the Oval Office and stumble back to bed, my mind spinning with questions. Until this moment, it hasn't mattered to me who killed Jack. It didn't occur to me to care—Jack is gone, our life over. But now I need to know. My children won't be safe until I know. Is Bobby protecting Jack from revelations about his philandering and ill health, or is there more?

Later Bobby knocks on my bedroom door. I open it. His suit is disheveled, his breath smells of whiskey, his eyes bloodshot and ringed with madness. He pushes me against the wall and kisses me hard, kicking shut the door with one foot.

"What in hell are you doing!" I manage to croak.

He sweeps back my hair and presses his jaw on my cheekbone, panting, holding tight. His desperation frightens me.

"I need you, Jackie. I'm dying. I can't . . . I can't—"

He pulls me to him, one hand behind my neck, his other on the small of my back, pressing his mouth to mine, his tongue thrusting between my teeth. I shove him away, furious. "I am not yours, Bobby. I won't be passed around like one of Jack's bimbos."

"You're all I have," he says, approaching again. "It's just you and me now." He kisses me behind my ears, down my neck. He groans as his lips taste my skin and I hear Jack's groan, a groan not of sexual excitement but of pain. "I love you, Jackie. I need you. I need Jack."

"Bobby, stop it!" It shocks me, appalls me—his sexual urgency as demanding as the need for oxygen, powerful as the will to live. I kick his leg, pushing him away.

He stumbles back onto the bed, the plywood underneath Jack's horsehair mattress clacking against the bedframe. His face crumples, shocked at himself and at me. I reach for a chair to steady myself. I feel raw, hungry, and hurt—aroused and repelled. Part of me wants to submit, to make violent, desperate love, to infuse myself with some kind of molten primal energy, to purge and hurt myself, to make us whole, to find Jack and bring him back.

Bobby begins to sob, his hands over his face. He flings himself over, burying his head in a pillow, howling into the feathers, whining and gnashing his teeth.

I sit beside him and rub his back, combing his hair with my fingers as I would a feverish child. He moans softly, and I wonder why, over thousands of years of evolution, it is the women who cradle the children and men, comforting them from pain, loss, and despair.

Who will comfort us women?

WIDOW

1963–1968

EXILE

*W*hen I awake, there is a brief moment of relief before I remember who I am and what has happened. The sheets are cool, the pillow soft, the predawn air moist and silent. I drift lazily down a slow gray river. Then I open my eyes and it comes crashing down on me—Jack is not here beside me and never will be again.

There is no refuge anywhere for me. I wish for cool soil over my face, a weight of stillness over my body—I wish to lie in eternal darkness, he next to me, his lips an inch from my lips, forever.

My body aches for his body, my spirit for his spirit.

No one will ever know what a big part of me died with him.

"I'm so glad you are finding comfort in God," says Ethel. She doesn't know how close she is to getting her face ripped off.

Every morning Blue Suit and I go to St. Matthew's, not to pray, as Ethel assumes, but to be alone. There the dark pain I feel lifts briefly like a fogbank at noon, only to return as the afternoon wears on and I return to the White House.

The priests know not to bother me. The Catholic Church is filled with silly little men running around in black, but they do understand death. It's the one time when their obsession with ritual makes sense, giving us a map to find our way out of the dark maze of despair.

My eyes fall on a stained-glass image of Christ holding a lamb to his heart, another sheep at his feet looking up adoringly at him. I think of the children and am nearly undone.

I kneel in a pew halfway down the nave. The church is cold, the damp chill of a crypt, a cold more penetrating than the below-freezing temperatures outside. The discomfort of kneeling and the cold make my pain more tolerable.

I feel so alone. I am hollow with failure. I try to sense the presence of God, the spirit of Jack. I pray for some sign that Jack is safe, out of pain and loved, that we will be all right.

Why didn't the bullet hit me instead of you?

Because the sniper wasn't hired to miss.

What am I going to do without you?

Take care of the children. Do that, and you will be safe.

Safe from what? Jack?

Was it his voice I heard? No. Only one of those ghostly conversations that spin around in my head. I am left shivering with paranoia.

A young priest I don't recognize watches me, his eyes tentative, feeling their way over to me, then jumping away, excited as a boy who sees his older brother's girlfriend walk into his father's soda shop. I've seen that look before. He is gathering courage to make the most out of an opportunity.

He makes up his mind. He clasps his hands together in front of him—they disappear beneath his long black sleeves. He walks over to me and stands a foot away. He smells of mothballs. I suspect the cold weather has driven him to dig through summer storage for a heavy wool robe.

"Mrs. Kennedy, I am available to hear your confession."

"My husband has been murdered. Exactly what would you have me confess?"

His head snaps back, shocked. I almost laugh, my scorn delicious. But the priest is smarter than he looks. "Your bitterness," he says.

"Confession is for the living. I am dead."

"You must ask for God's forgiveness for losing your faith. God will lead—"

"Fuck God."

"I know you are grieving, Mrs. Kennedy . . ."

Given the opportunity, he'll never shut up. My sauciness dissipates like air from a balloon. But I won't let this pompous puppy see me cry. "Go away," I say with a languid flap of my hand. "I don't want anything to do with you or your God."

The great thing about priests is that you can speak as nastily as you feel and it won't get published in a tabloid. He bows his head and shuffles out of the sanctuary.

I try to find that place of quiet I had before, but it's useless. Jack is gone, and I am filled with nervous confusion. Purgatory, it appears, is another curse of the living.

Maybe if I hadn't been so dreamy and happy and involved with my own thoughts, I would've been more vigilant, glancing around at the buildings the way the Secret Service do.

Maybe if I had insisted harder for the bubbletop to keep the wind from my hair, you would've relented.

Maybe if I had jumped up when I heard the shot, the sniper would've been distracted and I could've taken the second bullet.

But I didn't. I tried to save myself. I dove off the trunk, trying to get away from the target, away from Jack.

Would've, could've, should've—I exhaust myself with maybes.

Blue Suit isn't Catholic, but when I look over my shoulder, I see him in a back pew, praying. Sometimes I think he's the only one who knows what I'm going through—the only one who cares.

We share a special bond—our guilt. We both feel we should have saved Jack. But Blue Suit's first impulse was to save me. We both know that this means at some point he will ask to be reassigned. Not soon, I hope. I don't think I could bear that. He is the only one who makes me feel safe.

We step outside. It's very cold, and I realize I haven't been warm since the motorcade in Dallas. My fingers and toes are numb—a chill lingers just below my sternum.

We walk toward the Washington Mall. The city is bleak and desolate. As I look at the Jefferson and Lincoln Memorials, and the Custis-Lee Mansion above Jack's grave across the Potomac, Washington appears to me as one vast cemetery.

"We should get back for the birthday party." Blue Suit reminds me of my promise to the children—and my only reason for not shooting myself.

Sorting and packing—the curse of the living.

I don't want anyone to help me. I sit with half-filled boxes all around me. As I wrap each item in newspaper, it's as if I'm burying part of Jack.

I wonder what to do with Jack's clothes. Give them to a Catholic charity? Neither Bobby nor Teddy fits his suits. It amuses me to imagine homeless men wearing Jack's thousand-dollar suits, custom-made from fine Italian wools by Sam Harris in New York, shuffling through snowdrifts on the Washington Mall, wiping their noses on hand-stitched cuffs.

Decisions have to be made. What to take with us and what to store, where to hold the White House school. Perhaps Lady Bird will let it remain at the White House until Christmas.

A panic grips me. Where am I going to move? Our close friend Averell Harriman has offered his town house in Georgetown. I can't turn him down—I have no other place to go. I have to find a place of my own. Quickly. After losing their father, I can't have the children feeling homeless. Children are like dogs—they like routine and are very territorial. I can't imagine how it will be for them, living in boxes, the rooms filled with other people's possessions that mustn't be touched, drawers that mustn't be opened, the fabrics filled with other people's smells.

How am I going to provide for my children? How am I going to protect them? I need some staff, but how am I going to pay them? I have little money of my own. The money Joe gave me is tied up in trusts until the children turn twenty-five. I will get $10,000 a year from the government and something from Jack's will, but I don't know how much or when. I can live at the Harrimans' for only a few weeks. There is no room for us at Merrywood, and I refuse to let the children be raised at Hyannis Port. I can't bring them up at Wexford, our country house in Virginia—it's too remote. I'll put it up for sale when I can, but I will have to wait until Jack's estate is settled.

I've always counted on Joe Kennedy, but he can't help me now. I feel certain that if it weren't for Caroline and John, the Kennedy clan would wash their hands of me. Even Bobby.

I will sell some jewelry, discreetly. I couldn't bear it if the Harpies discovered the widow pawning her jewels. I suspect the Kennedys will veto my getting a job, terrified of newspaper headlines lambasting them for being so cheap that the president's widow has to work for a living.

I start in on my clothes closet. Suddenly it seems overwhelming. I'll send everything to storage and sort through it later. I look at the shelf above the racks of gowns and suits. All those pillbox hats! What will I do with them? I despised wearing hats—now I will never have to wear one again. I will send them to Encore in New York for resale. I drag a chair into the closet, stand on it, and begin taking them down, one by one.

My crowns of cloth, each a masterpiece. I can't resist opening the boxes and stroking the silk ribbons, the brims of mink, the soft cashmere. I am surprised when I discover a box with two hats jammed inside. Did I do that? Provi wouldn't dare be so careless. It makes no difference now.

I nearly fall backward when I take down the last box. It is extremely heavy. I set it on the floor and open it—inside are tapes, files, and photos. I dump everything onto the rug.

The pile feels like a ticking bomb. I walk around it, afraid to touch it. Why did Jack hide these things in my closet? Or did he?

I close my bedroom door, put on a sweater, and sit cross-legged on the floor. I start with the file on top.

It is filled with memos to Jack from various people. Some of the names I recognize: Richard Helms (CIA), Desmond Fitzgerald (CIA), McGeorge Bundy (Jack's national security advisor). Others I don't recognize. I read the top memo.

The memo describes a detailed plan for overthrowing the Castro regime, scheduled for December. Beneath it are similar memos going back to 1961, with various scenarios for killing Castro. Many seem absurd. Poison pills? A pen filled with Black Flag-40? An exploding cigar?

My heart is beating hard. I get up and circle the pile like a wild animal trying to outsmart a trap. I think of taking everything to the White House incinerator. My curiosity is too great. I sit back down and open the next file, which is on Vietnam. Jack wants to pull out but argues that he can't until after the election—"I can't look soft on communists."

I'm appalled. How dare he sacrifice the lives of children for his own election? I open the next file—a memo from Bobby about squeezing Johnson off the '64 ticket, scandals about Johnson he can use. Why does Bobby hate him so?

Beneath the files is a stack of glossy photos, mostly of naked women on the rosewood bed in the Lincoln Bedroom. The photographs are high quality—the lighting and sharpness of the images make me think of the work of one of the White House staff photographers, the one who takes photos of the children at play. The thought makes me sick to my stomach.

That leaves the tapes. My muscles are charged, my mind obsessed. I lug a heavy tape recorder from the living room, and wind on the tape the way I've seen Jack do. It's Jack and Pierre Salinger talking about a book written by amateur genealogist Louis Blauvelt, who did his family tree and listed Jack as the third husband of Durie Malcolm, an eleventh-generation Blauvelt. I'm appalled. Jack swore to me on the heads of our children that the marriage story wasn't true, that it was nothing but a drunken skit, married by the head chef of some trendy club in Palm Beach.

Another tape is Bobby and Jack talking about Jack shacking up with a German woman named Ellen Rometsch, who might be a communist spy. Bobby is afraid of a scandal like John Profumo's—the British minister of war who got caught lying to the House of Commons about sharing a prostitute with a Soviet naval attaché. He was forced to resign in June.

The sexual betrayals hurt, but what angers me more is Jack's recklessness—nonchalantly endangering his family, his presidency, and the stability of the U.S. government.

I fast-forward to the next conversation. I recognize her voice, chirping up the scale, giggling. It's Jack I have a hard time recognizing. His voice is soft and husky, and I realize he's probably masturbating.

"Hey, Lancer, how's your lance? It's Lollipop."

"You really shouldn't use my name. It's bound to irritate the Secret Service."

"Oooops. Sorry, sugar. You won't guess where I am. I'm in a bathtub. Naked!"

"I should hope so."

"You won't believe it. My breasts are floating. Like marshmallows on hot cocoa."

"I'd like to see that."

"Gosh, I wish you were here, too. I'd love a bubble bath with you. [splashing sounds] Bubble bath, bubble bath, bubble bath!"

Suddenly the room flashes white. I gasp and snap around. Bobby stands with his hand on the overhead light switch. "She has a nice voice, doesn't she?" His face looks as if he's smelling something foul, his upper lip curled, nose flared, chin tucked. There's a nasty quality to his tone.

I snap off the machine. "She *had* a nice voice," I say. Bobby recoils, and I realize Marilyn's death meant something to him. "How does she manage to say 'bubble bath' like that? Like she's getting pricked by a pin."

"It wasn't a pin she was getting pricked by."

"Where did these tapes come from?"

A false veil of nonchalance slips over Bobby's face. He saunters into my room and throws himself down on my fainting sofa. He puts his shoes on my Chinese silk pillow.

"Jack had a tape-recording system in the Oval Office and in the Cabinet Room. He also had a Dictabelt recording system for his phones downstairs and his bedroom. He had a switch on his desk that flashed a light in Evelyn's office. She'd then turn on the Dictabelt system."

I think of the broken receiver and missing cord in my bedroom and remember how Jack often seemed to know things, small things, like what toy John broke or how much an outfit cost, things I'd never told him. "Did he bug my phone, too?"

"No."

I realize that when Bobby holds his gaze too steadily, he's lying. He's lying now. "How many tapes are there?"

"Probably two hundred or so."

"These are the greatest hits?" I point to the dozen or so tapes on the floor.

"Yeah, you could say that."

"You took it out on Friday, didn't you?"

"What?"

"The recording system."

"I couldn't have Johnson asking about the tapes."

"You put them in my closet, not Jack."

He neither confirms nor denies.

"Is it true—what the files and tapes say? That Jack was married before me? That he was fucking a German spy? That he hired the Mafia to assassinate Castro? What else, Bobby! Tell me!" I fly at him, scratching his face, kicking his legs. He grabs my wrists and we roll off the couch onto the floor. He pins me, spread-eagled. I kick and thrash, tears pouring down my face. "It's all lies, isn't it? Our entire lives? How can you mope around like he was some great fallen leader?"

"Don't be naive, Jackie."

"You knew all along. How could you let him?"

" 'He is prosperous who adapts his mode of proceeding to the qualities of the times.' "

"You're quoting Machiavelli to me? Who *are* you?"

"Jack did the best he could."

I roll out from under Bobby. "People who do their best don't have orgies in the White House!"

"I'm sorry, Jackie. I'm sorry you had to find out."

"Damn you! Damn all of you!" I throw a glass at him. It shatters and cuts his chin—droplets of blood sprinkle over the white carpet. More Kennedy blood ruining my fine fabrics. A hysterical laugh snags in my throat and I struggle for breath. "You know, don't you," I say.

"Know what?"

"Who killed Jack."

"No. Of course not. Why would you think that?"

"I want to see his files, Bobby. The ones you had moved from the Oval Office. I want to know everything."

"No, you don't."

"I deserve to know! I'm the mother of his children."

"Johnson's ordered a commission to look into it—"

"Fuck that! You have no intention of letting Earl Warren look at those files. You won't tell him anything. You won't testify."

"I can't. Goddammit, Jackie! Do you want to see everything Jack worked for go up in smoke? Do you want his children to grow up thinking their father was a disgrace to his country? Do you want the Kennedys to be shamed forever?"

"I want you all to burn in hell."

"Your children are Kennedys, Jackie. Don't you forget it."

I feel entirely defeated. I've been robbed of even my grief. How can I grieve for a man who betrayed me so outrageously, who hired gangsters to murder the leader of another country? Who lied to me even when he vowed he was telling the truth?

There is nothing to hold on to. Nothing is real. For a moment I think it would be better for me to die and the children, too, rather than have to live through this. No, I love my children too much.

"What will happen to it all?" I ask.

"I'll assign someone to catalog everything. Then it will go to the Kennedy Library."

"Someone who will use his editorial discretion?"

"A friend of the family."

It occurs to me that what I desire to know is not in these files or tapes. They are merely the flotsam of a massive shipwreck. "We'll never know who killed Jack, will we?"

"Not in my lifetime," he says. "Not in yours, either."

PRISONER

It is eleven days since I buried Jack. The White House staff, afraid to look me or one another in the eye, pours affection and parting presents on the children. They stand at attention as I take Caroline and John by the hand and leave the White House forever.

I vow never to return.

I wear the same black dress I wore to the funeral; the children, the same blue coats and red shoes. This, too, is part of my funeral procession.

I know I have no right to love the White House as much as I do, but I created, with all my heart, a thing of beauty and importance. I feel that it is my home. I've lived here longer than anywhere else in my adult life. It has been untimely ripped from me like an unfinished canvas from an artist's hands.

I am frightened to step outside. I imagine snipers hiding around corners, ready to gun us down. If the Secret Service couldn't protect Jack, how can they protect us?

I feel the chill that has been with me since Dallas. I carry it out of the White House into the world. It has become part of me.

I cling to Caroline's and John's hands. We leave through the Rose Garden. The bare, pruned bushes are capped with cones of snow. The ground is icy; the air, harsh and cold. Each breath freezes my lungs and stings the inside of my nose. My eyes, swollen from crying, see watery stars around the edges like an antique photograph.

Each step feels treacherous.

Pop, pop, pop. The sound makes me jump. It's only photographers. I giggle nervously. Reporters fire questions and you stand there watching me, not with pity but with cool assessment. I am too afraid to answer questions. I seem only to be able to squeeze out a light whisper. "Thank you, thank you, God bless you."

We climb into the car and drive to someone else's home.

The children and I escape to Brambletyde on Squaw Island for the holidays. I worry about Caroline. She sits in her room clipping photos of Jack from magazines, then tapes them on the wall. The dogs go with us wherever we go—Shannon, Clipper,

Charlie, Pushinka and her puppies. I told Maud Shaw to let the dogs sleep in the kids' beds if they want them. I take Clipper for myself.

From the kitchen window, I see a small figure down by the beach. Fifty feet behind, a Secret Service agent keeps guard. I wonder what they think about during their watch, staring off at the gray sea, then glancing every few moments at the small, lonely child who hugs her knees.

He hesitates, then, as if he can't take it anymore, Blue Suit takes off his jacket, walks up behind her, and places it gently around Caroline's small shoulders. He retreats several paces to give her solitude. He knows, as I do, that she needs to be alone.

I give her half an hour.

I don't want to bother Provi, so I heat some cider and pour it into a thermos. I gather sweaters and mugs for her and Blue Suit, slip on my Wellingtons, and head to the dunes.

The sky is gray and the cold sand crunches under my feet. The surf, churned up from last night's storm, caps the waves with beige foam. Driftwood litters the beach.

A foghorn blows out in Nantucket Sound.

The landscape has changed. No, I realize *I* have changed. Something frightens me about the water—it seems relentless and threatening.

I hand a sweater to Blue Suit and pour him a cup of cider. He knows it's Jack's sweater. He stares at it, frozen. "Please put it on," I say. He nods silently and slips it on.

I walk down to sit beside Caroline. I wrap the blanket around our shoulders. She combs the fringe with her fingers. I pour her a cup of cider, and she takes it. The rising steam makes droplets on her eyelashes and her eyebrows.

The air smells of apples and cinnamon and the sea. We sip our cider in silence.

Later that evening, after the children have been put to bed, I sit, vodka in hand. I press the glass to my forehead. I must think. My mind is numb and doesn't respond, as if worn out. Concentrate. I must figure it out. I can depend on no one. I must trust no one. I must protect the children.

I have no weapons to defend us. I have but one thing—my image as the president's widow. For what it is worth, this is the weapon I will deploy.

A storm howls outside. The waves pound against the shore, the whitecaps frothy and furious. Wind whirls around the house, sleet slamming against the window like rice. As jagged flashes of lightning shoot across the sky, bare black branches scratch against the pale gray horizon. Thunder rumbles through the ground, cracking like gunshot. The room blinks light, then dark, like the end trailer of a movie reel.

The storm makes everyone subdued, and I am left to my own thoughts. The dogs lie by the fire. A knock on the door. The dogs erupt, barking, scrambling to the door. A Blue Suit lets himself in. A stranger follows behind, drenched, eyes bewildered like a new servant at Frankenstein's castle. His soaked hat shines, and a stream of droplets fall from the brim onto his nose. Provi makes a fuss and takes his raincoat and hat. I invite him over to the fire. I offer him a whiskey, which he gratefully accepts. I pour one for myself.

After handing him his drink, I sit across from him in a yellow leather wingback chair. He's a man of about fifty who wears thick glasses, an old tweed jacket, brown corduroy pants, and L. L. Bean boots—the uniform for New England writers.

I know what I want from him and am pretty sure I can get it. I proceed cautiously. I pull one of the puppies up onto my lap to hide my nervous hands. "What can I do for you, Mr. White?"

He looks alarmed, afraid I've forgotten I invited him, afraid he's somehow bungled the date or time. But no, the Secret Service agent was expecting him. He shifts in his seat and begins to stutter an apology when I rescue him.

"Look at your shoes! They're soaking. We must get those off you." I kneel in front of him and unlace his shoes. He's flabbergasted. He thinks I've lost my mind. I hand his shoes to Provi, instructing her to dry them, then open the closet door and pull out a pair of men's sheep-shearing slippers from Scotland. I slip them on his feet. His eyes are wide with disbelief. "Yes," I say, "they're Jack's."

"Mrs. Kennedy, I can't—"

"You must . . . for me. If you caught a cold coming out to see me, I'd be devastated. Besides, Jack doesn't need them."

He swallows hard as if I've slugged him in the stomach.

"Provi is warming up some soup for you. Would you like a sandwich?"

"No, thank you, Mrs. Kennedy. I had dinner."

"We have the most delicious Genoa salami, and prosciutto from Perugia that's simply exquisite. I'll ask Provi to make us something to nibble on."

When I return from the kitchen, White starts to get up, then sits again, his face pinched and anxious. "I'm so grateful you braved this weather to come see me," I say.

"When I got your call . . . I want to do anything I can to help."

"Thank you." I listen to the crackling fire, waiting until he nervously sips from his drink. "I have great respect for your writing. Your prose is lean and evocative, and I've always sensed you had a certain understanding of Jack's administration."

"I admired your husband tremendously, Mrs. Kennedy."

"I know." The poor man is close to tears. Who knew reporters could be sensitive? "I believe you have an ability to see things in a historical context. What you wrote in *Life* about Jack's campaign was insightful and quite moving."

"Thank you," he whispers, then sips his whiskey long and hard. His eyes close halfway—apparently it's a better grade of whiskey than he's used to.

"I'd like you to consider writing an article about Jack. I realize it's a lot to ask," I say, knowing any reporter in the United States would do anything to be sitting across from the widow in Jack's slippers. "More than policy or social programs, Jack empowered our imagination. He led us to believe that each one of us could become something greater and could contribute to society. Jack used to love to listen to this old Victrola we have, late at night. His favorite song was from *Camelot,* and I've been thinking about the lyrics: 'Don't let it be forgot, that once there was a spot, for one brief, shining moment that was known as Camelot.' There will never be another Camelot."

"With all due respect, Mrs. Kennedy, isn't it stretching things a bit to compare Jack's administration to Camelot?"

"Perhaps. What I'm trying to get at is that Jack gave so much to this nation, something intangible and wonderful, and I'm afraid we will slip into cynicism. Does that make sense?"

"I follow you," he says noncommittally.

"If anything can be salvaged from Jack's death, let it be his idealism—his love of our country, his belief in the worth of service to our country. Please, Mr. White, our nation is in emotional turmoil. We need something to cling to—an idea."

I think I am winning him over. When we're done, White wonders if he can get his article in the next issue. "Why don't you use the typewriter here?" I offer, eager to have him get the story out before his editorial instincts kick in. He types it up and I review it—the word *Camelot* tops the story. Nearly bursting with his scoop, he calls in the story immediately.

The myth is launched. I've done the best I can to protect my children. I have cashed in my insurance policy—the myth of Jack, of Camelot—a myth so alluring that all the reporters and commentators will neglect to probe deeply. The secrets will come out, as all secrets eventually do. I pray by that time the children will have spent their childhood loving their father and will be old enough to understand and forgive him.

As soon as we move into the Harriman house, Caroline gets sick. It's not serious—a winter cold—but I nurse her night and day. Her illness saves me. I read to her, feed her soup, rub her feet with Vicks VapoRub, and bring her juice and aspirin. This becomes a religious ritual, healing me, freeing me to forget, forcing me to focus on what is important—the future of my children.

My grief, I realize, is essentially self-pity. This thought may help me find my way out. I need courage. Soon I must begin house-hunting.

Johnson is a man who says one thing while meaning another.

"Jackie, stay as long as you need," he says to me, while later I hear him bellow to an aide, "Why can't I sleep in my own house?"

"Jackie, anything you need, just tell me," he says, but the walls have ears and report him saying, "I've bent over backwards for that woman. I'm tired of this bullshit."

"Jackie, why don't you drop by on Christmas morning with the children," he says to me, when I know all he wants are publicity photos of the Kennedy children under the White House Christmas tree, unwrapping gifts from President Johnson.

"Jackie, please come to the White House for dinner. We miss you," he says, when I know he wants me to bring to his dinner parties what I brought to Jack's—sparkle, glamour, wit. I couldn't manage that even if I wanted to.

"Jackie, I'm dedicating the Rose Garden to you," he says. What he won't do to try to get a photo of me and him together!

"Jackie, you know you're always in my thoughts," and I know his thoughts are on the government in exile, Bobby and me, which he fears is plotting his overthrow.

"Jackie, would you be my ambassador to France? How about Mexico?" he asks. I know he yearns to get me out of the country and out of his hair.

I know the game well and reply sweetly, "You and Lady Bird have always been so kind to me. Make sure you take a nap. When Jack started taking naps, it made him a new man." What he wants from me are not health tips. "I love you," I say. "I love you," he says, neither of us meaning it.

I tell Bobby and he laughs perniciously. "That old fox doesn't know what he's up against."

"Of course not."

But . . . did I make a mistake? Maybe I should take an ambassadorship. Would my children be safer in another country? More anonymous? Would our lives be more interesting?

No. I'm not rich enough to be an ambassador. Tish once told me that when she worked for Evangeline and David Bruce at the American embassy in Paris, they entertained eight thousand people on July 4. Out of their own pocket, they paid for two thousand bottles of wine, two hundred bottles of Cointreau, two hundred bottles of cognac, and 37,000 items of food. The cost must have been staggering.

If I had financial security, I might have the courage. If I did not care for Bobby and want to please him.

Sometimes I'm happy when I should be sad, and then there are times when just the opposite is true. When I sort through Jack's things, I'm happy. When John shows me his soldier's march, I'm sad. When I think about making love to Bobby, I'm happy. When I make love to Bobby, I'm sad.

Bobby stops by the house every day, wearing Jack's old clothes, his hair recently tinged with gray, his dagger eyes lifeless, his speech halting as if he isn't sure life is worth the effort. He comes to me for love.

When Bobby is here, I can't help but compare the two. Bobby is lighter, more agile, his touch tender, his kisses soft, then hard. He loves foreplay. He doesn't mind showing his emotions or being silly. He lies beside me and touches my arm, my breasts, admiring their shape, memorizing, almost worshipping, the textures, colors, and smells. He touches me and watches to see how I react. He makes my whole body into a sex organ.

As much as Jack wanted sex, he didn't seem to enjoy it, a mad rush to orgasm. He didn't savor it. He didn't play.

I reached a certain level of intimacy with Jack, but I always felt that 30 percent of his mind was thinking about something else. It was frustrating, because I sensed that he knew what love was, what intimacy was, but that he didn't want to get caught up it, as if in losing himself in love, he feared losing his direction, feared that he might question his drive and ambition. I felt Jack disconnect during sex— my body could have been any woman's body—and as I saw him drift away, I, too, disconnected from my body, feeling less and less until my arousal disappeared.

Bobby is entirely different. Each time we make love, I feel him reaching deeper and deeper inside of me—in loving me, he discovers new resources in himself.

I can't help but wonder if Bobby and I had had sex before Jack died—our mutual attraction has always been there—if I had known this was possible in sex, if I had been able to draw Jack deeper into myself, to nourish him, somehow he would be alive today.

I no longer blame myself for Jack's death, but had I been more aware, had I been the person I wish I were rather than the person I am, maybe I could have saved him.

I sit on the floor in the living room of a house I just bought. Already it feels like a mistake.

My eyes fill with angry tears, but I am not angry. I don't have the energy to be angry.

It is a three-story brick Georgian in Georgetown, much like the first house Jack and I bought at 3307 N Street. I didn't have time to figure out what is truly best for the children, so I did what I've done before. This time without Jack. Now I see that it was foolish to try to re-create the joy we had setting up our house after Caroline's birth. This place feels empty and temporary. It is not a home, but a shadow of home I once had.

I unpack boxes that we never unpacked when we moved into the White House, boxes filled with scrapbooks, photos, books, souvenirs from trips we took together, Caroline's drawings. I choke back sobs and have to remind myself to breathe.

I swallow my emotions and work on automatic pilot—books go on the bookshelf, pictures on the wall, goblets in the cupboard, clothes in the closet, toys in the kids' rooms. Decorating decisions are too much. I called Billy Baldwin to duplicate John's and Caroline's rooms from the White House.

My efforts are useless. I am creating the artifice of a home, like hanging up pictures in a hotel room. I tell myself I'm doing it for the children, but I wonder if they wouldn't be happier someplace else.

Caroline comes and sits on a box, kicking at crunched-up balls of newspaper. She talks to me about one of the puppies, eager for attention, totally unaware that I hear almost nothing of what she says.

I cling to my children's simple needs—food, love, attention—to keep me sane. Without them, I would try to follow Jack.

Tour buses thunder by the house, blocking the narrow street, blocking my neighbors from leaving their homes. Their diesel engines poison the air. The floor vibrates, the windows rattle. They set up picnic tables and director's chairs across the street, binoculars trained on our windows. We live like moles, drawing the curtains to keep out their desperate, prying eyes.

We are political prisoners.

It takes a major act of courage simply to leave the house. I fight an urge to run back inside.

When I take Caroline to school, policemen split the crowd from our door to the car. This morning I open the curtains to let in the sun and look right in the face of a teenager who is standing on a friend's shoulders, his face pressed against the window, nose flattened, palms spread. He kisses the glass leaving a smear of saliva. When the children leave the house, strange women grab at them, shouting their names, moaning prayers, reaching out like frenzied religious zealots to kiss the shroud of Saint Francis.

Bravely, John turns as we climb the front steps. "Why are you taking my picture? My daddy's dead."

Day and night they chant, "Jackie! Jackie!" When they start breaking things, the police drive them away, but the next morning they're back. I can't even walk the dogs without putting them in the car and taking them to an obscure park, so the task falls to one of the Secret Service men. Our mailbox has been stolen, our bushes denuded. I walked out yesterday and a brick was missing from our sidewalk.

"What do they want, Mommy?" asks Caroline.

I have no idea. Are they waiting for a miracle? "They're all very sad Daddy died, and they want us to know they care."

"We know that. Why don't they go away?"

"When they feel better, they'll leave."

"I hope they feel better soon. This is weird."

I smile and continue brushing her soft fine hair. She has no idea the solace she gives me.

I recall the joy of wandering through Paris, and long to walk down the street and say good morning to strangers without being afraid, a simple privilege most people have. I long for that funny exchange with someone you don't know, when you walk away feeling great, and you feel for a moment that life is good, and you are connected somehow to all people, and they would all be your friends if only you had time to get to know them. I long to be anonymous just for a day, like Audrey Hepburn in *Roman Holiday,* to meet a man whom I will never see again, to enjoy that pure, invigorating feeling of talking to someone who doesn't know anything about you, but who makes you rethink who you are.

The joy of anonymity is lost to me and my children, the simple pleasure of discovering another human spirit.

I realize being anonymous in a crowd is one of the great pleasures in life.

At night I lie in bed fully clothed, afraid to sleep, thinking I'll get up and go through some more of Jack's papers. I have a vodka in my left hand, a cigarette in the other.

My eyelids close and I feel myself floating, rocking gently back and forth in a gondola. Jack sits beside me in a white polo shirt, and we watch the gondolier's back, red-and-white-striped, as he poles us through Venice. Jack reaches under my cotton shift, under my panties, probing with his fingers. People in the Gothic windows and on the banks of the canals point at us, laughing. The gondolier glances over his shoulder and gives me a lecherous grin. I push Jack's hand away, but he tells me it's okay—people want to see us make love.

The sun is hot, glaring off the canal waters. Excited, my body moves to the rhythm of Jack's fingers, his head rocking back and forth, blocking out the sun like a camera shutter.

Then, between the bursts of glare, I see, on a bridge arched over the canal, a man with a rifle aimed at us. He shoots. My head shatters like pink glass, which rains down over the canal. The top of my head with a pink pillbox hat flies off and lands on a woman's lap in another gondola. The woman tosses my scalp into the filthy water, brushes off my hat with a horse-grooming brush, then places it on her head like a tiara.

I see my scalp floating in the water, my hair pulsing in the waves like a sea anemone. A second shot rings out.

I wake up panting, my blouse soaked with sweat. I look in the corners of the room for Jack or the assassin, under the drapes, in the shadow of the divan.

I smell smoke. My cigarette is burning a hole in the bedspread. I rub out the red-edged hole with the palm of my hand, then twist the butt in an ashtray.

My nights are wracked with nightmares. Sometimes I am riding in a Cadillac or on a yacht or in a horse and carriage in Central Park. Each time, I see the assassin before he shoots me. My blood rains down over the earth, my scalp with a pink pillbox hat flying off like a kite with a broken string.

I stumble over and open the window. The cold air blasts my face. In the dark across the street, I see a dozen faces of my faithful fans, startled, blinking awake. I slam shut the window and draw the curtains.

Mary Gallagher and I start the long process of going through Jack's papers. I open a box of papers from his desk drawer in the Oval Office. I find two clippings that Jack kept from my trip to India and a French exercise book. At first I think the exercise book must be Caroline's, but then recognize his handwriting.

"He was trying to learn French," says Mary. "He wanted it to be a surprise for you. He was taking lessons from Caroline's teacher."

"He must have loved me," I say, surprised at the disbelief in my own voice. Mary looks embarrassed and busies herself with another box.

Gifts from the grave. My anger dissipates; my loss deepens.

It is a cold, crisp February evening. I part the curtains and look outside. The sun fades early, leaving the street painted violet and gray. Frost sparkles on the iron railings. A few snowflakes drift in the air. Our vigil has dwindled to a dozen hardy souls, bundled up in blankets, some huddled around propane stoves.

Caroline comes from behind, takes my hand, and peeks out. "They look cold, Mommy."

White scarves of vapor billow from their mouths as they breathe. "Yes, they do."

"Could we make them some hot chocolate?"

I've been so worried about Caroline, wan and silent, more so than John. This is the first sparkle in her eye in weeks. I glance again at the mob. They don't look so terrifying now. "Yes, why not?"

We go into the kitchen. I pour a gallon of milk into a stockpot. Caroline stands on a stool by the stove and stirs.

"How many cups are in a gallon?" I ask.

"Sixteen," she says without hesitating.

I run my finger down the page of a Betty Crocker cookbook. "We need one-quarter cup of sugar per cup. . . ."

"That's four cups of sugar."

"And two tablespoons of cocoa powder per cup. . . ."

"That's two cups of cocoa. Thirty-two tablespoons."

"Smarty-pants."

John charges into the kitchen, wanting to help. "I wanna stir, I wanna stir."

"You're too short," says Caroline firmly.

Before an argument erupts, I let John count as I add tablespoons of cocoa to the pot: "Twenty-eight, twenty-nine . . . uh . . . twenty-nine plus one . . ."

"Thirty," prompts Caroline.

Just before it boils, I ladle cocoa into twelve mugs, then place them on two trays. Blue Suit takes one tray, I take the other. The children put on their coats. I get a nervous feeling in my stomach, worried that the mob will rush us, spilling the cocoa on us, burning our skin, but Caroline's face is determined. She opens the door.

Cold air slaps our faces and tingles our scalps. Snowflakes catch in our eyelashes.

The huddled figures glance up, almost as if we're disturbing them. As we carefully descend, they slowly unfold their frozen bodies.

"You want some cocoa?" shouts John.

They mumble affirmatives and reach tentatively for the mugs like refugees stumbling upon a lawn party.

Curious at our unusual behavior, the dogs slink down the steps behind us. Shannon bites at the snowflakes while the others sneak a pee on the neighbors' bushes.

"Daddy loved hot cocoa," says Caroline.

I hear one woman whimper. Silently they drink their cocoa, pressing the hot mugs to their chests between sips. The dogs sniff their shoes, their coats, their crotches, and the refugees scratch behind the dogs' ears and bury their fingers in their warm fur.

"Bye," says John. "Mommy says you can keep the mugs."

When we turn and climb back up the stairs, I realize that by some miracle, no one has taken our picture.

We escape to Antigua for Easter at Bunny Mellon's—Bobby and I, Lee and Stas. No Ethel.

Bobby and I water-ski on Nonsuch Bay. We stroll on Mill Reef Beach, arms around each other. We read Aeschylus to each other. As a crescent moon rises over Half Moon Bay, we sit on the terrace, quietly holding hands. When the evening dampness brings out the smells of jasmine and hibiscus, we dance, looking into each other's eyes. For a moment it feels like a honeymoon, a luscious escape, until I realize that for me, there is no escape. I live in a prison of love and dependence. Bobby is my prison guard.

Perhaps if we did not cling together like two children lost in the woods, perhaps if we did not swear never to leave each other, perhaps if his passion didn't take me deep inside myself, deep below the crust of consciousness where my blood turns into hot lava, perhaps if he did not whisper in my ear the things every woman desires to hear—"I can't live without you, Jackie, you are all women to me"—and those words that Jack could say only under duress—"I love you, Jackie"—his lips on my neck, his hand tracing the soft spot below my breasts where my ribs meet, whispering as he nibbles my ear—"I love you, Jackie"—perhaps then I could be free of the Kennedys, free of this widow farce, free to leave this country forever, to live in France and send my children to school in Switzerland. Free to be myself.

No. I don't have enough money to be free.

Now that the estate has been settled, I discover Jack left me about $70,000 and the interest from his trust, about $100,000 per year. That would be more than enough if my children weren't Kennedys. I want to work, but the Kennedys will never let me take a job. I know how it feels to be a penniless stepchild in a wealthy family, never granted the same status as the other children, always knowing you are the poor relative, always knowing your social position is precarious without the security of power or money. I will not have Caroline and John feel so vulnerable.

I feel so trapped. I begin to cry.

I hear Jack's voice—*For Christ's sake, Jackie, what are you crying about now?*—but it's Bobby who folds me into his arms, kissing me, letting me sob. "I love you, Jackie. I'll never let anyone hurt you or the kids. Never."

What I hear is that he'll never let me go.

NEW YORK

od bless you, Jackie! We love you, Jackie! We adore you, Jackie!"
As I step out of my car onto the sidewalk before my newly purchased pre-war apartment on Fifth Avenue, a congregation of fifteen appears stunned, as if I am an apparition of the Virgin of Guadalupe. They applaud and shout, reaching for me with their fingertips across the police barricade. What are they applauding for? They hold out photos of me to sign, babies to kiss. Two professionals blind me with their flashes, squatting, lunging around bodies, their cameras whirring and clicking—*pop, pop, pop*—as oblivious to the traffic as hunters to the dewy moss and forest flowers beneath their boots.

The Blue Suits plunge forward, gently pushing back the crowd. My heart races, terrified—I plaster a smile on my face and look straight ahead. I wish I could disappear.

I walk through a black wrought-iron gate into a lobby of black-and-white marble tile. Above, a crystal chandelier over a table with a vase of flowers. The elevator takes me up fifteen floors to a foyer with gold-framed mirrors and French landscape paintings.

The apartment opens into a large gallery with fourteen rooms radiating out. The living room is forty feet long. Its fourteen windows look out over Fifth Avenue and Central Park. The dining room is wallpapered in red damask and has a view of the George Washington Bridge. The furniture is eclectic, antiques mixed with comfortable sofas. In the corner, a large telescope aims at Central Park. I step outside on a wraparound terrace, where crabapple trees bloom in the cerulean blue planters so common in Provence.

The rabble is far below. I can't see them without leaning over the side.

A cool breeze blows over the park, carrying the scent of cherry blossoms. My panic subsides. I take a deep breath. I have gotten through another day.

This is how I live, sleepwalking through the motions of daily living. Memories float into my consciousness, usually of Jack and the children, down by the beach, with the dogs. I fight off panic, stabbing my leg with my nails, wrenching myself back to the present. I laugh and play with the children, but it feels hollow. I fear I have permanently lost my capacity for joy.

I have to admit that I'm lonely.

I know I can love. I feel it bottled up inside me. This life with Bobby is stran-gling my heart. I need to move on, but how?

Jack used to talk about how he felt the navy looked down on him because he was a captain who lost his ship. I feel that way about losing Jack—that somehow I'm damaged goods.

I want to live again. I want to love again. I want to live the fantasy of love, the airy dream of love, the drunken spinning of love. I ache for that love.

But I am afraid. I feel so vulnerable, as if my skin were healing from horrible burns, my nerves raw and sensitive.

The world seems new and terrifying.

"You need to keep your juices flowing," Lee tells me. "If Brando can't do it, no one can."

Lee wants to cheer me up, wants me to get out and see people, to stop "mop-ing around." This is what they all tell me, and I accept that they must be right, be-cause I don't trust myself to make decisions anymore; because to make decisions, you must weigh things by their value, and nothing for me has value any longer. She means to be kind, my younger sister. She arranges a double date with the Greatest Living Actor and his producer, whom she's dating, who worships the Actor and wants to meet the famous Widow, so the four of us go to a swank dance club on Lexington Avenue, the famous Actor, the famous Widow, the famous Producer, the famous Princess.

"We'll have fun," Lee says.

Lee and I giggle like teenyboppers because it seems so naughty: she, still mar-ried; me, a widow—playing at bad girls, even as we approach middle age. The club is expensive. The excitement and noise take my breath away. We all drink martinis and smoke.

Across from me the Actor radiates apathy. His body is as dense as lead, muscu-lar with a layer of protective fat like a wrestler. He reminds me that in the not-too-distant past we all evolved from apes. But there is something oddly feminine about him, the shine of his skin, his long eyelashes, his sleepy almond eyes, his full lips. He leans back in his seat, like a bored teenager sitting out his detention. He despises my class—"horse ladies," he calls us—but he's mildly curious about my act.

"Whatever happened to that pink suit?" he asks.

He is offensive in every way. Yet, Lee is right—I do feel pulled in by him, a desire that is half revulsion, half lust.

The Sexiest Man Alive. If Brando can't get your pump primed, no one can.

On the dance floor, under the pulsing lights to the throbbing music, he rubs against me like a bear against a tree, his eyes half closed, his eyelashes fluttering, watching in scorn.

I want to sink with him, follow him into the quicksand, cover myself in mud. He's revolting, and I want to rub him all over me.

Is this what Jack liked? Anonymous sex. Sex that feels like a punishment. Sex that has nothing to do with love or attraction or pleasure, and everything to do with dancing with death.

I sneak my palm under his sweater and feel his slippery skin and a soft roll of fat. I whisper in the Actor's ear, "Would you like to see my French Impressionist drawings?"

Suddenly five paparazzi, informed by the dessert chef, burst into the club, flashbulbs popping, their hard-soled shoes scuffling on the dance floor, shoving aside elegantly clad couples, spilling a woman's drink—*pop, pop, pop*—wrestling with the waiters to get another shot, and you are there, grinning at me as if you have caught me shoplifting.

Lee and I stand gaping, but M.B., who has had much experience with these fellows, jolts awake, grabs me by the hand, and pulls me toward the swinging door to the kitchen. The Producer throws a hundred-dollar bill on the table, grabs Lee, and follows.

As we dash through the kitchen, a soufflé crashes to the floor. Alarmed cooks spin around, guarding the handles of sizzling skillets. A dishwasher shows us down a hallway, over crates of tomatoes and lettuce, over empty bottles, mops, cans of grease, under swinging animal carcasses, into a dark alley.

You follow me, your long camera lens pointed at me like a missile launcher. I wait for the bullet to rip open my chest.

M.B. yanks me down the alley to the street and flags a cab. We climb in, giggling nervously, thinking in our excited panic that this is almost fun, because this game is new and we don't yet know they will come to terrorize our lives. But M.B. knows. He throws a twenty at the cabdriver and shouts, "Lose them," like in a gangster flick. We look over our shoulders to see the men with cameras running out of the club, waving down cars that aren't even cabs. As you stumble around the corner, you lower your weapon and let us go, spitting on the sidewalk.

We flee to my place on Fifth Avenue and ride the elevator up. A frowning Blue

Suit lets us inside. Our giggling begins to sound forced and tinny, our escapade showing itself as tawdry silliness.

Shamelessly I try to re-create the demon dance. I turn on the record player. The Princess and the Producer dance. The Actor and the Widow dance.

The Actor has taken off his shoes—there's a hole in one of his socks. He staggers against me, drunk. Desperately I cling to the dark erotic feeling I had. I tell myself a hole in a sock is nothing, merely the absence of yarn, but I am disgusted.

The moment has been lost; everything is different. The children are sleeping down the hall. Blue Suit stands outside my door. The maid clatters dishes in the kitchen. The furniture, the art, the books press their normalcy on me. I am no longer anonymous. I am the former First Lady. I fight the sober dawn of reality. I want to return to the devil's harem, to sink in murky darkness, in foul lust, in teasing, erotic pain.

I pull his buttocks to me. His body tenses. Slowly he pushes me away and takes my hand from his shoulder. "A lady like you shouldn't bite her nails."

Within a few minutes he finds his leather bomber jacket and stumbles out.

"Is that her?" "Where?" "Over in the corner, whispering into the ear of . . . her brother-in-law?" "Which one? Bobby?" "Isn't he married?" "Look at them! Just look at them!"

New Yorkers like to observe.

I imagine how they see us, spotted holding hands under the table and nuzzling in the bars at the Algonquin and the Sherry-Netherlands. I wear a white cashmere turtleneck and slacks; Bobby, in a polo shirt and khaki pants, looking rumpled and sleepy. We sit very close in a corner banquette far from the glow of the Tiffany lamp over the bar. I don't hide the smile on my face. A pained smile? they guess. A lazy postcoital smile? Bobby drinks Johnnie Walker Black Label, taking big gulps as if it were medicine. I sip a gin and tonic. As the jazz trio plays Cole Porter to a nearly empty bar, his hand disappears under the table. I shift closer to him and lay my head on his shoulder. In an impulsive gesture, a gesture so relaxed and graceful that they hardly notice it, I lift my chin and kiss his neck. Sometimes he is observed to laugh at something I whisper in his ear, not a boisterous laugh that shows his headlight-white Kennedy smile but a sad chuckle. Sometimes he is seen hunched over the table on his elbows, his face in his hands. Is he crying? they wonder. When he looks up, his face appears anguished with deep crevices in his forehead, his normally clenched jaw slack, his lips moist. I sweep my palm down the side of his face. I cradle his hand between mine, bend down to kiss it, then, with my head tilted to one side, hold it gently as if keeping warm an injured bird.

"Did they sleep together in the hotel?"

"We didn't see them go up."

"Those two have been through so much."

"Don't you think if something was really going on, they'd be more discreet?"

We are observed going to the ballet, the opera, and the theater, me wearing gorgeous gowns once worn at White House concerts. Tongues wag, scandalized— "The colors! Pink, lime green, baby blue! She's a widow!" Bobby, in a black tux, appears bashful. Why bashful? Because he, a Kennedy, doesn't know much about classical music, doesn't really like it, and feels out of place among people who know so much more than he. We appear as a couple, smiling for the cameras, mine gleeful, his slightly goofy. He takes my arm and leads me to our box seats, where, during the long second movement of Mahler's Fifth Symphony, his hand is observed to reach for mine.

Afterward we are observed entering Bobby's sister's apartment at 950 Fifth Avenue at two in the morning, walking leisurely hand in hand.

"He's a member of her family, after all."

"But aren't the Smiths out of town?"

We are observed skiing in Sun Valley and in Aspen, in New Hampshire and Vermont, riding together up a ski lift, me clutching him, laughing as he pretends to jump. We are seen piled together in a toboggan, grabbing each other, tumbling into a snowbank. Soaking in a steaming hot tub, our arms stretched languidly over the rim, Bobby clutching a cool drink, I am observed, just for a moment, as if to tease him, to straddle his lap. Later, in the lounge in front of the roaring fire, as we curl up together on the worn plaid couch, the flames casting dark shadows behind the exposed timbers, the sound of carolers singing below, he lays his head in my lap, and I am seen combing his bangs with my fingers, slowly, rhythmically, as if calming a feverish child.

"At least they were there with their children. Weren't the Lawfords there as well?"

"Yeah, but where was Ethel?"

"She stayed home. The young ones are too little to ski."

"It's her own fault, letting herself get pregnant again."

"How many do they have now? Nine? Ten?"

We are observed walking hand in hand on the beach at Montego Bay, me in a teeny bikini, our arms around each other, skin touching skin. We are seen walking down the streets of Provincetown and Chatham arm in arm, and, on Long Island, where we both rent summer places, we are seen stumbling out of a horse stall with straw in our hair, he fastening his belt, me stretching my arms wide, head back, laughing, spinning like a schoolgirl in a pinafore.

"Frolicking!"

"Nuzzling!"

"Hugging!"

"Kissing!"

And in the early morning, just after dawn, we are seen—by a Pakistani taxi driver, a black postal worker, an Italian bread-delivery man, a Puerto Rican maid, an actress rushing home from a bad date, a gay couple, and an insomniac with a toothache—exiting various hotel suites.

"Who wears a strapless evening gown at five in the morning?"

"Have they no shame?"

The tongues wag, and I don't care.

Bobby is draining me. I don't have the strength for him. He needs me too much. He's become an obligation I can't seem to shake. He thinks he's taking care of the widow, but it's me who gives him strength. It's killing me.

I keep thinking his desperation will fade, but it doesn't. Again and again he says he's in love with me, has loved me from the first time he saw me, but I know it isn't love. There is no future here. He cannot divorce. Not ever. It would be easier for Prince Philip to divorce the queen than for Bobby to leave Ethel. She tolerates us, barely, because that's what Kennedy women do. Perhaps she understands that it is part of his grieving.

But he isn't getting past it.

"Screwing isn't going to bring him back, Bobby."

He looks as though he's been slugged, and immediately I'm sorry. *Compassion,* Jack tells me. Compassion for how long? I am ready to move on—my patience is running thin.

He wants me to stand by him as he runs for senator from New York. I want no part of it. I am not his wife—I am done with politics. He can't co-opt me as if I were Jack's campaign manager. I was not born for self-sacrifice, yet this is what he wants, cloaking it in noble-sounding words. I cannot live up to his expectations. I need a life of my own.

A shout goes up when we enter the Greek restaurant. Men jump to their feet, clapping. *"Megalos!"* The big boss. Each one offers a chair at his table. Ari waves politely and leads me by the elbow. The restaurant owner, a lively spider of a man, runs up to Ari and kisses him on both cheeks. They talk in rapid-fire Greek. The owner points to a private table tucked in the corner, but Ari gestures with his chin to one in front.

"Don't worry," he says to me. "These people are my friends. No paparazzi will get in here."

As soon as we sit down, a bottle of champagne arrives. Ari waves his acknowledgment to a fat man dining under the mural of Ithaka in the shadow of a potted palm.

The restaurant is dark, lit by candles and wall sconces. The tablecloths are white. The patrons are comfortably dressed. It is a restaurant run for Greeks by Greeks.

Ari's mood is festive. He orders a little of everything. "This is real Greek food," he says proudly. Soon the table is covered with little white saucers filled with three or four bites: mousaka, dolmades, souvlaki, octopus, eggs of sea urchins, crisp fried fish the size of a finger. When I ask Ari why he's eating so little, he says, "I don't want to take my eyes off of you."

He removes his darkened glasses and sets them on the table. His eyes have huge puffy bags beneath them, and his skin is darkly tanned, with large, visible pores. I think of ostrich leather. He sweats through his fine Italian suits, making dark oval rings like feedbags under his arms. Under his spicy cologne, he smells of sardines.

Oh, yes, Aristotle Onassis is an ugly man.

Yet he radiates energy, passionately involved in everything around him. His voice is low, raspy, and very sexy. His hands are cool and soft.

The dishes set before us are swimming in gleaming liquids—glistening olive oils, gelatinous meat sauces, thick tomato sauces, slippery lemon sauces. I take a bite of a fig soaked in liquor and honey. Flavors—oranges, hazelnuts, raspberries, cinnamon, whiskey, and something earthy like the warm mossy smell of a pine forest—burst in my mouth.

"You're smiling," he says.

"The food is so . . . sensual."

"A little sensuality is good for the soul."

"Thank you."

"For what?"

"For bringing me here. You won't believe this, but I hardly ever get to dine out."

"Because of the paparazzi?"

"Yes. Jack and I hardly ever went to restaurants."

"Not even before he was president? I'm sorry. We don't need to talk—"

"No, it's okay." I feel myself blushing. "Jack hated to linger over dinner. As soon as he took his last bite, his body tensed, ready to go. I dreaded eating with him in restaurants. Sitting was uncomfortable for him. Sometimes I think there was more to it—that he feared the intimacy of sharing a meal." I find myself getting emotional. "I'm sorry. How rude of me, to be talking about my husband."

Ari wipes the corners of his mouth delicately with his beefy fingers. "This is not a state dinner. You don't need to follow protocol. This is food and friendship. Relax."

His understanding moves me. "Everyone has this exalted image of Jack. They don't want to know that he was just a man, a flawed, insecure man."

"Every man is insecure."

"Not you."

"Sure, I am. What makes me want to be around beautiful women? Because I look like a troll—a rich, powerful troll."

"I think of you more as a pirate." I see this pleases him. "A pirate that plunders the world and steals off with the princess."

"That's exactly what I intend to do."

My temples tingle and I feel warm. There is something atavistic about him, something primal, something real. A man of appetites—for food, love, sex, and life. I find myself . . . aroused?

But he is ugly. Oh, brother, is he ugly.

A fat woman in a long dark blue dress and maroon shawl walks across a small stage in back. Her black-dyed hair is wound up in a bun. She calmly looks around the stage as if remembering what transpired there long ago in her childhood. At first I take her for the restaurant owner's mother. She walks deliberately, her palms pressed together in front of her. Young musicians—a guitar, fiddle, bass, and accordion—scurry around her, setting up stools, arranging themselves. One brings her a glass of water, which she accepts and sets on a small table placed beside her. She turns to the audience and bows her head. She looks as if she's falling asleep.

Ari watches me watch her, grinning from ear to ear.

The musicians begin to play a slow folk tune in a minor key. It sounds like a cross between Italian folk and Arabic music. The fat woman stands perfectly still, then lifts her head to sing.

Her voice is husky, strident, and nasal. Her song is sad and mysterious. Each note seems squeezed out of her body, a plaintive moan filled with torment. It is beautiful and heart-wrenching. Listening to her is almost physically painful.

I blink back tears, dig my nails into my palms, and shake my head—I don't want to spoil the evening. Why did I have to bring up Jack?

"She's a famous rembetíka singer in Greece," says Ari. "It's the music of my people. When the Greek army invaded Turkey in 1921, the Turks retaliated and drove two million refugees of Greek ancestry from their homeland in Asia Minor into the mountains. Many of my family in Smyrna were killed. The lyrics tell of our suffering, exile, poverty, and pain. And, of course"—he smiles—"unrequited love."

"It's extraordinary." I feel as if I have stumbled into a huge dark cavern inside of myself. I begin to think that this strange music and this troll-like man can teach me something I need to know, something about mortality, about my soul.

Ari waves across the restaurant. "Costa! Over here."

I look over my shoulder. A tall, distinguished-looking man dressed in an impeccable English suit makes his way to us between the tables.

"Jacqueline, this is my oldest friend in the world, Costa Gratsos. We grew up together in Smyrna. He's vice president of Victory Carriers, my shipping division. Costa, may I introduce Jacqueline Kennedy, who needs no introduction."

"How do you do?" I say.

"Pleased to meet you." He takes my hand and kisses it, bending low. I notice his lovely, full head of white hair, longish, wavy, combed but not excessively neat. Just above his ear, a few greasy gray hairs stick out. Is he wearing a wig?

"Didn't I tell you she was beautiful?" asks Ari, taking my hand that was just kissed and sandwiching it between his. His palms are soft and cool.

"You are fortunate, Ari, to have such a lovely dinner companion."

"Thank you," I say.

"Your features would look beautiful onstage. But you would need a voice to match your beauty."

"All the world is her stage," says Ari briskly.

"Yes, why limit yourself?" Costa says, smiling obsequiously.

They exchange a few sentences in Greek—Ari does most of the talking, his face suddenly hard and intense.

Costa leans down between Ari and me. He wears the same cologne as Prince Philip of England—rather too much of it. His manner is restrained, too polite, as if he feels he is more deserving of success and fortune than Ari. I get a weird feeling from him.

Costa bows again and leaves us to join another table of diners.

Ari's beaming rascal face is back. "I apologize, Jackie. Business tends to follow me wherever I go."

"Don't apologize. I liked watching you."

He blushes like a schoolboy. "You'll have to forgive Costa—that business about the stage. He is fond of Maria Callas and gets jealous of any other woman I have dinner with."

"I thought it might be something like that."

"It's nothing. You'll like him. Any friend of mine is a friend of his."

"Why don't you marry her?"

"Who? Maria?" A flare of anger shoots across his eyes like a comet, over in a nanosecond. Then he smiles warmly. "Because I plan to marry you."

"How could you!" I scream at Bobby, shaking a newspaper in his face.

He looks startled, standing in the doorway of my apartment in a black tuxedo. "Why aren't you ready for the ballet?"

I fly at him, beating his chest. "I hate you, I hate you, I hate you."

"For crying out loud!" He looks over his shoulder at Blue Suit in the hallway, then pushes me inside my apartment and closes the door. "Jesus, Jackie. What are you talking about?"

"How could you, Bobby?" I say, shaking his shoulders, sobbing, knocking my forehead against his chest. "When will it all end, Bobby? When?"

"Jackie, what are you talking about?"

I fling today's edition of *The New York Times* in his face. Still clueless, he snaps to the page I have folded over, buried in the back of the business section. He glances at the article, then tosses it on the couch. "Oh, that."

"Oh, that? You knew her. You liked her. You probably slept with her. How could you?"

I grab the paper, and read it aloud.

" 'The body of a woman identified as Mary Meyer of Washington, D.C., was discovered today on the towpath along the C&O Canal, where she was known to take early-morning walks. Police investigators describe her murder as an 'execution-style' murder favored by mobsters. "She was hog-tied, then shot below the cheek-bone," reported one forensic specialist, "with her tongue cut out." A young black man was arrested at the scene, then released after questioning. The police are looking for leads and invite the public to come forward with any information that may lead to an arrest.' "

"Why is it always the women who take the fall?" I ask.

"I have no idea what you're talking about."

"Don't you?" I say coldly. "Marilyn, now Mary. You deported Ellen Rometsch before the Senate Rules Committee could talk to her."

"None of that's true, Jackie," he says so calmly that I almost believe him.

"Don't. Just don't!" Wobbly, I back away at least ten feet so I won't feel his sexual pull. "You had Marilyn killed, now Mary. Did you have Phil Graham killed, too? Just because you thought they might embarrass the great Kennedy family? Does human life mean so little to you? They were just women in love."

"I would think you'd be happy. Both women were Jack's mistresses. You hated them."

"Oh, Bobby. I never hated them. You are as ruthless as everyone says you are."

"There's nothing to your story, Jackie. Marilyn was a suicide. And you know Mary. She was into all sorts of mischief. It could've been drug dealers. She was into marijuana, cocaine. Even LSD."

"Oh, Bobby, don't lie to me."

"I would never lie to you, Jackie."

"Dammit! Leave me alone." I run to the other side of my apartment and collapse in a chair, hugging myself. Bobby watches me in silence. "Tell me you didn't do it," I whisper.

He walks over to me, lifts me from the chair, and stares me hard in the face. "I didn't do it."

I believe him and I don't. "I'm sorry, Bobby. I'm sorry for thinking that. It's such a shock. I'm so frightened all the time."

He cradles me in his arms. "There are things you don't understand about politics, Jackie." He kisses me gently. "Hey, I know what this is. You're picking a fight because I'm leaving on a campaign trip."

"Oh, Bobby." I am too weak to fight him, too weak to do anything but melt into his arms, wanting, wanting, wanting my mind to be wiped clean.

"Mommy, Caroline says he looks like a frog."

John grins at his sister. Caroline freezes—her big blue eyes pop open, mortified. He squeals, delighted, dashing out of her reach.

I try hard not to laugh—I mustn't encourage him—saving myself by bending down to slip on my shoes, flats, of course, because Ari is so short. I relax my lips and try to look stern. "You shouldn't tattle on your sister, John."

"Why not? It's true! She said it."

"You shouldn't tattle, because then Caroline might tattle on you, and who is more likely to have something worth tattling about? You or she?"

"Me?"

"What do you think?"

"Oh." His brow furrows, images running through his mind of little-boy secrets that he's sure would shock me. "You mean I should never ever tattle?"

"Not unless it is important."

"How important?"

"It has to be worth losing her trust. Like if someone might get hurt."

"Oh." The concept is too grown-up for him, but he gets the general idea. "Can I go bike in the park?"

"Yes. Be sure to ask Mr. Worth to go with you."

"He follows me whether I ask or not."

"Yes, that's his job. But it is much more polite to ask."

John scampers out of the room. Caroline, who's listened to this exchange, her hands behind her back, worried, says, "I didn't mean frog in a bad way, Mommy."

A laugh explodes from me—delighted at her intelligence, moved by her anxiety about offending me, and, yes, nervous that both she and John like him. "You are perfectly right. He does look like a frog. But he's a very nice frog. You'll see."

She considers this somberly, then brightens. "I guess that makes you a princess."

"Do you think if I kiss him, he'll turn into a prince?"

"Oh, Mommy, you won't kiss him, will you?"

"Could be."

I see how hard she's working not to squinch up her face and say, "Ugh," or "Gross." She is such a dear—she never wants to hurt anyone's feelings.

Ari does treat me like a princess. Every morning he sends me flowers—red roses after a date—with a note signed J.I.L.Y.: Jackie, I love you. Unnoticed, we do the romantic things impecunious young New York couples do when they're in love. We ride to the top of the Empire State Building or take the ferry to Staten Island and back. He rows me in a boat in the lake in Central Park.

His desire for me arouses me. His attentive eyes look deep into me, thawing a frozen black river inside me. He trembles with passion, his body quivering the way Caroline quivers when she runs out of the ocean in May, her first swim of the season. He acts as if he will die if I don't touch him, kiss him, love him.

He is so vital, so energetic, it is hard not to be bowled over by him.

He loves to dance, the tango, the waltz, his body alive with music and rhythm. Kennedy men don't understand dancing—they see it as an unpleasant form of exercise. Ari knows dancing is the language of love. I close my eyes and lean back in his stocky, muscular arms, leading me, turning me, bending me. He makes me feel beautiful and sensuous. He makes me feel like a woman, a woman of the earth, a woman full of color and life. He makes me feel sexy.

He recites poetry to me, not the death poems Jack knew or the jingoistic poems Bobby admires but love poetry, erotic poetry, poetry to seduce a woman, poetry of Sappho, Catullus, Ovid, Pablo Neruda, or—while eating a peach, its warm sweet juices running down his chin—D. H. Lawrence.

I can tell him things I could never tell Bobby, like how frightened I am so much of the time, unable to breathe. How I sometimes want to kill myself. How I sometimes hate the Kennedys. How guilty I feel to be alive and Jack dead. How when I think about my life with Jack, I feel as if daggers are stabbing me, as if my brain is going to explode, and all I want is never to think about him again.

"We Greeks have a word for it: *kaimos*. It means nostalgia for something lost, a painful memory of something that was once pleasurable. A painful presence of an absence."

"I don't want to remember anymore."

"Marry me and you won't."

There is something in his land and his culture that I need. My soul aches for it. I need it to survive.

He understands me better than I understand myself. He knows what I need. What I desire. He loves my children in a way that even Bobby doesn't. He delights in their quirks and mischief, as I do, and respects their tenuous young dignity.

He makes me feel safe.

"Just how rich is rich?"

He owns:

A fleet of fifty oil tankers, each a corporation onto itself.

Pier facilities in Greece.

A bank.

A half of Olympic Towers, a fifty-one story skyscraper in midtown Manhattan.

One-quarter interest in New York's Pierre Hotel.

Olympic Airlines, which includes the local carrier Olympic Airways.

An island in Greece, Skorpios.

A 315-foot yacht, the *Christina*.

Fleets of automobiles and private planes.

Residences in Athens, Skorpios, Monte Carlo, Montevideo, Paris, and New York.

Extensive real estate holdings in Greece.

Millions of dollars' worth of art and jewelry.

Tens of millions in stocks, bonds, and other liquid assets.

"Is he worth a billion dollars?"

"More or less. No one knows."

"Over my dead body!" Bobby rocks back and forth like a bantam rooster, his face gorged with blood, his eyes bloodshot. "I forbid you to marry that rogue."

"You forbid me? Who are you to forbid me anything? I am not your wife!"

"For Christ's sake, Jackie!"

"You reminded me of Jack just then."

Jack's name deflates him a bit. "Oh, Jackie! Not Onassis. He owns half the casinos in Monaco. You can't run casinos without organized crime. He's in bed with the Greek dictators! He does business with Nazi war criminals. He's a gangster, for crying out loud! He was arrested in 1953 for manipulating American laws. Hoover's got a file on him an inch thick."

"You don't want me to marry anyone."

"He's divorced. He isn't Catholic. I will lose five states if you marry him."

"Damn you! Don't you care about anything but getting votes? What about my happiness? I have a right to live my own life. I have a right to love."

"You think he loves you? He's only using you."

"*Et tu, Brute.*"

"I love you, Jackie."

"No, you don't."

"Jackie, I came here to tell you good news, and you spring something like this on me."

"What news?"

"Johnson. He's pulled out of the primary. He's not running for reelection."

"Why not?"

"Who in hell cares? It leaves the pathway open for me. Don't you see? If you marry the Greek, you'll ruin it for me. I need you beside me. You've been through it all. You coached Jack in his speeches. Help me. We'll work together to carry out Jack's dream."

"If you can't win without the support of some helpless widow, maybe you shouldn't be president."

"That's unfair."

"You can't become Jack, you know," I say cruelly.

"I'm not trying to become Jack. I'm doing what he would've wanted me to do."

My anger softens. "They will kill you, too, Bobby. I don't think I could live if that happened."

"They wouldn't dare. I'm too tough for them. Their bullets wouldn't even break my skin."

"Oh, Bobby . . ."

"I don't see why you have to marry at all."

I don't trust the Kennedys. Rose has already complained about my expenses. If anything should happen to Bobby, I fear they will cut me loose without a dime. "I'm not strong enough on my own. I need and want the things every woman needs and wants. Someone I can share my life with. Someone for the children. Someone to grow old with. Someone I can always count on."

"You can count on me."

"No, I can't! It'll be Ethel and you in the White House. There isn't room for two First Ladies. You'll toss me aside. You'll have no choice. Don't you want me to be happy?"

"Why Onassis?"

"Because he wants me."

"At least wait until after the November election. Will you wait? For us?" He kisses my neck and slips his right hand up my inner thigh. "Will you wait?"

SECOND DEATH

*T*he year was 1968. A year of turbulence, of student revolutions, riots, and assassinations. The world was having an epileptic fit, a nervous breakdown, a temper tantrum. The world was cracking up like ice slabs over a stream during a spring thaw. Everything was off balance. Fear raged between rebels and authority, between young and old, between black and white. It was an existential calamity between community and individual, hegemony and independence, and family and self.

It was the end of America and the beginning of America.

Police clubbed demonstrators at the Democratic National Convention in Chicago. Martin Luther King Jr. was assassinated in Memphis. The country exploded—riots in 110 cities, 39 people killed, more than 2,500 injured. Four thousand troops were sent to Washington, D.C. Students at Columbia held hostage a university building for a week, finally ending when a thousand policemen stormed the campus. In Paris *les événements de mai* turned the streets into a war zone of police and student protesters.

The year was 1968. Bobby was murdered.

Five surgeons work on a dead man.

They have worked on him all night at Good Samaritan Hospital in Los Angeles. I arrive by taxi from the airport. As I march into the hospital, nurses part before me like the Red Sea.

I meet Chuck Spalding in the hallway. "How bad is it? Tell me straight."

He squeezes my hand too tightly. "It's not looking good, Jacqueline." He calls me by my proper name—it gives me a burst of authority. I nod while at the same time pulling away his wrist with my left hand, releasing my other hand. I brush Spalding aside and continue down the hall.

I see Ethel in the lounge, Kennedys clinging to her like drones around a queen bee when the temperature drops. The drones look up as I approach. Their faces appear hostile, bewildered, and wild. I stop cold.

Then it hits me like a wave heavy with sand. I am not the wife. I am not the one to make decisions here. *What is my role here?* I ask myself. Comfort the wife, the widow-to-be. I walk toward Ethel. Cautiously.

Several weeks ago, in May, the family was in Hyannis Port celebrating Bobby's victory in the Indiana primary. We were all exuberant, flying high, and carelessly I exclaimed, "Won't it be fun when we're back in the White House." Ethel turned and said archly, "What do you mean 'we'?"

A cold wind blew through my heart. All her bitterness through the years—from the time Bobby kissed me at my wedding and said in front of Ethel, "Jack doesn't know what a lucky guy he is," to now—released with five short words like a primordial vapor from beneath a glacier. I suddenly had new respect for her. For some reason I never thought she had much to do with Bobby, as if she were nothing more than a morning chore, an obligation once met, easily dismissed and forgotten. In five short words, she claimed her right as wife.

That was the last time I had seen her.

As Ethel lifts her head, her face is blank. I'm not sure she recognizes me. The drones give me room to draw near, and I realize what I interpreted as hostility is merely fatigue.

I lay my hand on her shoulder, half expecting her to jump away like a hissing Medusa, but she puts her hand on top of mine. I know it isn't a gesture of forgiveness. She recognizes that I know more than anyone what she is going through.

"Let me see how it's going," I say.

"Please." She squeezes my hand, then drops it.

A surgeon steps out of the operating room for air. He tells me there's no hope, but they're still digging around in his brain for bullet fragments.

We wait for hours. One of the men smuggled in a bottle of Jack Daniel's, and everyone is getting plastered. I step out for half an hour to get coffee for everyone.

When I return, I see they have rolled Bobby into the intensive-care recovery room. Ethel is collapsed beside his bed, her head on his thigh. The respirator thumps and hisses like a sleeping dragon. He is enslaved, shackled by tubes and wires.

His head is wrapped just as Jack's was, and for a moment I see Jack there. I remember the oddest thing—Jack playing with John around the White House pool, teasing him, pulling him down into the water by his trunks, and John turning in mock annoyance and saying, "Daddy's a foo-foo head," Jack laughing, delighted.

I mouth the words *foo-foo head*. The drones notice and reach for their coffee, assuming I am muttering a Catholic prayer.

A doctor walks in and hesitates a moment before laying his hand on Ethel's shoulder. "There is no brain activity, Mrs. Kennedy."

Slowly she sits back in her chair and looks at the doctor. "There's no hope?"

"None. None at all."

"Turn it off, then," she says, but no one touches the machines. One Kennedy, drunk, shoves the doctor in the chest, demanding that he do something. The doctor flees the room along with two nurses and an attendant. Ethel becomes hysterical. Her besotted siblings embrace her in a tight hive, more to shut her up than to comfort her. By the time Ethel calms down, the others sink into their chairs, exhausted.

No one speaks.

The respirator wheezes on.

I take off my gloves and walk to the right side of Bobby's pillow. I feel the black cord in my hand. It's warm from the electrical current. A false warmth, not the warmth of life. I tighten my fingers around the cord. The doctor returns and sees what I'm about to do. He switches off the machine. Bobby's lungs expand and contract a few times, then stop. The room is quiet.

Teddy looks at me, his fat, oatmeal face a mask of dread, as if a young recruit volunteered by older soldiers to lead a suicide mission. The entire weight of the Kennedy clan falls on top of him. He's it. He knows he doesn't have a chance. He begs me with his eyes: *Get me out of it, Jackie, please.*

If it didn't hurt so much, I would laugh.

1:00 P.M., June 8, 1968. Eight hundred people ride a train twenty-one cars long. Black locomotive, no. 4901, leaves New York, goes under the Hudson, across New Jersey, Pennsylvania, Delaware, Maryland, to Union Station, Washington, D.C., clanking over 225 miles of track.

Eight hours on the train. Eight hours of delirium.

Outside, images pass by of small towns and the squalid underbelly of urban life—clotheslines, fire escapes, back alleys, backyards cluttered with rusty cars, doghouses, lawn mowers, toys, tires, and paint cans, abandoned properties with torn hurricane fences.

They say that as you die, your past flashes before you. I imagine it will be something like this—the mundane, the ugly, and the forgotten flashing before my startled eyes.

People gather at stations with signs, some weeping, some singing, some reaching out to touch the train, their palms falling on the sides of the cars in a syncopated beat, wiping away stripes of grime from the train like tears on a dusty cheek.

This is the funeral train.

They murdered my husband. Again.

I panic, staggering back through the train. Are they here? The men who killed Jack? How about that man by the window with his hat on, or that one wearing sunglasses? My legs nearly give out. I rest my weight against the back of a seat.

No, these are friends of Jack's and his family—reaching out to touch my hands as I pass. Where are my friends? Don't I have one friend whose shoulder I can lean against, a friend who with a glance says all that needs to be said? Where is Bobby?

Faces look up as I pass by, pretty faces of movie stars I've always admired but have never met. I assume Jack slept with them.

Each of them has an image of who Jack was and what he looked like. For a moment I see their snapshots of him projected on their foreheads, a youthful Jack, speaking at the podium, playing football, cramming a sandwich into his mouth after sex. How many are remembering his penis inside them, their thighs straddling his bony hips, his grin, tight with pain? How many desired the weight of his body on top of them, the weight of his maleness? He wasn't willing to give even that much of himself.

Jack! Why did you leave me!

Men stand as I walk by, touching my elbows, my hands, mouthing kind condolences, pledging to help me if I need them. "Anything, anything at all, let me know." One man takes both my hands in his. A big man with big hands. Then I think I hear, "Jack loved you," and I say, "Yes, I know he did." The train jerks. As my eyes snap open wide, I see a look of confusion on the man's face. I realize he didn't say, "Jack loved you," but something else, and I can't figure out what it was until I see a glass of liquor on a tray beside him and guess he has asked me if I would like a glass of Jack Daniel's. "You're so kind," I say. "Thank you for coming."

Then I remember—Bobby's coffin is on this train, not Jack's. I am not the widow here. I'm letting my mind slip—I must regain control.

"It's all my fault, Jackie," Bobby once said, insisting that it should've been him and not Jack who was assassinated.

"No, Bobby, it isn't."

"It is. I was the one who indicted the mob—after they helped get Jack elected."

"What do you mean?"

"Joe used Sam Giancana to funnel money to local politicians in West Virginia. He got him to falsify election returns in Chicago. They hired Oswald to kill Jack."

"You don't know that, Bobby. Nobody knows."

"It should've been me."

And now Bobby is dead, too.

The train sways. I walk past the dining car.

Poor Teddy, sobbing, so alone, hides in the bathroom, his shrieks barely covered by the rattle of the train. He comes out staggering and bleary-eyed.

I continue down the aisle, imagining myself tossed about on rough seas, these people, strangers, packed into a lifeboat with me, numb with astonishment as the luxury ocean liner, the white linen tablecloths, the musicians, and the chandeliers slip down into the dark water to the bottom of the ocean. We are the survivors. It fills us with guilt and confusion.

The train enters a tunnel as I step into the last car. I see the coffin set on three chairs. An American flag draped over it touches the floor.

I look to my left. Seated by the window, Ethel stares at me with pure loathing. I nod my head, but she doesn't acknowledge me. Perhaps she doesn't see me.

She now knows how it is to hate with all the disease and pestilence of the world.

I let her hate pass over me like a storm cloud on the way to the mountains. She has been tolerant over the years, keeping her witches inside her heart, crouched tightly over a caldron of anger, spicing their brew with resentment. Not once did she accuse me of seducing her husband. Now the witches fly out of her pupils.

She sits by Bobby's coffin, her hands clasping a cross and a Bible. She clings tightly to her faith, but she is lost to despair.

Ethel's hate saves me. Her hate makes me strong. Her hate keeps me from throwing myself on the coffin and weeping. As her ego disintegrates, mine grows stronger. I stand as if in a line of prisoners watching as one of us is singled out for torture. My desire to live grows stronger as she cries out in pain.

I don't worry about her. She has her God. She'll find some way to make sense of it. Or not. My coldness toward her shocks me. But I dare not give in to compassion. I must save myself and my children.

Her pregnant belly droops over her knees as she leans into the coffin. I fear for her children, but I know there is nothing I can do. They are like milkweed lost to the wind.

I pass by without comment. She can't hear anything, anyhow, except the screeching steel wheels against the train tracks.

I walk to the observation platform at the rear of the end car. The air is cool. Thousands of people standing beside the track shout my name. I wave. The sun is warm on my cheek.

Outside Elizabeth, New Jersey, a northbound train comes toward us from the opposite direction. The crowd runs, many carrying misspelled signs—*Bobby, may you rest in haven, Bobby, we luv you*—which blocks the approaching train. One man stops to pick up a copy of *Profiles in Courage* that he's dropped, causing a pileup. Black and relentless, the train blasts. Panicked, people start pushing and shoving.

The northbound train whooshes by, crushing one of the men.

We rattle on. I feel nothing.

"We're going to get you, too, bitch."

"Who is this?"

"That's not your heart ticking, honey. That's a bomb. Ticking away in your sweet little house right now."

I hear a click, then a dial tone. What time is it? My heart races, I can hardly catch my breath. I reach for the alarm clock: 4:20 A.M. I think first to dial Bobby. A cold blade stabs my chest. He's gone, too. Who can help me? Frantic, I dash out of my bedroom into the hallway, out the front door, into the private foyer. A Secret Service agent jumps up from his chair just as the elevator arrives. We both look at a note taped to the elevator door. Block letters in black Magic Marker read, TICK, TICK, TICK. DIE, BITCH!

The elevator doors open. Another Secret Service agent jumps out, eyes big as saucers. "We just received a bomb threat. They called the security guard downstairs."

"How did that get here?" I point shakily at the note on the elevator.

"They must've slapped it on in the basement or from one of the other floors."

"That means he's here? In the building?" A bolt of terror shoots through me. I don't wait for an answer. "I'll get the children."

"We're evacuating the building. The police are closing the street and handling the adjacent buildings. We called Lee Radziwill and told her you'd be over in a few minutes."

I wake the children and calmly tell them to get dressed. "We're going to surprise Aunt Lee. Come, quickly, put on anything."

"Is it her birthday?" asks John.

"It's her half birthday. She'll never expect us. That's what makes it fun. Hurry. Before she wakes up."

Caroline looks skeptical but doesn't make a fuss. She senses my panic.

"We're bringing the dogs?" asks John.

"Of course. They like a party, too." What should I take? I look desperately around the apartment. I grab the photo of Jack and cram it into my purse, know-ing how foolish it is, but feeling more in control for having it. Is there anyone else in the apartment? The maid and butler, both out. I suddenly stop dead in my tracks. Is that a coincidence? I will have to fire the staff in any case.

"We need a present, Mommy. Can I take her my *PT-109* model?"

He's only seven—I mustn't lose patience. "She'd like that, John. Run and get it." Hysteria flounders in my chest like a salmon in the shoals.

Caroline tilts her head. She doesn't think there's a party, but then . . . you mustn't go to a party empty-handed. "I'll give her the cashmere shawl Emperor Haile Selassie gave me."

I try to control the terror in my voice. "Get it quickly, if you can, Caroline." She hesitates, then scampers down the hall. I'm about to scream.

"We need to wrap it," she says when she comes back.

"We'll worry about that later. Where's John?"

John scrambles out of his bedroom. He's changed his sweater to a blue one. I want to strangle him. "Let's go, honey."

Blue Suit opens the front door and escorts us to the elevator.

"What's the hurry, Mommy?"

"No more questions now. Let's go, children. Quickly."

When we get outside, police are clearing the street, escorting the stubborn by-standers down the block, their heads turned, straining. "There she is! Jackie! We love you." I don't look. A Blue Suit hustles us into a dark blue sedan.

"Happy half birthday, Aunt Lee," yells John. "Look what we brought you."

Lee, sleepy-eyed with tousled hair, stands in her hallway, bare-legged in a man's button-down shirt. She immediately catches on. "Wow, I'm so surprised. I have a surprise, too, in the kitchen. Blueberry muffins. You two go get yourself some. Then we'll have a breakfast party."

"Oh, boy."

"What's going on?" she asks me as soon as the children are on the way to the kitchen.

My knees suddenly begin trembling. I wobble to a couch and sink. Whatever courage I had is gone. Tears start pouring down my face. "I can't take any more, Lee. I'm so scared. All the time."

"Jacks, tell me what happened."

"A voice on the phone. A bomb threat. He called me 'bitch.' He said he won't stop until all the Kennedys are dead. I'm so frightened. Last week a woman grabbed Caroline's hand and tried to drag her down the street. She started screaming, 'Your mother is a wicked woman who has killed three men.' Lee, we were walking out of church! How can I protect the children?"

Lee looks ashen.

"None of us is safe. Anyone with a gun can shoot me or the children."

Lee hasn't moved. She doesn't say a word, her eyes wide and fixed, imagining the twisted face of the madwoman, her gnarled fingers yanking at Caroline. For some reason her shock calms me.

The doorbell rings. "I've got to get dressed," Lee says. "Everyone's off today. Would you get the door, Jacks?" She shoots down the hall, her bare feet slapping against the marble.

I open the door to find a squat man in an impeccable suit. I fling myself into his arms, hugging him as I've never hugged anyone before. "Oh, Ari. Save me! Get me out of here."

Out of this town, out of this country, out of this world.

THE GREEK

1968–1975

THE MANIKIN

He comes to me like a vampire in the night, his massive black wings blocking the moonlight as he lands on my balcony.

He pulls his hulking body up onto the bed with his long arms and powerful peasant shoulders, carefully tucking his little stick legs beneath him. He perches there like a gargoyle, his eyes glowing yellow, his wings folded at his sides. He looks at my naked body and smacks his lips, his white teeth glinting.

"I've been waiting for you for a long time," he says. His breath, thick with cigar smoke, creeps over me like a smoldering fire. His sweat reeks of ouzo, sweet and bitter as vomited candy.

He squats over me, licking my toes, my ankles, tickling my shinbone with his tongue, his large, slippery, soft hands kneading my muscles.

He seeps over me. The folds in his belly are moist and smelly. My nipples contract in revulsion. His sagging old-lady breasts. The prickly hair on his ass. His papery neck, wrinkled and thin-skinned as a crone's hand.

He grips the back of my neck and presses his mouth over mine, a hard, angry crush. A kiss of dominance and appetite. Pulling my chin down between his stubby fingers, forcing his tongue into my mouth. I am suffocating. I struggle, confused, frightened, which he mistakes for excitement, grabbling my breasts, scrubbing them in circles as he plunges his tongue.

He sits back and shows me his fat clublike penis, wagging it at me, an old man with a young man's penis, a fat, blood-sausage penis. A drop of semen sparkles at the tip. Grinning, he dips his finger in the semen and rubs it on my lips—it tastes of fish and burnt leather. He rubs himself over me, over my breasts, in my neck, in my mouth, choking me with it like a rubber hose. I gasp for breath, gagging at the smell of sour milk, gagging at this serpent trying to suffocate me.

My body itches with disgust. Something squirmy with razor talons scratches to get out of my groin. Raw and tremulous, shivering with self-loathing, I yearn to be torn open. I want to be hurt, I want to be punished by this ugly old toad, who puffs and grinds against me, his belly flapping against my body. I want him to pulverize me, to grind me into dust so I can scatter over the earth where I belong. Kill me, please. It's my fault. Kill me.

I scream in sorrow, and as he tears at me, something quivers in my groin, building in pulsing concentric circles like a bomb blast, my hips bucking, and I feel his name pressed against my teeth, and only a fine thread of self-preservation—*Don't break, no, don't break!*—keeps me from sobbing Jack's name.

The black-winged thing ejaculates with my orgasm, grunting, lurching, pumping like an old farm machine, then herky-jerky wheezing, squealing like a pig. He collapses on me, crushing me with his potato-sack weight.

I feel relief, followed by a clinical coolness, as if I have finished a particularly distasteful chore. As I roll his body off me, I can't believe that I will do this again. I loathe myself that I want to.

I kiss Ari's sleeping brow, an obligatory motherly kiss, and leave him to shower.

"How could you do this to me?"

"Do what, Lee?"

"You took him from me! Like you take everything. Anything you want. Take, take, take."

"But you are married already, Lee. Your affair with Ari ended years ago. You knew we were dating."

"Dating, yes. But you're marrying him. It's so unfair."

Unfair?

"You stole him just like you stole Berenson."

Berenson? I am dumbfounded. She hasn't mentioned his name since our trip to Italy as teenagers. "What do you mean?"

"Berenson was mine!" Lee shouts, working herself up into a tantrum, as she used to at Hammersmith Farm, in her white pinafore and curled blond hair, writhing and pounding her fists on the floor—*Mine! Mine! Mine!* "I'm the one who read his books. I'm the one who wrote to him. But you took him like you take everything."

"That was twenty years ago!"

"You must stay up at night trying to figure out ways to hurt me. You're so selfish. You always had to be queen of the circus. I could be the lion tamer or the trapeze artist, but you never let me be queen."

"Lee, you've got to be kidding. That was a game we played as kids!"

"You can't stand the fact I'm more intelligent and more beautiful than you. You ruined my acting career. You've ruined my life."

I am flabbergasted. "Lee. You're not making sense. How did I ruin your acting career?"

"The press couldn't go after the precious widow—*oh, no,* not the president's widow—so they shredded me. They never gave me a chance. They laughed at me." A sob catches in her throat.

I never saw her performance—she asked me not to come. I only heard reports that her Tracy Lord in *The Philadelphia Story* was wooden and artificial. She blames me? It wouldn't help to remind her that I advised her not to go into acting, not because I doubted her talent—which I had no reason to question at that time—but because it would make her so vulnerable. Theater reviewers are bred to be unkind.

"I could have married Jack, you know."

"Have you been drinking, Lee?"

"Right . . . sure. Now I'm an alcoholic. Well, if I am, it's your fault. You don't care about anyone but yourself. You stole Bobby. You even stole my kids' affection. Fuck, Jackie, if you want them, you can have them."

She slams the phone down in my ear.

I feel my heart break into a thousand pieces.

I must be guilty of some of what she says—how could she be so bitter without cause? Did some part of me do these things to hurt her? The thought horrifies me.

When I bought clothes from the same designers as she, she saw it as competition, whereas I saw it as a compliment to her excellent taste. When I included her in the excitement of the White House—the concerts, the dinners, the trips to France and India—she felt I was forcing her into the role of lady-in-waiting. When I called her first at my personal tragedies, she felt I used her. I turned to her in my greatest success and deepest despair—she was my friend.

I did none of these things to hurt her, yet I feel both sullied by and guilty of her accusations.

Like Lee, the world can't believe what I've done to them.

As I walk down Panepistimiou Street in Athens, shopping for antiques with Ari's older sister, Artemis, we pass an international newsstand. Newspapers from all over the world are stacked so headlines can be easily read. My face is on every one of them.

Rome's *Il Messaggero:* JACK KENNEDY DIES TODAY FOR A SECOND TIME.

West Germany's *Bild-Zeitung:* AMERICA HAS LOST A SAINT.

London: JACKIE WEDS BLANK CHECK.

The New York Times: THE REACTION HERE IS ANGER, SHOCK AND DISMAY.

Stockholm Express: JACKIE, HOW COULD YOU?

On the streets in Paris and New York, strangers cry out to me: "How could you betray your country by marrying a Greek?" "Jack is rolling in his grave!" "You've gone from Prince Charming to Caliban!" "Traitor! You have debased America."

It is open season on Jackie.

Their rage shocks me. I have not merely fallen off a pedestal, I am dragged through the streets, shoved into a pillory in the village square, targeted with rotten tomatoes. They rip off the scabs over wounds not yet healed, the sorrows of my life, pouring salt into the raw flesh.

Only the people of Greece approve. Shopkeepers invite Artemis and me into their stores, open a bottle of retsina, and drink to my marriage. They ask me to kiss their children. I leave with a small gift and, of course, their business card and an invitation to come back to browse. Onassis women are known for their love of shopping.

"See, my dear," Artemis says, "we are a very civilized and hospitable people."

Greek paparazzi jump around us, dipping and bobbing like marionettes, tripping over one another, lenses smacking against competing lenses, cameras flashing—*pop! pop! pop!*—each one shouting to get me to look at them. The shopkeepers chase them away like dogs, and like dogs, they wait for us to come out again.

From the chatter, I pick out a few words I know in Greek: *wedding, bless you, happiness*—and the name Maria. "What are they saying about Maria?"

Artemis flips her hand, which returns to finger her ruby-and-diamond necklace. "*Phft!* They are just paparazzi. Vermin. Don't pay attention."

"No, tell me, please. What are they saying?"

Artemis hesitates, then says, "They are asking what you did with Maria."

I am shocked, appalled. "What I *did* with her?"

Artemis adds quickly, "Many Greeks expected Ari to marry his Greek mistress. They are ignorant. You will see how much Greece welcomes you."

On our wedding day hordes of photographers and journalists descend on Athens from all over the world like desperate refugees, their bags and cameras swinging off their necks. Their red eyes dart around hungrily, their trigger fingers trembling with fatigue and coffee jitters and the excitement of the big hunt.

Like a general under siege, Ari grounds Olympic Airways, which he controls.

He has all foreign correspondents rounded up and put under house arrest in the Hotel Grande Bretagne in Athens. His security force and Greek navy gunships patrol the waters around Skorpios. Yet dozens somehow get to Levkás, a small island nearby. Helicopters with bullhorns swoop over, warning journalists to stay away. They sneak on anyway. Like marines, paparazzi jump off motor launches, charging up to the chapel, stopping only to focus and fire, then advance.

Finally relenting, we allow a few photographers to take photos outside the tiny whitewashed Chapel of Panayitsa—the "Little Virgin." We are nearly crushed by them as we step into the chapel.

Inside, the chapel is dark and cold, the air heavy with incense and the cloying smell of roses. Rain rattles the stained-glass windows. Caroline and John grip long white tapered candles, the golden flames flickering on their serious faces. They look both curious and frightened, as if attending their first séance—*What's going to happen to us now?* Relatives—Ari's sisters, Lee and Stas, and a few Kennedys—stand in uncomfortable bunches. It amuses me that neither Rose nor Teddy came, sending in their places lesser Kennedys Pat and Jean, who seldom make headlines. They don't want to appear to sanction the marriage and hope that when the newspapers hit the stands the name Kennedy will be replaced with the girls' married names, Lawford and Smith. Also stewing in disapproval are Ari's grown children, Christina and Alexander, huddled in the back like two vultures, wearing black, heads bent, sulking and furious.

Who is that lurking behind them? A tall figure, hidden in the shadows, candlelight illuminating his thick mane of white hair, his hand briefly squeezing Christina's shoulder as if to reassure her. Ah, yes, Ari's dear friend Costa Gratsos. For some reason I am surprised he is here. He nods respectfully as I walk by.

A Greek Orthodox priest, looking like Merlin in a long black beard and gold robe, chants in Greek for forty-five minutes. I feel Ari's weight like lead beside me. He's thinking hard about something—I sense it's not about us but about some deal he's cooking up. He taps his fingers against his thumb, figuring sums in his head. Janet, too, figures sums, her eyes darting around the chapel, evaluating the cost of flowers and the ladies' dresses and jewels, calculating how long she should wait after the wedding to ask for a loan. Lee's eyes are glazed over the way they did when she was a child when the grown-ups talked.

A young boy walks around the altar, swinging incense. Fat snakes of smoke curl around the chapel. The ceremony begins to feel more like an initiation rite to a forbidden cult than a wedding. I feel something pulling at me, beckoning, like a cool stream deep in the woods, something ancient and primitive.

The air in the chapel becomes almost impossible to breathe. I worry about

Hughdie's asthma and am relieved when he steps outside to wait out the ceremony.

Ari and I exchange rings, then drink red wine from a silver chalice. The Greek sisters crown our heads in wreaths of *stefana* blossoms, switching them back and forth three times. As we circle the altar, dancing the measured steps of the *issaia,* the crowd throws rose petals and rice over our heads.

The children look dazed. I laugh and embrace them. I, too, am nervous and unsure.

We step outside into the chilly rain. "Rain is good luck," say the Greek sisters. Close to shore, the *Christina* bobs in the gray sea, lit up with white lights like an ocean liner. Boats bursting with paparazzi ring the island like lifeboats after a shipwreck, waiting to be saved.

Soon after our honeymoon, Rose sits on deck of the *Christina* in a huge straw hat with plastic cherries and kumquats around the brim. She wears a cotton dress, white with red hyacinths.

She seems oddly liberated by Joe's death—gleeful, livelier than I've seen her in years. She quite enjoys her new position as head of the family. She juts her sharp chin into the air, leans back, and closes her eyes.

Ari treats her with deference, as if she were his mother-in-law, welcoming her, chatting with her pleasantly, making sure she has a drink, offering her the Chris-Craft for her shopping—"Just have the bills sent to me"—then casually excuses himself—"I'm most sorry to have to leave you to entertain yourselves." For days. I teasingly accuse him of hiding.

"Oh, Ari. The richest man in the world hides from his wife's ex-mother-in-law."

He looks at me sheepishly, "The richest man in the world has a strong sense of self-preservation."

I wonder what she wants. She was the only Kennedy who didn't object to my marriage to Ari. I'm sure it wasn't out of concern for my happiness. Why then? Was she delighted to get me out of the country so when people spoke of "Mrs. Kennedy," it would be understood to be Rose Kennedy, not Jackie Kennedy? Was she glad to have me cut off from the measly Kennedy stipend she allowed? Or did she think—wrongly, as I did—that married and living in Greece, my name would stop appearing in the headlines? Is she here to demand the return of Jack's house in Hyannis Port?

Shrewdly, she doesn't show her hand. She plans to spend her vacation watching me scurry around, catering to her every whim, something that I refused to do when I was her daughter-in-law but now seems impossible to avoid under the laws of Greek hospitality. She enjoys seeing me kill myself trying to sustain a conversation with her, smiling, rattling off pleasantries and compliments. Why she wants this power over me is more than I can comprehend. Revenge, perhaps? For stealing away her two precious sons and allowing them to get killed?

"I hate it when you get around the Kennedys," Ari fumes. "You get all jittery and subservient. You are Mrs. Onassis. They are nothing. Don't let them get to you." With a poetic purposefulness that particularly delights me, Ari gives her a gold bracelet of an asp with emerald eyes. Yet even wily Onassis can't figure out what she wants.

After several days it becomes clear.

She sits in the deck chair that she has claimed as her own and, as she sips an insipid tropical concoction that she equates with vacations and balmy climates, says, "We are concerned, Jacqueline, that Mr. Onassis will want to give John and Caroline his name," and "We are concerned, Jacqueline, that you will school Caroline and John in Switzerland, and they will grow up knowing nothing of their family," and "We are concerned, Jacqueline, that the children will spend their vacations here in Greece rather than Hyannis Port and never get to play with their dear cousins." Dear cousins, indeed, who rampage around the Kennedy compound, trying to murder one another.

I am amazed at this matron in her big straw hat—"to protect my dewy Irish complexion"—using the royal we. Who are we? We are dead. Jack, Bobby, Joe. Who's left? The women and Teddy, the family buffoon. In the power vacuum, Rose barks orders like the queen in *Alice in Wonderland*—"Off with her head"— with just enough authority to make my life miserable.

"We would never want to withdraw their trust funds, but it could be done," and then, "We certainly don't want to go to court over this, my dear. I'm sure your husband wouldn't like his new wife's name entangled with negative publicity. They are Jack's children, and I have to insist they stay in the United States. They belong to us."

A shiver shoots up my body. Those words—*they belong to us*—so deliberate, so simple, bearing the weight of the entire Kennedy fortune. Joe may be dead, but I do not underestimate the power of the Kennedy lawyers. They would happily destroy my reputation. Without my reputation, my worth to Ari would plummet like a bad stock.

A pink tongue darts out of the asp's mouth, licking a drip of vermouth on the lip of her glass.

It's a trap she's set. She is demanding I choose between my husband and my children.

I boil over in rage. It is so clear what Rose wants. She wants me to disappear and leave her the children. I will never let that happen.

They hate me. Oh, how they hate me!

I give them presents I think are thoughtful. For Alexander, records of musicians I know he loves: Frank Sinatra, Joan Baez, Nat King Cole, and Paul Mauriat—even a record once owned by Jack and signed by Louis Armstrong. For Christina—because she apparently has no interests other than complaining—jewelry, which she normally adores. My gifts go unopened, left outside on the *Christina,* to get ruined or washed overboard.

When I enter a room, they leave. They refuse to address me and, if I ask them a question, answer me through a servant. "Please tell Madame that, no, I will not be joining them for dinner." They insult me to others, but close enough so I can hear. "My father needs a wife. I do not need a stepmother," says Alexander, packing his bags, refusing to return until I am gone. "I no longer have a home."

Their hate is something vile released from deep within the earth. They walk in a cloud of hate. They walk into a room and drain it of color, turning the pink Mediterranean light into a somber gray. They hate me with an uncompromising, nonnegotiable hate. I have known hate—Janet's hate for Black Jack, the hate of segregationists, the hate of jealous socialites, Ethel's hate—but this is beyond any hate I've ever experienced.

This is not Newport hate. This is Greek hate. The real thing.

I escape to my lovely house. My little pink house. I feel more secure here than anywhere in the world, yet I realize that in many ways I am a guest.

The Pink House sits on one of the lower hills on Skorpios. The island is merely four hundred acres. It has a view of the mountains of Ithaca and the small islands Levkás and Madouri. Until Ari bought it, it lay barren except for a few olive trees. He brought in water from the nearby port of Nydri, then planted cypress, almond, walnut, and fruit trees. There are eight little houses for Ari's guests and, over a hill, more modest homes for his employees.

But the Pink House is mine, a little two-bedroom stucco building with views from all the windows of the purple Ionian Sea. Ari prefers to eat and sleep on the *Christina,* which is moored in a little harbor—a fifteen-minute walk down from the Pink House. No one has ever tried to make it a home. That's my job.

Under the watchful eye of Marta Sgubin, their new governess, and Janet, the children are finishing the semester in New York. Soon they will come join us on Skorpios. School in New York, vacations in Greece—Rose's compromise, to which I grudgingly agreed. My panic has passed, but I worry about them. I tell myself that between the Blue Suits and Ari's men, they will be as safe as they can be. We take the *Christina* to Puerto Rico and fly the children down on the weekends. It's not enough. I miss them so much, sometimes my heart hurts. While I wait for them, I busy myself with the Pink House.

I buy beige and white flokati rugs to lay over the terra-cotta tiles. I study traditional Mykonos homes and decorate with Greek antiquities I pick up in my treasure-hunting trips on the mainland. I design new patios so the small inside spaces gracefully lead to outside spaces. I paint watercolors of the island to hang on the walls.

I feel guilty at how much I love this little house.

As I fix up the house, I sense that I am fixing myself, making order where there was only disorder, harmony where there was only anxiety and despair. Ari understands this and encourages me to buy whatever I want.

It is, I hope, if not a work of art, a work of meditation. I sit in front of each window, imagining a composition in which the interior colors, furniture, and art create, with the view, a *tableau vivant,* a living painting. The light peach of an interior wall accents the vibrant pink bougainvillea outside, against a backdrop of purple water. A sculpture inside mirrors a rock formation outside. The lavender white paint used on the window sashes picks up the light purple wisteria blossoming outside. The curve of the back of a chair matches the curve of a hill outside, its olive-patterned fabric mirroring the olives on a branch that shades the window. A painting of a sailboat positioned by one window looks as if it sailed from the sea onto the wall.

The view from each window is an assemblage, creating harmony between the interior mind and the external world, a harmony I have never known but seek to find. No one will ever know how many hours it takes me to create these compositions. It is my secret.

I love the solitude here. In solitude, I put back the pieces. In solitude, I learn and grow. In solitude, I can reach out to the world from a safe distance. If there is loneliness, it is like a clean, cool breeze on a winter's morning. In solitude, I heal.

Every day I swim in the ocean and climb the hills. The paths wind through wild herbs warmed by the sun, fragrant and full of bees—lavender, rosemary, thyme, sage, and wild garlic. In the spring the hills are carpeted with buttercup, shepherd's purse, field marigold, and chamomile. As warm thermals rise from the crevasses and cool maestros blow off the water, smells assail me, bringing back memories of Provence and Cape Cod.

On these walks Jack comes to me. Bobby less so. Silly memories of how Jack liked to crumble crackers into his clam chowder, rubbing them between his palms, or how Bobby liked me to scratch the back of his calves. The memories seem far away, as if from another person's life.

I climb to the highest peak and look out toward Ithaca. An eagle that nests in a silver poplar tree on the craggy north side swoops and spirals, riding the air currents. Often I bring my sketchbook or camera, or sit for hours doing nothing.

I know that when Ari leaves me on business, he works in a visit to his mistress in Paris or Rome. As I stroll along the cliff path, picking wildflowers, I find myself thinking about Maria. She doesn't torment me the way Jack's women did. I am more curious than jealous, wondering what they have together, imagining a soulful connection that goes beyond eroticism and passion, something I have never experienced.

I saw her sing once—her gala performance of *Tosca* at the Metropolitan Opera in New York.

Maria spoke her first word, "Mario," offstage. She floated into view wearing a crimson gown, her black hair loose down her back, her eyes, nose, and lips vibrant. Her voice trembled with despair of the finite, and terror of the infinite. Her jealousy was electric, ferocious, possessed—a rage against mortality and human imperfection. She sang from suffering, embodied it, in every chromosome of her body.

I flinched and squirmed during the scene where Scarpia tortures Tosca's lover, Mario, his backstage screams filling the opera house—*Stop the opera, please! Somebody help him!*—while Scarpia calmly eats a piece of fruit, taunting and tormenting Tosca—*Will she betray her lover's secret to save him?*—and when Tosca flings herself across the stage, writhing in agony, her silhouette backlit in a haunting nightmare. When Maria sang her aria *"Vissi d'arte,"* I understood why her fans risked hypothermia to hear her. "I lived for art, I lived for love," she sang, not only as the character Tosca but as Maria, the impassioned singer, the artist. She squeezed the notes from her very being—her voice became the soul and voice of all women. As she sang, *"Perchè, perchè, Signore, perchè me ne rimuneri cosi?"* my hands flew to my chest, pressing against my heart to keep it from flying out of my body, tears gushing down my face—*"Why, why, Lord, do you repay me like this?"*—my ribs aching with sobs—*Oh, Jack, Jack, how could you leave me?*

I wept as those around me wept, purged of our individual sorrows, sharing the despair of human existence. I felt my soul lifted up and knew, despite Jack's murder and my constant terror, that I could go on. As Maria took her bows, I was overwhelmed by my own littleness. This was a fully realized woman. An artist. A priestess. She was the embodiment of something elusive I felt I lacked.

Through the curtain calls—six, seven, eight, I lost count—my heart ached as it had never ached before, but I felt it expand, filling the opera house.

I remember that ache now. I don't think it has left me since that evening. I long to hear her sing, her voice echoing over the hills of Skorpios. I know why Onassis loves her—part of me wants him to love her. He finds something in Maria that I understand but cannot give. I wish I could, but I can't. Perhaps I am too shallow ever to plunge that deeply.

I hear a rumble and look over my shoulder. Two white stallions charge over the hills below, then disappear around a cypress grove, magically, mythically. It gives me the sense that Skorpios is not of this world.

Suddenly a loud shot. I jump to my feet in terror, sweat bursting from my temples, my heart thumping wildly. When I realize it's a gardener's truck backfiring and not an assassin's bullet, I collapse into a squat, weeping rib-cracking sobs, sobs I've held in for seven years, driving something out of me, purging myself as I did when I heard Maria sing.

Slowly my terror dissipates, and my heart fills with love. Love for Ari, for the children, for Jack. I sense I am working through something in this strange life I lead, this perverse relationship with Ari.

One day I will understand.

LEVKÁS

*A*ri and I dine in a tavern perched on the cliffs on the island of Levkás. We sit at a little table on the terrace and look out at our island home in the distance.

I imagine how they see us. The man, much older than the woman—thirty years, at least—must look like a prosperous businessman from Athens relaxing on vacation. He laughs as she runs her index finger around his large ear, affectionately, as if she can't resist touching him.

She is definitely not his daughter.

Though the woman is tall and reed-thin, the man is solid with a big barrel chest. He wears white trousers and a tan cotton square-cut shirt. When he leans back in his chair, smiling, eyes closed behind his sunglasses, he looks as content as a tomcat basking in the midday sun.

The woman wears a brightly colored cotton shift and sandals. Her shoulder-length hair is dark and tangled. Her sunglasses are neatly folded on the table.

We enjoy our solitude, no doubt appearing very much like any other man and wife at their local tavern. Indeed, it is the closest restaurant to Skorpios.

There are only a handful of other people on the terrace. It is too late for lunch, too early for dinner. There is a timelessness about the afternoon, the hot sun filtered through the leaves of the grape arbor above us.

The waiter, the bartender, the fiddler, the flower and newspaper vendors, the street urchin who sells reed flutes—all know Ari. He buys whatever they have to sell and waves off the change, even though the change is several times the price of the newspaper or rose. They thank him and depart quickly.

Ari drinks Johnnie Walker Black, I sip an Americano. Between us sits a basket of fried *calamaraki* and a plate of dolmades, stuffed grape leaves. I occasionally nibble the corner of a piece of squid, wiping my fingers meticulously each time. Ari ignores the food, then in a burst of hunger shoves several pieces into his mouth and chomps noisily.

I imagine we appear happy and relaxed, as if we own the place. Perhaps we do.

After I whisper a story in Ari's ear, I touch his hand with my index finger, pause, then deliver the punch line. Ari explodes in laughter, the rumbling, furniture-shaking laughter of a much bigger man, the laughter of a man who never laughs alone. He waves over the waiter and has me repeat the story. Initially, I am shy, uncomfortable, unfamiliar with the waiter, uncertain of my command of the Greek language, but I warm as I tell my anecdote, delighting as I see Ari's eyes dance in approval. We all laugh a little too loudly—the waiter eager to show respect, Ari eager to show the world his majesty, I eager to please. Ari orders a bottle of champagne—the very best in the house.

Are we here to celebrate? they wonder. Yes, to celebrate life, abundance, and the beautiful afternoon.

Ari begins a tale, leaning on his elbows over the table, which tips with his weight. I listen raptly, running my long fingers over my glass-bead necklace, my eyes large and sparkling, head tilted slightly, as if my life depends on catching every word. Perhaps it does.

Whatever the tale, I hardly breathe while I listen, completely absorbed in his story.

He finishes by drinking a full glass of champagne in one gulp. I press my hands together and laugh appreciatively. He gloats with pride.

"Oh, Ari. I never know whether to believe you or not. What a story!"

"I don't know if I've lived so long so I'll have stories to tell, or I've lived so long so I can tell stories."

"Is it true?"

He smiles slyly. "What is the truth, my dear?"

I love it when my pirate becomes philosophical. Even platitudes coming from him seem profound. Because of the accent? Or because they come from his experience?

Suddenly the air explodes with lights. A Greek photographer leaps out from behind a hedge of oleander bushes, snapping his camera, his flash—*pop, pop, pop*—circling the table with his Cyclops eye.

Ari flies out of his chair, his face purple with rage. "Who do you think you are, you son of a bitch! You're insane. Leave my wife alone. Go away. Get out of here. You want money? Here!" Ari throws a fistful of drachmas on the floor. The photographer scoops up the money into his pocket with one hand while continuing to snap pictures with the other. But he doesn't leave. *Click, click, click.*

Who tipped off the paparazzi?

The photographer dances around the table like a demon possessed, shouting in halting English: "Look at me! Over here! Here I am!" Squatting, leaning, leaping. The waiter rushes to the table and tries to shoo him away, snapping his white towel, to no avail. People on the street stop and stare. The other diners stop eating. One man stands up as if to help.

By now the photographer is out of film and is using his backup camera.

Ari grabs me by the hand, yanking me roughly out of my chair. He swings me in front of him and pulls up my dress. "Is this what you want, you son of a bitch? Are you happy now? Here, take her picture. Then get the hell out of here!"

I sway, about to faint—mortified—my crotch exposed to the world. A woman gasps; a glass crashes. It is as if all the air has been sucked out of the room. The waiter stares, pedestrians stare, diners stare. Everyone stares.

A cool breeze tickles my silk panties.

Click, click, click. The photographer squats, snapping away, then disappears between the tables, through the bushes, down an alley.

The Cyclopses come like wraiths in the night, springing on me wherever I go. Pursuing me like bad memories that won't be forgotten. Pursuing me like a thousand starving children clinging to my skirts, begging, demanding. Pursuing me as if I owe them something.

How much will Ari's secretary pay this time? How much did she pay for my naked butt high in the air, fucking Ari in a rowboat? *The Billion-Dollar Bush!*

Even on the island they sneak up like assassins, hiding in the bushes, stealing photos, zipping by in speedboats, buzzing by in helicopters, their long lenses like elephant trunks. Once when I was water-skiing, a paparazzo drove a speedboat between me and the lead boat, snapping my towline. Gleefully, he clicked away as I sank, nearly drowning, paralyzed in terror.

Why won't they leave me alone? Even Ari can't protect me.

I smooth my skirt and wobble back to my seat, my lips pressed together, trying hard not to be sick.

Ari sits down, furious at me. "If you didn't make such a goddamn fuss all the time, they'd leave you alone."

"You are right, Ari."

The happy mood is broken. The day ruined. We sit in silence for a few moments, then I excuse myself to use the restroom.

Yet there was much tenderness between us. Many good times. Those first few years.

"Do you know what I love best about our marriage, Ari?"

"What?"

"You let me be both a mistress and a wife. A mistress is about passion and eroticism. A wife is about security and friendship. You give me both, and I love you for it."

This makes him smile, even though he frowns slightly when I say the word *mistress* because we both know he still sees Maria.

He is far more sensitive than I ever imagined. A sentimental man. A loving man.

"You're my little bird," he says. "You can go wherever you desire and do whatever you wish."

His generosity to me and to everyone else is astonishing, not simply in the extravagance and abundance of jewels and hospitality, but he is the first person I've ever met who doesn't at some point feel taken advantage of by his generosity.

He desires to please me delighting me with stories. He wakes me in the morning with pearls on my breakfast tray. He stuffs love notes between my bottles of perfume. He seeks out new restaurants for us to visit, new islands to explore. He introduces me to Greek scholars and art experts who satisfy my insatiable curiosity about Greek culture.

Ari loves to saunter beside me as we walk down the streets of Paris, down avenue Foch to the Arc de Triomphe, down rue du Faubourg St.-Honoré to look at the art galleries and leather stores, down the Champs-Elysées. He is so proud of me. And even though I realize he is less proud of me than proud of himself because he has me, it makes me feel happy and loved.

He even cooks for me, *octapi* the way his mother once made it.

He is a poetic man, far more concerned about matters of the soul than Jack was. His spirituality is tied up with the earth, sea, and ancient myths. His understanding of death and resurrection, of tragedy and catharsis, feels more real than Christianity. And when we stay up late at night, talking, the *Christina* rocking softly beneath us, the stars shining above, we talk of yearnings that stir something in the pit of my stomach. He unleashes in me an awareness I never knew.

I try to please him. I flatter and fuss over him as I see his sisters do—"Ari, let me get you a sweater." "Ari, please take your vitamins." I praise him to his sisters and employees, which I know gets back to him: "Ari is such a brave businessman." "He's so strong and clever." I play First Lady for General Papadopoulos and other businessmen he entertains. I amuse him with caricatures I draw of him. I learn Greek and everything I can about Greek culture. I praise his sisters and court his staff. I make love to his troll-like body.

I call him my Odysseus, which flatters him. He likes to think of himself as the hero, wily and clever, who travels the world, winning wars, then comes home to reclaim his throne in Greece. I wonder if what I mean is that through him, I am trying to find my way home, trying to find out who I am. He is my Odyssey, my journey through temptation and hell. He is my landscape of exploration. My Scylla and

Charybdis are his anger and expectations—I navigate carefully between them. He is my Calypso who offers me immortality, yet imprisons me. He is the lotus eaters who ensnare me with mindless pleasures. He is Circe, who turns my family and my values into swine. He is my Siren, who seduces me with jewels only to destroy my self-respect.

Perhaps I am Penelope as well, unraveling the bandages over my past to keep from giving in to intimacy.

This, I fear, is what makes Ari so mad. He knows I'll never love him. He is furious that I am not jealous of Maria Callas but, rather, grateful to her. She is always there between us—my protection.

In a way, I feel as many of Ari's employees do, that she has greater rights to Ari than I. They understand each other—they meet in a place that Ari and I will never see.

Yes, we had many happy days. Those first few years.

GRAND CENTRAL TERMINAL

*F*ifteen floors above Fifth Avenue, I sit in my window, partially hidden by white gossamer curtains, peering through a telescope at the people below. At first, I follow a boy, not small but not yet a man, tearing through the park on his bicycle, cutting across the grass to a path, standing up on his pedals up a small hill, careening down over a favorite bump, where he launches himself into the air. He lands, wobbling, looking back over his shoulder at a man in pursuit. The man struggles to keep up, his blue suit tight and constricting, laughing at the rambunctious boy who makes his job difficult but fun.

No. I won't spy on my children.

"He will be fine," I tell myself, a mantra I chant along with all mothers of young boys. I have to believe he'll be all right. I have to ignore the knot of fear in my stomach that never goes away. I should scold him for making the Secret Service agents his playmates, but I won't. He is an affectionate boy, and the Blue Suits love him. How could they not?

Ari fumes, but I spend most of my time with the children now. I worry so about them. Caroline, thirteen, retreats into her shell too often, hurting in a way I'll never be able to comfort. She plasters her room with pictures of Jack. She must imagine conversations with him. I wonder what he tells her. John, ten, is wild, reckless, irrepressible—a danger to himself. I wonder what it is that makes him hurl himself at the world—some anger. I don't know. I worry so. Yet they are wonderful children. I would be nothing without them.

I wait for them to return from school. I swivel the telescope to the street, catching glimpses into the private lives of my fellow New Yorkers. My small but satisfying revenge. On the steps of the Metropolitan Museum, a mime tosses apples, oranges, and bananas. He drops an apple, which rolls down the steps. A messenger jogging by with a letter marked URGENT in red scoops it up, wipes it on his shirt, and takes a bite—he waves at the mime. A woman in a pink and gold sari pushes a perambulator. Nannies chase after toddlers by Conservatory Water. Japanese tourists swivel their heads, snapping pictures. Kids jaywalking across Fifth Avenue jostle one another as they head into the park with baseball bats and gloves. People with brown skin, tan skin, yellow skin, pinkish skin, black skin—all New Yorkers.

A man in a tan uniform with short black hair buys a tabloid from the newspaper stand, sits on the museum steps, and opens his bag lunch. He lines up his food on the step—a sandwich, chips, an apple, a bag of peanuts. He unwraps his sandwich—liverwurst, I imagine—his thick fingers struggling with the cellophane, lifting the top slice of bread to check for mayonnaise, then takes a bite. He sets down the sandwich and opens the tabloid with a picture of me on the front—JACKIE JOINS FIGHT FOR GRAND CENTRAL STATION. He turns to the sports page.

A pretty young woman in a shirtdress and sensible pumps slips into the museum on her lunch hour, probably college-educated from New England, full of hope for a career in publishing or art, struggling with boredom at an entry-level job at Random House or Sotheby's yet thrilled by her adventures in the city.

An older woman dressed in an elegant skirt and blouse sits on a bench, reading. The young mothers all know her and wave when she looks up. A towheaded toddler drags his nanny over and demands a boost onto the bench beside her. The older woman pulls out *The Ugly Duckling* from a canvas bag with the New York Public Library lion logo. The boy sits quietly, eager for her to begin reading.

I lean back in my chair and close my eyes, struck by a sudden, powerful longing. My shoulders and chest ache with that empty full feeling of being in love. Then I recognize the feeling for what it is: It is a sense of belonging.

Yes, this is my home. A place I love. Where my children live and play. Where my people live.

Once, I fled—frightened and persecuted—but now the city tugs at me, not letting me go.

What about my marriage? What about Skorpios?

I cannot live in two places. I need a home base. Not simply a place that feels like home, but a center of orbit.

I realize that when I am in Greece, I think of New York, but when I am in New York, my life in Greece is a distant memory.

Without my knowing it, New York lays claim to me.

Up and down the gleaming escalators—New York, Athens, Paris, London. I relish the hunt—the right scarf, the right perfume. The excitement evaporates my memory, drowns out the past. I feel victorious, as if I have accomplished something.

For a moment it takes away the pain. Gone are my feelings of anguish and insecurity. For a moment I forget myself in beauty. I feel a rush of euphoria. The cashiers, excited to wait on a celebrity, thrilled by the promise of a big sale, smile and laugh. It's Christmas for everyone.

"Nothing but sex and shopping. You must be the happiest woman alive," says Lee.

I buy furs, shoes, handbags, lingerie, fabrics, cosmetics, scarves, baubles, bibelots.

I buy massages, facials, manicures, coiffures.

I buy clothes from Valentino, Courrèges, Saint Laurent, Madame Grès, Lanvin, Dior, Givenchy.

I buy presents for Lee, Rose, Caroline and John, Ari, the Greek sisters, and anyone else I can think of.

By the time I get home, my purchases are dead weights. I am depressed again, filled with remorse. How many black sweaters can one woman wear? Guilt-ridden, I send the merchandise back. I feel guilty for overshopping, guilty for sending it all back, guilty for not doing something more constructive in my life.

To shake my depression, I go shopping.

A woman like you, wasting her talents! It's a crime.

Who is that? Black Jack? Bernard Berenson? Quiet! You're dead. Shut up!

You can write, you can draw and paint, you can mobilize people to support the arts. So much a woman like you can do.

No, I can't. I'm not strong enough. Don't ask me to show my pain. Don't ask me to deal with people.

You say you want to enjoy a full life, but you live on the surface of life, skimming along on its pleasures, experiencing nothing.

You are unfair. You are too hard on me.

Look at someone who really lives. Maria Callas, creating from the depths of her soul.

That's Maria. I can't do that. There's not enough left of me. I just can't.

Only because you don't want to. You have the soul of an artist.

You leave my soul alone!

"You think I don't know what you do with all those clothes you charge? You go to New York and sell them!"

At first I'm taken aback. Ari has never objected to my spending before. He has always said, "If it makes you happy, you can have anything you want." He was proud to read in the papers about what I had bought and for how much. It showed the world how rich and generous he was. It got his name in the papers. Why is he fussing now?

"Of course I resell them, Ari. Every well-dressed woman in New York sends her clothes to Encore to resell. You know I can wear a gown only so many times. If my picture is in the paper every day, I can't wear the same thing over and over. Do you want me to throw them out?"

"I paid for them. They are mine."

"Oh, Ari, when would you have time to deal with a bunch of out-of-date women's clothes?"

"How can any woman spend thirty thousand a month on clothes? I never see you in anything but jeans!"

"Ari, that isn't fair. It doesn't go just for clothes. I have two households to run, servants and schools to pay for, clothes and toys for the children, checks to Janet, upkeep of the horses, charities. Your sister spends far more than that."

"She is not my wife."

"Ari, you don't want people to say you are too cheap to buy me a new outfit, do you? You are so very generous. It would pain me terribly to have them say that about you."

"I am going to divorce you. You are too expensive."

I laugh. "Too expensive for Aristotle Onassis? Thirty thousand a month—what's that, a thousand dollars a day? That is too much for the wife of a man who makes fifty million a year?"

"What do I get out of it? You are never here when I need you! A Greek wife stays by her husband."

"I have responsibilities in New York."

"You have responsibilities here!"

"Do you think I want to go to back to those awful Kennedy ceremonies? Do you think I want to relive what happened ten years ago?"

"You love it. You roll in it like a pig in mud. If you don't want to go, don't go. The wife of Onassis doesn't have to do anything she doesn't want to."

"Yes, Ari. But I have commitments."

"What about your commitment to me!"

I know it's not my spending he objects to. His threats of divorce are empty. He wants to control me. He wants me to spend more time with him. But when he is so ugly to me, there is little incentive.

"Where are you going?"

"I'm taking a Chris-Craft to go shopping."

"No, you aren't!"

"Let me go!"

"You are my wife. You do as I say." He grabs me by the hair and slaps me across the face. He drags me to the nearest utility closet. I let him have his way.

I sleepwalk through the ceremonies. The date on the program—November 22, 1973—starts me trembling, and I can't stop. I couldn't make it without the children. John stands, twitching in his suit, his long bangs hanging in his face, slightly furious that he has to give up a day for some ceremony that means nothing to him. He was so young. Only three. Caroline looks reverent but a bit lost, trying, trying, trying to remember a shadow that slowly fades despite her scrapbooks.

I kneel, I bow my head, I walk slowly with a sad smile. I manage to utter a few rehearsed words. I plaster a smile on my face as Teddy mumbles a tedious speech, attempting to look dignified but failing miserably, his face bloated, his suit straining over his fat torso, his eyes puffy and bloodshot. This is what has become of us? His voice mimics the rising pitch of Jack's oratory but sounds stilted and empty, like a child reciting Bible verses he doesn't understand.

Are you here, Jack? I wait for his voice, but I hear nothing. Without understanding why, I feel deeply ashamed.

"Nothing has been touched since Jack died." Rose stands by the door to our house on the Kennedy compound in Hyannis Port. "I thought you might want to stay here tonight, so I had the sheets changed." She smiles, victorious, the curse of the ex-mother-in-law working its lethal magic. "If you need me, I'll be up at the house."

My eyes follow her up the hill, then gaze out at the ocean so desolate in November. A line of yellow foam, like a long, ugly stretch mark, wavers between the gray water and the sand. An algae bloom? Or perhaps a toxic spill? The air in the house smells of mildew. I throw open a window and smell salt air and the stench of dead fish.

The room is eerie. The furniture is exactly where we last left it—issues of *The New Yorker* and *Time* from November 1963 on the coffee tables, antique bottles I bought at a garage sale, which someone had dug up behind his house, a tiny ceramic dalmatian Caroline bought me at the same garage sale, baskets that once held our picnics, Jack's books, marked with napkins at his favorite passages, John's antique chest full of toys, watercolors I painted of the bay.

I open the bedroom closet. His suits and shirts hang there still. Someone has sprinkled mothballs around. I open a drawer and smell his sweaters. They still smell of him—of cologne and something bitter like the rue I've smelled on Skorpios, wafting from a ravine. Rue—the smell of sorrow and remorse.

I feel a terrible pressure in my chest and gasp for air. How long was I holding my breath? A minute? Ten years?

Let me go, Jack. Please!

"You are my wife," screams Ari.

"You are a Kennedy forever," taunts Rose.

"You are a Bouvier," says Black Jack.

I run out the door, down to the beach, running as if pursued by a thousand stinging hornets. Leave me alone! All of you! Just leave me alone!

"You see, Mrs. Onassis, the facade of the terminal is a unique representation of turn-of-the-century Beaux Arts design. The sculpture of Mercury above the central portal is sixty feet wide and fifty feet high, and weighs fifteen hundred tons, and is one of the most beautiful pieces of monumental sculpture in America."

The tweedy gentleman who leads me up the steps to Grand Central Terminal cringes slightly when he says, "Onassis." It's not the Onassis name he hopes will save his station.

"Penn Central Corporation wants to build a fifty-eight-story tower over the concourse, completely destroying the front facade. The city designated the building a historical landmark, but Penn Central is suing the city for sixty million dollars. The lower court judge ruled in their favor, and we're terrified the city will cut their losses and not file an appeal."

As we enter the main concourse, sunlight filters through the enormous central lunette window in long, broken shafts. Early-morning commuters shuffle by with steaming cups of coffee, and cool spring air seeps into the station, carried on the trains from the woods of Connecticut and New York. In an hour the concourse will be a mad frenzy of commuters. Now, when it is mostly empty, the moist morning air vibrates gently with a nervous flutter of anticipation—the ineluctable excitement of a train ride.

"The ceiling was painted with two thousand, five hundred stars showing Orion, Pegasus, and a menagerie of zodiacal constellations. Sixty of the brightest stars are electrically lit. There's Betelgeuse and over there, Aldebaran. You might notice that all the constellations are backwards. It's supposed to depict how the stars would look outside our solar system."

It wouldn't occur to me except that I have been helping Caroline with a science project. "You wouldn't merely have to be outside the solar system. You'd have to be on the other side of the universe."

"Well, yes, you're right. But it is a charming idea, don't you think? I sometimes wonder if the workmen flipped the drawings and it wasn't caught till later."

"And their publicist came up with an excuse?"

"Exactly." He chuckles in that way that academics chuckle at small scandals. "We need you, Mrs. Kennedy. New York needs you." He doesn't appear to notice that he's begun calling me Mrs. Kennedy.

I feel something tug at my heart—I push it away. "That's very flattering, but I don't see what I can do. I would be happy to donate—"

"We want your name, Mrs. Kennedy. Your endorsement. You can do as much of the committee work and lobbying as you would like. We'd be incredibly grateful for anything. But what we really need is publicity. You did such remarkable work restoring the White House and saving Lafayette Square in Washington. We need you to do the same thing for New York."

"Where's that smell coming from?" Hypnotized, I follow my nose, leaving the professor spinning in the middle of the concourse. Is that smell butterscotch? I discover a small bakery, glowing and golden, near the main staircase. The air bursts with the smells of fresh coffee, bagels, and the most delicate, buttery, golden brown croissants. "May I have one of those . . . please?"

A round, gray-haired woman behind the glass case blinks twice—then her eyes pop open wide. I nod—*Yes, it's me.* "Could I have that one, please," I say, my mouth watering. Her fingers tremble as she carefully uses tongs—*Don't crush it, please*—about to place the perfect creation in a small white bag, when I say, "I don't need a bag, thank you." In an instant I close my lips over the flaky pastry—*Yes, butterscotch, with just hint of something nutty, perhaps?* It melts in my mouth. As I close my eyes and let escape a small moan, the tweedy professor runs up to me with a panicked look in his eyes.

I hold up my hand. He halts, silent as I take another bite, inhaling as I open my jaws, diving into the buttery smell. I eat the entire croissant slowly. I wipe my buttery fingers on a napkin, then turn to the professor.

"What is the first thing we need to do?" I ask.

He claps his hands gleefully, then takes me by the elbow and leads me back to the four-sided brass clock in the center. "Publicity's the thing . . . speak to the press . . . in front of the statue of Cornelius Vanderbilt . . . Oyster Bar ramp . . . perhaps the end of this week?"

I agree to everything—committee meetings, press conferences, letter writing, editorials, telephone campaigning—knowing that in truth I am committing to something much more, agreeing to be a New Yorker, to be an American, to make my home here, a commitment that feels as strong as motherhood itself.

How dare they try to destroy our city's history! It must be preserved!

Our history, our city, our home.

I feel a passion, an almost mystical connection to the city—to the creamy marble floor under my feet, to the twinkling backward constellations above, to the screeching taxis outside, to the smells of fresh pretzels and onion rings from the Oyster Bar, to the Empire State Building, the Waldorf-Astoria, and the Frick, to Central Park, the Reservoir, and Conservatory Water. They are me. Riverside Drive is me. Fifth Avenue is me. St. Patrick's Cathedral is me.

After my meeting with the professor, I walk down Lexington Avenue, nearly breaking into a run. I smile and wave to every New Yorker. "Good morning," I say. "How are you? Beautiful day, isn't it?" I feel like Ebenezer Scrooge, enlightened, rejuvenated, joyful. Saved!

Yes! This is my home! My home! My home! MY HOME!

BETWEEN SCYLLA AND CHARYBDIS

*A*rtemis, I don't understand." As the two of us browse for antiques on Voukourestiou Street in Athens, I relive my shock from what I recall in the morning papers: *Jackie O. spends $6,200 on dogs, $1,325 for flowers—Jackie O. buys $60,000 sable—Jackie O. spends $5,236 on lingerie—Jackie O. exceeds $30,000 monthly allowance.* "How does an American tabloid find out how much I spent in a jewelry store in Paris? Or the other stores? They report exact dollar amounts. Sales managers and owners would never tell. They wouldn't risk losing me as a customer."

She pretends not to hear me. "Jacqueline, look at this perfect Greek bust of Homer. I'm sure it is museum-quality."

"Do you know, Artemis?"

"I think we should call Professor Georgakis and have him authenticate it. Wouldn't it make a lovely present for Ari?"

"Artemis? Please tell me."

Her face falls. She presses her lips together and runs her fingers over the curvy spout of an antique oil lamp. "Oh, Jackie, I didn't want to tell you. It's Costa Gratsos."

The image flashes in front of me of Ari's friend, the tall, dapper Greek who has always treated me with stiff politeness. I meet him occasionally at parties on the *Christina* and when I greet Ari at the airport after business trips. "What about him?"

"He looks through the bills when they cross Ari's secretary's desk. Then he tells the tabloids."

"What? Why would he do that?"

"Oh, Jackie. There's so much you don't understand about us Greeks."

"That's how the paparazzi know where I am all the time? The headlines about divorce and my spending—it's all Costa?"

"Yes, my dear."

"And my flight schedules? I suppose Alexander tells him."

"Yes, Costa has turned Ari's children against you."

"That's so malicious. Why?"

"The way Costa sees it, he has given his life to serve Ari. When Ari dies, he expects to have a large share in the control of Ari's empire. He sees you as a threat."

"Enough of a threat to ruin my marriage?"

"Yes, my dear. He wanted Ari to marry Maria. He knew he could manipulate her, but he's afraid of you and your New York lawyers."

"What New York lawyers?"

"This is the way he thinks."

"What can I do? You are so wise. You give me such good advice. I would never have been able to handle Ari without your help."

She smiles almost imperceptibly, but I can tell the flattery pleases her. "I told Ari not to listen to Costa, but they have been together for seventy years. Besides, a Greek man will always take the word of another man over a woman, even if that woman is his sister or wife."

"What can I do?"

"I don't know, dear. That's why I didn't tell you before."

"Iago had his handkerchief, Scarpia his fan, and Costa my note to Ros Gilpatric."

"What, dear?"

Ari rages over my note, a good-bye letter I wrote to my friend Ros Gilpatric after my wedding to Ari that somehow got published. It was nothing so terrible: "I hope you know all you were and are and will ever be to me." But Ari is Greek and enjoys his jealous rages. He uses my guilt to manipulate and control me.

I repent. I try to make peace. I play the good Greek wife, cooing and praising, catering and fawning.

Ari is having none of it. He feels violated in some way neither of us can explain. He is relentlessly nasty.

"You are nothing! What did you ever do? Have you ever held public office? Saved a life? Built a fortune? Run a company? Created a masterpiece? Sung an opera? You can't even carry a tune. You do nothing but shop!

"You are coldhearted, calculating, and shallow.

"You are such a bore. Who could stand a woman who reads all the time?

"You disgust me! Do you know how ugly smoking makes you?"

He humiliates me in front of his staff, contradicting everything I say. He insults me in front of guests, pretending it's a joke. "Don't worry about breaking the crystal. My wife will buy new ones. At least she's good for something."

I try not to take it personally—he has become nasty to everyone.

I know his anger is about losing control. His daughter ran off to Las Vegas to get married. His business is faltering, one deal collapsing after another. His ex-wife married his archrival, Stavros Niarchos. And he can't control me.

He is sliding into powerlessness, greasing the way with ouzo. He's setting himself up—an accident waiting to happen. I've seen it before. I know it's coming but am helpless to prevent it.

My tolerance of his abuse is exhausted—I spend most of my time in New York while the children are in school, making short trips to Greece. Still, I try to keep the peace. I don't know what else to do.

"Nikos, could we have red roe caviar out on the table with those spicy meatballs Mr. Onassis likes so much?"

"Certainly, Mrs. Onassis."

"I want the evening to be perfect. Mr. Onassis has been under so much stress, lately."

"Yes, madame."

I smooth the tablecloth, fastening the little clips to keep it from blowing off the deck. I arrange flowers I picked on Skorpios this morning in an antique Greek pitcher.

The evening starts out rocky. Costa Gratsos was in Athens, so I had to invite him. He smiles broadly as he takes a seat opposite Ari. So he can watch me? I see something sinister about the man I missed before, a suppressed appetite, a malignant greed.

For every polite compliment offered by the guests, Ari slams me with an insult. Do I imagine it, or do he and Costa appear to have an understanding? When Ari takes a snipe at me, he glances at Costa, who fights a smile.

"What a lovely meal, Jackie," says one of the Greek wives.

"You should tell the chef. She can't even boil water."

"What a lovely dress, Jackie."

"You should see her most of the time. She runs around in jeans and a T-shirt like a hippie."

"That was a lovely speech you gave at the commemoration for Jack."

"That's all she thinks about. She is obsessed with dead people."

"What a lovely necklace, Jackie."

"Cost me a fucking fortune. When I married her I thought I won the prize cow. This cow cost me fifty million."

The guests look shocked, then embarrassed. The kindest thing they can do is to ignore me entirely, to keep me out of Ari's line of fire.

A new waiter, a simple Greek boy, tips over a glass. Ari explodes. "You idiot! You peasant! You have the brains of a gnat! Get out of my sight!"

"It was an accident, Ari," I say calmly.

"Shut up, woman! You are a bigger slob than he is. At least he's a better fuck than you."

The guests are mortified. Even Costa flinches. Desperate, I try deflection. "Nikos, let's have some music."

"No! No music. No more music!" He stands abruptly as if to leave, then falls back into his chair, clutching his head.

"Ari, are you all right?"

He flips his hand. "More ouzo! Can't the richest man in the world get a glass of ouzo! Where are you going?"

"Please, Ari, I've had enough."

"Sit down, woman!" He jerks me back into my chair so violently that my sunglasses fly off onto the table. One of the female guests gasps at my blackened eye.

"What are you looking at?" snaps Ari. "Every Greek beats his wife." He laughs unpleasantly. "It keeps them in line." I sit down, pour him a glass of ouzo, and fold my hands on my lap. Immediately his mood changes again, engaging the guests with jokes. He ignores me as if I don't exist.

I retreat to my children, who keep me sane—that is, until they drive me insane.

They both think I ride them too much. I guess I do. Caroline is at the age when she refuses to listen to anything I say. She doesn't talk back so much as ignore me.

Why do I fuss about her weight? I know she will lose it when she sees a reason to. I think of Janet carping at me—"Keep your gloves on." "Stand up straight." "Don't smoke." I don't want to be like that. But the tabloids will be ruthless to her. She's growing up so fast. I'm afraid I won't be able to protect her anymore.

And John—what can I do?—in constant motion, a whirling dervish of energy—he's already taken a liking to Ari's Johnnie Walker Black Label scotch and Greek cigarettes. He has no interest in school.

I get panicky sometimes when they are not home—Caroline off working on a PBS documentary about east Tennessee coal miners for six weeks, John terrorizing the city. I have to let them go. They must make the world their own.

Like Ari, I am afraid of losing control. I fire Ari's servants for no good reason,

I run in panic from the Cyclopses. I starve myself—deluding myself that if I prevail over my body's need for food, I can prevail over my fears, I can somehow keep my children safe. If I can resist the temptations of baklava and lemon mousse, I can resist the temptation to give in to rage. I try to hold tight, but I am spiraling, spiraling, spiraling.

I have to hold on for the sake of the children.

THANATOS

*A*re you ready to take off, Alexandros?"

"Yes. Have you heard from my father in New York?"

"No."

"Good."

Alexander is madly in love and secretly planning to marry an older woman against his father's wishes. He is sensitive and intelligent and looks like Ari did when he was young, but tall and slim. He is proud of his job as manager of one of Ari's companies, Olympic Aviation, a small fleet serving the islands. As he unbuttons his dark blue blazer and dons a flight jacket, he calls in his flight schedule—he plans to train a new American pilot on the Piaggio.

He is a little cocky today, in a gleeful mood. Even though he has been brooding for the past few weeks, since his mistress lost their baby—a baby they hadn't anticipated, hadn't wanted, but now grieve for—he is optimistic, determined to go through with his marriage, despite this dread omen. He is young, a mere twenty-six, so he depends on the older employees under his authority to know their jobs and to do them well. He is confident in the competence of his copilot, trust that he has checked the aircraft for safety. Learning to gain the respect and trust of his father's employees, he jokes and compliments them, lets them know how valuable they are to him. Since he succeeds at this, he glows with a quiet charisma, which, the employees remark, is more dignified than his father's intense tyranny.

The dynasty is in good hands.

The three men—Alexander, the copilot, and the American pilot—all trot out to the Piaggio that sits waiting on the runway in Athens. Even though it is a little late for training, after three o'clock, the weather is clear. They expect to have a good flight.

He is cautious and thorough by nature, a trait his father has failed to appreciate. As they settle down into their seats, Alexander asks his friend and favorite copilot in back, "Did you complete the safety check?"

"Yes, sir."

"Let's take her up, then." He addresses the American pilot to his left. "You'll love the way the Piaggio handles. We'll take her up a few thousand feet and then let you take over the controls."

"Fabulous," the American says, and because he is nervous and wants to impress his Greek host in the way boys on the playground try to impress one another, quotes from an American movie he's never seen: "Damn the torpedoes! Full steam ahead!"

The plane slowly rolls down the runway, gathering speed. It lifts off into the hazy late-afternoon sun—fifty feet, one hundred feet, two hundred feet—then plunges nose first into the runway.

I bolt awake to a loud noise. The room is dark. The curtains billow into the bedroom. Clouds streak across a full moon. The outside shutters bang wildly against the house. A cold maestro wind blows over the island, howling through the olive groves, whistling through the rugged shale cliffs. I hear a strange sound. Cats yowling?

I look out the window and see a squat figure staggering. He lifts a bottle to his lips and dances a wobbly *syrtaki* in the gale, his white shirt unbuttoned, flapping like a sail. He is singing or cursing, his hands clawing at the night, as if through a beaded curtain to a private room in a Greek *bouzoukia,* but behind this curtain is another curtain, then another—a curtain of nightmares.

Quickly I dress. As I grab an umbrella at the front door, thunder rumbles in the distance. Within minutes rain pelts down—thick, heavy drops. I can hardly see him weaving up the hill to the chapel we were married in. He jumps onto a low stone wall, balances, spins on his back foot, rocks toe to heel, kicks out his front foot, spins, and hops down. He mustn't be as drunk as he looks, yet he sways from side to side up the cobblestone path. He tears off his shirt, his shoes, his pants and underwear. He stands in front of the chapel, crosses himself, then staggers behind to the small cemetery. Swaying, he drinks from his bottle, then pours ouzo over Alexander's grave. He screams, throwing himself facedown in the freshly turned dirt, beating the ground with his fists. He pushes himself to his knees and yells in Turkish, flailing his arms back and forth. Then he stands, his mood suddenly somber and dignified. He walks behind the chapel to a gardening shed and returns with a shovel. He begins digging next to Alexander's grave, driving the spade into the ground with powerful thrusts. As rain washes down over him, filling his hole with water, his feet sink into the mud. He tires and flings away the shovel, as if it disgusts him. He squats by Alexander's grave and talks to the gravestone.

I walk up behind him. I hold the umbrella over his head—it takes him a minute to notice. He turns, his eyes squinting, suspicious.

"Oh, it's you."

"I was concerned. I followed you from the house."

He looks at me in a way that frightens me, like a kidnapper wondering how to have fun with his captive. "You want to help me?" he asks mockingly.

"Of course, Ari."

He stands, picks up the shovel, and hands it to me. "Then dig my grave."

"Ari, no. Why are you doing this?"

"Do it, woman! How much do I ask of you? Dig!"

He grabs my wrist and yanks me down on top of Alexander's grave. He rips off my blouse and pants. I try to roll away, but his arms are like steel. "A Greek man needs a son." He smacks me across the face. I think he's going to rape me; but he is limp. He smacks me again, then throws himself into the mud, howling. I scramble away, slipping in the mud.

As I put my blouse back on and button it, I sense he is no longer dangerous, his pale body heaving in the mud, then still. I touch his shoulder. "Come, Ari. Come back to the house. This won't bring him back."

He lets me help him up. We stagger back to the house, the squat naked man, the woman without pants or shoes, huddled under an umbrella, carefully picking our way down the flagstone street.

I watch a man dying before my eyes. I watch a man call death with every fiber in his body. I watch a man will himself to sickness.

With the death of Patrick, Jack and I grew closer. Our shared sorrow gave us a chance to heal. With the death of Alexander, Ari drives me away. He drives life away. He wants to die.

I try to comfort him. I make sure there are two fresh blankets set beside Alexander's tomb every evening with a bottle of ouzo and a small basket of bread and fruit. I invite a trio of folk musicians whom we met on the slopes of Mount Parnassus to come play on the *Christina*. I make him comfortable on a deck chair, bring him sweaters, entice him with food, then leave him alone with his thoughts. I am solicitous and deferential as any Greek wife.

I use every trick I learned nursing Jack, distracting him from his pain, but Ari scorns my efforts. "What do you care? Alexandros hated you."

"I care about you. I know how it feels to lose someone you love."

"You know nothing."

Overnight, his hair goes from gray to white. He drinks ouzo all day and stays up all night, wandering around Skorpios. His temper is treacherous.

Out of habit, he conducts business but without enthusiasm. He throws temper tantrums and confounds his colleagues. "Everything Midas touches turns to shit," he says. He knows he's slipping. First he loses Project Omega, a $400 million joint venture with the Greek government to build an oil refinery, aluminum plant, shipyards, and air terminal. The dictatorship falls, and the new Greek government forces Ari to sell Olympic Airways back to them. Then the voters in New Hampshire defeat his plan to build oil refineries on their coast. And now, because of the oil embargo, half his fleet is idle. Ari doesn't care.

"Why aren't you here when I need you?" he screams, but when I am with him, he dismisses me at best, abuses me at worst. I fly to New York to my children and leave the Greek women to fuss and fight over him. They call in doctors who diagnose him with myasthenia gravis. I don't bother to find out more. I don't quiz specialists. I don't run to a medical research library. I don't tell him, "We can beat this thing together." No one can cure a man who wants to die.

I saw Jack die at the height of his power, Bobby before he achieved power, and Ari as his power withered away.

The cruelest death by far is the third.

When I arrive at the American Hospital in Paris, hordes of paparazzi are camped out in front. The sidewalk is jammed with klieg lights and cables, and boulevard Victor Hugo is packed with television vans. A cold mist hangs in the air. *Please, God, just get me through this.* I tell the taxi driver to go around the block. I enter the rear of the hospital through the back near the kitchen, take the elevator to the sixth floor, and step out.

Christina, already wielding the power of her father's money, closed down the floor except for Onassis visitors. I walk into his room, where I've visited him over the past month. Clean and empty. A nurse directs me downstairs to the chapel, which is next to the morgue.

The chapel is dark, dimly lit by candles. The Greek sisters sit in back, keening together like the three witches in *Macbeth*. They hiss as I walk in. I hear them whisper, *"Atyhya, atyhya, atyhya."* There she is—the curse. Their gnarled fingers reach for the heavy gold crosses around their necks. *"Atyhya."*

Christina sits alone, a zombie until she sees me. She gets up abruptly and walks

down the hall. I notice the bandages around her wrists from her last suicide attempt. The sisters get up and follow her, leaving me with the corpse.

Ari lies on a bier in a blue suit with a white rose in his lapel, like on the day we
were married. His suit, too big now, is gathered, pinned, and tucked beneath his
corpse. A heavy gold Greek Orthodox cross lies on his chest. His face has been
covered with makeup, his cheeks painted with circles of pink. His eyes are closed,
the lids a dark mauve.

While I was in New York, Ari collapsed from a gallbladder attack in Athens. I
rushed back to pandemonium—specialists flown in from New York, Switzerland,
and Paris, all arguing about what was wrong. Some wanted to send him to Paris to
have his gallbladder removed, others to New York. Ari didn't care. He had
stopped eating and weighed no more than ninety pounds. His face was gaunt, his
eyes dark tunnels. His spine curved like an old woman's. He looked like a gargoyle with its eyelids taped up.

For no reason other than not wanting to discuss it anymore, he let the Greek
sisters talk him into flying to Paris for a gallbladder operation. That, of course,
killed him.

I look at his shrunken body, and think, *I am a widow. Again.*

As I gaze at the deep shadows cast by the flickering candles beside Ari's face,
craggy as the cliffs of Mount Athos, I can't believe I ever had anything to do with
this man. It seems so unreal, as if it never happened. I try to think of the last time
we spoke with any affection, and draw a blank.

But we did love each other. Once. Didn't we?

I think of Maria Callas—probably because she, of all people, should be here.
The Greek sisters won't allow it. I remember a day only a few months ago. Ari
and I were eating breakfast when he summoned his helicopter pilot.

"Where to, Mr. Onassis?"

"I will tell you when I get on the helicopter," he snapped.

I knew he was going to visit her.

I imagine their rendezvous on some isolated Greek island. When he steps out
of the helicopter, she runs to him like a parody of a TV commercial for hair color,
her heavy thighs jiggling, a chiffon sarong, meant to disguise her weight, blowing
behind her. They come together: he, frail and shrunken; she, huge and lumbering.
All he sees is her tremendous smile. She can tell he is ill, but says only how handsome he is. They lock arms and chatter together in Greek and in French, walking
along the beach. She has a basket of wine and cheese. They sit on beach chairs and
look out at the Ionian Sea, as they have together so many times before. She sings to
him softly, not an aria but a Greek folk song he once taught her. He gives her a

box, perhaps the ring she always wanted, and perhaps he tells her what a fool he was not to have married her, which makes her cry. He watches her swim—he doesn't join her, doesn't want to show her his deteriorated body, doesn't want to worry her—watches her squeal and play in the waves, imagining, perhaps, the life they could've had, the child he wishes he hadn't had her abort, because then he might still have a son and his heart wouldn't ache to die. She runs out of the ocean, an opulently curvaceous woman, laughing like a child, throwing herself down beside him, sprinkling him with sea water, and he smiles as he combs out her wet hair. Perhaps there is a small cottage nearby to which they retire for a few hours, not to make love—he is too weak—but to lie beside each other, holding each other, both wishing to turn back the clock, to rewrite their lives, to revise their decisions that they fought so hard over and that now seem so trivial.

As the sun begins to fade, the Greek tycoon and the opera star stagger out of the cabin, hugging, tears running down both their faces. They embrace again, and he tells her good-bye. As he steps into the helicopter, the blades whirring overhead, Maria's scarf flapping in the wind, they both know it is the last time they will see each other. Perhaps she sings an aria as he takes off, the beach her last stage, the song—lost in the noise of the helicopter—her last performance. She no longer has anything to sing about.

I become infused with calmness. I feel as if I am somehow a participant in Ari's love for Callas and her love for him, as a child participates in her parents' love for each other. It seems more real to me than my own love for him.

She should be here.

I walk to the nurses' station and ask to use the phone. I dial her number, slightly embarrassed that long ago, in a fit of pique, I memorized it, fantasizing about making that ugly, jealous, "you keep away from my husband" phone call. I am glad I didn't. I am glad I never asked him to stop seeing her. The phone in her apartment rings and rings. Finally, someone picks up.

"*Allo?*"

"*Allo. Est-ce que je peux parler avec Madame Callas, s'il vous plait? C'est Madame Kennedy au telephone.*"

"*Je regrette,* Madame Callas is in the United States. In Florida. May I take a message, madame?"

"Please ask her to come to the funeral. As my guest."

"I will tell her, madame."

There. It is done. I doubt she will come, but she will know that I respect the love they had. This, I hope, will bring her some comfort.

I leave the hospital, leave the corpse to Christina, who needs it to mourn just as she needs me to hate for a life that hasn't turned out her way. I would like to tell her that Ari is fine, that she is fine, but it would do no good. I see how the Greek women are wrapped up in some ancient ritual of chants and dead bodies that seems as remote and as inexplicable as the changing constellations in the midnight sky.

I have tasted this black passion—it is not mine.

I return to our apartment on 88 avenue Foch. It feels like a stranger's house, as if I have no right to be there. The antique Louis Quinze furniture, the tapestries, the Chinese carpets, the impressionist paintings—nothing feels familiar. It smells funny, like the house of old people. I spend the afternoon packing things I want shipped back to New York. There isn't much. I remove a Degas from the office wall and spin the tumbler behind it. I collect a few pieces I have stored here, expensive but garish presents from Ari—the famous gold-and-ruby Apollo II ear clips, and a 40-carat Lesotho diamond ring—jewelry I seldom wear.

I think how death has always meant packing to me—taking what I need and moving on.

I close a suitcase, then fly to Greece for Ari's funeral.

The cortege of cars and buses winds slowly from Athens to the fishing village of Nydri, where we will take boats to Skorpios. Peasant women in black shawls line the road and throw small bouquets of purple flowers over the hearse. Men hold battered hats over their hearts. Through every little village, church bells ring out. All the villagers run out to pay their respects.

In Nydri the coffin is loaded onto a launch. Everyone else piles into waiting boats.

Skorpios is obscured in mist and fog. The air is still, the water flat. As we pass a flotilla of small fishing boats, we hear the voices of women moaning and wailing. We see nothing but vague shadows and specks of light. It feels dreamlike, as if we were crossing the River Styx.

When we land, six pallbearers carry the coffin up the street to the chapel. A traditional Greek band plays a mournful dirge. Hundreds of Ari's employees—chefs, waiters, gardeners, sailors, maids, airline pilots, shipping executives—line the streets, all holding lit candles.

I follow the Greek sisters, superstitious crones dressed in black, hunched over, heads together. How quickly beautiful women can turn hideous. They showed me great kindness, opening their hearts and homes as few American women would ever do. Yet, as with the Kennedys, as soon as Ari died, I am clearly no longer part of the family.

I don't mind. I have been to too many funerals. They have no meaning for me anymore.

I see myself as if through a long telephoto lens—a woman in dark sunglasses and a long black leather coat, her hair loose and damp, with a tight smile on her face. I feel strangely detached, like a reporter allowed to trail in back. The morbid procession seems slightly ridiculous. Such a drama! It seems so pagan, yet clothed in the garb of a Christian ceremony. Doesn't the Church preach that there is no death?

Alexander's mausoleum sits beside a cypress tree. Ari's grave is adjacent. A village priest reads a scriptural passage, a small choir sings. We file by and kiss the icon on his coffin, each leaving a white flower on top. Christina flings herself on the coffin, wailing and moaning until her bodyguard gently pries her off. The coffin is lowered into the concrete vault beside Alexander.

A sudden terror, all too familiar, flashes over me. What do I do now? Who will protect me? Where can I hide? How do I save the children? What do I do with myself? As the mourners drift away, I tremble with a sense of isolation.

I look out at the *Christina* bobbing in the water, a shadow in the fog, lit up with white lights in the shape of a cross. Is that Ari? In an armchair on deck, a Havana cigar dangling from his mouth, eyes laughing behind dark glasses, in shortsleeves and baggy shorts, his shirt unbuttoned, his relaxed thighs akimbo. In one hand he holds a glass of ouzo. With the other he waves.

CENTRAL PARK

1994

see him as soon as I cross Fifth Avenue and turn the corner around the museum steps. He follows me. He keeps his distance. He glances right and left, his eyes pealed for cops. His Cyclops eye zooms in, scoping me out like a sniper's rifle. He comes after me like iron to a magnet, oblivious to everything but me. He shuffles with his camera pressed to his face, bumping into tourists, darting between cars, flipping a finger to honking taxis—"Fuck you, sweetheart"—skipping around businessmen, then ducking behind a hot-dog stand.

Some of those who stumble in his wake look to see who he's so ardently pursuing—*a girlfriend? a movie star?*—and think they see a slim dark-haired woman walking swiftly, alone, peeking over her shoulder, slipping around corners, zigzagging as if to throw an alligator off track. Their spines straighten, chins lift, delighted to have a story to tell over dinner: "Guess who I saw by the Met today?"

On he comes, never ceasing. His feet splayed in a duck walk, hitting his heels hard, his dark slacks slightly wrinkled, his polished leather coat flapping against his thighs. He comes, a comet in orbit, a predator after his prey, a pilot fish after the whale. Unerring, undeflected, unmitigated. On target.

By Conservatory Water the children in red-and-white sailor *maillots* prod toy sailboats with sticks. Dried leaves swirl in spiraling gusts. The oak trees and crepe myrtle bend lightly in the wind. Weary Park Avenue au pairs chat with their friends in foreign tongues as their toddlers take tentative steps toward one another. Tourists take off their shoes and rub their feet.

He stands on the other side of the pond, his black proboscis probing the shadows until he finds me.

I turn and flee, up the path back toward the museum, under the tunnel that leads to the Great Lawn. At the end of the unlit tunnel, I stop and wait. He charges in, lenses rattling. He stops abruptly when he sees a figure leaning against the wall. He hesitates, not knowing if the figure is me or perhaps someone who will stab him, grab his cameras, and kick him in the face. His is not an easy profession—he's had his share of smashed cameras and flying fists, curses and shoves, at bars and private parties, in marble foyers and majestic driveways. His bones ache from such assaults, broken fingers, bruised ribs, now healed but painful in the autumn damp. He has learned to be cautious.

The tunnel is dank and narrow, smelling of pee, beer, and moss, the kind of place where bad things happen, the kind of place New Yorkers run through, holding their breath.

He takes a step toward me. I'm sure he still can't make out my face. Water trickles down the side of the tunnel. He wheezes, his breath is shallow. Does he have asthma or emphysema? Is my stalker ill? I can smell him, his whiskey breath, his body sweating in leather, frowsty like an old man. My stalker is aging with me.

I hear the tinny clank of his light meter knocking against his second camera. "Oh, Jac-kie," he taunts. The tunnel explodes in white light. *Click, click, click.* His camera whirrs.

I spin on my heel and dash out into the gray-yellow light, through the piles of dead leaves, my ankles twisting on horse chestnuts underfoot.

I see him laboring, his brow beaded with sweat. Yet on he comes.

I run across the Great Lawn, through the wild Ramble, down to the Lake, my feet slipping where the grass has worn to mud. The Lake is still and gray. A rowboat in the middle drifts as a man and a woman look at each other from opposite ends.

I pause on Hernshead Rock under the London plane trees and look out. The Lake seems so tranquil, out of a Seurat painting, the fall colors edging the water in orange and yellow like a cuff of leopard fur. The sun breaks out from behind a cloud and makes an amoeba-shaped jade patch on the Lake.

The photographer runs out of the woods. When he sees me, he stops and raises his camera.

I could run right toward Columbus Circle, or left toward the zoo. But I have come as far as I want.

I turn and face him.

I guessed what the young doctor would say before he said it. Then he surprised me.

"The CAT scan here shows you have enlarged lymph nodes in your neck and armpit. That's why you've been having pain. There are also swollen lymph nodes in your chest and abdomen. We did a biopsy on one of your neck nodes."

He pauses, and I hate him for it. I think of a politician just before he announces his own election results. The polls don't indicate victory.

"The tests indicate you have non-Hodgkin's lymphoma. The cells we looked at were anaplastic, which means they are undeveloped. That means your cancer is highly malignant and may spread to other parts of your body."

He suggests an aggressive chemotherapy. I'll have to lie in a hospital bed for several hours and get the chemicals through an intravenous drip. He compliments me on how calmly I take in the information. He says that the survival rate for this kind of cancer is 50 percent after five years, but I can tell he doesn't think I'm part of the 50 percent who will live. Doctors, like politicians, reveal more by what they don't say than by what they do.

"I thought I took such good care of my health." I smile wanly. "How could I get cancer?"

"That's the million-dollar question."

"I have a million dollars. Several."

He looks shocked, then laughs uncomfortably, not liking, as a doctor, to talk about money, as if the mere mention of it challenges his ethics. "Some studies indicate it's caused by viruses, such as the Epstein-Barr virus, sexually transmitted viruses, or even an untreated bacterial infection."

"Bacterial infection?"

"Yes, such as Helicobacter pylori, a bacterial infection that causes ulcers, or chlamydia. Over time and under stress, the viruses or bacteria weaken the immune system so your lymphocytes begin to divide uncontrollably. Of course, these are only theories."

Sitting in my paper Johnny, cold and vulnerable, I feel the words clash like cymbals in my ears—*sexually transmitted viruses, bacterial infection, chlamydia*. I feel dizzy.

The doctor reaches out his hand to steady my shoulder. "Are you all right, Mrs. Kennedy?"

Many of the doctors call me Mrs. Kennedy. As if somehow it would be unpatriotic to call me anything else. I begin to laugh. Jack visits me again. And again. The legacy of his sexual exploits. He killed my babies, Arabella and Patrick. Now Jack is killing me. It seems inevitable. After the pain, the suffering, and the forgiveness, he visits me again.

"Would you like me to have the nurse call someone for you? You shouldn't be alone."

His look of concern is endearing. I think of John at three, holding my hand—*Where is Daddy?*—wondering why everyone was so sad, why Mommy couldn't stop crying.

Jack visits me again.

"Mrs. Kennedy? I would suggest we start aggressive treatment right away. Would that be possible?"

He assumes I want treatment. He assumes I want to lose my hair and suffer the agony of chemotherapy. He assumes I'll do whatever he thinks is best.

"Sure." Why not? He'll be so disappointed if he can't try to keep Mrs. Kennedy alive. For the rest of his career, he will be able to say at cocktail parties—"Yes, I was Jackie Kennedy's doctor. Terrible tragedy. What a loss. She faced it bravely, though."

He is young and earnest, and I hate him. I would hate any doctor who told me I had cancer, who told me I could no longer ride my horses or run in the park. So why should I make his career for him? My illness and its treatment will guarantee his success. Guarantee his Westchester ranch home, his vacations to Hawaii, Ivy League educations for his sons. A lucky break for a doctor so young. And the hospital will only gain in reputation. All because they experimented on Mrs. Kennedy for a few months. But she died anyway. What a shame. Perhaps if she hadn't been so healthy, we would've discovered the cancer sooner. She had to fall from her horse for us to find it. Swollen lymph nodes in her groin.

"Sure," I say. "Can I still work?"

Momentarily taken aback, he then remembers that his client works as an editor, not because she has to, of course, but because she wants to. "You can do as much as you feel up to. Don't worry, Mrs. Kennedy. We'll beat this thing together." He pulls back his shoulders and looks me straight in the eye, a move he practiced in medical school, no doubt, in front of the mirror glued to the inside of his closet in his dreary dorm, a rehearsed optimism that seems so familiar, and I realize it's the bogus optimism of politicians—*Vote for me and I'll cure poverty. Vote for me and I'll cure cancer.* It's not a lie if he believes it. And just like a good politician, he does believe it.

In a flash, I see he will mourn my death more than his own mother's. I feel full of pity for him. I wonder about his wife, if he's too busy, too ambitious, too wrapped up in his patients to spend enough time with her. He looks pale, skin like oatmeal, tense around the eyes, and I wonder if he takes care of his own health. I wonder if when he was in medical school, poring over his oncology textbooks, he knew that most of his patients would die.

"Do you play golf?" I ask.

"Yes. I don't have much time for it."

"You should make time. My husband always felt calmer after he played golf." He blanches, recalling whom I probably mean by *my husband,* embarrassed that I should express concern for him, a mere servant of his medicine god. I enjoy his discomfort, then relent. "I'll make an appointment with your nurse on the way out. Don't worry," I tell him, "I'll pull through."

Then the anger hit me. Oh, yes, I was angry.

I railed at the poor priest, tears flowing down my face, my knees aching from kneeling so long. Why me? I've tried so hard to be a good mother. I've tried so hard not to be angry. I've tried to take care of my body. Yes, I smoked, but I exercised. All those push-ups! All that dieting! My body has served me well. Why betray me now? I am happy.

I railed at the trees in Central Park. I loved you! Why have you let me down?

I railed at the city, the historic stately buildings, the busy streets, the ineffable throbbing energy. Haven't I defended you?

I railed at my horse Frank, although it wasn't he who threw me during a foxhunt in Virginia, sending me to the hospital, the start of my decline. Haven't I cared for you? Haven't I given you the very best?

I railed at Jack. All those infections you gave me! All the humiliation and anger you caused! It's your fault!

I railed at God. Haven't I taken everything you dished out? Why me? Why now? I still can do good in this world. Let me live. You'll see.

But God wasn't listening.

Maurice takes the news in stride—better than I did. I can see in his eyes that he has suspected something was wrong for some time.

Even as we vacationed together last June, he had that look, a vacation that felt like a honeymoon, floating on a barge down the Rhône, through Avignon, Arles, and Aigues-Mortes, watching fields of lavender drift by, Provence farmers cycling with bread in their baskets, wild white horses along the Camargue glancing up from their grazing, flamingos bursting against the blue-white sky. Lying in his arms, I was so happy to be still, happy to be a nobody, to be nothing but a lazy body and a pair of eyes. It was a honeymoon we would never have, because we are beyond such things and know our friendship is all that counts. As we floated under the linden trees in blessed lassitude, the late-summer sun dappled our faces, the misty blue light like faded silk scarves across our cheeks. He held me softly and looked down at me, sweeping my hair out of my face. We floated down the Rhône in the present and in the past but never the future, floating in memories we don't have to share, he in his world, me in mine, because in the end, all we have are pleasant memories.

Without speaking of it, we shared a golden infusion of gratitude—for our lives, for our family and friends, for each other. Carried along, I felt safe, comfortable in the inevitable, comfortable in mortality. The feeling of gratitude was so overwhelming, so profound, it felt like being in love.

Maurice Tempelsman, the cello in my life, mellow and loving, my best friend. He is kind and generous in ways I have never known, and teaches me that fidelity is not matrimony or monogamy but concern for someone else's happiness over your own. He placed a white cashmere shawl around my shoulders, because he sensed I was cold, because he saw a chill pass over me, a memory I can't avoid that visits me every day. He didn't ask but leaned over and kissed my forehead.

We have no secrets from each other, yet we ask no questions. Our pasts are our own. The remembrances we share with each other are like lines of poetry that we don't try to understand, beautiful words that seem so right, made more beautiful for being left unscrutinized, drifting in the distance. We do not try to figure each other out. We do not search for meaning but see and listen and enjoy. In not marrying, we choose every day to be with each other, again and again. Willingly he is my escort, as if he has always known that this was his life's calling.

Yes. Maurice took the news well.

The children wept, but I do not worry for them. Caroline astonishes me with her resourcefulness, integrity, and good sense. She will be fine. After my death, I suspect that John's state of perpetual befuddlement will fall away and he will slowly come into his own. Like Jack, he will find purpose and commitment in his forties.

I worry sometimes if I've done right by them. Was I too hard on John? Did I share too much of my pain with Caroline when she was young? I relied on her so much for my sanity.

It is wonderful to have grown children—they are so beautiful—John with his chiseled handsome face, Caroline with her kind, soulful eyes. They constantly amaze me—I must've done something right. And the grandchildren—Rose, Tatiana, baby Jack. They are such a joy—their impish laughter, their earnest questions. Through them I see the world with fresh eyes.

I love to lead them on treasure hunts through the apartment, uncovering pirate loot behind the furniture, Gypsy trinkets in the cabinets, beaded necklaces in the bookshelves, listening to them squeal as I spin an adventure tale, and wish with all my heart they will find their way through life discovering and delighting.

I recall what Bernard Berenson told me as he eased his aching bones onto a bench in his Tuscan garden, that as he grew older he lived so much more in people, books, works of art, and the landscape than in his own skin, and I find myself seeing and identifying with the world around me—in the grandchildren, in the art in my home, which holds so many memories, in Maurice's face. As Berenson said, "A complete life may be one ending in so full an identification with the not-self that there is no self left to die." I sense, somehow, that this is true.

I worry most about leaving my writers. They will panic, frightened that their books will be orphaned by new editors with little enthusiasm for finishing up a prior editor's projects. I worry that they may give up on their work, or even give up on writing altogether. I wouldn't want that for all the world. I exact a promise from their publisher to see my projects through to publication. I will not let my writers down.

Sometimes it takes a suggestion from someone you don't know very well for you to put your life into perspective.

I felt so aimless and withdrawn after Onassis died. The fight over my share of Ari's estate kept me focused for a while, but 26 million dollars later, I felt lost. I didn't need to find male protection—I could buy it. Caroline was seventeen, John, fourteen—they didn't need me as much as they once did.

I made myself accept almost every social engagement. This was an obligatory lunch— with a former White House employee, a woman who has always seemed a bit too forthright to me, who has managed to go through her life on clearly marked trails, without doubt, without major mistakes. She thinks she knows how the world should be run. Perhaps she does.

I dreaded the lunch but knew I couldn't and shouldn't get out of it. I reserved a table at a busy bistro, hoping the lunch would be made short because of the restaurant's bluster and noise.

"So, Jacqueline, what are you going to do with the rest of your life?" As usual, before I could answer, she gave me her opinion. "You need to get a job."

"A job? Me?" I respected Tish enormously. She was married and had children yet ran her own public relations company with international clients. But me? A job?

"Working would give you focus and a sense of accomplishment. You'll be too busy and tired to shop," she said, smiling wryly. "It might keep those paparazzi at bay as well. No one wants to see the most famous woman in the world going to work every day and sitting at a desk in a windowless broom closet just like them."

"What kind of job?"

"Well . . . I don't see you as a writer. . . ."

I recoiled, offended. I'd written all my life—as Inquiring Camera Girl, letters, parts of Jack's speeches and *Profiles in Courage,* the *White House Tour Book.* I was proud of the two projects I did while married to Ari—the afterword to Peter Beard's book *Longing for Darkness: Kamante's Tales from Out of Africa* and an article in *The New Yorker* on the opening of the International Center of Photography.

During the two years I wrote my column "Inquiring Camera Girl," I thought I wanted a career as a writer. I really did. I showed John White one of my short stories while at the *Times-Herald.* He tore it apart. He was nice about it—told me the things I needed to do to make it better. He offered to read it again if I worked on it.

I wasn't discouraged, but I didn't rewrite it, either. I realized that what I wanted to get out of the story, I got in the first telling. I realized that writing a good article or a moving short story or novel is very hard work. And apart from spending delightful hours in café repartee, writers are people who write about life rather than live it. I realized that what I really liked about writing my column was meeting and talking with interesting people.

I knew I couldn't make myself do the rest of the work.

I understood the satisfaction of discipline—I could work with a horse for hours and hours—but I knew I couldn't survive the repetition of working a phrase over and over until it sings, until the person who reads your prose feels your emotions as strongly as you do.

"Why don't you contact your friend Tom Guinzburg at Viking Press?" asked Tish. "Tell him you can get celebrity memoirs. He'll snap you up in a second."

"What would I do?"

"Edit, of course. You're a natural."

There. She said it. Oh, how I resented her at that moment. I didn't want to hear it. How dare she point out something about me, as if she'd known it all her life? But she was right—as she often was. Apart from my letters, much of my writing had been editing more than creative composition. I had been drifting in this direction my whole life.

I could not resist the truth.

So I worked at Viking and then at Doubleday. I loved traipsing through subjects I adore—French and Russian history and art, dance, architecture, photography—without devoting my life to a single book. But it wasn't the celebrities with whom I worked that thrilled me, although there were plenty—Michael Jackson, Martha Graham, Gelsey Kirkland, André Previn, Diana Vreeland—but the novelists, struggling so hard to get it right. How grateful they were for a clear read, a little direction. How satisfying it was to help them express what they ached to say. It was like that explosion of joy, that eruption of laughter, after struggling to communicate with someone speaking a foreign language, when you finally understand what he is trying to say. This is what editing was for me—pure delight in clear communication.

Becoming a writer is a solitary and uncertain apprenticeship. I was happy to be an editor. I enjoyed the excitement of discovery without the pain. Let someone else bare his soul. I have sacrificed as much of myself as I can in this lifetime. It thrilled me to try to help another clarify his thoughts.

I was grateful for the routine and the hard work. It was like a prayer to me, a monastic ritual, my *opus dei,* bringing me closer to God. The routine began to heal me.

I leave a message with Lee's maid. Again. I want to talk to her. But I hold little hope that she will return my calls. Eventually word will get to her that I am sick. Maybe then she will call.

I miss the days when we were pals and could giggle with each other. I need to tell her I'm glad she is my sister. I need to tell her I love her. Isn't that what dying people do? Ask for forgiveness.

When I think of Lee, I am filled with such sadness at how she wasted her talent, intelligence, and beauty in her avaricious pursuit of money and grandeur. If she ever loved her husbands, her children, or her scores of lovers, I doubt that it was ever a love in which she gave anything of herself.

Her bitterness toward me crushes my heart. She blames me for destroying her life, for sabotaging every chance she has had for happiness. She says she hates me.

Any act of generosity, anything I try to say to mend our relationship, only makes her more hostile. I suspect that no matter what I did, she would feel this way—my generosity interpreted as dominance or manipulation. Do all little sisters feel this way toward their older sisters? I hope not. Our lives have been lived in extremes, and in extremes such feelings are exacerbated, like a ten-ton truck on a weakened bridge. Now the bridge has collapsed and there's no way from one side to the other.

Oh, Lee! What happened to you? Was there not enough abundance in your life that you always felt passed over, deprived, undernourished?

You live in your scary castle high on a cliff, black skies and thunder storming over your towers, with your heart buried in a dungeon deep beneath the earth. Just as part of me died when Jack died, part of me lies buried in that dungeon with you.

We have managed to create loss where there should be only joy.

I did not think there were any pieces left in my heart to be broken but, little sister, you break my heart.

I have lunch with a dear friend at Le Cirque. I am saying good-bye. Perhaps he knows this, but he doesn't let on. We have a merry time, eating and joking, as we always do. The sound of his voice is like music—his vowels rich and full of love. What a dear, loving man, I think. I am filled with gratitude for such wonderful friends.

At the end of the meal, the owner of the restaurant sends over a spread of desserts, tempting me. I peer at them closely, my nose inches away—a lovely tiramisu, chocolate cake with raspberries, a flan with apricot puree, baked pear with chocolate sauce, a strawberry tort. All so beautiful. I taste one—"Oh, isn't that marvelous." As I take a third and fourth bite, my friend looks at me with astonishment. He thinks, I'm sure, that I've lost my mind—that I've given up hope and have decided to make up for lost time.

I absorb the desserts through every pore in my body. I breathe them in and take them to the core of my being. It seems as if everything that has happened in my life, every meal I have ever eaten, all the pleasures of my life, have led to this moment. Chocolate and raspberry melt in my mouth. Oh, what joy! I feel as if I've never been as aware or alive before. With the apricots, I am transported to Tuscany, the strawberries to Switzerland, the chocolate to Paris, the cream to Ireland. Ah, what a marvelous vacation—a glorious world tour.

I know my body will never travel again, but that will not keep me from seeing Provence, or Acapulco, or Rome. Not as long as there are desserts to eat. Not as long as I have friends. When Niki Goulandris calls, I smell the wildflowers in Skorpios. And when Bunny Mellon calls, I am there again, walking on the sandy beaches of Antigua.

"Shall I have the waiter clear the table?" my friend asks worriedly.

"If you do, I'll stab his hand with my fork," I say.

I think of all the desserts I've denied myself, and I feel awash with the glorious bounty of this world. "God's love is inexhaustible," my priest says. I wonder why it has taken me so long to understand.

My body grows weak and frail. My face is thin, my hair is gone. Within weeks I have turned into an old woman with all of age's aches and wrinkles and slowing down. In a way I see my ugliness—my rapid aging—as a gift. It will make saying good-bye easier for my children and my family, for the people I love.

I adored Jack's body, his hands, his legs, his face, his stomach. After he died, my body ached for his warmth and gravity—his beauty. I think how much easier it would have been if Jack had died when he was old and ugly, if the physical loss were more gradual. Aging prepares you for death. Just think if you are ugly and in pain, how much easier it is to say good-bye to your own body.

I am ready, I think. Although I will miss so many things.

The smell of horses and of roasting chestnuts in the park. The sound and smell of the ocean, Maurice's soft, fatty cheeks. The grandchildren—who amaze and delight me. These I will miss most of all.

What did the medieval mystic Julian of Norwich say? "All will be well and every kind of thing will be well."

All there is now is the waiting.

The doctor says the cancer has gone to my brain. He wants to drill a hole in my skull and pour in chemicals. The image makes me laugh—like some nineteenth-century political cartoon. I suppose I'll let him experiment on me. I hate to disappoint him. I want him to feel he's done the best he can. But there is a limit to what I'll put up with.

"Will I lose my mind, Doctor?"

"You may find some impairment in your cognitive abilities."

"Well, I guess that's it, isn't it?"

Even now I have trouble remembering things. I make lists, then forget where my lists are. There is surprisingly little I have to take care of. I signed over my properties to John and Caroline. The lawyers have taken care of the will, all thirty-eight pages. I think I have remembered everyone I wanted to. My only regret is Lee. I will leave each of her children half a million dollars—but her, nothing. I forgive her bitterness, but I cannot reward it.

I write to all my friends whom I will never see again. I feel such gratitude for each one of them—they have given me such joy. I have to write it clearly. I cannot leave it to implication.

I think a lot about you, Jack. I will see you soon. You died on November 22, 1963. That's thirty-one years ago. That's a long time. But I think of you every day. Are you happy at last? At peace after all those years of restlessness? I understand your pain now. I have it in my back and my legs and my arms. I have headaches that feel like horses stomping on my skull. I don't mind it so much. There is almost a comfort in it. It makes me closer to you.

I am weak, yet my spirit stirs. It is eager to get on with things, I suppose.

I worry that you won't recognize me, Jack. That I'm too old and wrinkled. Life's final cruelty—your face will forever be young, yet I have aged.

I will not ask my doctor to give me a final dose of morphine. He would turn me down, and it would shake his confidence. To him, death is an enemy. Death means his failure. I will not try to change his mind.

But I am tired, so tired. I ache for the steady drip of morphine as I ache for Jack's embrace. I want to die at home.

Yes, I am ready.

I tell Maurice and the children that this is what I want. I want my room filled with photos from my life. I want my dearest friends around me. I want to hear the soaring tones of a Gregorian chant. I will squeeze their hands one last time, then close my eyes.

They nod their heads in silence. I know seeing me like this frightens them more than my death.

"Is that you, Jack?"

"No, it's Maurice, my dear."

"For a second, I thought you were Jack. Isn't it just beautiful today? Such a lovely spring after such a long, hard winter."

"Yes, it's beautiful."

"Where is the ocean? I can't see the ocean."

"We're in Central Park, dear. We're looking at the Great Lawn."

"Oh—I thought we were on the Cape. Why is that man looking at us?"

"He's a photographer. Do you want me to ask him to go away?"

"No. Let him take all the photos he wants. He hasn't much longer. Do you think he will lose his job?"

"No, Jackie. There are lots of celebrities to take pictures of."

"There will be my funeral. He'll want pictures of that."

"Probably."

"Life will go on."

"Yes. Of course."

"He followed me in Greece, you know. I remember him. He took a picture of Regent and me at my first dog show. She was a white bull terrier. He was at my debut. He's always taking my picture."

"Those photos were taken by many different photographers, my darling."

"They all seem alike to me. With one eye. I've kept them busy, haven't I?"

"Yes, you have."

"What about you, Maurice? What will you do?"

"I'll wait for my time, floating on a barge down the Rhône."

"Do you remember the horses, Maurice? The white horses charging through the marsh along the Camargue? Water splashing, manes flying?"

"Yes, I remember."

"Ah, it was so beautiful—so wild, so free. I love horses."

"Let's go back to the apartment, Jackie. It's getting a little chilly."

AUTHOR'S NOTE

This is a work of fiction. Most of the historical incidents in the novel have their basis in fact, filtered through the author's imagination and selected to represent the protagonist's emotional life rather than to record the past accurately.

For the millions who followed the glamorous and tragic turns of her life, Jackie—even when alive—seemed more mythic than real. My intention in writing this book was not to violate her privacy—I'm not sure that is even possible in fiction—but to get a sense of the woman behind the myth, the human behind the icon.

I approached Jackie's fictional persona as an actor approaches a new role. By writing in her voice and imagining her thoughts and feelings, I wished to explore the subtext of her historical life, psychology, personal history, and sexuality. Ironically, by exploring her emotional life, I began to see Jackie's spiritual evolution as mythical and archetypal—a Homeric journey through the trials and tribulations of the female soul.

Certain of Jackie's remarks used are from letters or chronicled conversations—the rest, fictitious.

Readers interested in a more historical chronology of Jackie's life may want to peruse her many biographies. Among those consulted by the author are *The Death of a President* by William Manchester; *A Woman Named Jackie* by C. David Heymann; *America's Queen: The Life of Jacqueline Kennedy Onassis* by Sarah Bradford; *Jacqueline Bouvier: An Intimate Memoir* by John H. Davis; *Jacqueline Bouvier Kennedy Onassis: A Life* by Donald Spoto; *Jack and Jackie: Portrait of an American Marriage* by Christopher Andersen; *Mrs. Kennedy* by Barbara Leaming; and *Just Jackie: Her Private Years* by Edward Klein. Books more specifically about the Kennedy administration include *The Dark Side of Camelot* by Seymour M. Hersh and *Four Days: The Historical Record of the Death of President Kennedy* by United Press International.

On Lee Radziwill, the author consulted *In Her Sister's Shadow* by Diana DuBois. On Aristotle Onassis, *The Onassis Women* by Kiki Feroudi Moutsatsos and *Ari: The Life and Times of Aristotle Socrates Onassis* by Peter Evans.

ACKNOWLEDGMENTS

I would like to gratefully acknowledge the support and assistance of the following people: Emanuela Bonchino, Susan Edmunson, Sandy Eiges, Nancy Folsom, John Houghton, Steve Lamont, Diane Reverend, and a very special thanks to Philip Spitzer.